C.S. Boag is a former journalist who has also grown potatoes, driven taxis and bulldozers and worked in a hamburger bar. Apart from his published short stories he has worked as a columnist for *Woman's Day* and the *Bulletin*. He won the Walter Stone Memorial Prize for Literature in 1986. He lives on a small 'green' holding near Bathurst, NSW, with his wife, Judith. He has five children.

www.csboag.com

By the same author

Bullets at the Ballet
Cock Robin Killer
Morgue the Merrier
Nightmare in Nimbin

C.S. Boag

MISTER RAINBOW

in the Case of the Hood with No Hands

XOUM PUBLISHING

Sydney

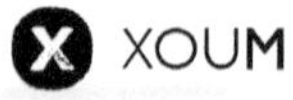 XOUM

First published in this edition by Xoum in 2017

Xoum Publishing
PO Box Q324, QVB Post Office,
NSW 1230, Australia
www.xoum.com.au

ISBN 978-1-925143-55-3 (print)
ISBN 978-1-925143-56-0 (digital)

Cataloguing-in-publication data is available from the National Library of Australia

Cover design by Xou Creative, www.xoucreative.com.au

Papers used by Xoum Publishing are natural, recyclable products made from wood grown in sustainable forests. The manufacturing processes conform to the environmental regulations of the country of origin.

Chapter 1

RENDEZVOUS WITH A DAME

The name's Rainbow.

You can spit on my card, bend it, twist it, rub it with your shirt sleeve or blast a hole through it with a .38, it will still read: Bruno Scutt's Detective Agency, brunscutt.etcetera.com and down the bottom the catchy little phrase:

'No Care Taken, But All Responsibility'.

Means as much as anything these days.

Whatever it says, I'm still Rainbow.

The card's so I look respectable.

No matter that I live on a boat, crappy little number, grubs munching their way through the hull, engine a lottery, only thing functions is the automatic bilge pump, gizmo that squirts out the water just that bit faster than it comes in and keeps me out of the teeth of sharks.

So does getting cash up front.

Might sound like I don't trust people.

Might be right.

So when this dame responds to my ad in the Personals of *The Sydney Morning Horrible*, that well-known navel-gazing bastion of political correctness tacked onto the only good thing about the rag – the comics – that's the first thing I ask her.

Not how long have you been suspicious of your husband or are you seeking a short-term relationship with a private detective aged forty-five, no ties he'll admit to except the ones he gets at op shops, suspicious of aliens, but prepared to walk barefoot on beaches in the moonlight, if that's what it takes.

None of that.

Not straight up, anyhow.

No, when she telephones and asks in the echoey sort of voice that can only come out of a bomb shelter in Beirut or an ancient telephone booth in an Australian country town if I can check up on her old man, I tell her

"

only if she produces the requisite number of dollars at a reasonably early stage in the proceedings, like immediately after the Hello-I'm-Bruno bit.

That's how I find myself in Dashiell, a biggish and crappy-enough rural proclivity in NSW's west, lurking under a Cinzano umbrella in a caffeine-den next to a funeral parlour on a coolish morning in March, battered Panama on the table before me, gulping down my third triple-shot for the day and reading the pulps, in this case the flirty-and-dirty women's magazines, as provided by a socially responsible management.

I'm just learning how I can keep my fanny in shape when up she slopes, in that tentatively confident manner peculiar to seriously beautiful women, the greatest knockout since Buster Douglas floored Mike Tyson in anno Domini 1990 – tall, willowy, blonde and about as born-to-rule as John F. Kennedy, before he was assassinated.

'Mr Scutt? I'm Sally Kane.'

Pale-grey pantsuit, pale-grey eyes to match the pantsuit, aristocratic stoop; it's like Sally Kane has spent her whole life trying to descend to the level of ordinary mortals; and the hand in mine is like something out of a waxworks.

I look at her inquiringly – that is, with the head to one side and the left eyebrow raised, never having perfected the right eyebrow lift, although God knows I've tried.

'Of course,' she says, letting go my paw and reaching into her bag, a monster of a thing with Gucci and pure class written all over it, hauling out a smaller bag of the brown-paper variety with nothing on it but promises, 'the money.'

The straw-haired character second table from the left glances our way, as does the dame wearing nothing but star-spangled swimmers and goose-bumps selling red roses out of a cigarette tray, but I bring the loot up to my face, sniff at it like it's lunch, and stuff the dough-re-you down the front of my schnauzers.

'Best not do too much in the way of advertising.'

'I'm sorry.'

Sweet voice, all rounded vowels and rolled r's and an even sweeter manner about her.

'It's okay,' I tell her, 'but don't do it again.'

Waiter hovering.

Could only happen in an Australian country town.

Sally Kane requests a skinny latte, I order yet another black-as-night zinger, and when the boy finally wanders off I turn the magnetism of my bloodshot eyes upon her.

'So what can I do you for?'

'It's my husband.'

Well, I want to say, I know it's your bloody husband, but it's her time and she's paying, so all I say is, 'What's he done, this husband of yours?'

'That's just it. He hasn't done anything.'

It's okay, I tell myself, I've got the dough.

'Right.' I drag the notebook and biro that were on special in the two-dollar shop at Newtown out of the side pocket of my Vinnies jacket and write, *Husband does nothing*, before looking back at her perched on the other side of the table with an anxious expression on her dial-up. 'And you don't like him doing nothing?'

The waiter deposits our coffees and Madame Kane colours.

'I'm sorry,' she says again, 'I — I'm not used to this.'

'Okay, why don't we start with the basics. What's his name?'

'David Jones. As in the department store.'

I write it down, looks professional.

'Address?'

She tells me the address: 48 Daisy Drive.

'And you're married to this joker?'

'Yes.'

'How long have you known him?'

'Six years come February.'

'Happy marriage?'

'I — guess so.'

Hit a sore thumb, mine if not hers.

'There are different kinds of happy. What kind was yours?'

I say *was*, it's instinctive. In my experience all happy marriages end up in the past. But if she notices, it doesn't show. Instead she answers the question. They've been married five years and the whole thing's amiable enough. He puts out the garbage, there's money to buy the groceries and they don't argue.

'So what happened?'

I busy myself writing. Always relaxes them. *Top up mobiles. Buy Dettol for shaving. Bail out bilge.*

'It was as though . . .' She says *as though*, not *like*, I like that. '. . . he had been getting sick over a long period and I hadn't noticed until one day it hit me that something must be — awfully wrong.' She leans forward. 'There was something inside him, like some sort of growth, and on this particular day it struck him, and he became — even quieter.'

'A woman's intuition?'

'I would like to think,' she says, 'that it was an informed judgment.'

I write, *Attitude.*

'Anything else?'

'You don't think what I'm saying is enough. You want to know why it matters now.'

I shrug.

'All right, it's because I want to have a baby. But first' – she takes a deep breath – 'I need to know the true identity of the father.'

I write, *Biological time-bomb*, then glance up.

She's still beautiful.

'So what's he look like, this husband of yours?'

'Medium height' – she shoots me a glance – 'shorter than you, certainly. Symmetrical features. And again, unlike you – if you don't mind my saying so – handsome in a traditional sort of way. And there's a . . . restiveness about him, a wariness – as though he thinks he's being followed.'

I write, *Paranoid.*

'Employment?'

'He's an estate agent.' Then, like the job needs brushing up a bit, as a vocation, 'it's his own business.'

'Do you work?'

'Yes.'

'And what kind of work might that be?'

A little clothing store. She'd be right at home behind a counter. Or a volunteer with Vinnies, helping the underprivileged, because her husband can afford it. Or an assistant to a dentist. Those hands.

'I'm a – surgeon,' she says. 'Neuro.'

And then she looks behind her.

Chapter 2

THE MAN WITH NO PAST

But it's only the star-spangled dame selling red roses – except it's noses not roses and she's giving them away not flogging them – leaning down to say she hopes our stay in Dashiell will be a pleasant one and we'll visit the circus when it comes to town. She says it so nice that I take one of her schnozzles and palm it across to Sally Kane, who rolls it around the table for a couple of laps before tucking it into a pocket and telling me all she knows, which is nine-tenths of nothing.

They meet, they fall in love, they get married. Only they don't live happily ever after. On account of he's got no background.

I stop taking notes.

'What do you mean "no background"?'

She tells me what she means. David Jones's life began when he first met Sally Kane. He didn't talk about his past and she didn't ask. She got the impression he'd had a Struggletown childhood and he was naturally reluctant to talk about it. He was also something of a mechanical genius.

I don't tell her straight up, but my bet is another woman, possibly another wife, who one day appears out of the wide-blue azure to discover David Jones is double-dipping on her and decides to climb into him for a cut. It would make anyone go quiet.

'When he does talk, how's he sound? Drop his haitches? Say anythink? End his sentences with but? Talk like me, for example?'

Sally Kane takes a sip of her coffee. Doesn't gulp. Brain surgeon. 'No, nothing like that.' She dabs at her mouth with a serviette. 'David has what I would call perfect intonation.'

After half an hour I still don't get it. Might be a battler but talks good. Might not be a battler but he's got a past to hide. I pocket the notebook. All that money in my jock but I've still got to earn it.

'So what's the problem? He does the washing-up. Makes not as much as you do but still quite a bundle. Talks nice. And he's not playing around with teenagers. What's to complain about?'

She shakes her beautiful locks. 'Mr Scutt, you would have been to the theatre?'

I shrug. I might have attended the odd performance.

'Then you'll know how easy it is to be fooled.' She folds the serviette and turns her eyes on mine. 'That is, of course, if you want to be.'

I inspect my chapeau. There's a hole in the crown and the brim's torn.

'Look,' she says. 'I spent a long time studying. After school I did three years of Arts, majoring in psychology, followed by five years for my medical degree, then specialisation. No diversions.'

'None?'

'None. I was nearly thirty before I looked at a man who didn't need something doing to his brain.'

I take a swig of my coffee.

'Meanwhile, the hospital was having these meetings about its facilities, or the lack of them.' She fiddles with the salt. 'They were looking at property and David was in property. I met him at one of our meetings. I was thirty. I wanted to be fooled.'

'And he fooled you?'

Again the colouring. Brain surgeon with the emotional age of a schoolgirl.

'I – I don't know.' Again that hesitation. 'All I know is that I'm thirty-five now and want to have a baby.'

And would like to know who the father is. Or is going to be.

'So you decided to hire a private detective to check out your husband's bona fides before entering into a state of parenthood with him.'

She hunches her beautiful shoulders and says something. Her head's down and it's hard to hear so I ask her to repeat it and this time I manage to catch the answer.

'Please, I – I don't like doing this. Also, I don't want him to know about it.' Her voice is barely a whisper, like she doesn't want anyone else to know about it either. 'Do you understand, Mr Bruno – I'm sorry – Scutt?'

'Yeah.' The joker with the straw-coloured hair doesn't look up as I leave and the perfume on the dame in the swimmers smells of candy-stripe.

Chapter 3

THE DAME GETS COLD FEET

Detecting's a case of following the trail, like the babes with the breadcrumbs in the fairy story. Only trouble is, after six years there aren't many breadcrumbs left in the forest.

After I've done the train ride and the bus trip and rowed myself back to the boat, I climb aboard the *Wooden No*. She's struggling to stay afloat in its hidey-hole in Sydney Harbour, an old tub with no identifying marks on its hull bar the forged code and the bit of rough patching where she crashed into wharf number six on grand final day 1987, ghosts of passengers past wandering the wraparound decks, an overworked bilge pump, and a pair of kamikaze seagulls that have set up home in the wheelhouse. I call her the *Wooden No* so that when nosy parkers ask what she's called I can just tell them 'Wooden No'.

I like my privacy.

All right, I got a business card but business cards can say anything, which is pretty much what mine says.

For the rest, I got no phone of my own, no bank account, no driver's licence, my marriage wasn't really a marriage, Aunt Rube got my birth expunged from the records, emails come to the account of a dead man, and my address when I've got one's a boat. It doesn't make me the invisible man, but it does make it that much harder for jokers to find me.

I fight my way past the empty-nesters, disentangle the Toshiba from the fingerprint powder and the secret-ink solvent and the mini-cam and the rest of the paraphernalia pertaining to detecting, plant the mainframe among the flotsam on the map table, and dial up Natality, Mortality and Misery Inc, also known as the Department of Births, Deaths and Marriages.

Everything starts with Births, Deaths and Marriages.

That's where you're most likely to find the breadcrumbs.

There are thirty million one hundred thousand Joneses on Google, six hundred and forty-nine thousand when you narrow it down to the Land of Oz, and even after you chuck in the prenom 'David', subtract thirty-eight to get a birth year and put in a couple of half-baked applications using Sally Kane's survival rations, there's still too many babes in the wood.

A vessel ploughs past and the boat rocks. As you age you acquire presbyopia.

Nothing to do with religion and everything to do with long sight, which is why you see so many codgers holding *The Sydney Morning Horrible* at arm's length in public libraries in the vain hope of making some sense of their increasingly confusing lives.

I mightn't be able to delineate my toenails but I can see what they've done to the name.

While the vessel might once have been called *Bullet*, now it's *Ballet*.

One word over another. Aunt Rube would have called it a palimpsest.

The mobiles are all out of credit so I take off the plimsolls, roll up the schnauzers, climb into the dinghy, row to the nearest patch of shingle, dig out some shrapnel, find a public phone that works, and dial up the digits.

'Dr Kane?'

'No, this is Reception.'

Reception's got a rising inflection.

'I wish to speak to Dr Kane.'

'I'm sorry but S. Kane is listed under surgeon so that would make it Mr Kane.'

I let Reception have it her way and finally get put through to Sally Kane.

'Scutt here.'

'Oh, yes, Mr Scutt.'

I imagine Sally Kane covering the speaker tube with one of her beautiful hands. Brain surgeons don't consult private detectives. They don't have private lives to consult private detectives about. Like the Queen they probably don't even go to the toilet.

'It's difficult to talk just now.'

Forty cents left. Says so in the little window.

'Look, I just need to get a handle on this husband of yours. David Jones could be an invention. He ever call himself anything else?'

Sally Kane's ready with her answer. 'His driver's licence says David Jones, all accounts are in both our names – again it's David Jones – and no one calls and asks for anyone called Freddie.'

That answers most of my question.

'I need to see him.'

'And tell him I hired you?'

'He won't know a thing.'

'Mr Scutt?'

Twenty cents left.

'Yeah?'

'Oh, I don't know, it all seems so – wrong.'

'What does?'

'This – spying business.'

Ten cents left.

'Look, lady, we just need to find out if your Mr Jones is who he says he is. If it turns out he is then everything's fresh cream straight from the cow, if not –'

But our time's up and so is my money. I get myself back to the smack, push it off the shingle, row back to the *Wooden No* and climb aboard, my body on deck but my mind off in Neverland. I'm just starting to pack the overnight for a return trip to Dashiell when the Port Jackson Jazz Band breaks into *Hot Nights in Hawaii*.

Chapter 4

ALWAYS CALL THEM DARLING

The racket's coming from the pile of mobiles in the bilge and I finally locate the offender – Phone No. 7, the Sony-Payola – and hit the little red button to shut it up, but when the music restarts I accidentally thump the little green handset instead.

'Is that Mr Rainbow?'

A bill collector or the taxation department or a pal of Pandora's.

'No.'

'Have you got another name now, Daddy?'

A kid.

One of mine.

'Sorry, darling.'

Always call them darling.

That way you can't get the name wrong.

'You forgot your name, didn't you, Daddy. But you didn't forget the circus as well, did you?'

'What circus?'

Silence.

I don't like silences, not from anyone, but especially not from kids.

'You still there, darling?'

'When you took me to Red Rooster I was playing with one of your mobiles, remember? And you promised to take me to the circus if I gave it back to you so I gave it back to you.'

Pause.

I figure the kid's fighting back tears.

'It's the last day before they go to the country and they've got this clown in it and . . .'

I taste citrus.

'Look, darling,' I tell her, 'it's just that I'm on this case, see, and . . .'

More silence at the other end of the cellophane.

Kids are like humans. You break an appointment, they send you a bill. Only with kids the bill's an emotional one.

'Darling?'

'You promised me, Daddy.'

'Look, Sophie, I'm real sorry, but it's work and I . . .'

No reply.

'Sophie?'

'It's not Sophie, it's Imogene.' Then she hangs up.

My hands are shaking as I climb back up on deck only to discover that the zip on the overnight bag won't work because the salt air has fused the alloy, but also because my fingers have turned into thumbs and my muscles to jelly.

I'd ring the kid back, only all my accounts are running on empty.

I'm probably a bit low on credit with Imogene, too.

I pick up the bag and lug it to the diving board, tripping over a hawser on the way.

My eyes aren't seeing so good.

And it's not presbyopia.

Chapter 5

A NICE LITTLE LIFESTYLE

Dashiell's 'Jones, Jones and Jones, the Realtors You Can Trust' are situated just up from the barber's, Woolworths, a gentlemen's outfitter, an op shop for the underprivileged, a boutique for the spouses of solicitors, an apothecary, a funeral parlour, and the caff where I first met Sally Kane.

I pause to examine the Vaseline-smeared images of desirable properties in the window but all I see is the reflection of a joker wearing a hat that looks like it's been savaged by a pack of dingoes, fists jammed deep in his pockets, and a gormless expression on his phyzog.

Reflections are always of this joker when they should be of me.

I head back to the outfitters where for eight slices of Dr Kane's homespun I'm sold a pink shirt with white detachable collar, a set of hot-burgundy cufflinks in the shape of tommy-guns, a pink tie, red braces, a pair of orange-and-white brogues, a pale-green fedora with a feather in the side, plus a yellow-check bag of fruit with an iridescent fleck in it.

While I'm waiting for the waist adjustment, I duck into the leech's for a haircut.

The facial and haircut take half an hour per itemo and set Dr Kane back another fifty clams but it's money well misspent because after I've packed myself into the shirt, the bag of fruit, the headwear and the shoes and got myself back to the dream flogger's, the image might still be of some other guy but now it's a guy who's had a haircut and facial and whose schnauzers don't bunch over his stogies.

The receptionist at Jones, Jones and Jones, the Realtors You Can Trust is a chirpy little number who might once have handed me over to 'Rentals' but now on account of the makeover decides I might just make it into 'Sales'.

She's armed with a telephone, a glass paperweight with fairies in it, and a vase of what might be nasturtiums.

'Good morning,' she says in a voice that's almost as bright as the flowers, 'would you be Industrial, Residential or Acreage?'

I nod the new coif.

Her face says: The customer's always right.

'We'll put down all three.' She busies herself with a ball-point decorated with a plastic replica of a yeti, on the end that's not used for writing. 'Name?'

I tell her a name.

'Very well, Mr Brown, now if you'd just take a seat, Mr Jones or Mr Jones will be with you shortly.'

I'm busy looking at the images of desirable properties plus the accompanying price tags and trying to figure how the two fit together when out trots Jones, looking pretty much like Sally Kane said he would.

'Mr Brown?' He holds out a paw. 'Very nice to meet you.'

We do the handshake thing and the How-are-you? thing after which he slips me his business card, takes me into his equally neat office, casts a connoisseur's eye over the papyrus the receptionist palmed him, nods, and consults his computer.

'How many Joneses are there?' I ask by way of conversation.

He keeps his panhandle on the computer. 'Several million, I believe.'

Those well-modulated tones and nice articulation that Sally Kane told me about.

'I mean here.'

'In this firm?'

'Yeah.'

'Just the one.' He brings his eyes back to me, the sort of eyes you'd want to buy property from. 'How many were you expecting?'

I keep the voice steady and the face as bland as a pizza base.

'Well, your business name suggests there might be several and your receptionist –'

'Ah, my receptionist . . .'

'– said that Mr Jones *or* Mr Jones would be with me shortly.'

Jones laughs just as shortly.

'It's our little joke, but also the suggestion of more than one principal implies stability, reliability and trustworthiness, don't you think?' He looks at me keenly before going back to his computer. 'But we're not here to discuss people's names, are we?'

I tell him No, we're not here to discuss people's names, so we discuss what we might be here for and after that Jones gets off his stool and I take a final shooftee around his office and Jones checks the street both ways plus one more time for good measure as we leave the premises, after which we climb into his nice, neat realtor's limo and hit the road.

Jones shows me a block of flats with cracks in it, a decommissioned Episcopalian church, and – just this side of a hill which I note possesses a little white cottage on the other side of it – a hobby farm that looks more hobby than farm, containing a driveway, a plough, a bunch of wombat holes, a couple of weather-beaten chooks, the odd gum tree, several acres of dust, and a shack.

'Nice little lifestyle farm.'

They got a language all their own, these realtors.

He waves a paw in the direction of the shack.

Its roof looks like a much-patched tyre, with a bunch of black squares all over it.

'They're solar panels,' he explains, like it's yet another of the joint's irresistible features. 'They don't feed into the grid, so you're not at the mercy of broken political promises, and although you run out of power when it's cloudy, the things are unbeatable when it's fine.'

Back at the office the receptionist's still smiling so I give her a big smile back, after which I tell David Jones I'll let him know regarding the farm, decant myself from the realtor's, head for the nearest signal box, dial up the hospice and ask for Mr Kane.

No argument over the title this time and the hospital receptionist puts me straight through.

'Dr Kane here.'

I cut to the action.

'Does your husband keep anything of any significance at home?'

'Not that I know of. Why do you ask?'

I ignore the query and move onto the next question.

'When do you expect him back?'

'He told me seven-thirty. Why?'

'He always return when he says he will?'

'Always.'

'What about you?'

'What about me?'

'When will you be back?'

'Oh, quite late, actually, because I have to attend one of those interminable meetings to save the hospital. Why?'

Because I need to visit her home and take a look around, that's why.

Only I don't tell Sally Kane that.

People get funny if you tell them you're going to break into their domiciles.

Chapter 6

THE GUN IN THE LEFT-HAND DRAWER

Number 48 Daisy Drive, Dashiell, is Location, Location, Location, just like any respectable realtor's property ought to be. Not the worst house in the best street but you could call it unpretentious, if you didn't happen to be a real estate agent.

At 7.13 pm on a dusty Friday evening I find a white picket fence with a hedge next to it, a BEWARE OF THE DOG sign so burglars can be sure there isn't a dog to beware of, and a lawn as trim as David Jones's manners that looks like it's been treated with floricides, pesticides, fungicides, and artificial colouring.

There's a white-painted house to match the fence, a neat driveway ending in a garage to match the house, and a garden that could pass for a neatly-tended graveyard, no flowers by request.

As night closes in it feels like the house is the one doing the surveilling, the way a statue can look at you out of sightless eyes.

I unpack the Smith & Wesson, park it under the hedge in the company of the coat, and amble up the driveway whistling *Give My Regards to Broadway*, a difficult number due to all the jerky bits, like the last thing on my mind's a break-and-enter.

Correction, *home invasion*, because that's what they call it now, the same galahs that decided shoplifting's shop stealing, actresses actors, and geographical locations need to be stripped of their apostrophes, for reasons best known to their mothers.

I track the alarm wire, flick the switch and turn off the power at the Main for good measure. I then smack the glass out of the back door with the butt-end of the torch from Vinnies and let myself into Chez Jones via the tradesmen's entrance, making sure I leave the hatchway wide open behind me.

The torch needs a good shake to make it function again, like a geezer experiencing problems with his prostate.

I make a detour to the bathroom where I unhook the glass from the porthole.

Then I start in on casing the joint.

There's an exercise bike in the middle of the living room floor and the torch gives up the ghost as the jewellery box from the master bedroom finds its way into one of my skyrockets, as a result of which I have to pick the lock to the study in the dark.

The study contains a chair, a desk and a lot of shadows.

I drag open the drapes.

At 7.23 pm, the desk's got nothing on it but a photograph in a gilt frame and several coats of lacquer.

There's just enough light to see the happy snap's a honeymoon shot and that Sally Kane looks just as good in a bikini as she should while David Jones looks like he wandered into the wrong photo parlour entirely. He's wearing a suit, but it's not of the variety you generally bathe in.

I use Mobile No. 9 to photograph the photograph before slotting it back on the lacquer and returning my attention to the desk.

By 7.27 pm, there's only time for one drawer so I choose the one on the left. I'm assuming Jones is right-handed and right-handed people keep items of consequence in their left-hand drawers, don't ask me why, I'm a gumshoe, not a shrink.

I step back, kick in the drawer, yank it open and Braille the contents. Inventory:

A packet of paperclips.

The expected miscellany.

And the unexpected gun.

The gat's a Vickers Luger with a four-inch barrel capable of firing nine-millimetre parabellum and possessing a 32-round snail magazine, fully loaded and with the magazine release off, all dressed-up and nowhere to go, de rigueur for every real estate agent afraid for his life.

I know what to do so I do it.

At 7.29 pm and 30 seconds by the radioactive indices of my chronometer, I return the banger to its hidey-hole and do a final finger dance through the left-hand drawer. I come up with something I haven't noticed prior because it's all neatly tucked up amongst the drawer's lapped dovetails – a scrap of paper the size of a sheet of Cottontail extra-strength – just as a set of tyres crunch onto the driveway and a spray of light sprinkles its fairy dust through the window.

In the brief illumination I make out the words *Singing-teacher* and *Debtor to H. Stowe* and what looks like an address, but the light quickly fades to black and footsteps sound on the gravel so I pocket the papyrus, slam shut what's left of the drawer, smear a fingerprint-removing sleeve over the top of the desk, drag closed the drapes, bang shut the hatch, and kick-start my way back through the desirable domicile.

That's when I knock over the exercise bike and that's when the hoofbeats outside break into a canter.

Just as I reach the bathroom, I hear David Jones throw open the front door and swear when he discovers the light doesn't work. He comes in anyway because this is his goddamn home. The through-draft tells him the back hatch is open, which means the burglar just left and the back door must have been his escape route.

I hear him hurtle through the living room, crash over the exercise bike, swearing as he goes, before heading for the back door just like I meant him to — that's why I left it open.

I chuck the torch out the bathroom fenetre, obtain some sort of footing on the edge of the bathtub, heave myself up through the aperture, and get set to make my departure.

Only it doesn't work like that.

Nothing works like that.

I land on the torch and go into an ankle-roll and in the all-enveloping darkness sense something in front of me and that something is David Jones. David Jones is putting the question and he's not about to take No for an answer, except using my greater reach I don't give him a No, I give him a Maybe in the form of an aikido-palm to the acromion process of scapula, borrowing the full force of the forward momentum of his fist to deflect his vertebra prominens into the wall behind me and Jones into cloud-cuckoo land. I then sidestep, roll, turn, stand, steady and reorientate, before hoofing it back down the driveway, gathering the coat and the armoury from the hedgerow as I go and getting the hell away from 48 Daisy Drive.

When my mother held me in her arms on that fateful evening forty-five years previous she couldn't in a lifetime of drug-struck hallucinations have imagined her only son catching his breath on a side street in an Australian country town in the middle of nowhere with stolen goods in his possession and no visible means of support, on the lam following a home invasion, having knocked down a law-abiding citizen in the process, busy packing an equaliser into his shoulder holster.

Except for the country town bit, I doubt it.

But then, I never really knew my mother.

Maybe she could.

Maybe she did.

Maybe that's why she did it.

'You what!'

Sally Kane looks aghast.

It's still night and we're perched on a street corner in Dashiell and pedestrian traffic's flowing around us like we're sticks in a stream. I've just informed Sally Kane that I broke into her home and smacked her husband about a bit in the process.

She seems to want to hear it again so I tell it to her again and when I've finished, she says, 'But why did you do it?'

'To obtain information regarding which you weren't all that forthcoming, when asked.'

'Such as?'

'Such as anything.'

'And what did you find?'

I don't tell her about the gun. Tell her about the gun and she's going to get colder feet than the pair of iceblocks she's already wearing on the end of her beautiful pins.

'A piece of paper,' I say.

'And?'

'That piece of paper might provide the clue we need to help us solve the mystery of David Jones.' I throw her a glance. 'By the way, you didn't tell me he sang.'

She looks like she might have made a mistake hiring me.

'He doesn't.' She frowns. 'Look, what do I tell him about the – home invasion?'

I dig out the jewellery box.

'You don't tell him anything, because you don't know anything. Instead, when you get home, you tuck this jewellery box under the hedge. Then you go to your room like you probably always do and when you come out of your room you tell him, Why, David, it looks like that awful burglar must have helped himself to my jewellery box!'

I pass it across to her.

'That supplies a motive for the burglary and at the same time puts you in the clear.'

She contemplates the jewellery box.

It contains diamonds and sapphires and maybe a lot of memories.

'After which you go outside and conveniently discover the jewellery box under the hedge. End of story.'

Sally Kane shakes her beautiful head.

'But it's never the end of the story, is it, Mr Scutt?'

I tell her the same thing I tell Imogene, that all stories end pretty much where you want them to.

The answer doesn't satisfy Sally Kane.

'So, meanwhile, what will you do?'

'I'm taking myself back to Sydney where I'm going to pay a little visit to a singing teacher.'

Chapter 7

THE DOG IT WAS THAT DIED

When I was a kid, going to see singing teachers wasn't in the curriculum.

In fact, when I was a kid, being a kid wasn't in the curriculum.

Because when I was a kid – after my mother left and my father dumped me on Aunt Rube and Aunt Rube pulled me out of primary school because my classmates were bullying me pretty well on a daily basis – my aunt became my teacher.

And the curriculum Aunt Rube taught was detecting, which meant that I didn't learn things like the capital of Siam and what Genghis Khan got up to and how to control a scrimmage and the point of any of the Grimms Brothers fairytales. I learnt centre-of-life stuff like self-defence, ballet, languages, knots, firearms and anatomy, with a bit of piano thrown in for good measure.

Supplemented by a lot of stories about hard-boiled detectives.

As a result I've learnt to take nothing for granted in this world.

As I approach the singing teacher's, my mind's full of unresolved suspicions. Why would David Jones take singing lessons if he didn't sing, unless he was using the lessons as a front?

And if he was using the lessons as a front, why didn't he tell Sally Kane about them?

Because the way I figure it, our friend Jones at some stage possessed a slice of activity on the side, in which case fake singing lessons would make a lot of sense by way of an alibi while he's in the process of making covert visits to his concubine.

It's not much of a lead but it's the only lead I've got.

I continue up Hesketh towards Valentine's – the apostrophe's mine – the park on the left full of codgers and prams wheeled by teenagers and dogs defecating on the tulips. The sun's midday rays are ricocheting off my white fedora and back into the hole in the ozone layer, my white-sided shoes are carefully picking their way between the potholes on the trottoir and my eyes are checking out the oleanders for hidden marksmen, the codgers to see if they're packing equalisers, and passing traffic for vehicles driven by assassins intent on killing me.

The address turns out to be that of a joint desperately in need of a visit from a bulldozer.

I shove aside a bush full of thorns the size of scimitars to proceed via a set of well-worn steps to a verandah that contains a leaking gas meter, a wooden bench well past its use-by date and cluster-housing for an extended family of arachnids.

The doorbell doesn't work because there's no need for doorbells in a graveyard, so I employ the knuckles with nil result. I'm just fishing out the good old skeleton keys when I hear what sound like wounded hoofbeats – one foot down, one foot dragged, a pause, a tap as of a blind man's cane coming down hard on bare boards followed by a dull thud as the first foot comes into action again, and the sound of the drag once more.

When the door finally opens I feel a prickling at the back of my neck like someone's behind me. Before me I see nothing but the darkness of a deserted hallway until I make out a sparrow of a woman leaning on a walking stick, wearing an orange hairnet, a dress that's busy fading to shroud, and the sort of footwear that wouldn't look out of place on Mickey Mouse's squeeze, Minnie.

'Mrs Stowe?'

The figure frowns.

'My name is Alice Cantor and I wish you people would stop bothering me.'

Half of me is watching something moving behind her while the other half responds.

'I'm interested in singing lessons.'

'I don't give –'

I don't hear what she doesn't give on account of the shadow in the hall's taking shape and there's no time for much in the way of evasive action.

The thing spears for me and I drop to the ground under it, a snarling, screeching Inferno-dweller of a being with more teeth than a piranha, against which a karate chop would be no more than an exercise in futility, but I manage to get my hands around its throat and hold it away from me, at the same time as I'm squeezing the murderous life out of it.

But the dame's got into the action now, screaming like a Banshee, and she's got her walking stick up and she's flailing away at my head with its steel-encrusted handle and it won't be long before she breaks it – my head if not also the walking stick – so I figure it might be a step in the right direction to release my hold on piranha-fangs and focus instead on defending myself from the crone.

'Let go of Rocket, you horrible man!'

So I let go and the crone leaves off with the stick but only in order to pick up the death dealer which I now make out to be a small, off-colour, nondescript-looking cur with a head too big for its body and badly in need of a haircut that has suddenly fallen peaceful in the close embrace of its materfamilias while I wipe the gore off my snout with a nose-wipe.

'Look, lady, I'm real sorry about the –'

She's a shaker.

'Mister, I don't want to know what you're sorry about, just go!'

I figure that departing right now wouldn't be the sharpest step in the pas-de-deux.

'I just need a minute of your time, lady.'

She takes a squiz at me.

'Are you a policeman?'

She's already called me 'you people' and now she's followed it up with an inquiry regarding the possibility of my being a rozzer so I'm beginning to see a pattern here that I'd be well advised to attend to.

'Lady, if I was the fuzz I'd have plugged Fido by now.'

She glances at me.

There's intelligence in the eyes and I see them soften.

'I suppose you're right.'

'All I need is a few answers.'

The crone gives it a couple of beats, during which the shakes turns into a nod.

'All right, but don't go upsetting Rocket again.' She waves a claw towards a hall stand. 'You can deposit your hat there.'

I do like she says but before I track the form twisting its way down the hall I toss a final Captain Cook over my background.

The denizens of the park are still there, with the addition of a kookaburra laughing fit to duff itself, a dame in an off-green tracksuit is lumbering past the duck pond, and a bunch of schoolgirls is making their way past the house in a flurry of soft hats, innocent faces and scatology.

Old dames have old kitchens and Little Miss Twisty's is no exception.

There's a table and chairs, a rickety old sideboard and a couch.

But what I'm pondering while the crone's wrestling with the Lipton's is, Where's the pianola?

'You must excuse me,' she says as she sets a couple of cracked cups in cracked saucers on the table in an equally cracked voice, 'but I've got out of the habit of visitors since Harry went.'

I look away from where the pianola isn't and back at Miss Twisty.

She's got eyes like burnt cinders and knuckles with lumps all over them.

'Did you say Harry?'

She gives me a queer look.

'Yes.'

'Was it you or Harry that was the singing teacher?'

'Harry.'

'And what do you mean, "went"?'

The crone starts splashing out the tannin.

'I mean that my Harry – passed on.'

I figure it's too late to make with the condolences so I stay on song.

'And Harry would have been' – I consult the scrap of paper – 'Mr Stowe?'

The cinder-eyes contemplate me for a moment over the orange-flavoured tea cosy before looking away as she fumbles the rug over the teapot and parks herself in a chair.

'That means you're definitely not from the police, Mr –'

'Green,' I tell her. 'Peter Green. But why would it matter if I was from the police?'

She shrugs, or maybe it's just part of all the twitching.

'Because if you were, you'd find yourself on the other side of the door.' She takes a sip of the tea. 'But if you don't mind my saying so, Mr Brown, while I do accept you're not from the police, there's still something decidedly – how should I say – *different* about you.'

She contemplates me over the cup.

'Who are you, what are you and what do you want from me? And don't say singing lessons again because if you do I'll puke.'

'I –'

That's when the dog starts barking, a high-pitched, constant yapping. I figure it's because someone's outside and the pooch is just doing the job it's paid for but I've got the crone to this point and if I depart now I might never get her back to it. So I stay right where I am, perched on a stool at the rickety table sipping tea and asking questions, but by the time the dog's shut up and the crone's showing me the door all she's discovered is

I'm inquisitive, and all I've discovered is:

Harry Stowe was a singing teacher;

Harry Stowe's pushing up daisies in Greenlawn;

Before attaining that status he taught David Jones singing;

All this occurred years ago.

The crone's handing me my chapeau and making with the felicities.

'Do you know Oliver Goldsmith, Mr Green?'

I can do blacksmiths but goldsmiths are a bit out of my league.

'Can't say I do.'

'Well you should. He was an eighteenth-century writer who wrote a lovely poem containing the line, "The dog it was that died".'

I look at the dog.

It's cradled in the old dame's arms, one eye in the shaggy head open and contemplating my nose.

'The townsfolk in the poem,' Little Miss Twisty says, 'were worried about the health of a man they believed to be beyond reproach. He'd been bitten by a mangy dog and they feared the bite might be fatal.'

She shifts her Minnie Mouse feet on the stoop.

'It turned out it was.'

She bends to put the dog gently back on the floor and with all the bending and twitching, plus the low voice, I have to strain to hear the punchline.

'Except that what happened was this man of impeccable character lived, and the dog it was that died.'

I nod but I haven't got the foggiest what the old dame's on about, unless it's that the barker that bit me might be going to cark it.

Chapter 8

INTERLUDE WITH AN EX-

It's late and public transport's missing presumed dead. As I make the approach to what in boat dwellers' circles passes for a front yard, there's a Black Hole of Calcutta where my coracle ought to be.

Dinghies are a live-on-board's lifeline.

You find your lifeline missing, you want to know why.

I select another dinghy from the forty or so on offer on the softly-lapping shore, launch it, remove my plates of meat from the whitesides, park myself in the driver's seat, fit the oars into the rowlocks, take the equaliser off Hold and put it on Maybe, and start rowing.

Twenty minutes later I come across my dinghy tied to the stern of the *Wooden No*. The shades are down and slivers of light sneak out into the harbour darkness around the edges.

I check about me.

The usual shipping, no unusual suspects.

I park the oars, clove-hitch the coracle to the stern next to mine, pick up the footwear and step sock-footed onto the swimming board.

Ferries are flat-bottomed and stable and the *Wooden No* is no exception.

Other tubs will list when a hundred-and-eighty-pound joker downloads himself onto it but not this baby.

I fist the gat, make my way to the hatchway and peer inside.

The interloper's back's towards me and he's leaning over the portside bench, a medium-height joker and slightly built, but it's the slightly-built jokers you got to watch in this world. They're the ones that have to defend themselves.

There's a good fathom between the two of us but I figure I can cover the distance using the bow thrusters. I park the hardware and am just preparing for take-off when the joker turns. The joker isn't a joker at all but a dame with a familiar face – but it's not a familiarity I want to carry further. This causes me to lose my balance on the launch pad, turning the fall into a tumble-turn, and I end up on my knees before Salina like I'm proposing to her all over again.

'Really, Rainbow!'

The dark roots are greying under the peroxide, the tall frame's on the gaunt side of svelte, and the expensive wardrobe's a mite worn, but the icy frigidity of Salina's being and the big, black, vacant-looking handbag on the table tell me I haven't made a mistake with the ID.

I get up off my knees fast.

'Where have you been?'

You'd think she was still my wife.

'Uh, seeing Sophie.'

'Who's Sophie?' She touches her hair as she makes the accusation. 'Another one of your floozies?'

I let the bouncer go through to the keeper, noting in the process that the wicket's in even more of a mess than usual – lockers open, drawers out, lids off jars, carpet torn away from the parquet – like she's been searching for the meaning of life even more desperately than usual.

'You've been through my stuff.'

'You should have been a detective.'

I find myself a vacant beer, operate the ring pull, take a swig to steady the peripherals and consider the situation.

Going by the number of empties, Salina has consumed four five-point-twos and is well into her fifth.

She always liked her lubricants, and that reminds me.

'How are . . .?'

'The kids?'

She frowns into her beer, remembers something and puts it into words.

'Imogene's fine,' her voice is chill as an iceberg, 'but I'd still prefer you stay away from Scarlet and Rhett. They're at a critical stage of their development and your visiting only disturbs them.'

The sea's coming up.

As is the request.

'I need more money.'

'I already paid you a year in advance' – I do the calculations – 'a couple of weeks ago.'

Facts don't cut much ice with Salina.

She's more an opinions person.

'I've spent it.'

It comes out *shpent*.

She uncrosses her eyes and slams down the can.

The boat rocks.

'Look, Rainbow, you wouldn't know, but bringing up kids is expensive.'

Then she goes for the big one.

'After all, they're *your* kids.'

She's not looking at me, like there's something stopping her.

I shrug.

It's only dough.

'Okay, I'll give you another grand.'

Her eyes harden.

Salina's strong on suspicion.

To her, Sophie's another woman and if I'm chucking her a big one without argument there's got to be a catch in it.

'Why?'

'You said you needed the money.'

Her face tells me she doesn't buy that and her words confirm it.

'There's got to be more to it than that.'

There is more to it than that only I've never been big in the bargaining department so I fish the dough out of my Y-fronts and am just handing it over when Salina pulls out her wallet, ripping it open so fast that something flies out and skitters across the chart table to me.

It's a happy snap.

In Wideascope, Wake-up-to-yourself and Technicolor.

Salina and Imogene.

And flanking them, a couple of medium-size but handsome brutes I might never have seen before, except that also I might have.

'That's not the twins.'

Salina looks uncertain.

You'd think she'd know her own children.

I reach for the snap.

'No!'

When people say No and also add an exclamation mark at the end of it there's got to be a reason and being in the line of work I'm in, naturally enough I'd like to know what it is.

I make to replace the moolah and that's when Salina removes her fist from the happy snap.

I check it out.

Salina and I have blue eyes.

So does Imogene, but the other two kids' peepers are brown.

Doesn't mean capsicums.

Blue eyes can throw brown.

Rube taught me that.

But Rube also taught me to look at the bigger picture.

So I look at the bigger picture and the bigger picture tells me that the twins in the happy snap are definitely not mine.

Chapter 9

GENES WILL OUT

I haven't clapped eyes on the twins since they were fat little maggots of ten.

After that there was no contact because Salina wouldn't allow it.

I was allowed to see Imogene but Salina didn't want the twins confused, disturbed or upset.

Then *she* didn't want to be confused, disturbed or upset.

Then she didn't want their uncle of the moment to be confused, disturbed or upset.

There was always a reason, even when there wasn't one.

When I last saw them, they were tallish, dark-haired and potato-faced and therefore could conceivably have been fathered by me.

But the kids in the chromatograph are short, blond and beautiful and therefore could only conceivably have been fathered by somebody else.

If teenagers are respecters of anything, it's genes.

It's just a suspicion.

But Salina confirms it.

'So now you know.'

That's the answer to one question.

Now for the second.

'When you suspected Tony –'

Her eyes are on the money.

So is her mind.

'Clint.'

That's the answer to the second question.

Clint was one of Salina's lovers.

He worked for Telstra, came to plug in our phone and ended up plugging Salina.

I always suspected there was more to it than that.

Now I know there was.

A set of twins more.

But I play it casual.

'Good old Clint still with the telecommunication shysters, then?'

Salina nods, like she suspects this isn't the question she's getting paid to answer, in which case she suspects right.

Now for the fourth question, the one she *is* getting paid to answer.

'When you first suspected Clint of cheating on you, how did you −?'

'Suss him out?'

It comes out *Shush*.

Tears spring to Salina's eyes and when she shrugs again it's with her orbs fixed on the last empty beer can. Her mouth is twitching, like the memory still hurts, like it all happened just the day before yesterday and it's my fault instead of anyone else's.

'In the way that every woman does.'

'Could you spell that out for me?'

I like having things spelt out for me.

Saves a lot of trouble when you look it up in the dictionary.

'I made friends with one of his fellow employees and persuaded him to get hold of Clint's telephone records.'

She goes to drain the can, remembers it's already drained and lets it slip out of her mitt to clatter onto the floor.

'And his phone records revealed text messages from hundreds of women, all of them wanting to be connected to Clint, or by him or with him or through him or whatever the preposition of the moment happens to be.'

She wipes the back of one hand across her eyes.

'Damn you, Rainbow!' She grabs back the photograph. 'Now, can I have my money and go?'

I chuck her the wad.

'Make sure you leave me my dinghy.'

Somehow it comes out sounding like *dignity*.

For a long while after Salina's gone I sit staring at the three-quarter moon, downing whiskies one after the other like they're water. I keep drinking long after the alcohol has ceased to do any good, long after the taste has stopped registering on my olfactories. The more I drink the emptier I feel of everything else.

The sight of Salina rowing off in the stolen coracle reminds me of the night she decided to pitch in her lot with Clint. Short, handsome, blond

Clint lurking in our little, narrow-gutted home, waiting for the suitcases to be packed so he could lug them out to his station wagon – the wheels I'd helped him choose long before I knew he was boffing Salina – with plenty of room to stow my wife and her suitcases and the kids in. He refused to look in my direction as I sat on what had once been Salina's and my bed of roses but was now a bed of Procrustes, wishing him somewhere I had never wished anyone before, even after my one and only visit to Sunday school . . .

About midnight, I start the engine and cast off – much like Ulysses after the fall of Troy except that I've got no Penelope to make my way back to – in search of yet another mooring, the dinghy dragging in the *Wooden No*'s wake like a codicil to yet another memory I'm busy trying to erase from my cerebellum.

After three hours and another half-bottle of Glenfiddich, I find what I'm looking for in one of the thousands of little inlets the Sydney coastline provides for husbands hiding from ex-wives and criminals and creditors and the cops – plus anyone else that might happen along, much like Pandora. The bobbing red buoy has mussels and slime hanging off it and looks like it hasn't been attached to anything for years, much like an ex-husband. I boathook the sisal out of the sea, fumble the line through the hawsehole and belay it to the cleat up in the prow of the *Wooden No*.

I straighten the mattress that Salina looked under and didn't put back right, listen to the groan of the bilge pump as it gets on with the Sisyphean task of keeping the *Wooden No* afloat, and fall asleep dreaming of Sally Kane and her beautiful peepers and the way they'll look when I finally tell her, Yeah, your husband's got a paramour but I'm available, with a love for Yours Truly that's deep, grateful, everlasting and impossible to ignore.

Or at least chuck another couple of grand my way so I can pay a bit more to my ex.

Chapter 10

FROM HERE TO PATERNITY

The Bell Telephone jokers aren't playing ball.

First up, they can't categorise me.

You're either an account-owing, an account-paying or a complainant, and if you're none of the above you're little better than a waste of potentially lucrative soundwaves.

I eventually score a humanoid, who says he's in this world for no reason other than to assist me. I know I'm asking for trouble but there's no other way.

'I need to talk to Clint Eastwood.'

Parents have a lot to answer for and that includes Clint's – Mr and Mrs Eastwood – and it's a while before the humanoid's able to reply, and even then he's still laughing fit to blow his connection.

'As in *The Man with No Name* in *A Fistful of Dollars?*'

I give him three beats to work it out of his system.

'Go ahead, punk,' he tells me, 'make my day.'

When I figure he's had enough time to get over it, I steer him back to rationality.

'He used to be in Sales.'

The humorist dredges his memory for another homily.

'Don't go away now!'

The recorded music tells me that Someone Just Called To Say They Love Me, which is more than the queue snaking out from the telephone booth does. By the time the father of two of my children makes an appearance on the other end of the telecommunications system, they're ready to turn-turtle me.

'Hi, mate!' Good old Clint, everybody's amigo. 'Who did you say it was again?'

I tell him who it was again and there's a series of clicks as Clint makes the connection.

'Mate,' he says at last.

Clint should be a chess master.

Then he could have all the mates he wants.

As it is, he has to settle for people who hate him and their husbands.

'I need a favour.'

'Anything, mate,' he says in a rush, 'you just got to ask.'

So I ask.

Not the hard question, at least not straight up, just the easy one, so as not to scare him back to where he came from.

'I need the boat swept.'

'Someone bugging you?'

You could say that.

Then again you could say a lot more.

Only I don't do either.

Instead, I tell him where the boat is and then make my way out past the hostile-eyed crowd.

First things first and the first thing is to meet up with Clint.

At which point I can get him to do the second thing.

My expectations are that good old Clint will be unchanged and that he'll arrive in a Telco van with advertisements all over the sides. But when he screeches to a stop at Leatherjacket Inlet at the far end of Yellowtail Park, it's in a red whizz-bang firecracker with smoke billowing out of its oesophagus and a fortune in effluent pouring out its bowels. He steps out onto terra firma and looks just like Santa Claus – bald head under a red cap bearing the words KEEP IN TOUCH! in silver foil, comfortable belly, cute little beard, everything bar the little red uniform, the belt and the free patooties.

'Mate,' he tells me.

'Mate,' I tell him back.

His eyes veer to the broken-down wharf where I've parked the *Wooden No*.

'This the boat?'

No, I want to tell him, this is a seaplane, heavily disguised, with its wings removed and its pontoons ripped off and yet somehow still afloat in the water.

But irony's a luxury I can't afford so I content myself with a simple affirmative, along with the rider that I need it checked out for listening devices.

It doesn't need a sweep but I don't tell him that.

He puts a hand on the *Wooden No.*

It's the same hand he put on Salina.

'I also require the Telefunken records of a real estate agent.'

'Of actual conversations?'

I shake my head.

'Of actual phone numbers – callers and called.'

Clint takes his hand off the boat, scrabbles a nose-wipe out of his Santa Claus outfit and uses it to towel the hand with which he's caressed Salina. He then replaces the nose-wipe, goes into doubtful mode and responds to the request.

'Look, I don't know about this, mate.'

'I don't know about an action for paternity, either.'

He takes off his cap and scratches his head as if that might be the way to better understanding, like praying to God or believing in the Australian legal system, of what constitutes the complicated social labyrinth of debt and obligation, in this world or in any other.

'Mate, you know as well as I do that accessing phone records is against the law.'

'So is living on a boat, but I'm doing it.'

'What if I get caught?'

'I've already caught you.'

He shuffles the cap back on his skull and because it's wrinkled it now reads OUCH!

He breathes like it hurts.

'All right. Give me the number and name of the subscriber.'

I haul out the card that Jones dealt me and give Clint the name and number of the subscriber. He keys it into a little machine that relieves people of the risk of writer's cramp or of having to use what might pass for a brain.

'That's not the department store, right?'

I ignore the riposte.

'How long will it take?'

'This sort of information's not just lying around waiting to be harvested, you know, it's all highly confidential. And if I get caught –'

'It's a question, not a debate and the question is simple: How long will it take?'

'It will take a while,' he says, 'before I'll be able to come up with anything and even then there's no guarantee it will be what you want, mate.'

So I remind Clint again what he's done and what I might do about it if he doesn't do it and he says, Mate, I'll try, but that's the best I can promise you, mate.

To which I tell him, Mate, you'd better do better than that.

Chapter 11

LITTLE MISS TWISTY REMEMBERS

I don't recognise the voice coming out of the Telefunken, in spite of the fact that it's using one of my monikers.

'Mr Grey?'

The voice is high-pitched and tremulous.

'Who's asking?'

The voice tells me who's asking but I don't recognise the name.

'The lady with the dog.'

Why didn't she say so in the first place?

'What can I do you for?'

'I've just remembered something.'

'Don't say anything over the phone. I'll come to you.'

'Can you come immediately?'

The dame sounds impatient, like if I'm too long she might forget what she's remembered, might even forget she had anything to remember, might even forget she's forgotten.

Normal detectives possess their own conveyance.

Only I'm not a normal detective.

Accordingly, I take the omnibus to Bondi Junction, underground-it back to the city, catch a cab to Camperdown and make with Shanks's pony down the home straight to the crone's joint. By the time I'm being meeted and greeted I might be in a lather of sweat but at least I haven't brought company.

'You took your time, young man.'

She's wearing a dress with purple diagonals against an orange background, too much rouge and an anxious expression on her dial-up.

'What I've remembered is —'

'Let's take the dog for a walk,' I interrupt, 'and you can tell me en route.'

The dame shakes her head.

'Rocket's never been for a walk in his life. He's an agoraphobe.'

'We'll take a walk without him, then.'

We park the pooch and I get the dame down the steps and across the road to the park.

'Do you remember, Mr Blue, my inquiring if you were from the police?'

'Yeah.'

'Well, the reason for my inquiry was that when Harriet died the police thought I'd done it.'

'Don't you mean Harry?'

'Harriet was Harry. Harry was a woman. We were lovers, Harriet and I.'

That's how she knew I wasn't from the cops.

The cops knew Harry was a woman while I didn't have a clue. I don't like not having a clue.

'What did you and Harriet being lovers have to do with the fuzz?'

We reach the lake and turn.

'Once they discover you're lesbian,' she tells me, 'you become fair game.

Despite all their talk of non-discrimination, if you're lesbian the police think you're guilty of all the sins of the world, short of creating the hole in the ozone layer, and they even keep their files open on that.'

I already know this because Aunt Rube has spent her lifetime in a similar situation.

'Second, Harriet died of an overdose of the painkillers I was taking for my rheumatics.'

She pauses.

'And third, because the police found traces of the painkillers in my system − why shouldn't they, for God's sake, I'm a cripple − they assumed that Harriet's death was the result of a suicide pact gone wrong.'

'Whereas,' I say, 'in reality, Harriet did herself in.'

The old dame shakes her head.

'Young man, Harry simply isn't − I'm sorry, wasn't − the suicidal type.'

'You think Harriet was murdered?'

'Mr Green or Brown or Grey or Blue or whatever your name is, I don't think Harriet was murdered, I know she was. The only thing I don't know is who did it. Or who would want to kill her for that matter.'

'Do you remember anything else?'

Miss Twisty frowns.

'Someone paid us a visit while I was pegging out the washing and that same person found my pills and forced them down poor Harriet's throat. Dear little Rocket was a witness to the deed.'

The dame staggers, pauses and rights herself before pointing her feet in the intended direction once more.

'Rocket barked the house down' – there are tears in her eyes – 'and I didn't do anything about it. Instead I just kept pegging out the washing.'

She shudders.

'When I came back inside – I recall it was just after midday – there lay poor Harriet, the love of my life, the empty pill container beside her, dead.'

'How come you're suddenly remembering all this now?'

She shrugs.

At least I think it's a shrug.

It's hard to tell with all the twitching.

'I haven't just remembered it, it's because I want to help you, Mr Brown.' She wipes her eyes with the sleeve of the dress with the orange background. 'I know what you're trying to do because you haven't once mentioned this niece of yours, the one who was so anxious to take singing lessons. Plus all your questions are about Harry.'

It's my turn to shrug.

'So what does that prove?'

She glances at me then quickly glances away and down at the ground because there are potholes in it and it's taking all her strength just to stay upright.

'It proves, Mr Green, that you're a private detective.' She takes a deep, shuddering breath. 'And that you just might discover who murdered my Harriet and afford me some finality in the matter.'

One thing the old dame hasn't remembered is to bring her house key, meaning I've got to enter through the side window. I then brave the acrid smell of an old dame's domicile, the dog smooching up like we're old friends and open the door. The crone taps her way straight past and on up the hall: she's racked with pain from her rheumatics and all she wants now is to lie down with Rocket on the couch in the kitchen. I pat the pooch on its funny big head before getting myself back up the hall and out the door.

Chapter 12

THE HARD CELL

The jail's a jail and there are two ways of getting into it.

One's by committing a felony.

The other's by taking a bus.

I take the bus.

Two things I don't like about jails.

One is you mightn't get out again.

The other is they take your shoes.

Every time I fight them over the footwear and every time I lose.

'So what's with the shoes?'

The screw chucks the two-tones in a bin, along with the belt, the wallet, the keys, the mobile, the bus money, the fedora and most of what's left of my self-respect.

'It's the rules, pal' – the screw's not taking any prisoners – 'and if you're worried about the restrictions to your freedom of movement, go see a chiropractor.'

Rube's seated with her hands on the prison-issue table, the shadows of bars lacing a rough noughts-and-crosses fretwork over her prison greens. She's ready with her favourite line from one of the talkies she used to screen on the dining room wall, the same line she greeted me with when my dad dumped me on her all those years ago.

'Here's looking at you, kid.'

I shrug.

I'm a big boy now.

It doesn't cut any gorgonzola with Rube.

'How they treating you, Rube?'

She moves her head but the fretwork stays where it is.

'Like you'd expect them to treat any criminal.'

'Only you're not a criminal.'

It's Rube's turn to shrug.

'Everyone's a criminal, it's just a matter of whether you get caught or not.'

'Look, I've got this case . . .'

Aunt Rube climbs down off her stool, ambles away from the bars, then turns and contemplates me.

'Who'd a thought,' her voice is a murmur, 'my little boy a Dee.' She shakes her head. 'I remember the day my brother dumped you.'

She's got this faraway look in her eyes.

'He was driving a Kombi painted all the colours of the – well, you know – and he had this blonde arrangement perched next to him wearing a set of boobs that could have been missiles set for take-off and he had an impatient look on his kisser like he had the world to save, his only problem being you.

You were spat out of that van like poo from a pig's bum on steroids.'

It's not a simile I'd use but Aunt Rube's Aunt Rube.

'He didn't even say goodbye. Your mother's body still warm and him with a new moll and here he is getting rid of his kid and he doesn't even get out of the van to do it.'

She shakes her head.

'Rube, he tells me, look after the brat, would you, there's a good girl.

'You did okay,' I tell her.

Her laugh is hollow at the best of times but this isn't the best of times, and the laugh comes out hollower than ever.

'Okay? Okay? Here's me, a private detective that looks like Mata Hari, reads old-time detective stories and watches nothing but movies featuring Humphrey Bogart and Edward G. Robinson and James Cagney, her head way back in the beginning of the last century, for God's sake, and her heart in crime, in charge of a kid who's in trauma.'

Again the laugh.

'You poor little bugger. What chance did you have? A name like Rainbow – which I made you keep because I decided it would be character building.'

She shakes her head.

'Okay, tell me what you need.'

I frown at her.

'I got this situation, see, namely a joker with no paperwork.'

Aunt Rube nods.

'What else you got?'

'I got his prints.'

'And now you want to see if he's got form.'

Everyone who's ever been in the nick has fingerprints and every set of prints comes complete with a name.

I tell her yes but also to hurry.

Because through the bars I can see a screw heading our way, which makes it a fair bet that the interview's over.

'Get in touch with Rory,' Aunt Rube tells me. 'Rory the Terminator. He knows all about you. But watch him. He can be a mite on the edgy side.'

Rube's just got time to add an address before the guard breaks up the party.

There's a new sadist at the door, and she advises me that the shoes will have to be destroyed.

'You don't just destroy shoes!'

The guard smirks.

She knows where it hurts.

'When we decide they're a threat to security we do, pal.'

She wants me to argue because that's when they can call in the support and when they call in the support is also when they're allowed to hurt you.

I see them shovelling Aunt Rube along the barred corridor back to her cell and the screws that are doing the shovelling aren't wearing kid gloves or any sort of gloves unless they're the ones with horseshoes in them, so I go quietly.

One, because I've got nothing on my feet to make a noise with.

But, and far more important, two, because I don't want to make things any harder on Rube than they already are.

Shoes are a dime a dozen.

But you can't buy yourself a new aunt.

Chapter 13

THE HIT MAN

The address Rube gave me is a prefabricated lean-to at the wrong end of the worst street on the crook side of the railway line in a burg at the bad end of the planet.

I'm not carrying a shooter because you don't visit jails wearing concealed and unlicensed weaponry unless you wish to become a permanent resident of the jail yourself. This makes me feel very naked and feeling very naked raises my anxiety level up around the danger mark.

I pick my way past an acre of dog droppings and a bunch of burntout jalopies to a falling down gate guarding a cracked concrete pathway leading to a door with an axe sticking out of it, at about the height you'd normally expect to find a door handle.

A buzzer sounds but no one answers my rataplan so I open the hatch by way of the axe handle and make my way along a hallway littered with empty whisky jars. The place in better times might have gone by the cognomen 'kitchen' but now is no more than a graveyard for cockroaches and a repository for the detritus of rats.

That's when I'm jumped.

I end up flat on my extended vertebrae with a little one-legged joker standing over me, head craning down on a too-thin neck, carving knife in one hand and a crutch in the other and intent on his face to kill me.

Rube did warn me Rory's a mite on the touchy side.

Also that he's a black belt in karate.

'Who are you?'

Well, he knows who I am because at some point in my existence Rube would have supplied a description. Only he hasn't put one and one together, so I figure I'd better help with the addition, because I don't want to die due to faulty paperwork.

'The name's Rainbow.'

I scramble to my hoofs and fetch my hat off the floor and replace it.

'What sort of name's Rainbow?'

I've heard it before and I'll hear it again.

'Rube told me to look you up.'

The one-legged joker's eyes soften in much the same way rock turns to molten magma during a volcanic eruption.

'So you're Rainbow?' He says it like nothing out of the ordinary's just occurred. 'How is old Rube these days? Still giving everyone a hard time?'

I inform him that in fact she's doing time.

'What did they nab her for?'

'They wanted to screw someone and they asked her to help with their inquiries but she wouldn't play ball so they framed her.'

Rory nods like it's just another game on the pinball machine and the little chrome spheres are bouncing pretty much like they always do.

'She want to be sprung?'

I tell him Rube might well want to be released from prison but that isn't the purpose of my visit. He asks me the purpose of my visit and I tell him and only then does he lower the cutter and only then does he start to relax a little.

I can see it takes a lot to relax Rory.

He's not a relaxed kind of guy.

'Who's the mark?'

I tell him who the mark is, checking the assassin out as I do so.

He's something under middle height and possesses the aforementioned thin neck. He's wearing words on his T-shirt that would have rendered him jailable even before they invented political correctness, and one leg of his crumpled trousers is pinned up over the vacant jamb. He looks like nothing more than the one-legged killer he is, but I remind myself he comes complete with a reference from Rube.

'So why do you need the check?'

'Request from the wife.'

'Any complications?'

'He could have a doxy on the side.'

'Anything else?'

'He doesn't exist.'

Rory nods.

He knows about people not existing.

In fact he's a specialist in people not existing.

'How can I help?'

'You can tell me if he's been through the sieve.'

I've obtained a copy of David Jones's prints from his business card using grey powder – the usual mix of chalk, mercury and powdered graphite – which I then took a happy snap of and this is what I hand Rory.

He scrunches it into a pocket without looking at it.

'I'll see what I can do.'

A figure appears in the doorway.

'Everything all right, boss?'

The lunk's so big he could double as a wardrobe.

'Took ya time to get here.'

The giant's tone turns to petulance.

'I warned you he was coming, didn't I?'

'And you reckon that's enough? Just rolling over in bed and pressing a button? For a start I didn't know who it was and for a finish all I had time for was to grab a knife and get myself behind the door.'

The lunk's whine turns into an even bigger whine.

'I was involved, wasn't I, boss?'

'Well it's time you got yourself uninvolved.'

Rube put me onto Rory as the best man for the job.

I remember the way he greeted me and now I see how he sends the big man packing and I understand why Rube put me onto him.

Rube knows I don't like hurting people.

Rory, on the other hand, kills for a living or lives for a killing, however you want to play it, and however you want to play it, Rory would have to be one handy little potato to have on your side.

Apart from which he clearly doesn't take No or Maybe for an answer.

'Is that all?'

'I might need you to do a bit of baby-sitting.'

'No killing?'

'None.'

Rory parks the disappointment.

'So who's the Mind?'

'It's a real baby,' I tell him, 'my daughter Imogene. It's worth a dee.'

'Five Cs!'

I'm running out of moolah but this case is starting to get a spread on it so five hundred's where the money pegs out as far as Rory's concerned.

'It's for Rube.'

Everyone owes Rube and Rory would be no exception.

He scratches an armpit, cocks an eyebrow, tugs at a lug, sniffs and eases his crotch.

Rory's an ease-his-crotch kind of guy.

'I need my head examined,' he says finally, 'but I'll do it.'

He grabs the crutch – the one with the big-bore barrelling in it, plus the sights and the breech and the triggering mechanism and all the rest of the accoutrements that go to make up an assassin's rifle – swings himself across the kitchen and deposits the knife in the sink.

In the backyard I make out a dog chewing on a bone.

It's a big bone, the size and shape of a human femur. It's still got plenty of gristle on it, and while the dog's a big dog, it's got its work cut out just gnawing on it.

I note the axe has been removed from the door and the lunk's chopping wood with it, like he's trying to get something out of his system. There's fat ballooning out of the armholes of his faded-blue singlet, and his pectorals are bulging. But just like I haven't asked about the dog or the bone, I don't inquire about the axeman, either.

According to Rube, Rory's always worked in mysterious ways, his wonders to perform.

Besides, the foot pinchers from Vinnies are killing me.

Chapter 14

THE MAN WHO HATED BEETHOVEN

Dashiell's turning bleak as I make my way from the station clutching my fedora. A wind whips about my ears at butcher-freezer temperature while a joker clings to a ladder hanging a sign over the main drag bearing a picture of a clown, together with a warning that Fate's heading for Dashiell, watch this space.

The wind drops for a moment and so does the sign, making it read 'Fete' not 'Fate', but tell that to my synapses.

When Sally Kane rang I was grubbing dry rot out of the hatchway and Panic was at Sally Kane's elbow.

'I can't go on,' she says. 'Tell me what I owe you and we'll call it a day.'

I wasn't in the mood to call it a day, a week, a year, or a month of Sundays, so I stare at the passing shipping and tell myself, None of us can go on, but we do, because it's what makes the world go round, from water birth to marriage, divorce to death, and funeral parlour to the wide blue verandah.

'What's the problem?'

'Can I speak over the phone?'

That's what phones are for, specifically.

'Shoot.'

'It's just that I – I think David knows.'

'Knows what?'

'Knows that I'm – that you're – Oh, I don't know . . . All right, that we're checking up on him.'

'What makes you think that?'

'He saw you at the house. He knows what you are, if not exactly who you are. I showed him the jewellery box but he wasn't convinced. He knows he's being watched and I know he suspects that I have something to do with it.'

'Thinking isn't knowing, people's minds –'

Sally Kane cuts across me.

'I happen to know about people's minds, Mr Scutt. I'm a neurosurgeon, remember?'

'I'll be there tomorrow.'

As per usual, Sally Kane has selected the trysting place and this time it's the hillside just around the corner from the farm with the solar panels on it. It's the same hillside overlooking the cottage I first noticed when Jones showed me the farm. The new shoes I got from the gentleman outfitters' slip while I'm climbing, the parcel I obtained is heavy under my armpit, and although I'm on time, it's another half an hour before I pick Sally Kane up on my radar, moving up along the ridge in a roundabout sort of way.

'I hope you haven't been waiting long,' she says on arrival. 'I've been at yet another of those meetings to save the hospital.'

Sally Kane's hair is glistening in the sunlight, her long dress wrapped around a pair of pins Mitzi Gaynor would have been proud of.

She throws herself down and while she's catching her breath I busy myself looking elsewhere – at the cottage, the sheep mooching around the cottage and, perched in the foreground, my new palominos with the dirt of the road still upon them.

I dust them off.

'I'm sorry, but I've changed my mind yet again, Mr Scutt. I think I – just wanted to see if you were – committed. Now I simply want to get to the bottom of this or I'll regret it for the rest of my life.'

She's agitated for about the length of a Baby Browning but collects herself, takes a swig of fresh air and finds herself ready to speak again.

'There is another matter, as it happens.'

'What might that be?'

She looks at her hands.

'I know it sounds silly, but David hates a particular piece of music. It's Beethoven's Ninth. Do you know Beethoven's Ninth, Mr Scutt?'

Rube always kept me abreast of the classics, so I'm able to tell her Yeah.

'Well, David came home one evening while I had it playing – the Naxos one with Nicolaus Esterházy conducting – and he simply hit the roof. He was so angry that he grabbed the CD player and hurled it out the window. And the window wasn't even open.'

'Sounds like he doesn't like it, all right.'

She looks worried.

'So what do we do now?'

'We put it all in the mix.' I give it two beats, like a thought has just entered my brain. 'You ever get to town?'

'I have a neurosurgeons' conference next week. Why do you ask?'

'Because by then I should have something for you.' I take a deep breath and the breath's got Sally Kane's perfume in it. 'I'd like you to make a reservation for the conference. Only you won't be attending, because we'll be taking a boat ride instead. Meanwhile, first thing tomorrow I'll pay another visit to your husband.'

I look down the hill towards the house.

The sheep have been joined by a shepherd.

They'll be safe now.

At least until they're trucked off to the abattoir.

Chapter 15

THE CASE OF THE RECYCLED RECEPTIONIST

First thing tomorrow it's cold and I'm hunched against the prevailing iciness behind a variegated pittosporum across the road from 48 Daisy Drive. I'm using the magnifiers to scan the frost blanketing the lawn which is just starting to thaw as David Jones – wearing a light-tan attaché case and a fixed expression – steps out of the front doorway and onto the porch. A dribble from the overhang splashes onto the left shoulder of his well-pressed suit causing him to flick a glance skywards. He checks out the sightlines to the left and the right of him before making his way along the seamless concrete pathway to the white-painted front gate. He lets himself out onto the footpath, looking back at the house like he's checking for something more than just rising damp and then both ways again as he clicks the gate shut behind him. He tucks the grip under his arm, turns right and picks his way with neat, precise steps towards town.

I follow, but at a discreet distance.

I'm garbed in the second set of gear the gentlemen's outfitter provided me with – vide licit, a brace of foot-pinching laughing-sides, white moleskin trousers, open neck shirt, oversize tweed jacket to accommodate the Smith & Wesson 645 in the shoulder holster, a pair of Zeiss binoculars crammed into a side pocket, the whole affair topped off with a curly-brimmed Akubra.

Accordingly I appear pretty much like any other denizen of Dashiell and therefore unlikely to excite much attention.

Jones doesn't spot the tail, even when my new boots upend me on the icy tar macadam outside the hot bread shop. (What do you do if you slip on ice when you're tailing someone? Rube would ask. Freeze, I'd tell her. Good boy! she'd reply, and I'd get the vodka.) He still doesn't see me, despite shooting a baker's-dozen worth of glances over his shoulder, like he's got a specific Nemesis in mind.

Beneath all the Circus and Fate signs as Jones steps into the caffeine den I note the unfamiliar girl stepping into the offices of Jones, Jones and Jones, the Realtors You Can Trust, just past the nice white Holden on the sun-favoured side of the carriageway.

Trust your feelings, Rube told me, on account of feelings is what distinguishes humans from automatons.

So I trust my feelings and my feelings tell me this must be the other woman.

It's not the receptionist I met, anyway.

Description: late teens, just the age to suit a mid-life-crisis male, even one married to someone as beautiful as Sally Kane, big goggly glasses, barber-tousled hair, neat black dress, everything shipshape and yet somehow something frazzled about her.

Like she just got out of bed and the bed had more than just her in it.

I'm still looking as Jones emerges from the caffeine parlour, brown Thermo-cup held away from his body so there's no chance of its contents soiling his bag of fruit, briefcase held just so out on the other wing, hailing and greeting passers-by like any good dream-flogger. He pauses at the bureau doors before entering to look at the For Sale signs. He seems alert and ready, but for all that like some sort of delicate sea creature, the sort that slips innocently through murky waters, hurting nobody, until something very nasty turns up and it finds itself dead.

The sort of thought that occurs to someone in love with another man's wife, desiring to discover hope where there is none, who assures himself, Yeah, someone's going to duff the poor bastard, it's only a matter of time, and when that happens I'll be available for a free consolation.

Bad thoughts, thoughts of which Rube wouldn't approve.

After ten minuets, Frazzle doesn't emerge but David Jones does. He climbs into the Commodore in the company of a young couple with moonbeams in their eyes and drives in the direction of out-of-town.

I wait until the car's gone before I cross the road, walk the block, surveill the sidewalk, de-walk the block, then enter the offices of Jones, Jones and Jones, the Realtors You Can Trust. Miss Frazzle is behind the reception desk.

'I'd like to purchase some property.'

Her eyes have trouble focusing, like she's just walked out of a cinema screening a movie in three dimensions and she's forgotten to remove her glasses.

'They didn't tell me anything about Sales.'

Blinking myopically, she peers at the pretty pictures in the window, like the answer might be there.

'I'm sorry but Mr Jones isn't in at the moment.'

She looks at the paperweight on the desk before casting her peepers back to me.

'There is one listing that's both, however. Mr Jones told me about it. Rent it or sell it, he said, it doesn't matter which.'

She pauses and considers me.

'Would you be interested in that, perhaps?'

I know that voice from somewhere.

'They've been trying to get rid of the place, oh, for simply ages, although maybe I shouldn't tell you that, you being a potential purchaser, so to speak, and also it's solar-powered, which is another pain in the butt because when there's no sun there's no power.'

She shoots me a gaze with a lot of vagueness in it.

'I'm new in real estate,' she tells me in case I hadn't guessed it, 'so I'm not altogether –'

She doesn't have to tell me what she isn't altogether because I've recognised the voice.

It's the receptionist from the hospital.

Miss Frazzle's been recycled.

'Mr Jones has already shown me that joint.'

'Oh.' She scrabbles among her papers. 'Well, if you could just tell me what your name is . . .'

I tell her what my name isn't and turn to go before stopping again, like I've just been slapped in the face with a flounder.

'By the way, what happened to the other receptionist, the happy one, the one with the gay demeanour?'

'Um, she was' – Miss Frazzle searches for the appropriate euphemism, can't find one, so settles for the truth instead – 'sacked.'

'Why?'

'She changed the ringtone on Mr Jones's mobile.'

Just like Imogene did to one of mine.

I'm still smiling, only now I've got teeth.

'She wouldn't have changed it to Beethoven's Ninth, by any chance, would she?'

Frazzle's eyebrows appear above her goggles.

'Goodness, how did you know that?'

The sentence ends in the air.

Only this time the rising inflection's justified.

Chapter 16

SETTING THE CATS RUNNING

Edith Burton?'

Good old Clint came up with the name after he'd romanced some dame several beaks above him in the Telco pecking order. The name stands out from a long list on the realtor's chat-lines because it's a regular contact, once a month, smack on the dot, reliable as the tide, and potentially just as relevant in the scheme of things.

'I understand you're a friend of David Jones.'

While there's no response from the other end of the Alexander Graham Bell, at least there's no hang-up either, no Bugger off and stop bothering me, so for the third time in this one-sided dialogue I drop my dulcet tones into the dropjaw.

'I have reason to believe there have been threats to David Jones's life.'

'Since when did department stores have lives?'

The usual joke but delivered in lead-weighted, drawly, deliberate Chicago tones.

No hint of anxiety, just the obvious witticism, like Edith Burton's had it all ready for a rainy day and doesn't need to look out the window to know there's a storm coming.

Then the follow-through.

'Who are you?'

Funny name time, to suit the joke.

'Mr Magenta,' I tell her, 'but friends call me Pinky.'

'Well, Mr Magenta, or whatever your name is, I hope you know what you're talking about, because I sure as hell don't.'

The records show that it's going to be another two weeks before Jones gets back in touch with his lover. That means two weeks of uncertainty, two weeks during which Edith Burton will berate herself for not paying more attention to this man with the obvious cryptonym, two weeks of barely endurable suspense, a fortnight strung out on those things they stretch sails on, also known as tenterhooks.

I suspect friend Burton's not the type to wait for the world to come to her – she's much more likely to get out into it and help herself.

The teeth of autumn are bared for their first nip at the winter cherry and par consequence I'm wearing a black sailor's cap and red sailor's windcheater over blue-jeans with a slight tear to the right upper-sleeve of the jacket into which I've inserted the micro-cam. I'm perched on the port side of the park bench with my arms folded in order to get the lens facing the right way and repelling all boarders while a pair of ankle biters squabble over a shovel in a sandpit, the leaves still on the trees because this is Australia, the natives are evergreen and everything in the garden's lovely.

Until something happens and it isn't.

'Mr Magenta?'

Edith Burton's out of the same mould as David Jones, someone who, on the Gemini principle, he could conceivably be attracted to. She's got a hint of Spanish olive to her but is neat as a pin, of middle height, with brown eyes and close-cropped hair. Her avocado-coloured parka is open at the front with the hood down, and underneath she's wearing a white T-shirt, joggers, close-fitting jeans with the zip at the front – which on women constitutes a design flaw, in my opinion.

'Just look at those kids,' I say, slick as oil. 'Now why is that spade so important to them?'

But Edith Burton isn't buying what I'm selling.

Finger on the button I click her frowning.

Snap of the competition to show Sally Kane.

'Look Mr Joke Name, let's forget the kids, shall we?' It might be cold but Edith Burton's got the gloves off. 'After you phoned I nearly called the police.'

I glance around.

A couple of jokers are taking in the autumn air and a gaggle of schoolboys are playing hooky from the reformatory, but there's not the barest whisper of the siege men, the boys in blue with the flame-throwers and the capsicum, so I bring my peepers back to lover-girl.

There's no threat of a concealed weapon – knife, toy gun, knitting needle, so forth – only you never know with illicit lovers, they're not always all that predictable.

She hunches her shoulders and spreads her fingers, the way dames can do these days, like they've put in more than the odd evening on the tae-kwon-do mat and they're dead keen to share the benefits of their training.

'So why didn't you?' I ask her.

She doesn't tell me why didn't she.

Instead, she makes with her own series of question marks.

'Call it curiosity.' She cracks her knuckles. 'But first I'd like to know what this Jones person could possibly have to do with me. Second, I'd like to know why it should concern you. And third' – she pats a side door of her avocado-coloured parka – 'I'd like to know why I shouldn't call the cops after all.'

I'm over the niceties.

'The answer to your fourth question, stated or otherwise, is that someone's out to get David Jones.'

It's a Mexican stand-off, without the wave.

I can't tell her that Sally Kane's hired me because she'd inform Jones of that fact.

And Burton can't admit to being Jones's lover because I could tell anybody.

'On the off chance I'm at all interested in what you're trying to sell me, Mr Spray paint, how do you know someone's out to get this person?'

'Let's just say I've got evidence.'

'And what might that evidence be?'

I stretch the truth and come up with another cliché.

'I have reason to believe that Mr Jones's life's in danger.'

I'm watching her closely but for all her reactions I could have told her that David Jones had turned Mormon.

'And what's your role in all this, Mr –?'

I glance at the kids then back at Burton.

'Let's just say I'm an interested observer.'

Burton hasn't shifted position.

She's still tense and she's still ready to launch into a flying fandango.

'So why bother me?'

I wait until my pulse steadies.

'Because I believe you might have a personal interest in the welfare of David Jones.'

Edith Burton has turned away and is watching the kids. I figure she thinks I am, too, only I'm not, because I'm watching her.

And because I'm watching her and she thinks I'm not, I see her stiffen, the slightest of backward jerks of the head. I snap a shot of that and several more unhappy shots as she gets up off the park bench and hurries away.

She takes small neat strides with her elbows close to her sides and speeds up as she disappears through a gap in the randomly planted evergreens on this cool autumn day with the kids held apart and spitting at each other from the safety of their respective mothers' arms, the spade abandoned on the ground between them.

I've put Edith Burton on the alert, which isn't a bad thing if you want to set the cats running.

And setting the cats running is precisely what I want to do. The object of this exercise isn't to discover the identity of David Jones's lover but to find out who Jones is and why someone like Burton might be worried if his life's in danger. I can only do that by spurring her into some sort of action that might be described as untoward.

Chapter 17

THE DESIGN FLAW

Ask me the precise moment I'm certain I'm being followed and I'd say it's when the omnibus drops me at the junction of Druitt and George, up alongside the Rathaus.

No one tailed me to the park, I'm sure of that.

I'm also certain I'm Omo-clean when I board the omnibus, there being no evidence of anything apart from a feeling.

And in this game, as Rube says, while instinct's fine, feelings don't butter parsnips, nor promise you anything but a lie-down role in a final farewell at a funeral parlour.

Several more punters get on – a blond kid clutching a scooter, a sum of accountants and an old dame lugging a green tartan granny cart – while only one joker boards the bus behind us.

I get off at Wynyard and take the third 412 that happens along, parking myself next to a geezer who looks like he ought to be on life-support instead of a bus. I plan to alight at the edifice named after our late and unlamented Queen Victoria.

I turn to help the codger whose hand is as thin as a coathanger, skin as dry as landfall after six months at sea and as cold as the polar ice cap. One hoof trembles on the running-board while the other waves about in the air like an antenna. I reach out to stop him tumbling into the gutter.

That's when I look back and that's when I see Edith Burton, only this time it's without the benefit of an appointment.

She's fourth out of the bus behind ours and if I hadn't been busy helping Herb – Herb's the name, just call me Herb, everyone does, even the dog – I wouldn't have noticed her.

When I last saw her she was wearing an avocado-coloured parka with the hood down. Now, the parka's black and the hood's up, and if she's got brown hair, you wouldn't know it. For the record, I only know it's her because of the way she moves: like a wildcat in the jungle with its claws sheathed.

I could call seeing her again a coincidence, only I don't call anything a coincidence.

Accordingly, I believe she's following me.

But I want to do more than believe, I need to know it for a fact.

Knowing things for a fact is what keeps sailors alive, knowing for a fact that all the cleats are in place, the rigging's secure, the steering cable's not hanging by a thread, there isn't a crack in the hull, and the bilge pump's fully operational.

It's also what keeps gumshoes out of the graveyard.

I set Herbie down, even more frail-looking now he finds himself at street level, and we have a little chat about the weather.

We both hope it will hold.

That's when I make my move.

In seven-tenths of a second I've completed the instep swivel-spin on the metatarsals and am clattering over the mosaics decorating the floor of the Queen Victoria Building, heading for York.

At Market I chuck a right, followed by a left into George – not to the ship circus in Darling Harbour but towards the Semi-Circular Quay. I then slow to five knots, anchoring long enough to glance in a shop window and nod at the mannequins wearing their post-summer finery. I tack sharply back into Wynyard, secreting the sailor's cap under the shirt while I'm in the Gents', but not the jacket, due to the fact the Smith & Wesson needs it for cover. I stop to buy a newspaper at the kiosk under the destination board, take the escalators back to York, then make the final preamble along the straight to the boat show, much in the manner of a middle-aged joker that's losing it.

And in all the glancing at reflections, doublings-back, stoppings and glancings between my knees, there's no sign of Edith Burton, in black parka or avocado-coloured turnaround or crimson top or no parka at all – no sign of her face, no sign of her walk, no sense of her presence, no glimmer of anything to do with the actual or soi-disant lover of David Jones at all.

Until I get to the boat show.

And then I spot her again, but only because I run into a fellow boater who's also wearing a red sailing jacket with blue jeans. After I palm him the newspaper and we separate, Edith Burton exhibits one of those dead giveaway nanoseconds of hesitation that can afflict even the most experienced of surveillers – she must decide which of us to follow.

She's stripped down to white T-shirt, jeans, and sneakers – the chameleon has turned into a sailor – but she's still Edith Burton and I still recognise her.

There are a number of ways of losing a tail.

First – Aunt Rube's Regola Numero Uno – don't let them know that you know that they're tailing you.

Well, it's too late for that, my friend, Edith Burton already knows that I know.

But it's not too late to apply the second rule, which goes something like this: be patient or be dead.

It's a truth, universally unacknowledged, that a surveiller has to eat, drink, sleep and go to the lavatory, just like any other micturating creature on this planet. This is why the well-trained surveiller always carries food and drink, plus something to pee in.

But that's only when they know they're going to be surveilling.

And that's something Burton couldn't possibly have known and therefore couldn't possibly have been prepared for.

I pay a visit to the toilet, in order to plant the concept 'toilet' in her mind.

Then I make for the marina where there are no toilets, just the heads on boats whose use by the general public is verboten.

After that, I saunter off to lunch, settling down at a table and tossing a serviette over my knees and ordering up big like I haven't eaten for a week and am getting prepared for a slap-up.

Five minutes.

Ten.

I see Burton haul alongside portside-aft and linger near the Damen und Herren.

The waiter passes into posterity.

I raise my wine glass and note in it the reflection of Edith Burton, secure in her delusion that I'm engaged in nothing more than anticipating my repast, while she's glancing longingly at the sign that says Damen und Herren.

Seconds later, she ducks into the Damen.

That's when I make my move.

You can't be followed into a kitchen, not without creating a serious disturbance.

One person might get away with it but in your average industrial-strength kitchen, two more's a crowd.

There's a chance that Edith Burton's still in the Ladies' but an even bigger chance she's done a hit and run and the bigger chance has won because I can hear her slamming the door open and following this joker she's only just had the pleasure of meeting. The big, awkward-looking affair has stuffed the gat down his jeans and chucked the jacket onto the gas burners and is now clutching his cap. He lopes past the pots, pans, sous chefs, bottle washers and waiters' assistants, the overseas students with garbage bins and mops in their hands and the future in their hearts and astonishment in their eyes, and out through the back door. He then belts across the promenade and clatters up the steps and into a carriage of the monorail just as the doors close.

I can see Darling Harbour laid out below me like a painting by Brueghel, a painting with too many people in it and all of them too much the same, until the carriage is halfway around the first bend and there she is, standing by a palm tree in the forecourt doing a 360-degree turn, slowly, deliberately, surely quartering the environs. As she does this, the fly on her jeans is open, exposing pink underwear, because a front-loading zip on women's jeans is a design flaw, and for Edith Burton, when she realised I was doing a runner, it was first things first, and the first thing was to relocate me. When she'd done that, or given up, whichever came first, then and only then would Ms Burton, professional follower, attend to the adjustment of her clothing.

Chapter 18

BACK IN THE SLAMMER

I present myself in the slammer wearing the purple-and-white pintos that got nailed in the last case but one – a slug through the portside aileron from a Remington Rolling Block 1871 – and it's icy like a morgue in winter. Me and Rube are in the south-wing visiting-cell, and Rube's in the sort of mood that makes me feel like a kid that's got caught stealing from the gift box on charity day at the poorhouse.

'Rory's just been to see me.' She's hunched and is staring out through the bars. 'He says he's fed up with all the killing.'

When Aunt Rube hauled me out of Baisson Primary and started in on my home schooling, I discovered that her idea of education was screening James Cagney movies on the cracked dining room wall, or handing me a book by George Harmon Coxe or W. R. Burnett or Hammett or Chandler, and dispensing her own particular brand of philosophy.

Along the way, I learnt the principles of logic, surveillance, self-defence, anatomy, pharmacology, body mechanics, several languages, ballet, and how to play piano.

I also learnt ethics.

'I told him killing's not on the agenda, Rube.'

Aunt Rube nods.

'But he's got a minder.'

'Who, Rory?'

'No, David Jones.'

I tell Rube about Burton – how she's in regular contact with the husband of the client, doesn't give anything away, and knows how to follow people.

'Prisoners on bail require minders.'

Rube's mind works like a computer, only faster.

'People can still have private lives.'

'That would make it a coincidence, Rube, and I don't believe in coincidence.'

Once upon a time that would have scored me a shot of vodka.

'I believe I taught you that, too, Rainbow.' Rube's silent for a moment. 'Tell me more about the minder.'

So I tell Rube more about Edith Burton and all the time I'm watching the screws prowling about us like dingoes around unattended babies.

'She could be anybody,' she says at last. 'ASIO, ASIS, CIS, DEA – any one of a number of acronyms.' She glances at me. 'That's words made up of initials, in case you don't remember.'

It's then that the door's knocked down or – the jail-place equivalent – the gate clangs open, and two screws – it's becoming a habit – charge into the room. While Rube's dragged kicking and screaming back to solitary by one of them, I'm advised by the other to get the hell out, visiting hours are over.

'What about the footwear?' I ask, leaving.

'Just piss off.' Which is jail speak for Goodbye.

I'm busy pondering Rube's take on Burton when Mobile C rings, its dial tone the theme from *Apocalypse Now*.

I dig it out of the portside aileron.

'That you, Rainbow?'

I've told Rory not to name names on the cellophane but I'm fast discovering Rory's not all that big in the listening department.

'No,' I advise him.

'Yeah, it is. Look, Rainbow, I got to see you.'

It's like Rory's brains have taken a powder along with the leg.

I hang up fast. Then I hotfoot it to O'Leary's. O'Leary's is doing a trade only it's not roaring. There's the odd piss-boy, a couple of travellers and a druggie in the midst of a delusion.

Rory's arrived before me and he's hunched over an ale with his eyes popping all over the place, even checking out Hank, the barman, and Hank's been here since Adam was a girl.

'Hi, Hank.'

'Hi, Rainbow, how they hanging?'

Hank pretends he's as butch as the next joker, hair poking out of the top of his pink singlet and muscles on muscles, when I know for a fact he shaves his shoulders.

I chuck him a frown.

He shrugs.

'It's just an expression, Rainbow.'

Hank gets over his agitation by rubbing hard at the top of the bar with what look like an unwashed pair of pink underpants.

'What's your poison today, Rainbow?'

'Same as it was yesterday and the day before that and the day before that.'

'That would be soda water.'

'That's exactly what it would be.'

'With . . .?'

'With carbon dioxide and a dash of potassium bicarbonate.'

I turn to Rory.

His face bears a hunted expression.

Rube warned me of his latest hang-up.

'Look, Roarer,' I tell him, 'if it's bullets you're afraid of, you might be in the wrong profession. But seeing you're in it, you can forget about being afraid, and tell me what you discovered.'

Rory shrugs.

'I put the prints in the system. I got this little mate, see . . .'

'Spare me the details. How long will it take?'

'What, the story?'

'No, the processing.'

'It's not a formal thing.' He shrugs again. 'Accordingly, it will take as long as it takes. Meantime, I'm staking out the kid like you told me to but it's giving me the creeps, because someone —'

I take a swig of the eau de nothing.

'Look, Roarer, you're a killer. Killers can handle killers.'

'Except I'm not all that crazy about killing any more, Rain, apart from which, this dame —'

That would be Burton, Madam Professional Burton, who would have done her own fingerprint check on me — courtesy of the Darling Harbour wineglass — and come up with Rainbow and via Rainbow she's come up with Imogene and having come up with Imogene she's also stumbled across Rory, so accordingly she's lurking with intent to discover what we're about, only I don't tell Rory that, the less Rory knows about things the better.

'Forget the dame and keep your eye on the kid.'

'I still don't like it, Rainbow.'

'You're not paid to like it.'

After Rory's gone, his eyes still darting about like a rabbit's at a summertime shoot, I linger a while with Hank.

'I need some advice, Hank.'

'Do you want that straight, too?'

I let the witticism pass.

'When you got out of the slammer after doing time for whatever you did time for – spare me the details – were you by any chance allocated a parole officer?'

Hank nods.

'We had to be in regular telephone contact.'

'How often? Daily, weekly, monthly?'

'Daily.'

'How long ago was that?'

He squeezes out the underpants in the sink.

'Years back, in the dark ages. Now they just stick a bug on you.'

Chapter 19

A DISTURBANCE IN THE NIGHT

The moon's on the wane but it's still as big as Cyclops's eyeball, rolling across the open hatch of the *Wooden No*'s aft cabin like the orb of the giant in *The Odyssey* as he tried to duck the poker that Ulysses was trying to jam into his one eye, preparatory to making good his escape.

The wind's shifting, from north-east to east.

The *Wooden No*'s on yet another borrowed mooring, a hempen line attached to a two-ton block of concrete on the ocean floor all that's stopping the drunken tub from smashing itself to smithereens on the rocks.

The moonlight reveals a crumpled doona and a pile of dirty clothes while the boat dweller's trusty jam jar and an empty bottle of Johnny Walker Red clatter this way and that across the marzipan like a couple of dice in a crap game.

Coupled with these sleep-inducing phenomena, the boat's crepitating, the fairy fingers of Fate tapping away at the superstructure like it's trying to decide whether to sink me now, or allow me a few more moments of uncertain existence before curtain time.

To top it off, one of the mobiles rings, the one containing the theme music from *Dr Zhivago*.

I scrabble it out.

'Mr Scutt?'

A dame's voice.

Play it again.

'Mr Brown?' This time I recognise the dulcets. 'I do hope I didn't wake you.'

'It's okay,' I say, 'I wasn't asleep. What is it?'

'I've just remembered something.'

There's a series of clicks like Miss Twisty's bones are cracking. I hear the sound of the dog snuffling about in the background.

'Shoot.'

'What did you say?'

'Forget what I said and just tell me what you remember.'

For three rolls of the boat all that comes out of the cellophane is shuffle-shuffle-shuffle, click-click-click, the clatter of teaspoon against cup, an old woman's memory playing ducks and drakes with the facts and then:

'Oh, yes, that's right, two things, maybe neither of them important, but I had to tell you or I wouldn't be able to sleep tonight.'

Make that two of us.

'First – Are you still there, Mr Green?'

'Affirmative.'

'What? Oh, you mean, Yes. Well, first of all –'

She goes silent again so I make with the prompt.

'Yeah?'

The clicks go into overdrive but after a bit she comes back online.

'First, you believed that Harry was male and that told me conclusively you weren't from the police because the police . . . Anyway, we sorted all that out. But second, you thought that Harry was a singing teacher.'

An old woman's midnight ramblings – of course Harriet was a singing teacher, didn't the receipt read: Harry Stowe, Singing teacher, Dr to David Jones, et cetera, et cetera and so forth?

'Yeah.' I think about it, then I don't think about it. 'Because that's what she was, wasn't she?'

'Yes, Mr Brown, she was. But she also taught voice.'

My mind comes into focus.

'Meaning?'

'Meaning, Mr Grey, that Harriet not only taught people how to sing she also taught them how to speak.'

Extract from interview with Sally Kane:

'How's he talk?'

'I told you. Nothing.'

'I meant his voice.'

'Oh, David has what I would call perfect intonation.'

I re-enter the present, during which time Little Miss Twisty is still busy explaining.

'Come again?'

Miss Twisty comes again.

'I was talking about Harry's students. There were children needing help after operations to correct problems like cleft palates, adults getting used to dentures, accident victims learning to talk again, people needing to change the way they speak . . .'

The click of teaspoon-on-cup metamorphoses into something else, a code that might be making no sense at all, but is still trying to tell me something.

'What sort of people need to change the way they speak, Miss Cantor?'

A sigh or it could be the wind.

'Persons who want to get on in this world, Mr Brown. Whatever people say, Australia is far from being a classless country and the wrong accent can be like a police barrier at a crime scene – yes, Mr White, I do read detective novels – and can seriously hold people back from somewhere they'd rather be.'

I absorb that little homily, at the same time as I'm leading Little Miss Twisty on to the next stage.

'There was something else.'

'What?'

'The second thing you remembered.'

'Oh, yes . . . Well, the series of lessons had just been completed when . . .'

Click-click-click-click-click.

'What's that?'

But the dog's started barking.

I picture Miss Twisty gripping onto a chair as she talks, eyes dulling as she winces with the pain, her joints cracking and the little dog – the dandie Dinmont or the agoraphobe or whatever it calls itself – prancing about and barking its crazy head off, at nothing more than the wind.

'Rocket, do be quiet! What on earth's the matter with you?' Then back to me. 'I'm sorry, Mr Black, what did you say?'

I tell her what I said but it's too late.

The barking has stopped, the clicks have ceased, Little Miss Twisty's voice has been cut off, the line's dead, and when I ring back all I get is the sort of signal that says the phone's engaged, you're wasting your time, call back tomorrow. After a while I give up, in case the reason the phone's engaged is that Little Miss Twisty's busy trying to call.

I'm still waiting when the arms of Lethe claim me and I'm still waiting again when I wake next morning, late, due to the disturbance in the night.

And I'm still waiting now.

Because Little Miss Twisty never rang me – or anyone else for that matter – ever again.

Chapter 20

DEATH AT NOON

There are chores to do on a boat in order to stop it sinking – the bilge pump to mend, re-pitching the hole in the hull that's reopened, and making with the bail out – so it's close to noon when I finally climb down into the coracle and close to an hour later when I step off the omnibus a couple of stops short of Miss Twisty's. I alight at the crossroads where the 437 chucks a right in order to make its circuitous way past the homes of politicians' grandmothers, then cross the park we traversed not all that long ago, moving this way and that in order to expose anyone that might be tailing me, but all the time heading in the general direction of Little Miss Twisty's.

I see no one.

That doesn't mean crabmeat.

Nor is there any traffic.

That's not unusual, either, except that there should be.

Not even the odd bus approaches along the carriageway. I can't figure the reason for this until I swing around the clump of trees at the southern end of the park and see the bus – just the one bus – and there's nothing odd about that either except for the mess of cops that's surrounding it, and the sort of barrier that Little Miss Twisty mentioned, that cops like to put up around crime scenes.

Six squad cars are spread across the road, red and blue fantasy lights flashing, twenty or so interested spectators craning for a glimpse of blood from the other side of the blue-and-white tape where they've been herded, an ambulance nosing its way towards the focal point, just to the fore of the bus.

I get nervous packing a gat around the fuzz.

They got X-ray vision for concealed weaponry.

I'm wearing the big jacket but am aware of the bulk of the S&W pressing against my ribs so I doff the trilby and park it over the equaliser. I realise I might appear to be paying my respects to whoever might require my paying my respects to, of which there might be a great need, or not much, depending upon your viewpoint in the matter.

That's when I see her.

Little Miss Twisty has never been straighter, a small, thin twig lying three-quarters of the way across the carriageway, arms by her sides, closed eyes facing heavenwards, so she might be asleep except for the marks on her face and the pool of what might be oil, but isn't, which has darkened a patch of her hair at the same time as it's matted it and which also appears to have glued the back of Little Miss Twisty's head to the tar macadam.

The marks on her face are consistent with her having been hit by a bus.

Or . . .

Three paces from the figure on the ground, someone in joggers is opening his heart to the rozzers.

From where I'm standing there's no way of hearing what he's saying so I work my way past the ambos with their stretcher and the gawkers, making especially sure to give a wide berth to the cop with the Sigourney Weaver face, until I'm near the back of the joker that's doing all the spraying and able to tune into the broadcast.

'She was going that fast. One minute there was nothing, the next . . .'

I miss what follows next, but then, 'Like a flash she was, like she'd been shot out of a cannon.'

Like she'd been shot out of a cannon?

Little Miss Twisty?

Miss Twisty could hardly manage a walk.

As I back away the cop's saying, But how do you account for the marks on her face?

No one seems to be paying any attention as I let myself in through the rusty gate and up the steps and onto the dark verandah under the laughing kookaburra etched in the fanlight and in through the still-open front door from where whoever-it-was hurled the body of Little Miss Twisty after what must have been many hours of doing a lot of hurt to her. I move along the darkened click-click-click floor of the hall and into the kitchen where the wall clock reads just after one in the post-meridiem. The pooch is cringing under the sideboard, just his funny little nose and glinty little eyes sticking out, staring up at me like I might be yet another person or persons unknown come to do him or his mistress further harm.

'Come on, boy.'

Or girl or thing or whatever you happen to be.

I bend down.

'Good dog!'

There's blood on Rocket's head but the wound doesn't appear to be fatal and he doesn't bite my hand or even attempt to, even when I pick him up, falling immobile in my arms like a child's toy, even when I accidentally knock his head against the window frame in my haste to get out, because there are footsteps and voices screaming Stop! as I exit and belt up the main drag as fast as I can in order to distance myself from the knot of interested spectators around Rocket's mistress's body. I take a left up a lane, the sound of my pursuers fading until eventually all I can hear is the clatter of my palominos on the sidewalk, the shuddering breathing of Rocket in my arms, and the myriad interrogatories echoing in my skull regarding the passing of Little Miss Twisty.

Like: Why?

And: Why just now?

Meanwhile, I've got a dog on my hands.

I call Rory.

'How are you doing with the surveill?'

'Apart from the dame that keeps making the guest appearances, good as gold.'

'Can you look after a dog?'

'What, kill one?'

He sounds appalled.

'No, look after one, as in care for it, feed, kennel it, that kind of thing.'

He tells me, Yeah, because it so happens the palooka just bumped his off and he's looking for a replacement – for the dog, not the palooka – so I find a cab driver that takes dogs and get him to take Rocket to Rory, after which I keep my date with Sally Kane.

Chapter 21

THE BLACK CABRIOLET

Keep dames at arm's length, Aunt Rube always told me, they can be bigger killers than the Thompson M1928 trench broom as employed by Al Capone's boys when they massacred seven of Bugs Moran's heavies in a Chicago garage on Saint Valentine's Day, February fourteenth, nineteen hundred and twenty-nine.

But Sally Kane isn't at arm's length: she's seated in the beam of the dinghy, pressing her hat into her nestful of beautiful curls with one slender hand and clutching the bulwark with the other. The wind's freshening as I haul on the oars that are carrying us into ever deeper waters, the only movement around us — apart from the rowing — a dozen bird-limed yachts abandoned on their moorings, the ripples on the surface of the harbour, and a bunch of seagulls tormenting a shiny black seal a fistful of fathoms to windward.

I keep reminding myself that the reason for the boat ride is not so much to get Sally Kane alone as to discover the raison-d'être for Edith Burton, given the Burton dame's a mite too handy in the tracking department to be nothing more than David Jones's extra-marital squeeze.

I get us to a beach and Sally Kane perches herself on a rock overlooking the water.

I've told her about the phone calls and also about Edith Burton and she's looked at the happy snaps but she still says she doesn't know the dame from Solvol.

'Do you think they're . . .?'

'Negative.'

'But why else would he be making regular calls to her, if she weren't, if they weren't —?'

'That's what I'm asking you.'

'Perhaps —'

'Perhaps what?'

'Perhaps . . . I don't know, perhaps they're — related. Didn't you tell me they're alike?'

'Yeah.'

'Well, then . . .?'

I look at the seal.

'Aren't they a protected species, seals?'

'What's protection got to do with the price of salmon?'

'Just a thought,' she says.

After the seal's gone plus the birds and all the romance that wasn't and we've piled back into the coracle and I've rowed us back to where we came from, I realise I know what that seal's got to do with the price of salmon. I've known all along, if only I could admit it.

A black, nineteen-twenties two-seater people-mover in the shape of an upright coffin with flat-foot running boards, oaken-spoke wheels and damask curtains to the windows tends to stand out in a crowd, which means that whoever's at the wheel isn't worried about being in possession of a profile. A dozen corpses laid cranium to metatarsal is about the distance the car's staying behind me. I've just seen Sally Kane onto her train, and the black car's keeping perfect pace as I foot it along the boulevard. Its forward progress – in the vicinity of five knots per honorarium – leads me to suspect that it's not just employed for transport – it's also a tail.

Chapter 22

RETURN OF THE AXEMAN

It's close to midday when Rory's voice filters through on dead-man's mobile No. 17.

'I'm outside the kid's place and there's something funny going on.'

'Shoot.'

'You know the dame I was telling you about?'

'Olive skin? Tall for a dame?'

'That's the one.

'Well, she's closing in on me and I want to know if I'm supposed to duff her, because –'

'No,' I tell him, 'I know who it is and she's only a minder, not a killer.'

'You could of fooled me.'

'Okay, rendezvous you-know-where in ten.'

'But it can't wait, Rainbow, I –'

'It's got to wait, pal,' I tell him, 'all of six hundred seconds it's got to wait.'

Rory's not you-know-anywhere when I get to O'Leary's.

I'm wearing the zebra-striped jacket and the new orange trilby I purchased from Serafino's to replace the fedora. While I'm hitting the sodawater I keep the head down because I'm not in the mood for socialising.

This isn't New York, it's not the nineteen-twenties and there's no Eighteenth Amendment prohibiting the manufacture, sale and transportation of intoxicating liquor, but that's just for the blatts.

It doesn't mean Sydney doesn't possess joints like O'Leary's.

It just means you don't hear about them.

'You waiting for Rory?'

It's the palooka, the one that just bumped off Rory's dog, the one with the axe.

The joker's an ape, and that's no compliment to primates.

He'd weigh in at about the two-hundred-and-eighty mark and there's a long, suspicious-looking bulge under his non-matching tracksuit.

Never trust a joker in a non-matching tracksuit.

'I got a message for Rainbow.'

Rory's just sacked this watermelon.

Accordingly, there are two ways he could know I'm waiting for Rory, and at least one of them carries ramifications that aren't all that pleasant to contemplate.

'What's it to me?'

Uncertainty flickers across the pug's face.

'Ain't you Rainbow?'

'If I'm a rainbow you're a moonbeam and if you're a moonbeam –'

The nice thing about O'Leary's is that when there's a contretemps, the clients tend to ignore it and continue indulging in their drug of choice while the matter's resolved.

So when I accompany the ape outside and Hank's busy clearing away the broken glass, the upturned stool, the blood and the axe, nobody looks up.

'What's the message, Sunshine?'

'Rory says he doesn't need to see you. The message he gave me is: Everything's good.'

'Who sent you?'

'Rory did.'

I convince him that Rory didn't, a discussion that involves smashing his jaw.

'So who was it?'

'A voice,' he manages through the jaw.

'You always do what the voices tell you?'

'This one I do.'

'Who was it?'

'I don't know.'

'You work for someone you don't know?'

He manages a shrug. 'They pay.'

Why would someone pay someone to tell me everything's good when Rory himself has just informed me that it isn't?

That's the first question.

The second question is, Where's Rory?

The answer to both is pretty much one and the same and suddenly I'm several street numbers down the road from the speakeasy, my palominos pounding the pavement, my breath coming in the sort of rasps that could spring Aunt Rube from solitary, the new trilby gripped in my hand, and fear clawing at my heart for Imogene.

Chapter 23

THE KILLING ON CASTANET CLOSE

It's a long time since I've been to Number 21 Castanet Close but I'm familiar with the address because this is where I send the major portion of my ill-gotten gains. Rory's across the road where he's meant to be, slumped in the driver's seat of the wide-bodied pink Caddie he uses when he wants to travel incognito, a miniature Colt pistol dangling from the rear-vision looking glass, and a little star decorating the driver's-side wind-up. He's got the sort of look on his face he'd reserve for moments of absolute calm, like when he's about to kill somebody. Only he's not about to kill somebody, because somebody beat him to it and killed him first.

I don't waste time on the autopsy. My first reaction is to charge into Number 21 Castanet Close, gun blazing. But my second is to stay alive, so I prostrate myself by the coupe and shoot a couple of Captain Cooks along the *camino real* prior to focusing on the narrow-necked brick-veneer lean-to with the pink geranium in the cracked pot out the front where in another life I used to reside, directly across the carriageway from the Caddie.

Imogene's room's the one on the right. The silhouette of the fairy I made for her hangs in the window under the half-drawn blind. The moving part of the fenetre halfway up the box frame reveals a Chinese lantern with witches etched on it and a part-open wardrobe with a child's drawing of a three-legged cat Bear-taped to the sliding door.

There's the shadow of a movement at about the point where the window turns into a sill.

Castanet Close is a wide street, wider still when there's a corpse in the car behind you, an even-money bet there's a second in the house in front of you, and the very real possibility the killer's still in the frame, all set to make it a trifecta.

The .45 is cocked but still in the cross-over under the jacket as I make my way – arms out, fingers spread, like Cagney in *Yankee Doodle Dandy* – to the front gate, at the slightest provocation ready to do the quick-draw, side-step and flip-roll onto the asphalt.

The side path's still got a slope to it like the Wall of Death at the Royal Easter Show, leaving enough room under the back of the house for Imogene to play hide 'n' seek in when she feels the need. The bell's still busted and the side door's still made of papier-mâché, so it's hardly a challenge kicking the hatch down. I whip out the Smith & Wesson as I stay on the stoop, right where I was when I kicked the door down.

Tripodi, Imogene's three-legged cat, has been lying in the hallway with a bullet hole through his brain long enough to attract flies, long enough to make clear he's never going to lurch about on his three legs again, but not long enough for the blood to complete its inexorable process of coagulation.

A sound comes from the direction of Imogene's bedchamber.

I dive over the dead moggie and into the sleepy-hole, Smith & Wesson at the ready.

Nothing.

No kid, no perpetrator, just a breeze through the open window with the fairy swinging in it, a Donald Duck clock on the green cupboard next to the bed telling me it's thirteen minuets after twelve, and too many memories – Imogene sleeping, Imogene unwrapping Christmas presents, Imogene . . .

I park the gat, tear the wardrobe door off its plastic slippery-slide, and yank Imogene's bed away from the wall.

Still nothing.

There's no blood in Imogene's room, I keep telling myself as I reupholster the gat and get myself in quick-time across to the window – there's no, repeat no, blood in Imogene's room.

The blind's hanging crooked, the fairy's still swaying at the end of its tether and there are marks consistent with footwear decorating the sill. But a quick shooftee tells me that apart from the Caddie on the other side of the carriageway, the street's still wearing the Vacant sign.

I stand with blistering eyes in the middle of Imogene's crumpled clothes, her books, her plastic macramé and her teddy dogs, trying to recreate in my mind what might have occurred a quarter of an hour prior.

The book on the unmade bed is *Where The Wild Things Are*, open at a page with a drawing of a monster with dirty big teeth in it, enhanced after publication, distribution and sale with scribbles of purple and blue crayon.

She always liked – make that *likes* – being scared, Imogene.

There's a real likelihood they got her.

They?

I don't know any They, only that Imogene's not here, and the street's deserted.

There's no blood in Imogene's room, I repeat to myself, nothing happened, or at least nothing that can't be fixed with an ice-cream.

I sense something behind me.

I spin around.

That's when I see Imogene, Imogene showing the effects of too many ice-creams, Imogene with an expression on her face halfway between laughing and crying, Imogene with dirt on her Levi's that can only have come from under the house, the place where I taught her to play hide 'n' seek in whenever there were people around that she needed to get away from.

I take a long breath, and I take it slow and easy.

'You all right, Immo?'

Imogene nods.

She's a small figure, shoeless in the middle of the hallway under the coat rack.

'What happened?'

'They hurt Tripodi.'

I cast an eye over the kid.

There are no marks on her, apart from the scars that must be all over her pysche, and the dirt.

'Who's they?'

I wait.

You don't push a kid, especially one that's just escaped something nasty.

She takes a deep breath, just like I taught her to.

'Mummy got a phone call and then she went away.'

I nod at the grey Telefunken that's parked among the detritus on the table at the far end of the hall.

'That phone?'

Imogene nods.

I cross to it, pick up the receiver, whack the necessary buttons, and the phone advises anyone that cares to know that the last call was from a private number, which therefore cannot be revealed.

I replace the receiver and turn back to Imogene.

'What happened after Mummy went away?'

Imogene manages to steady herself.

'I heard them climb in through Mummy's window and I knew it wasn't Mummy because Mummy's got a key so I took off my shoes and I ran out the back door and down the back steps and under the house and hid just like you taught me to and there was lots and lots of noise and I knew they were hurting Trippie and Trippie doesn't like being hurt so he made lots of noise and I wanted to go and help him but I knew I mustn't because you taught me not to so I squashed really hard against the water eater and then everything went quiet, and after that I heard your footprints so I came out.'

All in one breath.

I nod.

'Clever girl. Now you said "they". Can you tell me how many bad men there were, Immo? Think careful. You heard my footprints. Did you hear theirs, too?'

Imogene thinks careful but after thinking careful she can only shake her head, the tears brimming as she stares at the matted furball that used to be her cat, lying not all that far from the neat little row of bullet-holes drilled into the architrave.

'I tried to, Daddy, but Trippie was making too much noise for me to count them.'

There's no time for any more cross-exam.

I can hear Salina hurrying down the path. She's not going to be all that delighted about the wardrobe door being ripped out and lying on the carpet in Imogene's room. Nor the blood on the floor of the hall and the front hatch hanging off its hinges. Nor the guilt she's going to feel for leaving Imogene alone in the house to keep a rendezvous with someone that doesn't exist. That guilt's going to be converted into anger at yours truly so accordingly I shove the still-warm corpse of the moggie under my jacket and turn to face the mother, just as she makes her appearance in the hatchway.

Go on the offensive.

I can do offensive.

'You got to go into hiding,' I tell her.

Salina looks from the bulge under my jacket to Imogene then back to the bulge under my jacket.

She looks terrible weary all of a sudden.

'The usual place?'

I nod.

'The usual place.'

She sighs.

'The usual way?'

'The usual way. A cab hailed in the street – no phone bookings – not the first one, and one that's travelling in the opposite direction to the one you'll be going in. After you've ridden around for a while, get out, go through the shopping centre or whatever there is to go through and when you come out the other side hail another cab.' The cat's slipping; I shrug it back up. 'I know it's not a perfect process but it's better than the alternative.'

I look around.

'Where are the twins?'

'Your money bought them a holiday.'

She grabs hold of Imogene's hand, then glares accusingly at me.

'Why can't you get a proper job, Rainbow?'

The cat slips against my torso.

I shrug it back up.

'Sorry, Sal, but this is what I do.'

Chapter 24

BACK FROM THE DEAD

I bump against the pink wing reflector with Cadillac inscribed on the back as I slip into the passenger side of the wheels, the side that the slug with Rory's name on it exited, the side with the brace of Zastava M57 pistols on the seat, and shove them out of the way.

They don't explode.

Surprise.

Zastavas usually explode.

There's a sound like a sick dog gasping but there's nothing under the bench seat but knives and nothing in the glove box, either, if you ignore the dozen dead-men's driving licences and the fifty or so mobile phones, plus three revolvers and a bunch of grenades.

Ditto the back seat, apart from Rory's crutch, a Sokacz sub-machine gun, an Ero nine-millimetre parabellum, an Agram and an APS 95 with optical sights, all of them made in Croatia.

He always was a patriot, Rory.

The gasps ratchet up but there's nothing on his face except surprise and his hands contain only fingerprints.

I finger his pulse and it's then that I discover he's not dead, he's only in shock paralysis after growing a new throat, and that's where the dog's rasps are coming from.

Rube was big on anatomy.

Get on top of the body, she'd tell me, and you're on top of the world – defence, attack, diagnosis, prognosis, post-mortem, ante-mortem, the works.

So I get on top of the body and on top of the body is the head and the head is perched on the neck and in the neck is the larynx.

The larynx, says *Cunningham's Anatomy* – published 1909 and occupying pride of place on the top shelf in Rube's library between *Ashley's Book of Knots* and *Advanced Forensics* – lies in the interval between the great vessels of the neck.

Hit just about any of these and the possessor is dead – or at least in serious trouble.

But Rory's neither dead nor in serious trouble, just breathing like a sick dog. The marksman hit nothing but the merest whisper of the larynx.

There's got to be an advantage in having a scrawny neck and Rory just found it.

I dig out a handkerchief and wrap it around what's left of his breathing apparatus.

I can't afford to get sprung for driving without a licence.

A thump to the side of the head gets Rory functioning.

He's muttering something about praising the Lord.

Salina appears on the other side of the road with that look still on her face, an overnight bag in one hand and Imogene's paw in the other.

I give Rory another smack over the head.

'Can you drive?'

'How do you think I got here?'

His voice sounds like it's got blood in it.

So does his brain.

'I mean can you drive *now*?' They've reached the gate. 'Can you see straight? Are you compos?'

Rory puts his patella against the steering column, knees himself upright, and fumbles with the ignition.

Salina turns left, dragging the kid after her like a dinghy, and hot-foots it towards the introspection, where she waves away the first cab that comes her way and piles, as instructed, into the second.

'Okay, get going,' I tell Rory.

The eight cylinders burst into pandemonium, most of which bypasses the mufflers. Rory puts his foot down, the car lurches forward, and the armoury in the back of the chariot rattles like a bunch of bones in a graveyard.

The cab carrying Salina and Imogene recedes into the distance.

'What happened?'

I tell Rory what happened and he touches his neck during the telling. It seems only now that he realises a bullet's gone through him.

After I've finished, it's a long time before he answers, and when he does he's raving.

'God meant me to live . . .' The bullet missed his jugular and took out his brain instead. 'But why would anyone want to take a pot at me?'

Wrong question.

Why would anyone *not* want to take a pot at Rory?

He examines his mug in the looking glass, the one with the miniature revolver hanging off it.

'God wanted me to live,' he says again.

Something happened to Rory and it's not just a bullet.

'Forget God,' I tell him, 'and tell me about the gorilla.'

Rory shrugs.

'Well, Gandhi,' he begins and notes my look of incomprehension, 'that's the dog – had a go at him, because the ape was waving his chopper at me, so the ape sank his axe into the dog instead and cleared out, taking the axe with him.'

'Where's the other dog, the one I asked you to look after?'

He tells me Rocket has taken Gandhi's place in his affections and the pooch is safe at home. I ask him how he went with the shopping list, prior to him nearly becoming an item on it himself.

'A couple of years back,' he says, 'I did this little job.'

I nod.

Everyone knows Rory kills people.

'Who was the client?'

'A guy called The Red Dwarf. He was in charge of State Prisons.'

The morning's overcast and behind us there's not much in the way of traffic, while up front there's a hole in the clouds, and I'm beginning to see the light, too.

'So you called in the IOU?'

Rory nods.

'I gave him the name and the photograph you gave me plus the piece of paper with the name of the music teacher on it, plus the prints.'

'And?'

'The prints came up negative. The Jones dude's clean. He's never done time.'

Back to square one.

And in square one I can see, via the wing mirror – the one I knocked crooked when I got in so that it's angled my way rather than towards Rory – nestled amongst all the other vehicles on the road in much the same way that Rory's perforated larynx is nestled in the cluster of muscles, glands and arteries that go to make up his skinny little neck, a vehicle that shouldn't be there: the black cabriolet.

Chapter 25

THE RETURN OF THE
BLACK CABRIOLET

'Turn off here.'

Rory doesn't hear or, if he does, chooses to ignore.

I've unholstered the gat and I'm busy checking that it's got the requisite complement of slugs in its sidecar but Rory sails right on past the turnoff like I haven't said a word.

He might be dumb but he's not deaf.

'Next left.'

But he keeps his foot on the gas feeder and also keeps looking straight ahead, along the long pink bonnet with the Cadillac wreath on the end, focusing on chewing up tar macadam rather than taking orders from passengers.

'If we're stopping at all,' he says, 'we're stopping at McDonald's.'

That's when he looks across at me and that's when he sees the gat.

It's taken him a long time.

It's a big gat.

'What are you doing with the equaliser?'

'We're being followed.'

Rory's never been big on detail.

He goes around with his gun cocked, his attitude in neutral and his brain on safety and when some joker interferes with his lifestyle, he pots them.

Until then he's going for a ride in the country.

'Look, it might have escaped your attention, Rainbow, but we're on a road. And on roads some vehicles are in front of you, some are beside you, and some are going in the opposite direction, while others are behind you, following. It's called traffic.'

My eyes haven't left the looking glass.

'It's the black cabriolet.'

Rory looks where I'm looking.

'That old heap!'

He puts his foot down.

'No way that washing machine can keep up with us, man. This is a Caddie. Know what its engine capacity is? Eight-point-two. Against what?'

He answers his own question.

'A fly's fart.'

I wind down the window.

A typhoon swirls into the Caddie and tickles my trigger finger.

Arguing with Rory is like trying to reason with a stoat.

'Think, Roarer!' I yell at him. 'Use the old grey matter for once and explain to me how that old rattler is keeping up with us, unless it's able to!'

Rory was nervous about being shot even before he got shot.

He takes his foot off the speed dial.

'Okay, but put the cannon away, will you?'

The Caddie lurches into another lane.

The driver of a 120Y protests.

Rory aims the Caddie at him.

The 120Y takes a trip into the forest.

'Look, I admit it, okay?' he croaks, straightening up. 'Guns in the hands of other people make me nervous, because I know what damage they can do.'

Rory's orbs swivel between the road, the cabriolet and the shooter.

'Those things are like magnets. Shoot one and it attracts others, like iron filings in a lab.'

Rube told me Rory was going to become a scientist before he decided to kill for a living.

His teachers were impressed with his talent for pulling the wings off beetles.

Teachers aren't the fastest balls in the cartridge.

'So what do we do now?'

We compromise and we stop at a KFC, that's what we do now, offloading a couple of kids out of a window seat to enable me to surveill the action outside, while at the same time avoiding the sight of the Diet Coke dribbling out of the holes in Rory's neck.

But no black car swings into the KFC parking lot and there's no joker crouching beside the Caddie, looking over his shoulder while he's letting down the tyres or interfering with the steering or taking to the brake lines with a hacksaw.

'I'm sorry I'm late. I've just come from another of those wretched meetings to save the hospital.'

It's two hours later and I've just left Rory to get a visual of David Jones so he can describe him to the Dwarf. I'm on the hillside above the cottage just around the corner from the wombat farm when Sally Kane arrives, smiling out of a flushed face and smoothing down her hair, which is ruffled.

Being back on the mountain is like old times.

I like old times.

You can't get hurt in old times.

'Here's the progress report,' I say. 'On the one hand I've made headway but on the other hand I've made no headway at all.'

Sally Kane's wearing a sheer floral skirt, sensible shoes and a confused expression on her face.

The only thing she's not wearing is her money bag.

'I'm not following you.'

'You might not be but someone else is.'

I tell her about the black cabriolet.

'Someone's after your husband, Dr Kane, and it looks like they don't particularly care for private detectives poking around where it doesn't concern them.'

'Perhaps you should stop poking around, then.'

She's speaking slowly and all the while she's gazing down at the little red-roofed cottage, the one with the shepherd outside tending his sheep.

'It's too late for that, lady. Besides, like I said, I'm making headway.'

There's no point telling her too much.

She's scared enough as it is.

Instead I stick to what might have a direct bearing on the matter.

'On the name thing, I'm drawing a blank – David Jones still hasn't got a history.'

I let that sink in.

'When I ran out of proof that your husband might be having an affair – that is, failed to discover an affairee worthy of the name – I tried the next best reason anyone might have for desiring privacy, and that is that your husband might possess form.'

'What's form?'

Even surgeons can be ignorant.

'Gone down, done time, been inside, soiled his pants —'

'I'm sorry?'

'Been in jail.'

'Oh.'

Sally Kane smoothes down her dress but she doesn't look as surprised as she might be.

'And has he?'

I shake my head.

The Dwarf came up with David Jones's report card and it turned out to be as blank as the prints of a murderer wearing Latex.

'Not a whisper. Not under his own name and not under anyone else's. Hasn't even done an overnighter for speeding.'

Sally Kane goes quiet for a long time after that.

I can't even hear her mind operating.

Clients are strange.

Give them what they want and suddenly they don't want it any more.

'That's it, then,' she whispers.

I move my head by way of a negative.

There's still the black cabriolet.

Plus Rory and the kid nearly copped it. Harriet Stowe and Little Miss Twisty, not to mention Imogene's cat, are dead. And David Jones looks all set to follow in their wake.

'That's not it at all,' I tell her, 'in fact it's not even the beginning. Someone's after your husband and I've got to find out who. And why.'

I don't like loose ends.

They tend to flap around when you least expect it and end up hurting people.

'So you wish to continue your investigations?'

'Wrong auxiliary,' I tell her, 'I've got to keep investigating.'

Sally Kane takes a deep breath and when it comes out it's quavering.

She's changed her mind back again.

Time to apply for a withdrawal.

'I've run out of the necessary.'

Sally Kane smiles.

'I thought you might have.'

She stands and turns away to face the sunset. It's formed an outer ring of rose-pink around a bullseye of madder crimson. I sense that my complexion's acquiring much the same colouration . . . Sally Kane has hitched up her dress with one hand and is fiddling around beneath it with the other. When she finally turns to face me, her eyes are shining, her skirt's caught up, and she's gripping a fistful of fifties.

She notes the question mark in my eyes.

'When one is introduced to a new bank, Mr Scutt,' she says, adjusting her dress as she hands me the dough, 'it doesn't hurt to open an account there, does it?'

Chapter 26

THE CASE OF THE NERVOUS REALTOR

'What do you mean, pulled a gat on you?'

'What do you mean, what do I mean?'

Rory's still got the holes in his neck.

He's also still got the hole in his head where his brain ought to be.

We're on the road back to the City.

It's going to be a long trip.

'Jokers don't just pull gats on people, Roarer.'

'Well, this one did.'

I talk him through his interview with David Jones.

'You open the door.'

'I what?'

'That's what you did, right? Opened the door.'

'Opened what door?'

'The door to the real estate joint.'

'No.'

I try it in low gear, uphill, with the brakes on.

'Look, how could you get in, if you didn't open the door?'

'It's a self-opening door.'

'Okay, the door opens all by itself. Then what?'

'This doxy's there.'

Call me old-fashioned but I don't like dames being referred to as doxies.

Dames are dames or they're ladies, unless they're broads.

But I let it pass.

In some respects, Rory's beyond teaching.

'All right, then what happens?'

Then what happens, Rory tells me, is that the doxy comes onto him.

One look at Rory's sea-greens and she's yak-fat in his hands and melting, or that's how Rory describes it. She asks him if he's wearing coloured contact lenses and when he tells her no, she wants to know what happened to his leg. This gives him the green light to make with the story concerning his battle with the great white pointer, armed with nothing more than raw strength, sheer courage, and the shattered tip-end of a mizzen-mast.

That's when the guy appears in the doorway.

When he sees Rory, he turns pale.

'What do you want?' he asks.

Rory rounds on the newcomer, his crutch cocked.

'Who's asking?'

David Jones takes in the naked dame on Rory's T-shirt, the missing leg, plus the wrap around his throat and I begin to understand the gun thing, only I don't tell Rory that, because he's busy negotiating the traffic.

The realtor goes into realtor mode.

'Perhaps you'd be interested in purchasing property.'

Rory forgets the dame and remembers his mission.

'Yeah, perhaps I would.'

'Please come this way.'

Rory lurches after the dude, but not without bestowing a wink on the receptionist as he passes.

The two enter Jones's office and that's when Jones pulls a gun on him.

'Just like that?'

Rory makes like he's busy with the gear stick.

'There might have been a bit of a lead-up.'

'What might have been the lead-up?'

'The guy wanted to know who sent me.'

The skin on the back of my neck prickles.

'You're sitting down, right?'

Rory glances in my direction, wisdom in his eyes but not in his brain.

'How can I draw my gat when I'm sitting down?'

'You drew your gat?'

Rory never had family.

Consequently, when he meets people he tends to shoot them. He finds normal social intercourse challenging.

'You're dead right I drew my gat. The guy had a crack at me.'

'How did he have a crack at you?'

'By asking who sent me.'

'But someone always sends you, Roarer, that's what you do, you get sent, you're a killer.'

Rory's eyes go hard, like the Cadillac wreath on the bonnet is a rifle sight and he'd like to take out the world.

'Let's get this straight, Roarer,' I go on. 'Jones asks who sent you, so you go for your gat only he beats you to the draw.'

'It wasn't in the drawer, it was behind his desk.'

'Describe it.'

'What, the desk?'

'No, the gun.'

'Browning trombone-action rifle, 22 calibre, a pop gun.'

A very nervous and very hunted realtor who's so dead scared for his life he's got a handgun in his study at home and a rifle behind his desk at work.

'What happened then?'

'What happened when?'

'After he pulls the gun on you.'

'I answer the question.'

'You told him I sent you?'

He shakes his head.

'I told him I was there to take care of him.'

Rory's no expert in linguistics.

'He didn't seem to know how to take it. So while he was working out how to take it, I left. I believe God guided both my words and my actions. The receptionist wanted to continue our conversation but I kept right on getting the hell out of there.'

The black car's bouncing around in the wing mirror.

There are three ways you can deal with cars following you.

You can step on the gas and risk getting done by the cops, not the smartest cut on the breadboard considering the firepower the cops would discover on the back seat.

You can try shooting out the car's tyres. This isn't too smart, either, because given the crate's vintage, the tyres are probably made of solid rubber.

Or you can pretend the tail's not there, sit back, and count the daisies.

There's no choice, so I take it.

Chapter 27

THE RED DWARF

You got to pull yourself together, Roarer.'

It's mid-afternoon and we're at Rory's.

He's got Rocket on his knee and I've done as much of a debug as I can manage – checked the lightbulb, run my hands over what passes for chairs in Rory's joint and looked under the linoleum. I'm working on the gaps between my teeth with an Interden in the ongoing battle against dental caries. Rory's muttering to himself.

'Man, I just want to put an end to all this killing!' he says. 'I've found God and want to join the Hare Krishnas.'

'That's all very well,' I say, scraping the roach off my shoe with the pointy end of the toothpick before going back to the caries, 'but your conversion will have to wait until the completion of your contract.'

Roarer's eyes have gone murky, like someone just disturbed the seafloor.

'I can no longer be a party to senseless slaughter.'

It's like he senses what's ahead.

'Look,' I say, giving up on the teeth, 'the only guarantee with death is that it happens. But if there are going to be any killings, you won't be the one required to perform them.'

Rory seems satisfied with that, only you can't tell with born agains.

When you least expect it they can turn around and crucify you.

'So what do you want me to do?'

'We call in the IOU from your new best friend, the short person.'

'I've already called it in.'

'So we call it in some more.'

'And I won't be killing anyone?'

'Only if you don't drive careful.'

There's been talk that, as part of his conversion, Rory will be ditching the Caddie.

But it hasn't happened yet, so we take Sydney's potholed Western Highway that becomes The Parramatta Road that in turn becomes Broadway until it magically transforms itself into George Street. We finally reach a joint that's got a porn pedlar in the basement, a religious bookseller on the ground floor, and God knows what in the hereafter.

Rory parks the Caddie and we climb out.

The porn pedlar doesn't look up from behind his counter as we enter.

'Same-sex stuff's up the back.'

'We're not same sex.'

The porn pedlar's travel weary eyes come up off his comic book and crawl over Rory before returning, covered with grime, to me.

'Whatever you say, pal, if you know what I mean.'

Rory comes to the rescue – the porn pedlar's, not mine.

'We need to see Howard.'

Tupperware grimaces.

'I'll see if she's in.'

He presses a bouton.

'Two guys, Kevin,' he says into it, 'only they claim they're not guys, if you know what I mean. Three legs between 'em, the mono's got a crutch rifle, and the biped's packing a gat.'

He listens for a couple of beats then glances at Rory.

'You the killer?'

'I was,' Rory says, 'but I'm not any more, because I found God.'

The dealer squints through his cynicism.

I shove Rory aside.

'Yeah, he's the killer.'

Rory looks puzzled.

'But you told me –'

I shoot him a look, the one with the leg-lopping landmine in it.

'It's just a description, Roarer, okay? They only call you a killer, it doesn't mean it's what you do.'

The porn pedlar's back on the speaker.

'There's a bit of confusion over definitions here, boss.'

I shove him out of the way and grab the phone.

'There's no confusion, Howard, it's Rory all right, just tell us where we can find you and we'll come right on in.'

Kevin Howard's sitting on a stool when we find him and I can see that he's small, even when he's wearing a stool.

He's got hair the colour of a Jaffa, he's wearing a pair of horn rims that Buddy Holly would have been proud of, and he looks like the nervous type.

'What's the problem?' he asks.

'I got two names and I want to know where they came from.'

'Why should I help you?'

'Because you owe Rory and I'm with Rory.'

'I already helped Rory.'

'Then you can help him some more.'

'Maybe I can,' the small man says, 'but I'll need dates, places, names and descriptions.'

So I tell him maybe seven years ago, Sydney, Edith Burton, and I describe her.

I don't tell him David Jones because that's the name of a department store, but Rory describes the joker that wears the moniker.

'What's he done?'

What's he done, this husband of yours? I asked Sally Kane.

And Sally Kane replied: Nothing.

'Nothing,' I tell Kevin Howard, 'but someone wants to do him harm and I need to know why.'

'So why come to me?'

'Because everyone else that can help us is dead.'

'Does that mean I might go the same way?'

'Only if you're not careful.'

'Death's a high price to pay for helping people.'

I shoot him a look.

'You ought to know all about that.'

The Dwarf sighs and climbs down from his stool.

You can see how he scored the cognomen.

'You're right.' He pauses. 'Look, there's not much small people can do in this world except work in circuses, and the do-gooders are making even that difficult, because they claim that working in circuses is some sort of exploitation.'

He waits for me to say something, only I don't say anything, so he goes on.

'Because of these self-same do-gooders I had to give up my cushy number as a clown, because the circus I was in had a management you might describe as weak-willed, however through sheer perseverance and ability I was able to forge a highly successful career in the public service instead.

'Consequently, I found myself in charge of State Prisons and on the shortlist – all right, I've heard all the jokes – to become head of the Federal Department of Immigration.'

The Dwarf's expression turns sour.

'That's when the bastard who was supposed to retire duds me and decides he's not going to retire, after all.'

He stares out the window.

I don't know what he's seeing.

It can't be the view, because the sill's at least a foot higher than his head.

'Accordingly, I get Rory to top him.'

Rory moans.

Any man's death diminishes him, or at least his chance of getting into Heaven.

Outside a bell tolls and the way Rory looks it tolls for him.

'Rory stands in front of the limo and machine guns the dude as he's coming down the driveway of his Vaucluse mansion. He also takes out the chauffeur, and that wasn't even in the contract.'

Rory moans again, or maybe he's just praying.

'The trouble with taking out the chauffeur is it leaves no one steering the Rolls, as a consequence of which the vehicle runs into Rory, who's standing in the gateway clutching his equaliser, like Cary Grant in *High Noon*.'

'Gary Cooper.'

The Dwarf arrives back at the stool and somehow gets himself back up onto it again.

'Whatever. Anyway, I'm behind this bush making sure Rory does the job and that's how I see Rory get himself crunched between the limo and the cast-iron gatepost. I drag him free and that's when I tell him I owe him.'

He contemplates the desk.

'Of course, that's not going to bring the leg back, despite the best efforts, et cetera, et cetera.' His glasses look like they're in danger of misting over. 'Anyhow, the upshot was the stiff was dead, we framed someone for it, Rory lost a leg and I got the job.

And when I retired, the payout from a grateful government was enough to set me up for life.'

He looks at Rory and the look he gives him is one of the deepest gratitude.

'Which means I owe Rory, and accordingly I'll do whatever he asks.

I still possess the necessary contacts.'

By the time I get Rory out of there he's a mess.

'This all relies on me being a killer.'

'Don't worry, Roarer,' I tell him, 'life's not a retrospective.'

The bell tolls again and it belongs to the little stone church across the way. The tolling reminds Rory that his way to Heaven is paved with more potholes than the Great Western Highway. He asks if I'd mind leaving him alone for a while before turning and crutch-and-one-legging it across the road. The last I see of him (until the next time I see him) is a small, lonely, lopsided figure making its way towards the church, the common and garden variety traffic veering and honking and crashing around him.

Only it's not your common and garden variety traffic, because one of the vehicles in it is the black cabriolet.

Chapter 28

THE HOOD WITH NO HANDS

In a world without answers, the cabriolet is what comes after the question mark.

It trundles through the first batch of lights headed for Park, and I make off after it.

I'm not in peak condition, what with one or a hundred whiskies too many, and I can see that the traffic's not in the mood to cooperate.

But you don't solve cases waiting for traffic to cooperate.

Alice in Wonderland is showing in the movie parlours in George Street and kids are queued twenty-deep on the trottoir to see it.

I leap two of the ankle-biters but two more don't make it because they bob up their heads at the wrong time.

A mother voices a protest but I'm up for the greater good.

A geezer in a wheelchair hits the turf.

An old dame whirls like a top and follows him.

A couple of schoolgirls go down.

Collateral damage is never a good thing but sometimes it can't be avoided.

By City Hall, I'm close enough to the chariot to see the reflection in the windows of the joker chasing it.

It's clutching its hat and G-forces have got hold of its face as the boneshaker slows down to make the turn into Park and I make the leap.

The breath is punched out of me as my body thumps into the paintwork and I grab the nearside door pillar while the soles of my whitesides make contact with the running-board.

I need an ID.

There's only one way to make an ID under the circumstances, so I take it.

Sirens are headed our way, a wing-beater's fluttering overhead and the cabriolet's doing fifteen paces per second, not the speed of lightning in raw tabulation but sound-barrier stuff when you're clinging to a running-board.

It's now or forever.

My toes forming the fulcrum, I clench the bo-peeps, throw my body weight onto the ankle joints, in the same nanosecond placing my hands in the thumbs-in-fingers-out position. Someone inside chucks open the back-hinged door, which is when I adjust for the rear-thrust of relativity and back-arch over the hatch. I force my feet towards the bow to ensure the footwear lands on the running-board. At the same time, I drop into a full crouch, twist my head, and flick open my eyes, the rods and cones having had time to adjust during the hand-spring, in order to obtain a spot-check of the cabriolet's interior.

A glance is all I need.

Resist obvious identifiers, Rube always told me, hair can be cut, irises discoloured, and beards purchased at the nearest theatrical supply shop.

That's why hoods scowl.

Witnesses can remember the expression but not the perpetrator, to the ultimate benefit of the perpetrator, because next time they see him he's smiling.

I do the ID.

Squatting in the cabriolet's bucket seats are two figures in black, between them packing enough weaponry to make the pre-conversion Rory look like a pacifist – sawn-off shotgun, sub-machine pistols, mortars, handguns, a howitzer, everything but an ack-ack battery, and I can't even swear to them not possessing that.

Clothes can be changed and weapons are little more than fashion-accessories.

Therefore observe such factors as shoulder slope, face geometry, length of leg, hands.

I check accordingly.

Passenger: Baby-faced, hunched shoulders, big hands.

Driver: Regulation scar on cheek, shoulders squared, no hands.

I blink in the darkness.

Rods and cones playing tricks.

I look again, staring despite the pain in the fist where Babyface has grabbed hold of me.

But the driver's still got no hands, nothing but a couple of black coat-cuffs ending in two angry red stumps where the hands should be.

The case of the missing mana distracts me when I shouldn't have let it.

I wrench my fist free from Babyface and bang him over the skull. Too late I remember the bazooka and by the time my brain starts functioning again, the joker's had time to work out his counter move, bringing the weaponry back as far as he can. He rams it into my solar plexus, the result being my ribs hurt that much more, my lungs are deprived of breath, my blood finds itself deoxygenated, my brain swims, I experience vertigo, and I fall off the running-board.

Rube used to refer to it as cinematographic time warp but these days they just call it Fast Forward. This is exactly what the chariot does when I come off the running-board. I roll in the dust at the feet of a broad in red leotards who's standing on the corner of Denizen and William, smiling at passers-by as she enjoys a quiet cigarette preliminary to whatever she might be thinking of doing next. Meanwhile the cop cars close in and the eggbeater swoops low and I get to my feet, pick up the gat, reinstall my fedora, nod to the dame and take myself off towards the traffic tunnel.

I'm running from the cops.

But I'm also trying to shake the image of the handless hood in the cabriolet.

Chapter 29

INCIDENT AT ALCATRAZ

The tunnel's not built for pedestrians but the other thing going for it is there's no entry for choppers either. The whoomph-whoomph-whoomph of the eggbeater fades to yesterday amid the roar of the klaxons and the squeal of brakes as I head past the GO BACK YOU'RE GOING THE WRONG WAY signs and start burrowing underground.

I hang onto the hat and hug the wall as I hammer my way along the right-hand side of the carriageway.

The way to survive, Rube taught me, is not just to keep moving, but to keep the cerebrum humming along while you're doing it.

How do you survive?

Keep thinking, I'd tell her.

Good boy, she'd reply.

And I'd get a tot of the vodka.

In tunnels, the cops have got two sources of intelligence – the cameras on the walls and the jokers on their mobiles dialling 131700 and screaming there's a maniac loose in their tunnel.

The trick is to get them in synch and get them wrong.

The cameras are predictable.

What is also predictable is that lights start flashing and the electronic signs start purveying the false information that there's an accident ahead, so as not to unduly excite the populace, and drivers are kindly requested to throw out the anchors.

What is unpredictable is the pale-green Vespa wobbling through the stalled traffic, the rider in the matching green helmet ignoring all instructions to stop, which is the whole point of Vespas, until I appear in front of it waggling my arms and looking official, thereby causing it to squeak to a halt, at which time I dislodge the rider from his perch and take over the conveyance.

The pain in my mitt incurred during the incident with the jalopy has eased and I manage to control the two-wheeler with one hand as I manoeuvre it between the stalled traffic while gripping onto the fedora with the other. By the time the cops can get even close to realising what's on, I'm out of the southern exit of the tunnel and sliding into South Dowling and the maze of streets that go to make up Slurry Hills. I lose the Vespa before we become too attached to each other, under a tree that's pretty much the same colour as the scooter.

From then on it's hoof-time.

I've remembered the address of my old ballet teacher and that's where I make for: sub-unit 2960 on the twenty-ninth level of one thousand, two hundred and twenty-three-B Cortizone. It's an above-ground bomb shelter constructed along much the same lines as the hotel in California called Alcatraz, otherwise known as a New South Wales Housing Commission hell-hole. There are job lots of artificial greenery in pink plastic pots gracing the darker corners of the bricked-in balconies, to add that extra little touch of sheer fun to the surroundings.

The eggbeater's a distant memory as I reach the balcony of the twenty-ninth floor. I catch my breath and hammer with my good fist on the imitation wood door of sub-unit three-sixty, in the space between the cracked eye-peeper, the broken door handle, and infinity.

No one answers.

There's no eggbeater around so why am I experiencing this sudden feeling of panic?

It must be the surrounds, trapped as I am in a rabbit warren three hundred feet above ground zero, with nothing about me but unpainted concrete, plastic pot plants, and a lot of depression.

'Who's there?'

Who do they think's here, the Avon lady?

I tell them it's the cops and the door opens just enough to reveal a chain, an eye and a waft of foul air.

'You're not the cops,' the eye tells me.

'And you're not Madam Blavatsky.'

'Weirdo,' the eye says.

And the door slams in my face.

I make an attempt at a laugh.

Rube always told me that laughing is miles ahead of the alternative so I'm still laughing as I turn, shaking my head and rubbing the back of the mitt as I do so.

But when I raise my eyes it's to discover, standing between me and the fake pot plants and twenty-nine storeys of stratosphere, someone I don't particularly want to see. The hood with no hands. And he's holding the howitzer and it's pointing right at the place where I was laughing.

101

Chapter 30

THE MAD DOG

The scar on the cheek under the homburg looks like it's been excavated by a meat cleaver, the mouth is bitter gall, and the eyes are ashes. It's the eyes that stop me going for the gat. These eyes go back to the beginning of Time, when Neanderthals trembled in caves, things were alive that had no business being alive, and death crept abroad after nightfall. In these eyes hate has shoved aside reason. The irises are opaque, they're crawling with malevolence the way a long-interred corpse writhes with worms, and they're craving pain – other people's – because a quick death would be merciful, the sort of hate that needs to hear the screams of its victims echoing throughout all eternity.

Scarface waggles the tip of the howitzer. 'Move,' he murmurs.

There's no opening and closing of the mouth to indicate speech, I can't even be sure he's spoken, but I know what he wants, so I move.

It's a long way to the ground when you've started on the twenty-ninth floor, you're being forced to take the fire escape, and you've got a howitzer gouging into your back, held by a handless killer.

Don't ask me how he's holding it, it's not something I want to think about.

There's not much more light in the stairwell than there is in the eyes of the killer and I've got to rely on my whitesides to tell me there's several dead rats, a broken chair, and a job lot of what look like discarded body parts to negotiate on the way down.

At my back I hear the soft whisper of the hood's footfalls, and in case I think it's just noises there's the ongoing thrust between my shoulder blades of the business end of the howitzer.

I wait until the ninth before making my move.

There's a split-second when the hood finds himself caught up in a Queen-sized Sleepmaker Rest-Assured with a syringe sticking out of it. Meanwhile, I'm two steps down, and there's no guarantee I'll find myself with another chance like this one.

I feint to the left, do a double-turn with twist ending in a forward-thrust somersault, and the cannon goes off while I'm in mid-air and dropping, the thunder of its percussion hammering at my lugs as it smacks a crater the size of a baby's skull in the reinforced concrete wall of the stairwell, a millimetre away from my neck.

I keep going, because there's nothing else to keep.

Being handless doesn't slow the killer, who's busy redefining Ness's logic of movement at the same time as he's redeploying gravity, ricocheting off the sides of the fire stairs like a one-man avalanche as he tumbles down the companionway after me.

By the penultimate landing, my breath is searing my throat and the maniac's gaining, the clatter of his hoofbeats just one step behind my starboard Achilles tendon. Fast running out of options, I make the final turn to the exit and the promise of a taste of freedom.

It's then that I realise my mistake.

I've been focusing on the threat behind me.

Focusing's good because it concentrates the energy, at a time when the energy needs to be focused.

But it can also be bad, on account of it blinkers you to any danger that might be waiting for you elsewhere.

And it's bad now because before me and blocking my escape route, a mangy cur of a dog cringing beside him, is the second hood, the baby-faced one, and he's holding a submachine gun, the gat with the round-box magazine, the infamous M1928A1. It's the very gun that Al Capone's hoods used on that fateful St Valentine's Day all of eighty years ago. The baby-faced hood is smiling because such a simple trick has worked, and he likes simple tricks, in fact, the simpler the better.

I'm a rabbit at the mouth of a warren, there's a ferret fore and aft, and both have got their razor teeth bared and scalpel claws out, all set to tear me apart.

'Don't!'

It's Babyface, it's a baby's voice, and it's not addressed to me, but to the killer behind me with the howitzer.

'I said don't!' he squeaks again.

I sense the thug at my back park the machinery.

Babyface returns his attention to me.

'Unbutton your jacket.'

It's like open-heart surgery without the anaesthetic.

Babyface tucks the Thompson into one mitt, smacks me across the skull with the other fist, and relieves me of the Smith & Wesson, flicking the shells out one-handed before parking the gat inside his suit, never taking his eyes off me for a moment.

The mutt looks on with interest.

'Now the blade.'

The hood bends, removes the dagger from my shin scabbard with the gat-free mitt and tosses it onto the garbage heap that is Alcatraz's backyard. Then he straightens, all in the one movement, like he's just smacked a mosquito, pinched it between his fingernails, and is negligently disposing of the remains.

'The hat.'

I pass him the fedora.

He knows where the second blade is and how to remove it without cutting himself.

He also knows something else.

'Now the hand.'

Something clicks in my brain.

Somewhere deep in my subconscious, from the moment I came fascia to ugly mug with Handless Hood on the balcony, I've been trying to work out how they tracked me.

Now I know.

It's like Hank said: Why worry about people's location when you can plant a bug on them?

I hand over the mitt, the one that Babyface whacked in the cabriolet, the one I've been nursing ever since, the way you'd nurse a hand that's been bitten by a tarantula.

The hood's gripping the blade between thumb and forefinger.

It's a double-edger, hollow-honed blue-steel with the name Eversharp inscribed on the side, so you know what to ask for when you want a replacement, an Escher vase cut-out in the middle for fitting a hand-grip to, on the off-chance you might want it for shaving.

Babyface doesn't.

He grips my paw and it's not just because he's suffering a sudden attack of the friendlies.

Blood spurts out of the hand as he slices and the pain's severe, but I can do pain.

I watch as the thug disentangles the technology with the same degree of compassion that a vet might display removing a blood-filled tick from a horse.

The technology's small and black and when inserted under the epidermis, enables a follower to track the hand, plus anything else that happens to be attached to it.

'Here, boy!'

Babyface is addressing the cur.

The mutt wriggles excitedly, waggling its tail because it thinks that for once in its miserable life it's found a friend. Instead of patting the dog, the thug reaches down and with one deft movement tucks the bug in next to the mutt's right eyeball, just beside the tendo-palpebrarum.

The dog screams, spins wildly and careers down the rutted road, yipping and bleating and leaping in circles, the sound of its agony providing a suitable accompaniment to the murmur of approval from the thug with the baby's face and the torturer's heart. Soon enough, the animal has disappeared over the edge of the rubbish-strewn horizon.

But there's no time for empathy.

Babyface has got both mitts back on the gat and is motioning with it like he'd much prefer pulling the trigger to employing it as a pointer.

'Move!' he squeaks.

I move.

The second hood's beside me but I don't look in his direction because I haven't been invited and in these circumstances you only do what you're invited to do, as per Lesson Thirty-Seven in Aunt Rube's Manual of Survival.

The landscape around Alcatraz is all that was left in *The Book of Revelation* after the Angels of the Lord paid their little visit to a sinful world – nothing but bleak black towers and straggling weeds and bottomless pits and desolation and death and eternal misery.

In normal circumstances, it's just such a landscape that hoods like these would choose to do their killing in.

They are Book of Revelation people.

Only these circumstances aren't normal.

Because if they were, the hoods would already have done their killing.

Instead they prod me across the blighted landscape and when I stumble they force me upright and instead of exxing me they push me forward.

Nothing stirs in the black towers.

Seething tens of thousands of condemned souls dwell here but in the harsh light of day, with two black-suited and heavily-armed hoods conducting an abduction, the denizens are so many craven figures trembling behind blinds, primitive beings cowering in caves in the presence of forces they don't understand, offering this ritual sacrifice to the gods, namely me.

My gun and my blades are gone, but it's the bug I miss.

There was something comforting about it, like it offered the solace of ethereal attachment, even if that attachment was only a malevolent one.

But now even that comfort has been stripped from me, leaving me naked.

The hood screams, 'Forward!'

Hugging my bleeding paw to my bruised ribs, I manage to stumble into a trot.

Chapter 31

A CRIMINAL CONVERSATION

There's not much room left in a cabriolet after you've factored in two hoods, the armoury, a suitcase, the victim, and the body odour.

The handless hood is at the wheel.

Don't ask me how he works the gear stick, probably the same way he picks his nose, and while he's playing his ultimate computer game – tracking the final agony-stricken-journey-to-madness of the dog via the GPS on the dashboard – he's giggling.

In the back with me, the hood with the hands has ripped off my fedora and forced a balaclava over my head, backwards, and tied my hands between my knees. He's joined them to my neck with a slip knot in the time honoured manner of the criminal conspiracy, so that if I move at all, the noose around my neck tightens, and if I move any more than that, I'm history.

I fight down the panic.

Have one bad experience and it comes back to haunt you.

Have a second bad experience and it never goes away.

But bad memories never got anyone anywhere so I concentrate on the problem in hand.

Rube on logic:

Pick a number, double it, take away the number you first thought of, and what you're left with is the answer.

In other words: Follow your hunch. So I follow my hunch.

And my hunch is that if I hang around these two roosters much longer, I'm chalk.

These hoods are the psychopaths of my childhood, grown to maturity.

They eat, sleep, drink, fornicate, defecate, urinate, pick their noses, and kill people.

They've climbed dripping from their primaeval swamp, loped to Chicago's O'Hare Airport and flapped like a pair of pterodactyls to the Antipodes. They've then got hold of a souped-up jalopy and topped up their small arms collection. They didn't come all this way for the good of their health or anybody else's, because they've only got one thing on their minds – apart from eating, sleeping, drinking, fornicating, defecating, urinating, and picking their noses – and that is killing people.

I stress-test my bonds.

The action is rewarded with a tightening of the noose and a crack over the skull with the butt-end of the armoury.

I try reasoning.

'You got the wrong guy,' I tell the upholstery.

All I get for that is another crack over the skull.

You learn to listen in this game.

You got to separate the whisky from the water, the angel dust from the talc, the sand from the gunpowder.

They're taking me somewhere and I need to know where and I also need to know why.

And I'm not going to get to know any of that by asking.

Accordingly I make like I'm in the Land of Nod.

'That banana giving you any trouble?'

It's the handless one, the joker driving the jalopy.

They've done their fast-food stop and chomped through a Family-Pak from McDonald's and par consequence the interior of the cabriolet stinks like a soup kitchen in the middle of a summer heat wave.

Babyface gives me a thump.

I don't move.

'Nah, he's dead to the world.'

'Whadya say?'

'It's an expression, idiot. It means he's asleep.'

'Why didnja say so then?'

'Same reason I haven't told you why we're going to Dashiell.'

I can hear the rumble of the supercharged motor and the clash of the weld-hardened gears and the torque of the reinforced crankshaft but for a couple of semesters there's nothing from either of the hoods but breathing.

Then:

'Why are we going to Dashiell?'

Babyface gives me another thump.

I don't respond.

'Because that's where the answer lies, dummy. Remember we asked the boys to do the research, after the court decided to hand out the dough?'

'We wasn't happy.'

'Yeah, like you say, we wasn't happy. Meanwhile, the research resulted in a name, Dashiell. And when we Googled the name in the prison library, we were given the choice between a dead scribbler's moniker and an Australian country town. We took the town.'

'That's when we escaped.'

'And why did we escape?'

'To go to Dashiell.'

'And what did we find when we got to Dashiell?'

'A nosy detective.'

'And what did we do after we found the nosy detective?'

'We followed him.'

Babyface sits back.

'So what we're doing now' — there's satisfaction in his voice — 'is doing our sums.'

'And what sums might they be?'

'We're putting one and one together and coming up with the answer to our little problem, that's what they might be.'

The answer seems to satisfy Handsfree, but I still don't know raspberries from rhubarb.

Chapter 32

A MOUTHFUL OF BLOOD

A couple of hours later the cabriolet hits the dirt. I need to relieve myself only I figure I'm not about to be handed a toilet pass.

My ribs and the mitt are killing me but that's better than the hoods doing the job.

We pull up six hundred beats after the dirt starts. Babyface rips off the balaclava and removes the strangler-ropes, I get pushed out, a cock crows, there's a shot, the crowing stops, Handsfree sprouts a couple of hooks and picks up the portmanteau, and I get shoved forward.

You don't need to be a genius to work out where we are or what my fate's likely to be or that the clouds covering the sun are cumulo-nimbus.

What I don't know – in relation to the first two questions, at any rate – is why.

Apart from the dead poultry and another fowl or three still in the land of the living, I make out the rusty plough, the shack with the solar panels on it and several acres of wombat holes, any one of which could provide a convenient resting place for a dead detective.

'Why are we here?'

I'm not being existential.

'Because you led us here when we were following you, so we figured this place will lead us to our quarry – move!'

The hood with the hands encourages me into the residence with a clout over the back of the head with the Uzi.

Inside is a chair with arms on it, a table, and the absolute guarantee of a great deal of pain.

Handsfree tables the suitcase, Babyface shoves me into the chair, straps my wrists down with the ropes he's brought from the cabriolet, and stands back.

'All right, punk' – the squeak has risen to a screech – 'where is he?'

It's a good question.

I glance behind me.

Using his meathooks, Handless has opened the lid of the portmanteau.

The hooks look like they're carved out of somebody's grandmother and the portmanteau looks like the sort of box they store evil in.

I answer the question.

'He's behind me, removing his makeup from his handbag.'

Babyface force-feeds me the butt end of the Uzi.

'I asked you a question, punk,' he reminds me, 'where is he?'

I clear my throat.

It's not easy keeping up your end of the conversation with a mouthful of blood.

'Where's who?'

'Waddaya mean, wear shoe?'

I spit out a tooth.

'ID me, you moron, and tell me who you're talking about, on account of I don't happen to possess extra-sensory perception.'

I've regressed forty years, shouting idiocies back at the kids bullying me in the schoolyard.

'Waddaya mean, extra-cents-whatever-you-said?'

'I need a name, idiot.'

The hood's face clears.

Scarface has appeared beside him, he's chewing on a cheroot, and he's fitting together the contents of the suitcase.

He's also handed Babyface what I identify as the ingredients for a thumbscrew.

Suddenly I need to get out of there fast, and it's not just to go to the toilet.

'You expect us to believe you don't know?'

It's like we're playing join-the-dots, except the pencil needs sharpening, a lot of the dots are missing, and someone's mixed up all the numbers.

I tear my attention away from the joker with the hooks, and direct it instead to Babyface.

I need to focus on something.

There are too many memories, all of them bad.

'How did you guess?'

Babyface raises the gat, and it's not just to air-condition the barrel.

'Looks like we got ourselves a wise guy.'

It's not meant as a compliment, because in this fidget's lexicon a wise guy would rank somewhere below a disease-carrying sewer rat and just above the common earthworm.

'If I was a wise guy,' I tell him, 'I wouldn't be strapped to a chair facing certain death at the hands of a couple of goons with their brains missing.'

The sophistry earns me another crack over the skull with the firearm.

'I still don't know what you're talking about,' I manage through the blood.

That's when he tells me what he's talking about.

'Grimaldi,' he squeaks, his lips clenched. 'That bastard Josef Grimaldi.'

It's like some character has wandered into the wrong narrative entirely.

I tell the turnip I don't know what he's talking about, that, in a present day context anyway, I've never heard of Grimaldi, Josef or otherwise, and the name means as much to me as Gruyere, Sobrani, Camembert or Grana Lombardo.

That's when I do a recheck of Captain Hook's handiwork.

Not many punters are familiar with even the most common instruments of torture, because torture's not a commonplace occurrence in the everyday byplay of generally accepted social intercourse in this country.

Members of the John Q. Public, for instance, might imagine that quirt's an activity involving water, a flagellum's what citizens run halfway up a pole after an assassination, and a kurbash is something you do to a dog.

Show them a trebuchet, branks, iron maiden, scarpines, or a bed of Procrustes, and they could be excused for thinking they're seeing a no-longer-extant form of parlour game.

Only going by what Screwjaw's got his hooks into, these babies aren't looking for someone to make up a third in a game of tiddlywinks.

The modern-day rack has dispensed with the old labour-intensive cogs and ratchets and crank handles and pulleys.

Instead it's powered electrically.

Handless is kneeling on the floor beside Babyface attempting to assemble such a contrivance.

I'm hoping he doesn't get it together in a hurry, because all I've got going for me are two things:

The time I can filch from the hoods; and

The vulnerability of the knots that are holding me.

Chapter 33

THE BED OF PROCRUSTES

Aunt Rube taught me three ways of dealing with torture – fight it, ignore it, or avoid it.

I start with the fight.

'You idiots wouldn't have heard of Procrustes.'

There's no answer.

Babyface is having trouble with the thumbscrew and Handsfree's busy at the wall flicking switches.

'I'll take that as a no,' I say into the silence, 'in which case I'll have to tell you.'

Talking is keeping my mind off what they're intending to do to me.

Meantime, I'm working at the knots.

There's got to be some advantage in being a sailor.

'Procrustes, Damastes, Polypemon or simply Procoptas, take your pick, was the name of the world's first sadist.'

Two knots down, four to go.

'You two would have loved him, on account of you're his direct descendants. He'd hammer people out like he was flattening horseshoes, or he'd lop bits off them, in order to fit them into one of two beds he possessed, a short one and a long one.'

'Shuddup!'

Babyface has unfolded a sheet of paper with writing and pictures on it and he's spread it out on the floorboards next to the pieces for the thumbscrew. He's trying to read what's written in the semi-darkness caused by the cloud cover and scratching his head at the same time.

It's not making him any smarter.

'Procrustes possessed a rack much like the one that our idiot friend's put together.'

'I said, shuddup!'

I don't shuddup on account of shudding up's no longer an option.

'Where did you get the torture ware? Ikea? Or maybe it's a flat-pack from Bunnings and you're having trouble making sense of the instructions.'

I get a back-hander for that.

But I'm used to back-handers.

I continue with the ropes.

'Maybe you can't even read.'

Hit a sore spot.

I like hitting sore spots.

'Look, dickhead,' Babyface says. 'I ain't got no trouble reading nothing when it's written in American.'

He thumps the paper.

'Ring circle box-frame twice.'

He shakes his head.

'Call that American?'

I shrug.

'Buy cheap rubbish and you get cheap rubbish instructions.'

Scarface is hammering at the wall-switch with one of his meat hooks.

'Hey, I've found the problem!'

'What is it?'

'There's no power!'

'Try plugging it in.'

'It is plugged in!'

'Switch it on, then.'

'It is switched on!'

Babyface looks out the window then back at Scarface.

He's shaking his baby face.

'Didn't you happen to notice something when we came in, you moron? That this is a solar house and there's a heap of clouds covering the power supply?'

Scarface resorts to basics.

'You calling me stupid?'

'Well, you're the idiot that got his hands cut off.'

That stops Handsfree.

He's got his hooks raised like Freddie Krueger in one of his moods and he looks like he's ready to give his pal a bit of a scratch-up. That's when he glances in my direction and that's when he lowers them.

He's already got his victim.

One more would only confuse things.

I try bravado.

'What are you going to try now, idiot, Chinese burns?'

Scarface moves closer and he's making a noise like there's a fishhook jagged in his gills.

It can only mean one thing and that is I'm not likely to get out of here in one piece, even with only three knots to go.

'So we just wait for the sun to come out,' he says softly. 'Now why don't you fill in the down time by telling us how you got yourself a stupid name like Rainbow?'

I make like I don't hear him.

'I suppose it came out of some stupid weather report, like the clouds.'

I shrug; the shrug loosens the ropes a little more.

Telling the story will buy time, so I tell it.

'You're half right. My parents were hippies and the day I was born the weather was uncertain.'

I feel like I'm reciting my prayers, and maybe I am.

'There was sun plus a few clouds and my mother could see the resultant phenomenon, on account of she was in a dam at the time.'

Babyface is still trying to assemble the thumbscrew, but I've got Captain Hook's attention.

'What was she doing in a dam?'

I glance at Babyface.

The thumbscrew's a basic instrument of torture – a G-section fits over the thumb, a clamp attaches the machinery to the furniture, and the operator works the screw down into the victim's thumb at his leisure.

I concentrate on the knots holding my right arm.

'Giving birth,' I tell him, 'it's what hippies do.'

Babyface has turned the G-section of the thumbscrew around and if he applies it like that, while the thumbscrew won't work precisely like it was meant to, it will still work.

'She was going through an American Indian phase at the time.'

'Hey, give up on the electrics and get yourself over here!'

Scarface does like he's told, clamping my left wrist with one of his hooks while Babyface removes the rope holding my left radius and ulna to the arm of the chair and attaches the end of the upside-down thumbscrew to my thumb.

I'm down to one knot and after I've untied that the only thing holding me to the chair will be a failure of willpower – and the thumb.

I keep talking.

'She'd heard that Indians named kids after whatever was occurring at the time of their birth.'

The screw starts biting into the nail.

I clench what's left of my teeth and continue.

'And when I came into the world, what was occurring was an arc de ciel over the eastern horizon, also known as a rainbow.'

The screw has got through to the quick.

The device might have been put together upside-down and back-to-front but it's still working.

The only thing it's not doing is holding my wrist to the arm of the chair.

Nothing but the thumb's doing that.

The last knot's proving stubborn.

'That's how I got the name Rainbow. Meanwhile, talking of stupid,' I manage, 'how did you come by the conveyance?'

'What conveyance?'

'The straightback, horseless carriage, voiture, crate, landaulet, wheels, the cabriolet.'

Babyface turns the screw some more and the pain bites into my thumb some more. Scarface's eyes cloud over like the sun, not with any pain he might be experiencing, but because of mine.

I gouge at the knot.

'We needed wheels,' he murmurs, watching the blood seep out from my nail, 'and some punk possessed a hotted-up jalopy. He happened to be in jail at the time so the wheels were on offer.

We took him up on the offer.'

The blood's starting to trickle and now it's my eyes that are clouding.

'Now for the last time, you lowlife punk,' Scarface says softly, 'where's Grimaldi?'

I don't even know who Grimaldi is, much less where.

And because I don't know, if I sit here much longer, the sun will come out, the electrics will come back on, the stretcher will start working, and they'll strap me onto it and start chopping bits off me. I'm going to die and my death will be a long way from easeful.

But there's something neither of these roosters knows.

I've suffered pain like none of their victims could ever have suffered pain before. I suffered it at the hands of sadists much sadder than these punks could ever be and I suffered it young. Apart from all the foregoing, I'm a great believer in adages.

Especially the one that goes, What doesn't kill you makes you stronger.

I've undone the last knot.

My life is hanging by a thumb.

It's time to bid that portion of my anatomy adieu.

Chapter 34

AT LEAST THE COCK DIED CROWING

I don't like impotence, never have.

At least the cock died crowing.

I steady the pulse rate, flex the recta femora, tense the gastrocs, and focus my attention on the seat of the chair, because that's going to provide my fulcrum.

I hear the bone snap and the flesh tear and feel a spear of pain like no other I have ever experienced as I yank my mitt skywards.

It helps that Babyface put the thumbscrew on wrong because it means my wrist's unshackled and I've just got the one joint to pull free.

I leave half my thumb decorating the chair.

It doesn't matter.

It's just another joint.

I hurl myself at the hoods and go straight into a tumble turn, at the last moment switching to a one-hundred-and-eighty-degree spin. I end up two paces away, hunched in a full crouch, what's left of my thumb dribbling gore.

I assess what's left of the situation.

The hoods have gone for their guns.

Professionals anticipate and these two are nothing if not professional.

After the gymnastics, they expect more, so I don't give them more, holding the squat for half a beat longer than they expect me to. The first volley goes wide, converting the front door into splinters and going by the sound effects also taking out another rooster.

Then the hoods do like I know they will: they close ranks.

It's what professionals do.

Faced with a common enemy they go back-to-back.

It makes them a much nicer target than the one they'd provide separate and a lot better target than the one I'm giving them.

I'm supposed to retreat but in this game you don't do what you're supposed to.

Accordingly I shift my weight to my toes and take a flying leap straight at the goons.

One of my whitesides hits nasal cartilage and I've got good cobblers, which is where I catch the second one – a direct hit in the awls.

I don't like brutality, never have.

So I keep it to a minimum.

On a count back – apart from the shattered nose and the manhood problem – there's a broken wrist, half an ear gone, a splintered tibia, a broken rib, a couple of teeth that will never chew on a stogie again and, in one case, temporary paralysis.

There isn't much left to tie up, but after I tourniquet the forearm and wrap what's left of the thumb to stop it haemorrhaging, I drag the hoods outside and attach them – using number eight wire, almost thick enough to make a stiletto with – to the plough.

They're not knots a hangman would be proud of but they'll have to do.

I dig my gat out of Babyface's wardrobe and the fedora from the jalopy, park the gat, reblock the hat, jam it on my head, and return my attention to the hoods.

Scarface is getting his brain back from its visit to the cleaners, but the other one – the babyfaced one with the hands, the shattered manhood and the paralysis – is still out cold, cuddled up to the plough like he's married to it.

I tell Scarface there's more where that came from.

They're not words I'd use normally but this isn't normally.

Plus, I don't want there to be any confusion in the matter.

Scarface requests that I not punish him any more. I tell him I'll accede to his request given his continued cooperation, to which he says he'll try, and I tell him he'd better do better than try unless he wants to be further adjusted, to which he says words to the effect of, Please don't hit me.

It's enough of an introduction for two people just getting to know each other. Accordingly, I figure it's time to advance the dialogue.

'I know what you are and I don't need to know who you are.' I put on my American president look, the one that says I'll stop at nothing to save the world, even if it means destroying most of it in the process. 'What I need to know is *why*.'

'Why what?'

My nod takes in the shack and what has just occurred in it.

'Why the torture, bean brain?'

Handsfree wipes his nose on the plough, which gives me the answer to the nose-picking problem, but only when he's tied to a plough.

'We needed a few answers.'

It's a reply, only it's not the right one.

'We all need answers, but we don't go around torturing people to get them.'

'I mean concerning Grimaldi.'

As well as the shooting lessons and the Cagney movies, home schooling a la Rube included some of the gentler arts, which is how I know Grimaldi's the name of a clown that was around all of two hundred years ago.

'What's a dead clown got to do with the price of thumbscrews?'

But the hood's eyes have gone blank and I can see there aren't going to be any more answers in the immediate future, so I borrow his mobile and make a call.

Chapter 35

DESTINATION WITH DARKNESS

What happened to your thumb?'

'I put it somewhere it wasn't wanted. But I'm not here to talk about thumbs. Tell me what you know about Josef Grimaldi.'

I've left the hoods tied to the plough while I'm busy on the other side of the hill working through matters with Sally Kane who's looking exquisite in Givenchy. The shadow of the shepherd in the paddock below us is lengthening as the sun heads off for its destination with darkness. It's the second time I've trotted out the name Josef Grimaldi and the second time Sally Kane has shaken her beautiful locks and replied,

'I know that name only insofar as it relates to a clown.'

I try a different tack.

'Has your husband ever mentioned a person called Josef? Or told you that he's acting as someone's minder?'

'No.'

'Does he seem even more nervous than usual?'

'N–No.'

Sally Kane's hiding something, and it's not just her legs.

'Look, lady,' I say, experiencing a feeling close to exasperation, call it edginess, 'you hired me to check out your Benedict. Well, I've checked him out and it seems like he's Simon Pure. That fact alone should make you delirious but instead you're acting like you got a heartful of iron filings.'

Sally Kane takes a deep breath.

'But we still don't know . . .'

'You're right, we still don't know turnips. But for my money it's like you told me about the seals – just like they're a protected species, so is Grimaldi.'

'What do you mean?'

'Have you ever heard of a thing called a witness protection program?'

When Sally Kane answers, she trots out the words fast, as though she's already thought out her answer long ago but doesn't want me to know she has.

'Isn't that when — someone gives evidence that — how would you phrase it — puts someone away — and because of that evidence — other persons are out to — want to — get them — that is, punish them for giving that evidence?'

Couldn't have put it better myself.

'And you think this person Grimaldi —'

I nod, but something doesn't add up and I don't like things not adding up.

'By my reckoning, this Grimaldi gave evidence that got two nasties put away. As a result, Grimaldi was placed in a witness protection program.

After that, the two nasties escaped from lawful custody and now they're after Grimaldi.'

'And you think that David's minding this Grimaldi . . .'

Edith Burton bears all the hallmarks of a government agent and by my reckoning David Jones has been reporting to her.

'It would account for all the guns.'

'All what guns?'

I tell her about the gun in David Jones's left-hand drawer as well as the rifle in his office.

That's when Sally Kane starts to look guilty.

'Oh, poor David,' she says. 'So shouldn't we — drop the investigation?'

There's just the right degree of hesitation.

I think about the murder of a singing teacher, the killing of the singing teacher's soi-disant lover, Little Miss Twisty, the potshot someone took at Rory, plus what I strongly suspect was the near abduction and murder of my daughter, Imogene.

Not to mention the thumb.

'It's too late for that,' I say.

'What if I suspend payment?'

The sun's setting, the sheep are in the home paddock and the shepherd's shutting the gate on them but that's still no guarantee against the foxes.

I shake my head.

'Sorry, lady, but this caper's gone way beyond payment.'

From the direction of the wombat farm I make out the sound of a motor starting.

I say my goodbyes to Madam Kane and get myself back to the farm, fast. But I'm too late: the hoods have freed themselves and they and the cabriolet are no longer in residence.

I don't need Aunt Rube to tell me you need two thumbs to tie number eight wire.

Nor that the hooks that Handsfree wore on the end of his arms might make a very effective pair of boltcutters.

Chapter 36

THE CORPSE ON THE CHAISE LONGUE

Early next morning, having ridden the last train back to Sydney, caught the bus, walked the walk, rowed the dinghy, run the engine to charge the batteries in order to get the pump going again, had a few drinks and caught up on the beauty sleep, I shave, using the bailing bucket, the Dettol and the straight edge, rebandage the thumb, check my remaining teeth, drain my sixth coffee for the day, and feel more or less human again.

Then one of the cellophanes rings – the one with the wild African throb to it – and it's Sunday, so I get down to the bilge fast before someone gets it into their head to complain there's some gypsy living on a boat in the harbour, with nothing better to do than drag down the value of very expensive harbourside real estate.

'Rainbow?'

'Depends who's asking.'

It's what you say when you don't know who's on the other end of the phone, or who might be listening, before giving them something worth listening to.

'I'm sorry to bother you on a Sunday.' It's the Dwarf. 'But I couldn't raise Rory.'

If it's Sunday, Rory is down on his knees somewhere begging forgiveness, and he won't be getting up for anyone, unless that Someone happens to be God.

'I've obtained the information you requested. Two persons arrived from America at about the time you mentioned and went to the address given –'

'Not on the phone.'

'The usual place?'

There's urgency in his tone.

'The usual place.'

'Good' – the urgency changes to relief and relief to anxiety – 'as soon as you can make it.'

The usual place is closed owing to sex objects not being big sellers on Sundays. There's a sign in the window taped to the portside breast of a blow-up doll between a pink suspender belt and a pair of blue velvet handcuffs saying RING MY BELL. I do like it says and a dusty rattle echoes among the dildos, instruments of flagellation and sado-rags. While I'm waiting for a response I turn my back to the door and cast my peepers up and down the Boulevard of Broken Dreams.

I work my way back through the dialogue.

I got here as soon as I could but I've got a feeling that as soon as I could might not have been soon enough.

The door's got a Lockwood, a back-to-base alarm and a slide bolt weighted down with a double-thud Yale but there's no striker for the Lockwood and the door jamb's made of maple, meaning it turns into splinters under a nudge from the deltoid. A back kick en passant to the little black box via one of my whitesides disables the alarm.

The gat finds its way into my fist as I make for the back of the shop where the stairs are.

Nothing moves, not even the Lifelike Model with Edible Mammaries next to the DVD rack featuring post-Christmas specials, including the ever-popular *Naked Santa on Ice* and *The Orgy of the Christmas-Tree Fairies*.

The periodicals carry the usual quota of flesh but the stairs at the back of the shop feature nothing but yesterday's echoes.

I set the whitesides to Mute and start climbing.

Christianity's closed.

I could stay on the top step and wait to get myself thrown back down by whoever's in residence or I could get myself into the Dwarf's office fast.

I get myself into the Dwarf's office fast.

I dive as I enter, hitting the floorboards in the roll-ready position, what's left of the thumb tucked under me, gat held with the elbow in the 'L' shape of the quick shooter. I do a triple-loop with half-spin that takes me away from the window and towards the chaise longue, ending in a forward crouch by the bookcase at the foot of the recliner featuring a deluxe edition of *The Encyclopaedia Brutannica*.

There's still silence.

I hunch out of the crouch.

Then I stand out of it.

The swivel chair's vacant and no one's holding the broken cup adorning the Persian rug on the floorboards.

I turn to the chaise longue.

It's upholstered in white, there's a dame on it, she's naked as the day, and she's a looker.

Make that *was* a looker.

I place her age at time of decease in the vicinity of thirty-five.

She possesses cornflower blue eyes, a retroussé nose, ruby red lips, hair of a colour that all the available evidence suggests is original, and a shif sticking out of her chest at about the region where the heart should be.

Death's not a good look on anyone, least of all a beautiful blonde.

I shelve the gat.

The office clock says thirty minuets after noon.

I glance around the room.

There's still no one in it.

I turn my eyes back to the dame.

She's still dead.

I use the Dwarf's phone to call Rory and tell him to organise a house clean.

Then I ring the Dwarf.

He's short.

'Where are you?'

'The usual place.'

'I've just come from the usual place.'

'Where are you now?'

'The other usual place.'

There aren't that many joints you can get drugs on a Sunday and par consequence the boofs and sidlers and pants boys and ultraspans have flocked to O'Leary's like pigeons to the crone that dishes out day-old bread at the Fountain.

Hank the Barman sidles up on the other side of the counter wearing a natty little purple one-piece with *Suck Me* on one breast and a flower on the fob, doing a job of work on a decanter that looks like it's already done a couple of rounds with the Dishlex.

'Looking for the Dwarf, Rainbow?'

I adjust the fedora, grass-green with a metallic glow to the check but minus the feather – you attract less attention if you dress down – and chuck a glance around the hooch-parlour.

It's the usual crowd, and the pianola's empty.

'Something freaked him out. He said you'd find him on the Strip.'

When I finally locate the Dwarf, I also discover that he's edgy.

He keeps flicking his eyes about him as we hoof it along Macleay, surrounded by flaneurs acting like they're in Paris, and that anyone apart from them cares.

'Someone planted that corpse on me.'

'It's been taken care of.'

'That's not the point. The point is: why would anyone plant a corpse on me?'

'Pal, you had Prisons and after that you had Immigration. First you're locking people in and after that you're locking them out. It's not a situation that's going to win you friends.'

'Plus I'm a dwarf.' He goes all subdued on me. 'But even all that doesn't add up to a corpse. It's because I'm doing this job for you, right?'

'Probably wrong. What have you got for me?'

The Dwarf glances behind him again before bringing his peepers back to mine.

'I got a couple of names, but they're neither David nor Jones.'

He runs his fingers through his orange hair.

'Go on.'

'Every person that enters this country is required to fill out a yellow card, which is then handed to Customs upon disembarkation.'

'They'd be those little cards they hand out to distract you from the perils of landing and afterwards chuck in the shredder?'

The Dwarf shakes his head.

'They're not just to distract you and they're not shredded. They're assessed, filed, and the details are entered into a central computer.'

'Okay,' I tell him, 'so you tracked back ten annees like I asked you to and Edith Burton's name pops up on two of these little cards.'

'Seven years ago, to be precise.'

'And the reason Edith Burton's name pops up on two of these little cards is that two jokers intended staying with Edith Burton after disembarkation, right?'

'Wrong.'

'What do you mean, *wrong*?'

'They weren't jokers, they were dames.'

I don't like dealing with dwarfs, never have.

'Let's get this straight. You're telling me there were two dames, and both of them stayed with Edith Burton?'

'Like I told you, the cards are cross-referenced and –'

'What were their names?'

Name numero uno: Sarah J. Churchill.

'Description?'

He turns smug.

It's a little-known fact, he tells me, that with security the way it is these days – due to the threat of terrorism and the effect that acts of terrorism can have upon share prices – airlines no longer content themselves with what people tell them. They get out there and do some research of their own.

'Tall, plain, olive complexion.'

'And the other hoop-la?'

'Josephine Turner.'

'Description?'

'Blonde, little turned-up nose, and going by the description, a peach.'

The corpse on the chaise longue.

'Who we discovered subsequently moved to a second address.'

'One she went to after staying at Chez Burton?'

The Dwarf nods.

'So feed me the second address.'

The Dwarf tells me: 221B Baker Street, Craydon.

It still doesn't add up.

Two dames arrive in Australia, followed seven long years later by the hoods.

After which one dame decides to turn herself into a corpse.

Knowing the hoods, it doesn't take much to work out who killed her.

Now all I've got to discover is:

The dame's connection to the hoods;

The hoods' connection to David Jones; and

David Jones's connection to Grimaldi.

I return my attention to the Dwarf.

'I need you to check out two more arrivals. They're recent and –'

The Dwarf shakes his head.

'Sorry but I've just finished repaying any debt I had to Rory.'

'I'll need the prints back.'

'You know where to find them.'

The call to Rory takes less than a minute.

'Your pal the Dwarf just ditched us. We need a fix on an American dame, name of Josephine Turner.' I tell him the details. 'Your friend the Dwarf will supply you with the prints.'

'Willco.'

Rory did his apprenticeship in the army.

Chapter 37

THE LAST WORD

The mailbox at 221B Baker Street is overflowing, the washing's got dust on it and the lawn hasn't been vacuumed for a week.

I lift a Harvey Norman brochure out of the box, let myself in via the green ColorBond gate and make my way down the side path like I own the joint, the Taurus waltzing in three-four time against my pectorals.

I stuff the shooter down my schnauzers, take out the laundry louvres, stack them on top of a pile of dog droppings, place the jacket on top of the glass, stand on the jacket, and heave myself up through the aperture.

Drum-beats are hammering in the missing thumb, but I'm healing, and after I land in the laundry, I'm still healing.

Whoever was here last fully intended returning, otherwise there wouldn't be a Kentucky Fried extra-large rotting on the kitchen bench next to a sheet of paper with a corner torn out of it. I also wouldn't be holding my nose with the hand not holding the gun, the one that's still got the thumb on it, as I step over the stain on the kitchen linoleum and into the room where they kennel the television.

From the opening gambit I can see this is no permanent habitat, because the relevant issue of the *TV Times* isn't sitting on the lounge with programs rough-circled in blue, a pair of slip-ons isn't lying abandoned on the carpet, and there's no half-empty mug on the coffee table, with Pall Mall cigarette butts floating in the dregs, and lipstick marks on the cigarette butts.

In fact, there's nothing but a green Smith's alarm clock lying face-up on the rug, with the hands behind the little glass porthole freeze-framed at twelve.

The joint's got all the hallmarks of what's known in the trade as a staging post, a fly-by where jokers water the horses, pay a visit to the john, grab a kip and find themselves a schooner of chips and a warm beer before scampering back through the postillion to the stagecoach, and there's no one standing on the stoop to wave them goodbye.

It's like no one ever lived here, and even the dust's been dry-cleaned.

It tells me something, but it's to the tune of the gate clicking, followed by the sound of footsteps advancing along the footway, and I decide to make myself scarce before someone else decides it for me.

A cop – it's got to be a cop – is trying out the doorbell.

I'm back in the company of the chicken when I hear the wood in the front door splintering.

You got to do things in this business you'd never do in front of your mother.

The fowl next to the paper with the corner torn out of it tries to slide onto the floor as I shove a fist up its gizzards, putting my other mitt where the beak used to be in order to stop the thing slithering to the floor.

Hoofbeats are sounding in the hall, and it's a short hall.

A Rent-a-Crowd of maggots is doing a tango over the paper as I drag it out of the lucky-dip.

It looks blank.

I pocket it anyway, and am just leaving by the back door when the first of the hoods snow-boards in on the maggots.

While the paper's getting warmed by the blow-dry powered by the *Wooden No*'s auxiliary, I get the main engine up and running and spend an hour working the pump. The bilge is starting to look like your average suburban swimming pool. After that, but only after that, with the bilge happily spewing effluvium, I dust the paper with the grey powder and take a visual of the prints, matching them against the ones on a piece of the daisy-patterned china salvaged from the Dwarf's. They come up positive.

I then get to work with cotton wool soaked in a Condy's crystals and methylated spirits solution and eventually a bit of writing appears, in a nice shade of yellow-brown. It's a bit like the stain on the linoleum floor, the blood that should have been on the chaise longue but wasn't, the address on the piece of paper the Dwarf palmed me, the address that, going by the advertising material and the chicken, hasn't been lived in for a week, and the body carted off post-mortem to the Dwarf's, to add to the illusion that that was where the crime took place, in order to put the frighteners on the Dwarf.

Which means the corpse that used to be the living Josephine Turner but ended up dead on the chaise longue wasn't a random killing but a specially-selected and premeditated murder. Whoever killed the travelling companion of Sarah J. Churchill knew where Turner was and for what purpose she happened to be there as well as what to do with her after she turned into a corpse.

Someone needed to kill the dame.

That same party also wanted to put the frighteners on the Dwarf.

They decided to do two jobs in one.

And whoever they were believed that after they killed Turner they would be in the clear, that no one could trace them to the deed.

But in her last moments, the dame worked out not only who was coming for her but also what was in their minds while they were on their way.

That was why she wrote what she did on the bit of paper and why she stuffed it in the chicken, in the hope that, while her killer-to-be wouldn't be any the wiser, someone like me – or an accomplice like Sarah J. Churchill or the Burton dame – someone with the know how to search for a clue anyway, would find it.

The writing on the scrap of paper is scrawled like it was written in a hurry, without much concern for the slope of the characters or their shape, the way someone would write when her murderers were halfway up the hall, and it was a short hall, and she guessed one thing – apart from the identity of the killers – and that was that she was no more than a couple of hot breaths away from becoming a corpse.

The letters aren't all that clear but I can be sure of the last two, and they suggest the first.

This is how it reads:

Chapter 38

THE DEATH OF A FED

It doesn't make sense.

The dame had five seconds before getting bumped off and she uses them all up writing a word that means peanuts.

Doesn't make . . .

But there's no future sweating over a word that doesn't make sense.

I got to find myself something that does.

We're in a coffee joint at Bondi with the surf swelling and jokers around us with a lot of time on their hands. Clint's still Clint, he's still got the gormless expression on his face, he still looks guilty as hell, he still acts like he understands the meaning of life, and he also still looks like he doesn't.

The difference is that he no longer has a job, because the broad that gave him the list also gave him the sack after discovering good old Clint, everyone's mate, busy boffing somebody else.

'So I can't do what you're asking me to do, mate.'

'You got the numbers David Jones contacted. All I want now is the same thing in reverse.'

'Yeah, but –'

'If you can't do it,' I tell him, 'you can back-pay the price of your kids' education, not to mention what you owe me for all the humiliation and defeat.'

Clint bends his attention to his skinny latte.

'Mate, that's blackmail.'

I shrug.

'If you feel happier putting a name to it, that's as good a name as any. But whatever you call it, I want a list of the numbers the Burton dame called and you're the joker that's doing it.'

'You're not looking all that well, Rainbow,' Aunt Rube says. 'Are you sure you're getting plenty of protein?'

Rube likes to keep up with my protein intake.

There's been some sort of preliminary hearing and it's gone well so they've taken her out of solitary and we're out in the exercise yard, well out of reach of the prison's listening devices, but the cameras are still rolling and they've still relieved me of my pintos, belt and fedora.

'Yeah.'

Rube nods.

'The dames still treating you bad?'

'That's what I want to talk to you about.'

'Is it Pandora?'

I tell her it's not Pandora.

Pandora's been quiet of late.

She mostly is when I'm busy.

'So tell me,' she says.

So I tell her, especially about the word Josephine Turner wrote on the bit of paper and stuffed in the chicken. When I've finished, Rube gets me to describe the dames I'm talking about, including the corpse, and she listens intently all the while, the way Aunt Rube does, and after I've finished she's silent for two laps of the exercise yard, after which she's no longer silent.

'I been thinking, Rainbow. This word "Red" – was there any punctuation? A full-stop or something?'

'Nothing.'

'Let me see it.'

I palm her the paper and she shoves it in her kick without looking at it.

'Let's try another tack. What if this Chinchilla –'

'Churchill.'

'– and the Burton broad were one and the same?'

That puts me on Pause.

Rube has always been able to put me on Pause.

'How would that help us?'

'For a start, it would explain why the Churchill dame no longer exists.'

There's a commotion at the far end of the play pen but I pay no attention, on account of Rube's still talking, and when Rube's still talking I listen.

'Even though a name was given on the little immigration card, it doesn't mean the person existed, does it? So why shouldn't Sarah J. Churchill have simply become the person she was staying with?'

'Edith Burton?'

'You got it in one.'

'Hey, you!'

The screw puffs up like a loaded alibi.

'You the dude gave his name as Grey?'

The questionnaire will take its usual course.

'Depends who's asking.'

'I said, is Grey your real name?'

'As real as it'll ever get.'

'Have you got another one?'

'Close friends call me Fatty.'

That gets me back to Reception, as well as a black eye, my belt, shoes and fedora.

My mind's still swimming with ideas of what RED might mean long after I get back to the boat, check over the engine, catch a few hours' sleep, row myself ashore, call Rory from a public phone, and bus-it to the place where we agreed to meet.

Aunt Rube's given me something to think about.

Rory provides me with something more.

It's not yet dawn, with moonlight glistening on the airline billboards, as I crunch across the frosted foliage to the place where Rory's waiting, shivering in the early morning cold.

'Is the kid okay?'

Rory nods.

'I haven't seen the dame for a while. Apart from which I scored some intelligence.' Rory means that strictly in the sense of information. 'Tex owed me one.'

Everyone owes someone, it's what makes the world go round.

'Who's Tex?'

Tex turns out to be a Pittsburgh, US of A, housebreaker whose acquaintance Rory made during a little stay on suspicion of murder in a New South Wales correctional centre – make that prison – where Tex was residing while waiting to be sent back to wherever he came from.

'He's back in America where he got himself a job in Security, and I asked him to check out the names the Dwarf provided, and regarding Josephine Turner he came up with pure gold.'

We find a cab and I tell the guy the station.

'So what did he come up with?'

'He got a mate in the Bureau to check out the prints of Josephine Turner.'

The prints on the cup from the Dwarf's, the prints of the blonde that wound up dead on the chaise longue.

'Bureau?' There's only one Bureau that I've heard of, but I've got to be sure. 'You mean the United States Federal Bureau of Investigation?'

'That's right, the good old FB of I.'

'And?'

'The swab came up positive.'

'This dame's fingertips were on the FBI's records?'

Rory nods.

'You're dead right they were.'

'On account of she was a major malfeasant?'

The nod turns into a shake.

'So what was she, if she wasn't a major malfeasant?'

'She was an agent for the FBI.'

Chapter 39

THE MAN WITH THE STRAW-COLOURED HAIR

It's early morning and I've got a train to catch but Rory's still talking. I'm only half-listening.

Seven years ago US Federal Agent Josephine Turner flew herself into Sydney airport in the company of a second female – one Sarah J. Churchill – both giving the address where they'd be staying as that of Edith Burton.

At some point, Agent Turner moved out of Edith Burton's address and into the staging-post.

Where she lived on and off for several years – doing whatever it is that FBI agents do – until the hoods arrived on her doorstep and she was killed, joining what is turning out to be a very long string of corpses.

And all I've got is a word she wrote on a bit of paper and some joker's name, Grimaldi.

RED . . .

Short for Redhead?

In which case maybe the Dwarf killed her.

Or RED meaning Blood.

But why would a woman about to die bother writing Red meaning Blood?

'Do you know anything else about her?'

'She thought she was always right.'

I put the conundrum to one side and come back to the other problem.

'Okay, that covers Sarah J. Churchill. But what about Grimaldi?'

I find it hard to keep the urgency out of my voice, because something in the back of my mind has just made its way to the front of it, and that something is very scary indeed.

Rory shuffles his foot.

'Tex didn't want to say, because he reckons any debt he owes me isn't worth dying in the repayment of.'

'Why should he die?'

'He says that's what happens to people that mess about with Grimaldi.'

Which tells me something about Grimaldi.

Only I need to know something more.

'Can you get the Dwarf back on side?'

Rory shrugs.

'I'll try.'

'Okay, we got the name Grimaldi and it's coupled with the name of someone from the FBI. Now I want you to get Dwarfie to match the two names with Legal Action, US of A.

'I think we're closing in on the reason why the hoods are after David Jones.'

The train's an express so it's a few minutes after eleven as I climb out at Dashiell, discover from the timetable at the station that the last train out will be at five, and make my way along Main Street.

The sweat's working up a lot of enthusiasm under the shoulder holster as I near the ruins that pose as the local infirmary.

At three pounds fully loaded, the Smith & Wesson 686 is the heaviest item in my luggage rack.

The lightest is the stethoscope I picked up at the apothecary's in Main Street that I sling around my neck as I elbow my way through the swing doors of Dashiell Base Hospital and hoof-it along the corridor of Building numero uno, nodding to a cleaner in mauve pyjamas as I pass.

The odd nurse glances in my direction but I make like I'm a visiting doctor and they give me the benefit of uncertainty.

Accordingly, I'm making satisfactory progress until I get to Coronary, where I discover the flaxen-haired shepherd emerging from a door with *ANGUS MACIVER, M.D. M. Surg. F.R.C.S. Reparative Surgeon* neatly engraved upon the wall beside it.

The joker's wearing a suit and somehow he's got himself into the wrong paddock entirely but he's still wearing the thatch of straw-coloured hair and that's how I recognise him.

I also recognise danger when I see it and that's how I find myself shoving open a door and backing into a little room as the joker turns. I cop a profile that I've seen before, not only in the company of a bunch of sheep and at a distance, but also sitting slurping caffeine in close-up, as well as in several other locales.

I don't do coincidence.

Coincidence produces a lot more questions than it answers, and among the questions are:

Why has this joker been watching me and Sally Kane?

And what is he doing here now, posing as a doctor?

I've got the door half-closed and there's no way the joker can see me but I've caught a glimpse of the sort of all-seeing eyes you only find on the very guilty, and their owner's standing stock-still, like he's feeling my presence rather than seeing it and he's busy reaching out with his nerve ends to locate me.

I go into freeze frame, like when Rube would stop one of her movies to explain a Cagney dance step or what it was that Bogart was up to when the cops found him or how the P.I. worked out that the match-seller was a killer, and the shadowy images flickered on the dining-room wall, guns blazed, bodies sprawled all over the shop, and hoods kept the motors of their De Sotos turning over in the sunshine until the lesson was firmly implanted in my cerebral cortex, at which point Rube would remove her hand from the drive-spool and allow the movie to continue.

I count the seconds and there are five of them but it seems like an eternity before Blondie starts moving again.

Following him would answer a lot of questions, only I'm not about to follow him because just as I start out the door a voice from behind stops me.

'We'll have to stop meeting like this.'

I turn. Even though she's seated on a Fowlerware and her trousers are down around her ankles, Sally Kane's still as poised as ever, like she's just had a patient's head shaved and she's about to start in on a trepan.

'To what do I owe the pleasure?'

I turn away and address the door.

'I thought something might have happened to you.'

'It has' – the voice is still cool – 'I've discovered I can no longer rely on my privacy.'

Chapter 40

THE LADY IS A LIAR

Sally Kane's fully dressed and she's mooching about her office. The office is a cubicle with cracks in the walls and boards on bricks for bookcases and the books might look dishevelled but the red nose I gave her all those aeons ago looks very nice sitting next to the telephone. This is situated next to the biro-and-pad set that every doctor likes to have beside them for writing their death sentences on.

I'm in the swivel chair behind the desk.

I lean forward.

It exposes the gat but I leave the coat open anyway.

'Isn't it about time you levelled with me?'

The colour drains from Sally Kane's face quicker than water comes into the *Wooden No* when the pump fails.

'I – I have been – levelling with you.'

'Lady,' I say, and it's like we've come full circle, 'you haven't levelled with me since the moment we first met.'

The sounds of the infirmary grind on around us, someone coughing their last, the beat of witch doctors' bongos, and a hospital cleaner motoring around in the hall just outside the office with a vacuum.

At this stage in the questioning people have got two options.

They can go on lying.

Or they can confess.

Sally Kane does neither.

'I – was worried that you mightn't take on the case if I – told you everything.'

'So now you can be worried I won't stay on the case if you don't.'

Sally Kane drops into the chair that's normally occupied by the patient, and her voice drops to a whisper.

'The day we first met I – I was desperate.'

The Hoover's still hoovering and at any moment someone could bust down the door and let rip with a carbine.

I don't close the coat.

'I didn't know where else to turn.'

Sally Kane reaches out and picks up the red nose like it's a lifebuoy.

'All right, the truth is I – wanted a divorce from David because I – no longer loved him.'

'So you were lying when you told me you wanted to have his baby?'

'Yes,' Sally Kane whispers.

'Did you know anything about his history?'

'I – already told you. No.'

'I know what you already told me, lady, that's why I'm asking again. Did you know anything about his history?'

Sally Kane sucks in a lungful of hospital air.

'All right, yes, yes, I did! At least I – I guessed.'

Her voice is raised.

I like it when they raise their voice.

It means there's a chance they might be telling you the truth.

'You live with someone and there are hints, giveaways,' she goes on, 'and after that there are more hints and more giveaways until you end up putting together a profile.'

'A kind of patient dossier?'

Sally Kane nods.

'So how does this particular patient dossier read? The one you put together on David Jones.'

Sit someone in the right chair and they become what the chair says they are.

Sally Kane has become the patient.

She takes a deep breath before she continues.

'Look, I know paranoid as a word is unscientific,' she says, shifting in the chair that's normally occupied by the patient, 'at least it is the way people use it today. But using the word unscientifically, David shows all the signs of being paranoid.'

'Thinks jokers are following him, reading his thoughts, spiking his tea, out to kill him, and so forth?'

'Yes.'

'Why might that be?'

'Because there might be a good reason for someone to follow him.'

'So why didn't you tell me this in the first place?'

'Because I – wanted a second opinion. And I – didn't want to colour your judgment. Also I – was afraid you mightn't take on the job.'

A lot of reasons.

On a countback, too many.

'What about you?'

'What do you mean?'

'Is someone watching you, too?'

She reddens.

'No. All right, I mean yes.'

'Who?'

Pause.

'I – don't know.'

I try another approach.

'What makes you think you're fine and dandy when you say that someone's following you when the same thing on your husband makes him paranoid?'

Sally Kane sits up straight and takes another one of her deep breaths.

'Mr Scutt, you once asked if it was a woman's intuition that made me think something might be wrong with David, and I replied, No, it was an informed judgment.'

I remember.

'Well, I'm beginning to think intuition is nothing to be ashamed of.'

I've got one more question so I ask it.

'Does the word Red mean anything to you?'

Just then the telephone rings.

Sally Kane puts down the nose and answers it.

I look at the chronometer.

It reads just after midday.

Chapter 41

THE MAN IN THE MAUVE PYJAMAS

Sally Kane here.'

Dr Kane's all business as she bends her pearly to the business end of the receiver.

'Name?' She's got the biro in her hand and she's busy writing on the pad with it. 'How soon you can get her to the hospital?'

She makes with the Yeses, Noes, and Maybes, particularly the Maybes, before jamming the receiver back in its bassinet and responding to the unasked question I put to her.

'A car was forced off the road adjacent to the Dashiell abattoir, hitting the slaughterhouse at such speed that it smashed through the double-brick wall just above the offal chute. The driver was hurled the length of the killing room floor and onto a meat hook.'

Sally Kane's standing, no longer the patient, no longer even patient.

'Serious head injuries ensued, requiring immediate surgery. I'm sorry but I have to go.'

I get a feeling.

Call it intuition.

'Who was it on the meat hook?'

Sally Kane bends to the pad.

'The name on the licence read – Edith Burton.'

She pauses in her headlong rush to the door.

'Wasn't that –?'

Her pause enables me to get to the door before her.

I grab the handle, wrench it open and discover the joker with the Hoover down on his hands and knees. And he isn't dusting.

'Look, I really must go!'

Sally Kane's already said that. There's no reason for her to be between me and the joker on the floor, because the patient must still be all of twenty minutes away.

The parabellum's already in my fist and the words are already forming in my icebox.

'Hey, you!'

It's what you say when you want to grab hold of someone but can't because a dame's between you and the joker who's been listening at the keyhole, a joker who might be all dressed up in cleaner's pyjamas – cap, mask and gown – but is no cleaner than he ought to be, and who even now is hurtling past Reception and headed for the door marked ESCAPE.

I park the gat and turn back to where I last saw Sally Kane.

'Isn't that the joker who –?'

But Sally Kane's no longer there.

Lesson No. 103: faced with a choice between two pursuits, choose the one least likely to succeed.

In the light of Lesson 103 this is a no-brainer.

I know who Sally Kane is and where she'll be when I want her but I don't know anything about the joker in the mauve pyjamas except that I strongly suspect he can help me with my inquiries.

Chapter 42

DEATH BY FIREBALL

A codger in a wheelchair finds himself sprawled on the floor as I charge down the corridor after the cleaner. At least the codger's in the right place — a nurse is already helping him to his feet and stitching him back into the wheelchair.

Meanwhile, a figure crawls out of a broom cupboard wearing nothing but long johns.

I leave via the swing doors.

All I can see in the hospital grounds is sunshine.

I swivel on the path and pound my way towards the carpark.

An ancient green Toyota Coronary is at the boom gate and a mauve-pyjama'd arm is carding the auto-go.

I take three-point-five seconds over the hotwire of the early-model Mazda in the Nurses' lot, point-five seconds to lever the transmission onto the small cog, do a three-pointer, and launch the crate across the paddock as Mr Pyjama guns the Coronary southwards.

The thing about booms is they bust easy.

An alarm sounds as I rip past the sentry box, splintering the boom, and keeps right on sounding, a *whoah-whoah* that follows me according to the law of diminishing returns as I hammer the heap down Hospital Drive, left past the showground and around by the Christian Girls' Brainwashing Establishment, before swivelling right up the hill towards the racetrack.

The Toyota's drawing away.

Early-model Mazdas might be easy to break into but they're nobody's number one choice for a chase. Mr Pyjama's already past the guards and halfway up Nimrod Straight while the 121's still smacking the brains out of its pistons in Camshaft Canyon.

It's Sunday so something must be happening on Mount Goodyear and the something that's happening is a veterans' rally in celebration of the town's sesquicentenary. The crowd thinks we're in it as Mr Pyjama guns his jalopy into the first turn hard on the heels of the tailenders, while

I spin past the Guadeloupes at the barrier before starting in on the long grunt up Heartbreak Hill after him.

Your average punter loves death and nowhere outside a warzone is death more imminent than on a racetrack.

I'd put the crowd at ten grand and the starters at around the fifty-mark as the chequered flag waves us into the next lap, the two of us screaming into contention for line honours, even though neither of us is even entered in the race.

I hug the rails as a 1947 Buick Vee-Eight full of chromework and curves and superiority nudges the Toyota into the outfield.

The joker at the wheel of the Coronary might be able to handle a Hoover but he can't drive a car for pecans. As he comes into corner numero quattro, I note he's gone out too wide and his tyres are squealing so I paddle back to midstream as he throws out the anchors in a desperate attempt to correct the slide. This has an effect totally contrary to the one he was after.

The mob howls as Mr Mauve's rear end flicks around, putting him amongst the ads for spark plugs and beer and a holiday in Hawaii, scraping his portside fender as he goes into a wobble, and potential dingle or not, I go in after him.

I need to head him off, come up on the outer edge and go into a slide on his portside on the way out. The crowd sees the rescue coming, or better still, the possibility of bloodshed, and is on its feet and screaming for injury, but above all death.

It's then that I notice the cabriolet.

It's still black and it's still upright, it's ahead of the Coronary and it's enough to distract me from my good intentions. I slam on the sizzlers when I should be accelerating and the outside donuts to drag when they should be wheeler-dealing and the Mazda to flip, taking out an FJ, an XL, a PR, an APC and a couple of Plymouth Brethren on the way.

The somersault takes me over the ring board, I enter a planetary system unsuspected by your average astronomer, and there's not much left of anything by the time I come out of it. Thankfully there's more of me than there is of the Mazda, which appears to have been cobbled together out of no more than blind faith and goosebumps.

I locate what remains of my senses, decant the shooter and smash the dregs out of the windscreen. I then drag myself out of the car past the registration sticker, the wildlife pass and the next service reminder. The paramedics scurry my way with their little black bags and red tape and clipboards full of good intentions, so I dust down the Gatsby jacket and melt into the crowd.

The cabriolet's still burbling around the racetrack — I can see it wavering as it wobbles into Hell's Corner — but the Toyota's gone into retirement in Hawaii. The other crates are veering to avoid it as it lies on its back in the dust, wheels turning in the air, smoke elbowing its way out of the engine, and low-octane spilling down from the gas tank to join it, like lovers too long parted.

I can't handle fire.

Not after what happened to my mother.

Not after what happened to my sister.

Not after what almost happened to me.

The blond is a Rorschach blot against the driver's-side window, the sort of shape psychiatrists come up with using bits of paper and a splat of Waterman's ink, imperfectly symmetrical, with what might be fingers spread against the glass like a salamander's. The fingers are framing a central blob that could be an upside-down head or a heart or a lump of coal or a piece of faecal matter. Whatever it is, it's being pressed in place by the bulge of the airbag, inflated when the vehicle smacked into the circuit board, tea leaves on the inside of bone china, foretelling a hangman's future.

The blond joker's features have come into sharp relief and real fear is etched in his pale eyes. I can see the man's past like I'm doing his dying for him — a figure in the caff where I first met Sally Kane, a shepherd beside a cottage by a hillside, a doctor in the hospital, a cleaner kneeling outside Sally Kane's office door, and now a just-about-to-be-dead man at the wheel of an upside-down Coronary.

Unlike David Jones, the blond joker's got a lot of past.

What he hasn't got is a future.

The blast when the smoke says hello to the petrol reverberates around the mountainside and sends a burial shroud of smoke into the air. It also hurls me back up the hill whence I came. When I open my fire-scarred eyes, the blond joker's still there, only he's no longer blond, his fingers are no longer fingers and his face no longer has any features in it.

Flames are licking the sheen off the duco, the tyres are sizzling and the airbag's deflated, leaving what remains of the shepherd to sag against the Toyota's window like a fire-struck Lepidoptera that flew too close to the candelabrum.

The rest of the cars are still hurtling around the track and among them is the black cabriolet, dancing by on its third or fourth or fifth or sixth runabout. The passenger-side window is down and Babyface is leaning out of it, hard eyes scanning the scene like he wouldn't mind having been responsible for the wipe-out, as well as any other deaths that might be going.

I half-expect the business end of a machine-gun to appear cheek-by-jowl with the cherubic face and start filling the air full of sunshine.

Chapter 43

OPERATION DEATH

At 3.15 pm by her office chronometer, Sally Kane's got blood on her hands, and that makes two of us.

She shouldn't have, because surgeons wear gloves when they're surging, but there must have been a hole in her Ansell's or else she sliced them while she was gouging around in Edith Burton's brain pan digging out the bone scraps that had knifed their way into her cerebellum when she went through the windscreen at the abattoir.

And I shouldn't have, either, except that my past got in the way of me saving the shepherd.

I've rebuckled the holster, reblocked the fedora, dusted off the denims, and patted down the flapdoodles on the jacket's storage system. I've also put one and one together and come up with angst, so I'm not in the mood to pussyfoot around with anyone. I shove my way past the gurney with the green sheet over it outside Sally Kane's office and barge in without waiting to be invited.

Sally Kane looks like she needs treatment.

Accordingly, I apply the electrodes.

'Your boyfriend's dead.'

She turns porcelain.

'I don't have a boyfriend.'

She's right.

She doesn't.

Not any more.

'Dead and cremated,' I tell her, 'so you can stop pretending you were going to all those meetings to save the hospital, when in reality you were rendezvousing with your lover.'

I give that time to sink in.

'You can also start helping me with my inquiries.'

If her face were any whiter it would be risotto.

'Wh – what happened?'

I tell her and I don't spare her feelings in the telling.

She falls apart, and it's a long time before she falls together again – the little nose wipe comes into play, the sobs are real sobs, and for once the emotion is genuine.

I give her thirty seconds, because that's all I've got.

'I once asked if you knew anything about the word RED.'

Sally Kane shakes her head.

'All right, then I need to see Edith Burton.'

She takes one of her deep breaths.

'I'm sorry,' she replies, 'but Edith Burton was involved in a serious accident. It was touch and go but I believe we got to her in time. I've inserted a steel plate in her head, she's in a serious but stable condition, and if she's allowed good and sufficient rest she's got an excellent chance of making a complete recovery.'

Enough clichés to paper over most of the problems in the public health system.

'It just so happens that I can't allow her to rest on account of I need to interview her,' I say, 'and I need to interview her fast, and to do that I require a room number.'

'I'm afraid that's not possible.'

'Then neither is your staying alive.'

'Wh – what do you mean?'

They always want to know what you mean, even when they already know. I've got nothing to lose by telling her.

'The jokers that are after your husband have now bumped off everyone connected with him except you.

So – apart from your husband – you're the last man standing.'

'How do you know?'

They always want to know how you know, even when they already know. I tell her anyway, and at the end of the telling, Sally Kane's ready to agree to anything.

Edith Burton's in Room 327B, she tells me, at which point something starts squeaking on the other side of the door, and it isn't rodents.

'But I warn you,' Sally Kane says as I make for the hatchway, 'she mightn't make much sense. I've seen a number of such cases, and I know that such trauma can manifest itself in confusion.'

It's a chance I'm prepared to take.

Because now I'm prepared to take anything.

Chapter 44

A BULLET FOR BURTON

Intensive care units are like morgues.

The difference is that in morgues the corpses have stopped breathing.

The gurney with the green sheet over it looks familiar but I've got no time for familiarity as I hotfoot it up the hallway to Room 327C. I press the EMERGENCY button beside the bed, waiting behind the door until all available hospital staff have answered the call before slipping out, letting myself into Room 327B, and easing the door shut behind me.

Edith Burton is lying on the bed but she's no longer Edith Burton.

Instead she's a figure in a waxworks, a bundle of machinery humming around her, a mask over her face, wires attached to chest, arms and legs, and tubes coming out of her nostrils. There's a lot of dried blood, her head is swathed in bandages and there's a fearful look in her eyes that grows ever more fearful as I remove the mask from her face and seat myself on the visitor's chair beside her.

'If I don't return this,' I say, holding up the mask, 'you're going to cark it.'

'What do you mean?'

'Expire, cease to exist, extirpate, pass away, perish, die.'

It wasn't what she asked but it's what I'm telling her.

'I mean . . .'

'I know what you mean, lady, but what's important right now is what *I* mean and right now I need to know who you are.'

She shakes her head.

'Okay, play it the hard way – what's your relationship to David Jones?'

Again the head shake.

Maybe she's trying to clear it.

Or maybe she just wants to die.

'Why are the two hoods after David Jones?'

The front door to her transigence is locked, so I try the rear entrance.

'Tell me about the accident.'

She must be dead keen to get the mask back on because she tells me about the accident, but in the telling of it her voice is the rustle of a bloodstained gown on a sickroom floor and I can only just make out enough to understand half of what she's saying.

And half of what she's saying is that she was accelerating around Abattoir Bend on her way to Dashiell when a car appeared out of nowhere, forcing her vehicle across the road and into a stone fence and through the brick wall of the slaughterhouse.

But I already know that.

'Why were you coming to Dashiell?'

She stops to draw breath.

It's a long breath and there's a lot of blood in it.

Meanwhile, one of her mitts is creeping towards a button that looks very much like the one I pressed next door.

I make to chuck the mask across the room and Burton withdraws the hand from the button, fast.

'Now tell me who was driving the car.'

Burton shakes her head, which suggests either that she didn't see who was driving the car, she can't say, or she just doesn't want to live. Take your pick.

I hear the door behind me opening but I continue with my line of inquiry.

'Colour of car, year of manufacture, marque. Was it by any chance a black cabriolet?'

Edith Burton's not answering.

'Josephine Turner, then. Your fellow FBI agent. Tell me about her.'

'Disappeared . . . don't know what . . . happened to her . . . Arrogant bitch . . . liked to be able to say she could . . . work things out before . . . anyone else could . . . Can imagine her on . . . her deathbed . . . saying . . . I told you so . . .'

Quite a speech, only I'm not interested in speeches.

'What does RED mean?'

Edith Burton looks confused.

Also she's suddenly looking very afraid so I figure I need to forget the car and Josephine Turner and head back to the garage.

'Grimaldi, then. Who's Grimaldi?'

Edith Burton opens her mouth only it's not to speak.

Her head's turned my way and her eyes have still got fear in them only they're no longer focused on me but on a point just behind me.

When I see that, I immediately bring the interview to a close. I drop the mask and go for the gat, at the same time moving into a high-danger spin, the sort of movement that needs no flex-for-weight-transference and is therefore more or less directionless, but has the advantage of giving no warning of your intentions.

I manage to bring the drip feed down around my lugs as I go but I've effectively taken myself out of the line of fire so that when the shooter goes off and the bullet hole appears in the middle of Burton's bandaged forehead, I don't know if the bullet was meant for me or for Burton or for both of us. What I do know is that the mask won't be helping her any more, because her condition has suddenly deteriorated and a recovery of any sort is out of the question – complete or otherwise.

I swing my peepers in the direction of the door, disentangle myself from the drip feed, kick away the chair and dive back to the bedside, in order to catch whatever it is that Burton might have for me, in the way of last words.

'Gurgle,' she says, eyes rolling.

I check the damage and discover that the reason Madam Burton didn't die pronto was that the steel plate Sally Kane inserted in her head deflected the slug.

The bullet's still found its way into her brain.

And she's still saying Gurgle.

But she's also trying to say something else.

It sounds like 'cycle path'.

But why would anyone worry about cycle paths when they're just about to be dead?

Chapter 45

THE DEATH OF THE DWARF

Aside from the gurney – its green sheet trailing on the chessboard floor and whoever was under it gone – the hallway's deserted, with nothing to kick up a breeze in it but the doors.

I hurl myself down the passageway, gat at the ready.

A doctor, three nurses, the tea lady and a cleaner emerge from Room 327C, see me and demerge back in to it.

An attendant gets in the way, then gets the hell out of it.

An old dame with difficulty walking sees me, and suddenly has no trouble walking at all.

Screams come from a room on my right.

I slam open the door, crouch between the architraves, and brace myself in the knees-bent, legs-apart position, gun gripped in both fists at the ready.

A dame's lying on her back in pretty much the same position, and when she catches sight of me she stops screaming.

Maternity would be a lot quieter if they called in the assassins.

I shelve the gat and start back to where I left Sally Kane. I've still got some unanswered questions as well as the odd unquestioned answer and Sally Kane is now in very serious trouble indeed.

As I reach the weed-strewn lawn the last joker I expect to see is David Jones, but that's who I see.

He's strolling from the direction of the visitors' carpark whistling Dixie. He's moving with short, quick steps in the direction of the hospital.

He doesn't look my way as he pushes through the doors.

He's on his way to see Sally Kane which means she'll be back under his protection, and that frees me up for other duties. I reach for one of the dead-men's mobiles and en route to the station dial C for Clint.

'I need those telephone records.'

'Nearly there, mate, but –'

I tell him to get completely there and where I'll be in a four-hour train ride from now so he can hand me the results. He hasn't quite completed his side of the dialogue.

'I think I'm being followed.'

What is it with people?

'Look, pal, everyone's being followed, it's called traffic, just be there.'

I thumb the red button and phone Rory as I hoof it past all the sesquicentennial celebratory signs lining Main Street. I make it into a carriage just as the dame in the railway uniform flags away the riff-raff on the platform and the doors close.

It's just after nine in the pm when I reach Sydney Central. Rory's waiting on platform numero uno, and so is the latest obituary.

The Dwarf's dead, Rory tells me, but not before the little man managed to file away a stack of documentation about the size of a Patrick White novella. This is what Rory's got in the faded canvas dilly bag over his shoulder.

'Why aren't you watching Imogene?'

'I can't be everywhere, Rain!'

I shake my head and head off up the concourse.

Stations make me nervous.

So does Rory.

'Tell me what happened to the Dwarf.'

The Dwarf considered the devil and the deep blue azure and Scylla and Charibdis and a rock and a hard place and the frying pan and the fire and et cetera and so forth and finally came down on the side of incaution. This resulted in a bunch of papers being heisted from a courtroom in America.

Just after the Dwarf took delivery of the papers – but not before he'd safely parked them with Rory – he was standing at the window of his office when some person or persons unknown waltzed in and shot him.

I interrupt Rory's discourse.

'How do you know all this?'

'The porn merchant told me.'

'The porn merchant told you and you believed him? Did the porn merchant even see who did it?'

Rory shifts his foot.

'Well, he was at the Dwarf's when they came for the little man but he dropped behind the desk as they entered. He heard the shots, came out of hiding after they left, saw the row of bullet holes on both sides of the window and the Dwarf slumped on the floor beneath them, and cleared out. I found him downing hotshots at the hooch parlour – that's when he told me.'

Some things have to be taken at face value and among the things I have to take at face value are Rory, the porn merchant, and the death of the Dwarf.

No more than half a block away, I hear a car engine burble and die, a car door slam and the sound of hurrying footsteps.

A couple of beats.

Then the same again, like an echo.

Another dying engine, another car door, more footsteps.

I keep walking while next to me Rory keeps crutching.

It's getting dark as we head up Alum.

'Hang onto that bag,' I tell Rory.

'Where are we going?'

'We're meeting someone.' That's when I hear something. 'Shuddup!'

Someone's following us.

The list of suspects has shortened.

The shepherd and the Dwarf and Burton are dead.

Which just leaves the hoods.

I indicate east, and at the same instant head in the other direction, grabbing the fedora as I go and ending up in a crouch while the gat comes out for an airing.

The footsteps stop.

The world's reduced to a blob of light on a deserted footpath – courtesy of a single bulb lamppost – and a bunch of shadows.

I stay where I am.

Rory stays where he is.

The tail doesn't move.

The world stops on its axis.

The trick to moving quiet, Rube taught me, is the same as any other act of camouflage – imitate your surroundings.

So I imitate my surroundings.

And my surroundings are a Vinnies donations bin surrounded by sacks of donations, a lot of darkness and an office building possessed of faulty air-conditioning.

I do the air-conditioning.

It's no more than a muted clunk and whisper but that's what I do, picking up the sound and lifting it a notch or two, using my diaphragm like Ruby taught me and producing a continuous clunk and whisper that covers the shuffling of my feet as I move through the undergrowth that in this part of the world passes for landscaping.

The tail's standing by a bush.

I spot him because he's not imitating his surroundings.

His outline's fuzzy.

Rory's nowhere to be seen.

Lesson number one when you discover you're being tailed: assume the opposition's sharper than you are. You'll never be disappointed.

Lesson two: assume that patience in these situations isn't a virtue. It's a necessity.

And lesson three: assume nothing.

Chapter 46

THE END OF THE LINESMAN

At last count, there's half-a-dozen deaths, leaving eight lives remaining in my care, eight people to keep in the land of the living – Imogene and the twins; their mother; Sally Kane and David Jones; Rory; and last of all, Clint, who we're now on our way to keep a rendezvous with.

Whoever's out there is the enemy. I can't hear the enemy breathing but I can see it, great chunks of carbon dioxide metabolising whitely in the cold night air.

Lesson four: always let your follower make the first move because the first move will always be the wrong one.

The follower steps into the light.

That's when I recognise him and that's when he gets shot, hands flying up to his chest, body thrusting forward in an off-centre half-turn pirouette, legs crossing, followed by a free-fall, a pitching-forward and simultaneous crumbling so that all that's left at the end of all the fancy footwork is a ragged pile of clothes on the footpath, like just another donation to Vinnies.

Lesson five: stay where you are.

I stay where I am.

That's when another person steps out of the darkness.

Correction: another two persons.

The hoods.

Handsfree is carrying a gat and the gat's carrying a silencer.

He kicks the sack so it rolls over.

'He's dead.'

Babyface shakes his head, but it's not in wonder.

'No kidding.'

'I was just saying.'

'Yeah, well don't just be saying nothing, it's enough that you exxed the bastard.'

'Well, he was hand-in-glove with that Rainbow banana, wasn't he? Him and the cripple? Ain't that why we're following him? Ain't that why he was with them?'

'He wasn't with them, you ape, he was in process of keeping a rendezvous with them.' Babyface peers into the darkness, his baby face glossy in the half-light. 'And because you were so bloody trigger happy, we lost them.'

They're still dressed in black and they still haven't got a brain between them.

While Babyface goes through Clint's pockets, Handsfree stands over him with the Stechkin.

Babyface comes up with what have to be Burton's telephone records and shuffles to a spot under the light where he frowns over them.

Rory motions me to shoot them both and I motion him to stop motioning.

'Just a bunch of telephone numbers,' Babyface says to no one in particular. 'No names, just telephone numbers.' He stares at the paper. 'Except one's got a circle around it.'

He looks up, and under the one-bulber I can see inspiration on his baby features.

'So what do we do now?'

'We find out where this number is and we pay it a little visit.'

After they've gone, Rory crawls out of the woodwork.

'Why didn't you pin him?'

A killer doesn't break the habits of a lifetime overnight.

'Life's not just about pinning people, Roarer.'

'So what do we do now?'

'We get ourselves back to Dashiell, fast. But first we got to rid ourselves of a corpse.'

I don't hear the hoods' vehicle departing but that doesn't mean rhubarb.

We find a black garbage bag among the donations to Vinnies and wrap Clint in it.

After that, we get ourselves a taxi cab, one of those big ones that people cart wheelchairs about in, and get the corpse, ourselves, and Rory's dilly bag into it.

'Where you taking the garbage?'
I tell the cab-jockey the harbour.

Chapter 47

DESPERATELY SEEKING SAFETY

The harbour's a fine and lonely place.

At night, lights glimmer on its surface, the sound of ferry klaxons carry clearly across the inky water and corpses are weighted down and dumped in places where only the sharks can find them.

When we get to the rocks where the tinnies are I tell the cab-jockey to wait.

The depositing of bodies in the harbour requires a sound working knowledge of seabed geography and also tides and eddies, as well as a chain plus a large rock to tie the body to in order to stop it making like a soufflé and rising.

'It's a small boat,' Rory observes as we manhandle Clint into the coracle. 'It'll sink under our combined weight.'

'It won't sink under our combined weight because our weight won't be combining.' I get the boat into the water. 'Me and Clint are going for a little boat ride while you're taking the cab back to town and collecting the Caddie. And don't forget the dilly bag.'

I row to a spot just past Point Hopeless where I dump Clint.

There's no eulogy.

The black water closes over his body like he never was and I row back to shore that much easier for his passing.

We're in the Caddie.

Rory's at the wheel, we got the dog between us – the one with the big head, Little Miss Twisty's pooch, the dandie Dinmont – and there's not much in the Caddie in the way of armoury.

'Where are your tools of trade?' I ask Rory.

'I gave them away. But I still got the crutch. Where we heading?'

'Swing by the kid's.'

'What kid's?'

'My kid's, the one you're supposed to be protecting. But first, you can chuck me one of your phones.'

I ring the jail.

'Any further thoughts on that word, Rube? We're going in, and –'

'As a matter of fact, yeah.' Rube's voice is hollow, like she's talking from a death chamber. 'Remember we were talking about acronyms? Well, I –'

But the connection drops out. I check the little window. It says, OUT OF CREDIT.

'Anything the matter?' asks Rory.

'Yeah.' I chuck the dead phone onto the back seat. 'We're not moving.'

Salina answers the door and Imogene's beside her.

At least one of them looks surprised.

'What are you doing here?'

'I'm taking the kid.'

'Over my dead body you are.'

Once upon a time we used to love each other.

Now all we got in common is the language, and Imogene.

'Her life's in danger,' I say.

Salina sighs.

'All right. But if she goes, I go with her.'

I climb in the back seat with the kid and the pooch while Rory sits behind the steering wheel glaring at Salina.

'What's she doing here?'

'She's the mother.'

Rory thumps the wheel.

'I know she's the mother. What I'm asking is what she's doing here.'

Too many questions, too little time to answer.

'We're taking them to safety.'

'Where are you taking us to, Daddy?'

'Safety.'

Even as I speak, just up the street I think I see a shadow.

Maybe it's Pandora, maybe it's the hoods, or maybe it's just a shadow. But I got enough on my plate without worrying about shadows.

Chapter 48

THE MOMENT OF TRUTH

Imogene picks up on what she thinks I told her.

'Are you taking me to see my sister?'

People hear what they want to hear.

I shake my head.

'I said safety, not Sophie.'

'So when can I meet Sophie?'

I'm heading for a confrontation, only I didn't know it would be this kind of confrontation.

I like stand-ups, two men, two guns, kind of thing, I don't do subtle.

'Look, she's not where we're going, okay?'

'She's never anywhere we're going. Why can't I even meet her, if she's my sister?'

Sophie's been a great comfort to me over the years and I don't want to give her up but I don't want to risk losing Imogene, either.

'She's —'

My throat's seized.

The Caddie's rocking into the night, and if the two up front are talking, I can't hear them.

'She's what, Daddy?'

Salina cranes around.

'I'm sorry but did I hear right? You've got another kid besides Imogene?'

She doesn't add and the twins.

Instead she turns on Imogene.

'And you knew this but never told me?'

Imogene shrugs.

'Daddy told me not to say. He said it was our little secret.'

'Have you ever spoken to this sister you've never seen?'

Imogene turns away and stares out the window.

'I can explain,' I tell her.

But Salina explains for me.

'What Daddy's trying to say,' she tells Imogene, 'is that this so-called sister of yours doesn't exist. There's no Sophie, because — for reasons best known to himself — your father made her up out of his head.'

There's a lot of silence after that.

Imogene finally turns towards me.

There's more than just the dog between us.

'Is that right, Daddy, what Mummy just said?'

It's the moment of disillusionment, when the kid finally discovers her daddy's a fruitcake.

'Is what right?'

'What Mummy just said about my sister.'

I look at Rory's neck but there's no inspiration there, just a lot of dirt and a bullet hole, and Salina's staring through her side of the split windscreen.

'There's no Sophie?' Imogene's eyes are shining, and it's not with an excess of love for her paterfamilias either. 'And there never has been?'

I shake my head and nod it all at the same time, on account of Imogene's asking two questions and the answers to the two questions are totally different.

'There was a Sophie,' I say, when I finally manage to get the words out, 'only she wasn't your sister.'

Imogene frowns.

'Whose sister was she, then?'

I take a deep breath and when I do there's dust in it.

'Mine.'

Chapter 49

DEATH BY WINDMILL

Salina turns in her seat.

'Let's play Colours, shall we?'

'What's Colours?'

Come midnight there aren't all that many vehicles on the road and what there are aren't all that easy to see but somehow the game grows legs and pretty soon everyone's got a colour and forget they're locked in the car with a loony and are yelling, There's one! and Is that blue?, even Rory.

That's when I see it.

Imogene's won two out of three and I haven't been doing all that good but that's only because I keep getting dealt the wrong colour, when Imogene chooses blue, Rory's on red and Salina's got yellow, while Imogene's lucked white and I've been landed with the colour nobody wants, if you can call black a colour.

'Red!' yells Rory.

'That's not red. It's red and blue.'

'And yellow.'

'And white.'

I look where they're looking and where they're looking is at a B-double circus truck which accounts for all the colours, with pictures of ringmasters and acrobats and clowns all over it, and colours all over the clowns.

'That counts as one for everyone except Daddy.'

'That's not a car,' I tell her. 'It's a truck.'

'It still counts. And there's one for you, anyway.'

That's when I look in the looking glass and that's when I see it, dancing from lane to lane and having no trouble at all keeping up with the Caddie. It's souped-up just like the hoods said it was and its straight-up-and-down windscreen gives nothing away but reflections. It's the colour of death and just as welcoming: an upright coffin on wheels waiting for the next customer, all shined up and with somewhere to go.

I know why it's following us.

The hoods didn't depart after they killed Clint but waited around and followed us instead. They figured that our destination and the address of the phone number they pick-pocketed from Clint might be one and the same.

They're following us for the same reason that Fate follows anyone – because we've got a rendezvous.

We pass another circus truck only to find there's a string of the things, like elephants attached to one another's tails. Eventually they take their place among all the other clowns on the road while the cabriolet's still sitting bolt upright behind the Caddie and I'm the only one who can see it, because the world's moved on since the Colours game, but that doesn't mean Imogene's moved on as well.

'Where's your sister now, Daddy?'

'I don't think Daddy likes talking about his sister,' her mother says, 'so let's drop the subject and all have a little nap, shall we?'

These babies are gas-guzzlers but we've done the fuel stop and while we were at the gas station we've made the necessary trip to the Damen und Herren. All of us except Rory that is, who was happy to mix it with the dog up against the ice container. This was how he came to surprise the joker in the balaclava. The pooch went ballistic and the joker only just managed to escape to his conveyance and drive off.

Now Rory's curled up in the back seat with the kid and the dog, they're all wearing seatbelts, even the dog, and snoring their heads off, leaving me up front with Salina and too many memories.

It's started to rain.

'You tend to be full of questions,' she says, peering past the wipers, 'but you're not all that free with the answers.'

She taps at the wheel, frowning.

'This crate's handling funny.'

'It's a funny crate,' I say, 'or else it's the rain.'

The night's deepening and we've had the question-and-answer dialogue and the this-crate's-handling-funny conversation but sooner or later Salina's going to get back to what's really bothering her.

'You never told me about your childhood.'

I shrug.

'It was just another childhood.'

But she's not buying what I'm selling.

'As far as I can make out your sister died when you were quite young and for some reason you feel guilty about it, so guilty that all these years later you're still pretending she's alive.'

I don't answer.

It doesn't stop Salina.

'How old were you when she died?'

I feel the automobile shift from side to side, along with my world.

'Was it an accident? Did she fall off a cliff?'

'No.'

'So how did it happen?'

I can't stall forever.

'I was five and Sophie was three. Dad was a pusher and my Mum was a hop-head. You could say it was a marriage made in Heaven.'

Salina's wrestling with the steering.

'It was the nineteen-sixties and the whole world was hippy. People with names like Mahatma and Shava carved totem poles out of gum trees, power came out of windmills, parents did drugs, and kids did the best they could, under the circumstances.

We lived on a collective farm where one of the chief entertainments was something called "Orbiting".'

Even after all these years I shudder.

Or maybe it's just the way the car's handling.

'Any time of the day or night some hop-head could strip off and start twirling a length of wood with oil-soaked rags on the end, burning like fury.

Accordingly, there was always a lot of fuel around, plus the necessary matches.'

And people drugged out of their brains.

'There happened to be a windmill on the Collective and the hippies had rigged up some sort of seat on the end of one of the vanes, with a ladder up to it, and on windy nights people would strap themselves onto it and whirl round, waving their fire sticks and making like they were an integral part of the cosmic cycle.

'That's how she did it.'

'That's how she did what?'

I stare out into the darkness.

'One night my mother decided to become a Catherine wheel and thought we kids might like to be part of the fireworks.

She got hold of Sophie but I managed to hide behind a totem pole.'

We're heading downhill.

The Caddie speeds up.

'My mother couldn't find me so she contented herself with Sophie. She had a can of kerosene and a box of Redi-Lites and the wind was up and the windmill was straining at its ropes and next thing she'd strapped herself into the seat and had Sophie in her arms and she was lighting matches and laughing.'

The memories are on a roll, just like the car.

'In my five-year-old mind I thought the wind might blow the fire out but of course it did just the opposite. I thought I saw a figure by the windmill but it wasn't doing anything about it so I ran out from behind the totem pole and started climbing the stepladder beside the windmill. There was a lot of smoke but I kept on climbing and when I got close to my sister I reached out to grab her.'

I have to stop for a moment.

'But all I got was her shoe.'

Salina stares out into the darkness.

'No wonder you're messed up, Rainbow,' she says.

That's when the car goes into freefall, veering towards the edge of the precipice.

Chapter 50

A FREE RIDE

We smack into a vacant rock and spin around.

There's the stench of burning rubber and the shriek of buckling Caddie.

I find myself grateful for the invention of seatbelts and the solidity of big old American cars.

Half of us is dangling in space.

The other half wants to join it.

Behind us drivers are reining in their horses.

In front of us, brake lights flash.

Something white rips past us, heading hell for leather for Dashiell.

A truck looms out of the darkness, at the last minute its lights veer around us, there's the sound of people screaming, and a horn starts a one-sided conversation with the sky.

Tyres screech.

More horns blare.

Headlights play a kaleidoscopic cacophony among the trees.

A ricocheting wheel smacks into the Caddie.

The Caddie teeters.

And through all the smoke and the stench and the racket and the ricocheting wheels I hear the voice of Imogene, saying, 'Is this the safety you were talking about, Daddy?'

I reach over, grab the kid, fling open the door and roll us out into the mud.

I catch a glimpse of the dog and the others following.

Meanwhile, figures are slipping and sliding towards us from the truck ahead, the beams of their torchlights glistening on the wet road in between.

Voices in the maelstrom.

'Give her here!' Salina drags the kid out of my arms. 'Bloody Rory's bloody heap wouldn't handle, it was like trying to steer a Dodgem, the bloody brakes failed.'

Rory takes it personal.

'There was nothing wrong with the brakes, she just got the million-mile service.'

Salina shakes her head, glares at Rory and hugs Imogene.

'The brakes were useless, Rory. Ditto the steering.'

The figures from the truck have reached us.

'You lot okay?'

'Our car's stuffed. We need a ride.'

'We're going to Dashiell.'

'So are we. Chuck us a torch, will you?'

I motion the others to go ahead while I make my way back with the torch.

Steering doesn't just go, brakes don't suddenly fail and cars don't suddenly head for the nearest cliff, not even when they're eighty-year-old Caddies.

I lie on my back in the mud and shine the illuminator up under the chassis.

The steering's of the Gemmer-worm-and-Sector kind.

I don't know how it got into a Caddie but I know why it's no longer operative – the pump line's gone walkabout, while the rest of the system is pretzels.

I don't need to check the brakes, but I do it anyway.

In these crates, brakes require actuating rods.

But the Caddie's brakes have been de-actuated.

Someone's cut them.

I slide out from under.

The road looks like a landslide.

There's the sound of sirens, actuated by fifty or so mobile phones calling Emergency.

I don't want to be here when the cops come.

I make for the truck.

'Tell me about the rubber-necker.'

'What rubber-necker?'

We're squashed in the cabin of the truck, the truck's on its way past a quagmire of traffic trying to go the other way, and Rory's frowning.

'The one at the servo,' I tell him, 'the joker in the balaclava, the one you found checking out the Caddie, the one Rocket went ballistic over.'

'It wasn't a joker.'

'What do you mean, it wasn't a joker?'

'It was a dame.'

Chapter 51

LIFE IS A CAROUSEL

We're almost at our destination before the guy at the wheel breaks his silence.

'Time for you lot to get out.'

'Why?'

'Because this is our turn-off.'

I blink into the night.

I can just make out a sign.

It's the turn-off to the farm.

I make a decision.

'It's our turn-off, too.'

We're back at the farm. Because it's rained, the dust is no longer dust but mud. Although the place is as dark as a murderer's thoughts, I can still see the farm's no longer a farm but a circus, complete with Big Top and sideshows and a generator roaring in the front paddock and a crane rearing up into the night sky and arc lights picking out the shadows of workmen as they busy themselves setting up a ferris wheel.

'Where are we?' Salina asks.

'It used to be a farm.' The No. 8 wire's still there, with the loops in it where I'd tied up the hoods, along with the plough and the memories. 'It was leased to a couple of jokers that weren't farmers.'

Rory's down on his knee.

'Thou art the resurrection,' he's croaking, 'the truth, and the light!'

The rest of us slosh through the mud to the shack.

By the light of the torch I make out the black patches on the roof and a note on Jones, Jones and Jones letterhead attached to the door with the sort of tacks generals use in world wars while they're standing around converted billiard tables wondering what battalion to sacrifice next, complete with little red tips on them to indicate the progress of the enemy:

TO WHOM IT MAY CONCERN

Due to a lease being broken and as Dashiell Council considers it ideal for the purpose we have leased this farm to the circus.

Cottage still available For Lease. Inquiries . . .

'Hey, you!'

I spin around, torch in one hand, equaliser in the other.

The torch picks out a joker coming our way, squinting into the beam.

I lower the torch and shelve the gat.

'What's your game?'

I make it up as I go along.

'We're renting the house,' I tell him, 'what's yours?'

The joker jerks his head over his shoulder to indicate shapes of tents in the darkness and the crane swinging a steel section into place for the ferris wheel.

'I'm the circus.' He squints harder. 'Look, I'm sorry but I get nervous because we've got a lot of valuable equipment here and our security people have been held up en route.'

The crane swivels in the early-morning darkness behind him.

'There was an accident in the Mountains – some idiot nearly went off a cliff and the cops have closed the road while they investigate. Meanwhile we're supposed to be in the parade so I thought seeing you're here you might keep an eye on things and in return your kid can have a free ticket to the circus and a ride on the ferris wheel.'

I tell him yeah.

Tell people yeah and they get out of your way.

Mr Circus's hoofs gloop in the mud as he moves off and he's got to shout over his shoulder to be heard over the racket of the generator.

'You can pick up your free ticket at the booth, just tell them Pete sent you.'

After a while, the circus people drive off, leaving nothing behind but the Big Top, the sideshows, a few spare vehicles, and the ferris wheel.

The car approaches from the direction of Dashiell, pausing briefly at the gate before coming on again, a white car travelling out of an incipient sunrise along a dusty, weed-strewn track between straggling eucalypts next to the paddock in which stands the carousel, its skeleton sharp-etched against the sky, and its empty seats dangling.

Chapter 52

THE FIGURE IN THE BALACLAVA

The person climbing out of the Commodore's familiar.

I like familiarity.

It breeds contempt.

The kid, Salina, Rory and the dog have got themselves into the shack while I'm out front toting the Husqvarna, which to seamstresses spells sewing machine, but to me means gun.

The figure trudges through the mud towards me.

I store the gun and meet her halfway.

'Why, Mr Brown!' It's Goggle Eyes, the receptionist from the realtor's. 'So you decided to take the place, after all!'

I tell her yeah.

'Oh, goodie!' She claps her hands but after that looks warily about her. 'Look, I'm sorry we haven't cleaned up after the last tenants but they left in something of a hurry and it's so hard to find cleaners when you want them and they were behind in the rent and really we all felt so let down they seemed so nice, all dressed up in their black suits and the rest of it and it was me that did the renting, Mr Jones didn't even see them, and . . .'

From the shack behind me comes the sound of barking.

But I haven't got time for dogs.

'Where's your boss?'

'You mean Mr Jones?' The dame's no longer pretending there's more than one, apart from which she also appears distracted. 'He's – disappeared.' She switches the subject. 'I'm so glad you're taking the place. There was a real nice man with green eyes and a missing leg that was interested but he –'

Behind me the barking has turned to Frenetic.

'I need to find him.'

'The man with green eyes?'

'No, your boss, David Jones.'

'I've told you,' she tells me again, 'I don't know where he is.'

Behind me, the shack has suddenly gone quiet.

The dame glances over my shoulder before looking back at me.

'Is there anything else you need?' She seems in a hurry to get out of there all of a sudden, feet shifting in the mud, goggle eyes shifting in her head. 'I mean, anything apart from Mr Jones, that is?'

I tell her no.

She turns to go.

'You can sign the lease when you're in town,' she calls over her shoulder.

I watch her make her way back to the car.

Even from where I'm standing, I can see the dent in the fender.

She climbs in, starts the engine, lets out the clutch, turns and motors slowly up the driveway, the sight of her progress masked by the trees, stopping at the gate for what seems a long time before starting the engine again and continuing down the road and away.

I turn back to the shack.

It's as silent as the grave.

Houses shouldn't be silent as graves.

Not when they've got a kid and a dog in them.

Despite the cold I suddenly break out in a sweat.

The Husqvarna finds its way back into my fist and I break into a gallop.

My brain's been on vacation.

It's time I called it back to the workplace.

I smash in the fly-screen, enter on the half-roll and note as I climb to my feet why the house has gone silent.

There's no kid in it.

Neither is there a dog.

Rory's not in attendance either.

In fact, the only person still in the joint is Salina and she's trussed up in the same chair I was trussed up in when I donated my thumb to it, but she's gagged with a tea towel and she's struggling.

I untie the gag.

'Where's Imogene?'

'She took her.'

'Who took her?'

'The woman in the balaclava.'

I rip off the ropes.

'What woman in what balaclava?'

But Salina's already out of her chair and running.

There's a back door and she's out of it and she's screaming.

That's when I get out after her and that's when I see what she's screaming about.

There's no sign of Imogene and all that's left of Rory is a crumpled heap and the crutch by the tank.

At least he's moving.

Next to him lies the pooch.

It isn't.

I swing back to Salina.

'Give it to me from the top.'

So she gives it to me from the top and from the top Salina and Rory were inspecting the hut when the dog started barking like mad out the back, after which the dog stopped barking like mad, and Imogene burst in on the run.

'There's a woman here!' she screamed.

But it's all she manages to get out because the next thing they know a dame wearing a balaclava appears behind the kid with a rifle in one hand and Imogene in the other. Imogene stops running and starts crying instead.

The dame's waving the rifle.

Rory's been around enough murders to know when he's in the middle of one so he does what's required without the dame having to say a word, trussing up Salina while holding the dog under one arm and the crutch under the other before obeying the beckoning of the firearm and accompanying the kid and the dame outside.

Rory's coming to.

I turn my attention to him.

'What happened?'

When Rory shakes his head, drops of blood fly out of it.

'The dame told me to jettison the pooch, after which she whacks it with the butt end of the rifle before whacking me over the head, and decamping with the kid.'

'Since when couldn't you handle a dame?'

'She had the drop on me and she was a big dame.'

'Where's Imogene?'

'I told you. The broad took her.'

'Describe the broad.'

'I told you, she was big.'

I give him the cut-glass chandelier look.

'That's all you got for me, she was big?'

'She had this balaclava over her head, for Chrissakes, how can you describe someone you can't even see?'

Rory doesn't know anything else and he still doesn't know anything else as we get ourselves out of the shack, grab one of the circus cars from where it's parked near the Big Top, and head off back up the drive.

Salina's at the wheel.

'Where are we going?'

'To the land floggers. Fast.'

Chapter 53

LAST CALL

There's a sign in the window of Jones, Jones and Jones, and the sign reads VACANT.

I don't believe in signs.

I kick down the door.

The paperweight with the fairies in it is no longer on the counter and the joint smells of dust and criminal intent.

I hit Last Call on the Alexander Graham Bell and after that punch Call Back but the phone rings out into silence and tells me nothing I didn't already know.

I hoof it down the corridor to Jones's room.

That's where I find the paperweight.

Only as well as fairies it's now got blood on it and sprawled beside it is the girl, her goggle eyes shut tight and a patch of blood busy turning black on the back of her head.

I sling her over one shoulder and I'm just lugging her past Reception when the Alexander Graham Bell on the counter rings.

I reach out with the free mitt and pick up the receiver.

I don't speak.

Never answer a phone, let it answer you.

Sometimes it does, sometimes it doesn't, and sometimes it tries to sell you a holiday in Majorca.

This one does.

'Is that you, Mr Scutt?'

Only one person calls me that.

I give a grunt in the affirmative.

'I'm sorry but I missed your call. I'm ringing about our appointment.'

There was no appointment but I give another grunt in the affirmative.

'Remember we were to meet at twelve?'

I grunt again.

'Instead of twelve, can we make it one?'

I wasn't supposed to meet anyone at twelve.

I shift Goggle Eyes across to the other shoulder.

'Is Imogene with you?'

'Yes.'

'Remind me where we're supposed to be meeting.'

'The usual place.'

The phone goes dead.

I look at my chronometer.

It's going on for eleven-fifteen.

The usual place, Sally Kane tells me.

At one, she tells me.

Not twelve, but one.

I got to rely on nothing happening to Imogene in the meantime.

I carry Goggle Eyes out to the car.

'Is this another one of your little popsies?' asks Salina.

I ignore the commentary and park the dame in back of the wheels with Rory.

I've got to save Imogene.

But first I've got to see those papers, the ones Rory's got in his dilly bag.

'Hand me the papers.'

'What papers?'

'The papers I told you to get, the ones your pal Tex lifted, the court papers from the US, the ones in the dilly bag, the bag I told you to keep your eye on.'

'It's in the Caddie.'

And the Caddie could be anywhere.

I check my timepiece.

Five minutes have passed.

'We're nowhere without those papers.' I think for a moment. 'Give me the numberplate of the Caddie.'

Rory gives me the numberplate of the Caddie.

'Now a driver's licence number.'

Rory gives me a driver's licence number.

I get myself back into the realtor's.

The joint still smells of dust and criminal intent, the PC's still on screensaver, the nasturtiums could still do with a makeover, and the phone connects me to the cops.

'I'm the owner of a Caddie,' I tell them, 'and I want it back.'

'Name.'

'I just want the Caddie.'

'Name.'

I tell them Rory's name.

'Licence number.'

I tell them the licence number Rory gave me.

'Registration number of vehicle.'

Three minutes.

I tell them the registration number of vehicle.

The three minutes turns into seven.

Then, 'I'm sorry but that vehicle is the subject of a police investigation.'

'What investigation?'

'It was involved in an incident.'

'Where is it now?'

'That's not for me to say. First, you got to present yourself at Dashiell police station.' Suspicion enters the voice; suspicion always enters the voice. 'Were you the driver at the time of the incident?'

'The car was stolen.'

'Are you saying it was stolen at the time of the incident?'

'That's exactly what I'm saying. Look, I just need something out of it, and it's urgent.'

'Then all you got to do is present yourself at the station.'

I haven't got time to present myself at the station.

Present myself at the station and I can kiss the rest of the day goodbye.

I haven't got time to kiss the rest of the day goodbye.

Because it would also mean kissing goodbye to Imogene.

Madame Kane's got my kid, she's telling me to come and get her, I've only got until one in the post-meridian to do it, the answer to how I'm going to do it is in Rory's dilly bag, Rory's dilly bag's in the Caddie, and the Caddie's –

The cop shop's on the other side of Dashiell. They're clearing Main Street for the parade and accordingly we pass a lot of vehicles clogging up side roads and congregating in paddocks and cops manning the barricades and a long while after that we find ourselves at the cop shop.

From where I'm sitting I can see a building with a big blue-and-white sign on it saying POLICE. Poking out from behind it is a tall, pink tail-fin that could only belong to the Caddie.

Five more minutes have passed.

To go through the hoops will take more time than I got.

I tell Rory to create a diversion.

Goggle Eyes is still off in 3D land.

Rory tears himself away, slams open the door and crutches his way quickly to the cop shop.

Thirty seconds later I'm sidling around the backside of the Caddie.

I get down on my hands and knees and reach up to the door handle. It's locked.

The thing about driving with dogs is that people keep windows open just wide enough to let the stale air out, but at the same time keep the dogs in.

Just wide enough for a hand.

I reach up through the opening, unlock the door, open it, and crawl in.

The dilly bag's not immediately apparent.

I hear Rory yelling words to the effect of, Give me back my frickin' car, or else . . .! which should be enough by way of diversion.

I check the floor of the Caddie, but there's only footprints and breadcrumbs, and then up the back, where there's nothing but more breadcrumbs, a lot of mould and a noddy dog.

I reach in where the well-padded back seat fits under the well-padded backrest.

I find a sixpence dated 1927.

There's also a receipt from the Hillbilly Church, thanking Rory for the cash donation.

There's also something else.

The dilly bag.

I grab it, get myself out of the Caddie, ease the door shut, and head back to the wheels.

Chapter 54

THE STOLEN PAPERS

Salina's got the motor running.

Rory appears in the doorway of the cop shop and starts crutch-hopping across the concrete towards us, a covey of cops hard on his heel.

Rory can move when he wants to and right now it looks like he wants to.

I reach behind, sling open the door and Rory falls in on top of Goggle Eyes.

'Let's go!'

'Where to?'

The cops are nearly on us.

I glance at the clock on the dashboard.

Twenty-three minutes to twelve.

'Back to where we came from!' I tell Salina. 'The other side of Dashiell! Go!'

Salina goes.

I flick through the papers.

The name of the court's been blacked out and so have most of the names, but behind all the legal malarkey and the dead hand of judicial censorship, the facts are still there.

And the facts are that ten years ago, in a well-to-do suburb of Chicago in the US of A, one Josef Grimaldi was hacked to death at his place of residence in an attack of unprecedented savagery.

While Salina hammers the vehicle in the direction of Dashiell, I read on.

Grimaldi initially worked for the Mob – for Mob read Mafia – but subsequently turned informer.

And a few months into blabbing to the Federal Bureau of Investigation all he knew about the Mob, he suddenly finds himself dead.

But Grimaldi's fifteen-year-old son – hereinafter referred to as XB1 – happened to be at home at the time of the crime, running downstairs when he heard his father's screams over the noise of the radiogram, to discover his papa all chopped up in little pieces on the floor in the company of two men he happened to recognise, the taller of whom was waving a meat cleaver.

But – and this had to be one plucky little potato – while the hoods were standing around admiring their handiwork, the kid snatches away the cleaver and gets in a couple of good swings, forcing the perpetrators to flee, one of them minus his hands. The kid's left grieving over the remains of his father, which is the position in which a neighbour, alerted by all the excitement, found him.

The handless hood was arrested when he presented himself to be doctored at a nearby infirmary.

It wasn't hard locating his fellow assassin.

The kid did the ID on them and the two hoods were charged with Grimaldi's murder.

The legal procedure took a few years but the kid's evidence finally nailed the perpetrators.

The kid was subsequently placed under a witness-protection program to ensure that his fate didn't follow that of his father.

There's a hand-written addendum and like all good addenda it's brief.

Witness XB1, who has been equipped with a new identity and relocated and is understood to have started a new life, was subsequently awarded twelve million dollars in damages, to be paid by the Federal Bureau of Investigation as compensation for the death of his father. Grimaldi Senior was considered in the employ of the FBI at the time of his demise, and the Bureau failed in its duty to afford him adequate protection.

I look at the date of the addendum.

It's a week prior to the time Sally Kane contacted me.

About the time Sally Kane noticed David Jones to be acting even stranger than usual.

It's like tumblers falling into place when you're cracking a safe.

David Jones isn't minding a protected witness called Grimaldi.

David Jones *is* the protected witness called Grimaldi.

Josef Grimaldi Junior was hustled onto a plane to Australia disguised as a woman – namely Sarah J. Churchill – in the company of FBI agent Josephine Turner, who on arrival handed him into the care of special agent Edith Burton.

Josephine Turner then moved to a safe place – namely 221B Baker Street – from where she undertook other duties for the FBI.

Meanwhile, Josef Grimaldi Junior took lessons in voice to disguise his American accent, got plastic surgery which produced the regular features Sally Kane told me about, and then set up in Dashiell as a realtor, a business requiring the minimum of qualifications, and therefore ideally suited to a joker in hiding.

And met and married Sally Kane.

And they were all set to live happily ever after, except that four things occurred.

The surgeon that had done the work on Josef Grimaldi Junior moved to Dashiell, met Sally Kane, informed her that David Jones wasn't who she thought he was, and became the disillusioned Sally Kane's lover;

Josef Grimaldi Jr was awarded a lot of money;

The two hoods escaped and tracked Grimaldi to Australia, vowing vengeance; and

They found a private detective on the same trail they were and decided to follow him.

Which explains everything except all the deaths.

As I consider these facts, a sheet of octavo falls out of the sheaf of papers and finds its way into my mitt.

Chapter 55

THE TRUTH WILL OUT

We're nearing town, the traffic's getting heavy and we've slowed to a crawl.

It's nineteen minutes before noon.

I stare at the new bit of paper in my fist, where I make out the words DISALLOWED, INADMISSIBLE AS EVIDENCE and NOT TO BE USED IN COURT and underneath, translated by me into English:

1. The father maltreated both the child and the child's mother;

2. The mother is believed to have died as a result of such maltreatment;

3. Confused and disorientated, the child was mercilessly bullied at school;

4. The kid formed an intense hatred for his father;

5. Consequently that kid can't be trusted as far as you could kick him.

It's signed by a shrink and the observation could be about me, only it's not about me, it's about some other weirdo, and suddenly all the unexplained deaths can be explained. What can also be explained is why the hoods are after David Jones – make that Josef Grimaldi Junior – with a vengeance.

Grimaldi Junior killed his own father.

He timed the killing for when the hoods were due to turn up for their usual shakedown.

Then he framed the hoods for the job, lopping the mitts off one of them in the process.

Meaning Imogene's now on death row.

I turn my attention to the back.

Rory's telling Goggle Eyes how he got the holes in his neck in a sword fight.

'Shut up, Roarer.' I turn my attention to Goggle Eyes. 'Now tell me what happened.' I check the clock: seventeen minutes before midday. 'And keep it brief, there isn't much time.'

Goggle Eyes tears her eyes away from Rory.

186

'First thing this morning I was at my desk when Mr Jones came rushing past me then came out to Reception carrying something in a case that only later I realised contained a rifle.'

'Was there anything odd about his appearance?'

'He was dressed as a woman.'

'Well, of course I looked surprised but he told me that some jobs were best done dressed as a woman and he was my boss so I had to believe him. He ordered me to drive to the farm where he got out at the gate, telling me to go on ahead and keep you occupied while he tidied up.

'I did as I was told; I didn't want to appear incompetent or stupid. I didn't realise what he meant by tidy up until he met me at the gate afterwards.' The girl shudders. 'He was dragging a very frightened little girl by the hand and telling me to drive back to the office or he would "zap the kid".

'Those were his exact words, zap the kid. So again I did as I was told, this time because of what might happen to the little girl if I didn't.

'And when we got to the office, he whanged me over the head with the paperweight, and that's all I remember until –'

'Did he say where he was going?'

She shakes her head, and it's then that I hear the sirens.

There are a lot of them and they're heading our way.

I check the rear-vision.

The cops are in it.

But there's also something else.

The black car.

The hoods have picked us up on their radar.

They want Grimaldi as bad as I do.

But they've only lost a couple of hands.

I stand to lose Imogene.

Chapter 56

APPOINTMENT AT NOON

I check the clock on the dashboard.

It's going on for a quarter to twelve.

One o'clock, Sally Kane told me.

That's when I get an attack of the chills.

Because Sally Kane told me words to the effect of not twelve but one, and she told me it not once but twice.

But who said anything about twelve?

Only Sally Kane.

And the reason she said anything about anything was because someone was standing beside her, making her say it.

Adding the bit about twelve must have been her idea, which was why the call was suddenly terminated.

I haul out the papers again.

Page thirteen gives the details of the death of Josef Grimaldi Senior, including the hour of demise.

The hour of Josef Grimaldi Senior's demise was noon.

I do the recap.

Twelve noon was the time Harriet Stowe was dispatched, Agent Churchill met her end at noon, it was also the hour when the Dwarf appeared to have copped it, and little Miss Twisty ditto, as well as the time an unknown car collided with Edith Burton's at the abattoir.

They were all people who, one way or another, could have fingered David Jones as being Josef Grimaldi.

Like Sally Kane said, paranoid as a term is not all that scientific.

But it will have to do until something better comes along.

Like –

Cycle path, I thought Edith Burton said.

Try *psychopath*.

Patterns make sense of motel wallpaper, they tell you when to put money on a greyhound, and they help solve serial murders.

It's like I'm reciting my tables for Aunt Rube all over again.

Once twelve is twelve, two twelves are twenty-four, three twelves are thirty-six, four twelves are forty-eight, and five twelves are sixty.

But six twelves is mass murder.

Someone was standing beside Sally Kane at the time of that phone call, that someone could only have been David Jones, and the message he told her to pass on was to meet her at one.

But . . .

Sally Kane's one very smart dame.

Shortly after her marriage to the man of her dreams she realised he could be a nightmare.

She diagnosed him as having something seriously the matter with him.

That's why she set herself to leave him for somebody else.

That's also why she hired me, to see if I could discover the excuse she needed to rid herself of him, and also why she had her boyfriend riding shotgun, to protect her in case David Jones found out.

Sally Kane had done the diagnosis, and decided there was evidence of serious illness.

The only trouble was she diagnosed the disease as benign.

It was only later that she realised it could be malignant, and that's when she started getting her changes of heart.

But she also discovered there was a time frame.

A killing hour.

And that killing hour is noon.

Which is why she told me words to the effect of, Instead of twelve we'll have to make it one.

A band's playing, the ta-ra-ra of trumpets, the smack of drums and the evil hullabaloo of bagpipes mingling with the whoop-whoop-whoop of police-issue helicopters surveilling the parade from above.

Salina pulls up in a mess of brakes.

'The parade!' she screams. 'The parade's in the way! We can't move!'

In front of us a bunch of dancing girls is strutting their stuff, in front of them again is a brass band, marking time because the float that should be in front of the band – the one with the hospital team demonstrating for better facilities for the hospital – has got all snarled up in the process of getting out of a paddock, not going anywhere and blocking the parade's progress in the process, while we've got the cops closing in on us from behind.

'Get out,' I yell, 'we got a float to catch!'

The hospital truck's being driven by a clown, which is how he's managed to catch a corner of the truck's tray on the gate post.

I rip open the hatch.

'Get out!' I tell the clown.

I pull the clown's nearside arm and it comes off in my hands.

The sirens are all around us.

I chuck the arm back in the truck, shovel what's left of the clown onto the turf, and order Rory behind the wheel in his place.

'Move it! Move it!'

Rory moves it.

The truck's an old Leyland Hippo and normally it would be carting bulldozers but right now it's carrying an operating table. There's a bunch of doctors around the operating table, except they're not operating – they're staring wild-eyed at this bunch of desperadoes that's taking them to Hell, which wasn't their original destination, all they wanted was more money for the hospital.

The black cabriolet's almost upon us, behind them are the cops, and above them again is the chopper.

Chapter 57

AT THE TRYSTING PLACE

The black cabriolet's managed to get through, mainly because the hoods aren't all that interested in life, especially when it's other people's.

It's a rough ride for the jokers on the back while up front Goggle Eyes is nursing the spare arm in one hand and Rory in the other, Salina's tangled up in the gear sticks, and Rory's one foot's working overtime on the brake, the clutch, the accelerator and anything else he can put his foot on, as the road segues into dirt and I tell him can't he get the heap to go any faster.

'But we're here.'

We're at the gate to the circus.

The tents are up, hoop-las and sideshows have appeared in the paddock, and a kid's screaming happily on the ferris wheel, turning hugely and lazily against the sky, like it's detached itself from the Earth and is busy creating its own universe.

'What did you say?'

'I said, we're here.'

'Not here!' I have to shout to be heard over the generator, plus the truck's engine, the jokers yelling on the back of the truck, the distant-but-rapidly-approaching racket of the police-sirens and the kid screaming on the ferris-wheel. 'The next place, you idiot!'

The one around the corner, below the hill where Sally Kane and I used to meet, outside which her flaxen-haired lover pretended to be tending his flock when all the time he was watching Sally Kane. The other cottage, the lovers' trysting place where Sally Kane and her lover met when Sally Kane was pretending to be at all those meetings, the joint where Josef Grimaldi's holding Sally Kane and Imogene hostage, because that way he knows he can get me, at which time he can take us all out together.

The clock on the dashboard says twelve minutes to midday as Rory screeches to a halt next to the white car with the banged-up mudguard outside the house with the madman in it, bringing more shrieks from the passengers up the back as our sudden inertia causes them to pile into the back of the cabin.

I tell Rory to stay where he is and the other three ditto, climb down, haul out the gat, and start in on the approach.

Psychopaths like patterns.

Josef Grimaldi likes twelve.

But I like my patterns, too.

And my pattern is to arrive early, and enter by the front door.

Accordingly, I arrive early and enter by the front door.

Josef Grimaldi, also known as David Jones, is alone.

He's sitting on a bed, he's wearing black tights and a green dress. On the bed next to him is a balaclava and a Browning rifle, there's a clock on the wall behind him and something red on the floor near the door. He's got a Luger in his fist and it's pointed directly at my head.

He's smiling as he speaks.

'Drop the gun or you're dead.'

I drop the gun.

He checks his watch.

'You're a tad more than an hour early.' His accent has reverted to its native Chicagoan. 'I only just got back from my little excursion.'

'I'm still on daylight saving,' I say. 'Where's my kid, Grimaldi?'

The request doesn't register.

'They used to meet here,' he murmurs. 'They were supposed to be making money for the hospital but instead they were making – whatever it was the two of them were making.'

The clock on the wall behind him says ten minutes to midday.

'Tell me about the murders, Grimaldi.'

He considers the request, then comes to a decision.

'You'll be dead yourself soon so what does it matter?'

So he tells me.

They always tell you.

It's half the fun in being psychotic, the look on the victim's face while the killer justifies the unjustifiable, just before he kills you.

Nine minutes to go.

David Jones is no longer the easy-going realtor.

Instead he's a soft-spoken lunatic called Josef Grimaldi, with something to sell besides real estate.

His own madness.

Chapter 58

THE SELF-PITYING PSYCHOPATH

'First, I killed my father.' His voice is low, calm and reasonable; he might be talking about the weather. 'He drove my mother to suicide and bullied me. He ran a numbers racket under the protection of the Mob and the standover men were due to arrive to extract their regular payment from him.

I chose that moment to kill him, despatching him with the meat cleaver and chopping him up into lots of little pieces.

Then I waited.

He smiles.

'The standover men arrived right on time. I was in pretty good shape because of all the workouts I'd done to deal with the bullies at school, so I knew I could handle them, plus I had the meat cleaver and the advantage of surprise.

I managed to hack off the bigger one's hands before they fled.'

Eight minutes.

'Go on.'

So he goes on.

After he kills his dad, frames the hoods and obtains protection, he dresses up as a dame and calling himself Sarah J. Churchill (both Rory's and the Dwarf's description for Sarah J. Churchill was big or tall – but a medium-sized man would seem tall for a dame). He then emigrates to the Land of Oz, shacking up with his Minder, Edith Burton, while he gets his face and voice reshaped before moving to Dashiell.

Seven minutes.

'What about your other victims?'

This is his big chance, so he takes it.

'The voice coach was always going to be a problem, so I took her out early. And I would have got away with it, too, except that you started nosing around.'

The fault's always somebody else's.

'And the others?'

The expression on the killer's face remains bland.

'You could say it got to be habitual. I scored the compensation but that only brought the hoods after me, and I knew it was only a matter of time before they found me so I started covering my tracks by – well, attending to detail.'

He smiles shyly, like a kid that's scored high marks after being labelled incurably stupid.

'It also gave me – this might sound strange to you – a good excuse to go on a killing spree. I realised after I killed daddy that I – well, that I rather liked killing. Next came the old girl, the voice coach's live-in. She was on the phone to you when I killed her – after a prolonged bit of fun and games torturing her – and I would have got the dog, too, only it recognised me from the previous time and hid.'

He shrugs, it was all too easy.

'I hired the axe man to keep you away from the proposed scene of my next crime – I thought that was a neat touch – while I took out Peg Leg and your kid. Except that you twigged to it and showed up too soon.

'Through Edith Burton I located and killed Special Agent Turner and dumped her on your retired public servant friend as a warning, but somehow you got onto that, too.

'So when that failed, I just walked in with my trusty rifle and shot him while he was standing by the window.'

He steadies the Luger.

'Then I forced Edith Burton's car off the road into the abattoir – don't you just love abattoirs? – but thanks to my son-of-a-bitch wife and her skill with a scalpel, Burton stayed alive and I had to finish her off as she lay blabbing her heart out to you in the hospital, just missing you in the process.'

The cops must be getting close.

'That's when I came across you in the hospital grounds,' I tell him, 'pretending to be coming from the direction of the carpark. You must have moved fast.'

He shrugs.

'I kept in training.' I remember the exercise bike at Daisy Drive. 'It had become a habit. When people want to do you harm you've got to stay fit to survive.'

He crosses one leg over the other, neatly, still holding the Luger on me, also neatly.

'But you were always one step ahead of me, Mr Private Eye. You even robbed me of the pleasure of killing Lover Boy. But I can still look forward to killing all you lot, including the hoodlums, who I believe should be here any minute, plus, of course, your peg-legged mate, who unfortunately I couldn't shoot at the farm because people would have heard the shot.

'But I finally managed to kill that goddamn dog, the one that sprang me when I was attending to the Cadillac, the dog that barked whenever I was around.'

The madman's voice stays soft but his features have turned hard.

The gun stays aimed at my sternum.

Five minutes to go.

'Everything would have been all right,' he murmurs, 'if only you hadn't shown up.'

He's overlooked all the murders.

'Sally and I could have been together forever.'

Four minutes.

Tears spring to his eyes and his knuckles whiten on the Luger.

'All those people would still be alive and I would still be with Sally.'

Psychopaths like their delusions.

It's what makes them psychopaths.

'What about your father? Wouldn't he still be dead? And wouldn't you still have killed him?'

Grimaldi's got centre stage and he's making the most of it so he's crying a little.

He doesn't wipe his eyes.

He wants me to see the tears before he kills me.

But I've still got two questions before the big one.

'What was it with Beethoven? And why the obsession with twelve?'

I know the answer but I need to keep him talking.

I can hear the sound of approaching sirens.

'My father had *Song of Joy* playing on the CD player when I killed him. I turned it up full volume to hide his screams and forever afterwards that goddamn song has haunted me.' He shrugs. 'As for twelve-o'clock, that was the time I killed my daddy and it became a habit. While the song was an omen, the time was a talisman.'

The sirens can no longer be ignored, and neither can the time.

Three minutes.

'Where are they?'

That's when he smiles.

Psychopaths like justice.

Particularly when it's poetic.

'She had it coming.'

'That accounts for Sally Kane,' I say, 'but what about the kid?'

A set of non-pneumatic tyres screech to a halt outside but the sicko's so carried away with himself that he seems unaware of it.

He shrugs.

'It's enough that she's your kid.'

Suddenly there's the sound of running footsteps outside. Grimaldi straightens the arm with the Luger in it. He's sighting me along the barrel so that all I can see is the little black hole that the bullet's supposed to come out of. His finger is whitening on the trigger as he's squeezing it, but the gat doesn't work because I took away the bullets during my little visit to 48 Daisy Drive. There's just this ragged click as I look away. That's when I notice the little red thing on the floor and that's when I realise it's the nose I gave Sally Kane all those aeons ago. The nose is telling me something that Sally Kane wants me to know, and that is their whereabouts – hers and Imogene's. I hear the echoes of the kid screaming on the ferris wheel and I realise those screams weren't ones of happiness but of dreadful fear. It wasn't just some kid, it was my kid, and she's heading the same way my sister Sophie went. I turn and beat it out through the door, nearly knocking into the two hoods, hobbled by the injuries I gave them at the farm but still able to move fast enough, especially when their quarry's sitting on the bed behind me. The handless one is screaming, 'Get out of my way, he's ours!' and the two of them are waving machine guns. In through the door burst the rozzers and they don't see me because the action by the bed is filling all of their sightlines. I'm already out the door and heading for the truck that Rory has about turned, leaping aboard as it takes off. The jokers on the back are starting to scream again and Salina and Goggle Eyes aren't all that calm either. Rory's yelling 'Where to?' to which I reply, 'The circus, you clown, the circus!'

Chapter 59

THE WHEEL OF DEATH

The flames have already taken hold as we round the corner, the core of the conflagration a screaming meteorite as death's wheel turns steadily on its axis. The bile rises to my throat and I'm a five-year-old boy again and my mother and sister are tied to the windmill. Only this time it isn't a windmill but a ferris wheel and it's no longer my mother and sister but Sally Kane and my only daughter, Imogene. It's no longer a hippy farm in Nimbin in the nineteen-sixties but a wombat farm in Dashiell in the first stages of the 21st century. I'm no longer a boy and yet somehow I still am, with it all happening all over again, and I feel myself cringe until something clicks inside me like the Luger that Grimaldi was wielding. Well before the truck lurches to a halt I'm out and my fedora goes flying and I jettison the gun and the coat comes off plus the shoes. It's like all the props and bells and whistles I've been relying on all these years have come off and I'm pounding past the joker at the controls of the ferris wheel wringing his hands and screaming, 'I can't stop the machine! Someone's done something to the machine!' I remember Sally Kane telling me her husband was some kind of mechanical genius. I realise that just like he fixed the Caddie he also attended to the machine after he'd tied Sally Kane and Imogene to it. He poured fuel into the bucket under them and set the fuse burning and the wheel turning with the STOP button neutralised so that nothing short of a gun blast could stop it. He then drove back to wait for me. The empty bucket in front of the one with Sally Kane and Imogene in it is rattling past, so I leap for it, my fingers grappling for a handhold as it spins me high in the air. When I look down I can see the bucket's already well alight and Imogene and Sally Kane are rearing back from the flames while Imogene's frightened, wide-open eyes are staring up at me. It's my sister's white scared face all over again and my sister's screams all over again, engulfed by flames all over again. But this time I grapple for the knots, and missing thumb or not I manage to get them untied. I feel Imogene's small body hot against mine and I'm gripping onto Sally Kane while Imogene's clutching onto me and the ground's rushing towards us as the bucket descends and I can hear someone yelling, 'Jump! Jump! Jump!' But I can't jump because the wheel's turning too fast. I make out a figure and it's Rory and he's swinging up his crutch to aim it at the engine and even above the roar of the flames I hear the detonation and at the same time feel the wheel lurch to a stop. The burning bucket sways close to the ground and it's only after I hit the dirt, my body hunched around Imogene to protect her, that I realise the person doing the screaming is me. Hands reach out and break my stranglehold on Sally Kane and get the kid's hands untangled from mine. As I fade in and out of consciousness I note that the people attending to Imogene are the hospital team from the float. I make sure the kid's okay and after that I limp around among the wombat droppings looking for Sally Kane, only I can't find her . . .

Chapter 60

THE RETURN OF THE RED DWARF

The circus is a circus.

Whatever the do-gooders do, circuses are still circuses.

There might be no lions or tigers or elephants but there are still clowns and there's also still plenty of greasepaint, high wire and excitement.

Imogene was wary when I said I'd take her.

'You told me that before.'

'This time I mean it.'

'Didn't you mean it before?'

I lapse into silence.

Sometimes silence is the best thing to lapse into.

They kept us for observation, like they do, and then they let us go, like they also do. Imogene was just a bit shaken up and Sally Kane proved to be as tough as old rope. Salina was only suffering shock, but she's used to shock, and the hospital needed the beds, anyway. Sally Kane's paid what she owed and I've given most of it to Salina on condition that she let me keep Imogene another day. We've given the dead pooch a state funeral in a wombat hole, complete with a cross made out of the chair Salina was tied to. I can see the lights of the Big Top and hear the mutter of the generator and the shouts and screams of the kids having fun at the circus, only this time . . .

It's all over, I tell myself. Get a grip on yourself, Rainbow. So I do, at the same time as I take a grip on the crutch the hospital gave me, plus a grip on Imogene's paw, hard.

I focus on the signs.

They were flapping all over Main Street and dangling from gum trees, and hanging over the gate to the farm is the biggest sign of all, with trapeze artists smiling down from it and a ringmaster holding a whip, and in red and splashed across the sign like a spurt of blood, almost as an afterthought:

. . . and featuring, The Red Dwarf.

I feel Imogene's hand shake as we pass the ferris wheel, so I hold her mitt even harder, and also buy her a Triple-Blister Ice-Cream for distraction purposes.

Rory advised that he and Goggle Eyes would let us do the father-daughter thing but they would pick us up after, to drive us back to Sydney. But the ferris wheel's out of action due to the fire as well as Rory shooting up the engine and the fun in the Big Top hasn't started yet, so me and the kid are cruising down sideshow alley when we come to the rifle range.

'Can I have a turn, Daddy?'

The rifle's firing high but after I tuck the crutch under one arm and make the necessary adjustments and teach Imogene how to hold her breath and also how to keep the rifle as still as a rock and her eye on the target the way Rube taught me, she starts hitting most of what she needs to hit and also amassing a handy collection of kewpie dolls. I look over to see the flap of the Big Top closing.

'We better go in,' I say.

'Do we have to, Daddy?'

I think about that for a while and after thinking about it I tell her, No, we don't have to, because life's more than bread and circuses, life's doing what you feel you need to do at any given time and doing it often and doing the best you can under the circumstances. So Imogene goes on squeezing off the slugs and also goes on getting better and better at putting the slugs through the targets. Afterwards we tuck into a couple of big, sticky messes of red, yellow and blue fairy floss while the punters inside the Big Top are laughing and groaning and sighing like it's life on fast forward after a time warp.

'I like shooting guns,' Imogene informs me. 'Do you shoot guns a lot where you work, Daddy?'

I tell her, Yeah, I shoot guns a lot where I work.

'When I grow up,' she says, and here it comes, 'can I do what you do, Daddy?'

'It takes a lot of practice.'

'Does practice mean I get to shoot guns a lot?'

I tell her, Yeah, plus throwing people around and ducking and weaving and fighting bad people and rescuing damsels in distress, kind of thing, to which she replies,

'And rescuing boys, too?'

To which I tell her, Yeah, boys can be in distress, too. She seems to like the idea of saving boys in distress. By this time we're sitting on the plough that I'd tied the hoods to and we're watching the punters straggle out of the Big Top and Imogene's onto her fourth ice-cream when I feel the little body beside me go tense.

'Look at the little man!'

I look up to see a small joker coming out of the Big Top wearing a sugar-coated smile, clothes six times too big for his body, and hair you could cook a casserole on.

'It's just another midget.'

But I know it's not just another midget. It's a person that was too small to see out of his office window when Grimaldi took a pot at him, so that the bullets went over his head and the fall to the floor was a clown's ruse, making the porn merchant's report of the Dwarf's demise what might be called premature.

The Caddie's making its way past the blackened remains of the ferris wheel.

'Time to go, Sophie,' I tell Imogene.

Big pause.

Then, 'You were just joking when you called me Sophie then, weren't you, Daddy?'

I tell her, Yeah, I was just joking when I called her Sophie, but that doesn't mean she's not still gripping my hand hard as we climb aboard the Caddie.

Post-Mortem

A NIGHT AT THE SPEAKEASY

The speakeasy's doing it slow.

Hank's polishing the usual glass and gazing at the world through innocent eyes and a couple of stool pigeons are over by the Radiola offloading their hallucinations to a cop. A broad in an orange frock is wearing the dazed bright eyes of someone who's just shot up – and I don't mean lengthwise – and the pianola looks lonely. I carry my glass of aqua furiosa over to it, park the crutch, shift the controls to manual, spin the chair, lift the lid, and start hammering away at *Starlight*.

I forget the thumb and par consequence one or three notes find themselves in the Missing Persons Bureau, but you can adapt to anything in this world and so it is with *Starlight*.

Over by the bar I hear the Telefunken ring and Hank answer it.

I don't know what I expected when I took on the Sally Kane caper but it was never going to be a holiday in Bermuda.

Salina's taken a renewed interest in Imogene and Rory's busy converting Goggle Eyes – she's got a moniker, Janet – to his particular brand of religion while he's studying to become a minister. The hoods are back in jail where they belong and there was enough left of Grimaldi after the hoods had finished with him to join up the dots, crayon in the pretty picture and pack the remains back to the US of A to face the doh-se-doh.

Sally Kane's swapped Dashiell for Sydney, where she's doing a postgraduate course in psychopathology.

She's already done the practical.

'Play it again, Sam.'

Hank's so close I can identify his deodorant.

'The name's not Sam and it doesn't read that way in the movie.'

I sense him shrug.

'Have it your way, Rainbow. After all, you're the guy tickling the ivories.'

Hank's in one of his moods.

I'm playing it again when he interrupts again.

'By the way, I got a message from Rube.'

'So tell me the message.'

'She says quote unquote she's worked out what RED means.'

That makes one of us.

'And?'

'She says you got it wrong. The first letter isn't an R but a Q and the word's not a word but a bunch of initials.'

I put the music on Hold while Hank consults what he's written.

'That makes the initials – QED. Rube said you'd know what they mean.'

I know what they mean. They're the letters at the end of every chapter in the book Rube used to teach me geometry out of and as every kid that ever studied geometry knows, the letters stand for *Quod Erat Demonstrandum*, which is Latin for 'Therefore it's proven'.

The blonde guessed the truth and as the proof came up the hallway to kill her she had one thought in her head and that wasn't to identify the killer but to brag about how clever she was to her colleagues.

But I don't tell Hank that. Tell Hank that and I got more explaining to do than I need right at the moment.

So I turn my attention back to the music and after a while I hear Hank pad back to the bar.

That doesn't mean I'm alone.

Someone's standing behind me.

But I've had enough excitement for a couple of millennia so I give the joker the benefit of the doubtless and switch to Beethoven's *Ninth*. When I get to the bit with all the singing in it, the joker behind me starts in with the chorus.

The voice is familiar and by that I don't mean it's Enrico Caruso or Benjamino Gigli or Joan Sutherland or even Carlo Begonzi.

I drop the lid, spin the stool, raise my peepers, and find myself face to face with Pandora.

C.S. Boag

MISTER RAINBOW

in the Case of the Death of a Ladies' Man

For Sophie, Gemma, Max, Zola, Escher,
Matilda, Wolfe and Carter

*If you don't mind your own business in this world,
someone will come along and mind it for you.*

Chapter 1

STIFF LUCK

It's the winter of our discontent. There's no ice on the streets of Sydney town but there's plenty in the veins of the hitmen. And there's ice of a different kind in the track-riddled arteries of the junkie hanging around the fresh-minted corpse in the gutter.

The corpse is neatly parked, all lined up with the kerb nice and tight. It's a well-constructed cadaver, the sort you'd enter in a Mr Corpse competition, if they had such a thing, and it was yours to enter. The thing is, this particular corpse doesn't possess a head. Feet, legs, torso, arms, hands, neck – but no head.

An hour or so earlier, while I was busy bailing out my boat, the *Wooden No*, a dame called Annabel Franklin phoned on one of my deadmen's mobiles. She was worried for the safety of her lover because a person or persons unknown were out to kill him. Annabel saved my life once when Pandora tried to fold me on the cusp of the caper I filed away in the locker labelled 'SUN' – that's Solved Until Further Notice – aka The Case of The Hood with No Hands. Accordingly, I owed her one. So after she called, I climbed down into the scow and rowed myself across the wine-dark sea, took a bus to the city, and hoofed it to the pointy end of town . . .

But I'm too late – somebody's lifetime too late – and the remains of Annabel's lover are enjoying the siesta that never ends in a gutter in a side street in that salubrious part of Sydney town known as Kings Cross.

The body is togged-out nice and neat in jeans and T-shirt, lightly blood-spattered.

I calculate the armament employed to be in the elephant-safari category – with the accent on *gory* – small enough for a well-built joker to tote under a three-quarter coat, but big enough to blow a pachyderm's brains out. It was enough to take away this joker's skull, anyway.

Position of assassin: Directly in front of the victim.

Angle of fire: More or less head-on.

Distance of point of barrel to face: Somewhere around zero-range, or point-blank in the old money.

Executive summary: Someone didn't like him.

So what's new? To have known this joker was not to like him. Thomas L. Tycho was everybody's enemy, a trickster who played one trick too many on one too many people, a dirty dealer who dealt one dirty deal too far, a wide boy wide enough to keep himself alive until the moment he made the mistake of wide boys the world over – not getting a whole lot narrower when the gun went off.

How do I know all this? I'm not a detective for nothing, unless you're talking about what they pay me.

I shoot a Captain Cook along the boulevard and note three more items of interest.

One: It's a fine day.

Two: It's Kings Cross, so punters are passing by on the other side of the street in order to maximise their chances of enjoying the fine day.

And three: Both sides of the boulevard possess blank walls – one of them newly decorated with blood – thereby providing no convenient viewing platform for possible witnesses to a murder.

I've worked this much out before the cops rock up, with just enough time left over to catch up on a little light reading, kindly provided by the corpse in question. The words are in a ring-a-rosy conformation around the headless honcho's neck – right below where the fuse box neatly carved off his entablature – the sort of tattoo someone might wear in place of an inscription on a T-shirt, just to let you know what kind of guy he is, relieving himself of the time-wasting business of small talk.

That's how I know the body belongs to Thomas L. Tycho. I can't see all of the tattoo – Tommy's lying on his back and the punchline's busy talking to the tar macadam – but I know from memory how it goes, and how it goes is as follows:

Populus vult decipi – ut falleret . . .

No trouble with the translation, thanks to my Aunt Rube. She taught me Latin, along with how to shoot a gun, how to move, how to withstand pain, plus a whole lot of other stuff about the private detecting business.

The people wish to be deceived – so deceive them.

I straighten just as the police sirens wind up the decibels, while the pedestrians churn by on the other side of the street like they think they can escape Destiny – all they got to do is look the other way.

'It says –' comes a female voice from behind me.

I swing around. Annabel has appeared out of nowhere wearing an expression of horror on her dial-up and a frock that's hiding about as much as a wet bikini at Bondi.

'I know what it says,' I say. 'What I don't know is why he put it there.'

Annabel shrugs. 'Tommy always liked to make out he was smarter than everybody else. He –'

But if there's any more to an answer that makes as much sense as a law and order editorial in *The Daily Terrorgraph*, I'll have to put it on hold. The rozzers are hurtling around the corner of William and Hackberry, Glocks in their fists, justice in their eyes and the pockets of their blue serge playsuits bulging with unused ammunition.

'We need to find the emergency exit,' I say.

'But what about –?'

'Look, your Tommy might not be going anywhere but that don't mean we have to go there with him. Like the man in the poem says, we got to keep our heads while all about are losing theirs.'

There are three ways of reacting at times like these. You can come out with your hands up and buy yourself a one-way ticket to the goosepot; you can take your chances and go down in a fusillade of arrows; or you can join the pedestrians.

I choose number three – life. I grab Annabel's hand – badly scarred from where she crushed the lightbulb the night she saved me from certain death in the speakeasy – tip my fedora to the corpse, then get us out into the foot traffic heading towards the Coca-Koala sign at the Top-of-the-Cross, and resume the dialogue.

'I'm Smith.'

Cop cars nail the street fore and aft and enough persons in uniform emerge to start another war in Afghanistan.

'Shouldn't we stay and help the police with their enquiries, Mr Smith?'

'Lady, if we hang around any longer, we'll shoot straight to the top of the cops' target list. There's no need for an ID when the corpse already carries a toe tag, even if it *is* situated at the wrong end of its anatomy. Wearing a necktie like the one he's got, your late boyfriend doesn't need collaring. Some deaths go straight to the Unknown Victims department, but this one's what you might call a no-brainer.'

Chapter 2

BECAUSE OF THE STAIRS

The hand in mine goes tense – past and present tense, but a little shaky on the future. I figure I better elaborate. 'Look, *no-brainer*'s just an expression, okay? It doesn't mean – given Tommy's current condition – that I'm making him the butt of a bad gag. So let's just look straight ahead and keep running.'

Annabel does like she's told, and I do what's necessary to keep her mind off a bad situation.

'Why did you call me?'

'Because Tommy said they were out to get him. It was the last thing he told me before leaving the club this morning. I knew something terrible was going to happen and I also remembered the card you gave me after what happened at the speakeasy.'

'Did he say who?'

'Who what?'

'Who was out to get him.'

She shakes her head. 'No, he just said *they*. There were so many people who, you know, *hated* Tommy. It was all building up to a Ganymede.'

'You mean Runnymede.'

Annabel shrugs. 'Whatever. Anyway, the killer could have been anyone.'

A cop appears to starboard. 'Hey, youse!'

I slow the pace. Do more than stroll and the rozzer will laser us. He might also beat us to death and tell the Police Integrity Commission we were running from the scene of a decapitation and he was therefore duty bound to do whatever it took.

'Where do you lay your head?' I ask Annabel.

'What do you mean?'

'Hang out, reside, dwell, lodge, doss down, domicile.'

She tells me an address in Macleay Street.

'Okay, Anagram, you take the high road and I'll take the low, and I'll see you at your place in five.'

That's when we part company. That's also when the rozzer discovers that the plural form of the second-person pronoun isn't working for him any more, because me and Annabel have split into two singulars, so he shelves his Glock and goes back to doing what he's paid to.

The high road takes Annabel up to fairyland while the low road takes me into that part of the world known as Woolloomooloo, which could be a public convenience for livestock but instead is an expensive piece of Sydney real estate. Woolloomooloo lies beneath the shadow of a cliff that's darkened by the deeper shadow of too many unanswered questions. For example: How come the killer blew off Tommy's head so neat it was like a dotted line joined it to the rest of the body? And: How come the death occurred *after* I received notification, and not before, in the manner of most crimes?

I chuck a shooftee around me as I turn up the McElhone Stairs. No one's following, if you don't factor in my imagination. The McElhone Stairs – a hundred or so rough-hewn slices of Sydney mother rock worn lower than a Sister of Mercy's hemline – take me from Woolloomooloo up to Potts Point. I'm a long time reaching the top. And even longer by the time I'm hoofing it across Victoria Street to a brown-brick hostelry with a dinky little alcove nursing a dozen or so green security buttons. I enter via the grille door, and ring Annabel's ding-a-ling – in the only way I'm ever likely to.

There's no answer.

Thanks to the McElhone Stairs, some *fifteen* minutes have elapsed, instead of the agreed-upon five, giving Annabel time to prepare herself for my arrival. So why isn't there some kind of response?

The hostelry is pre-war but it's had a facelift that includes a new blanket of paint, a wheelchair ramp and a sign saying something like 'Hawkers Can Go To Buggery'. After I've considered all of the above, I thump the button with 303 next to it again, before trying 403, which would be the apartment directly above 303.

'Yes?'

It's a dame, only it's not my dame.

I say I'm the postman, with a special delivery.

'So put it in the letterbox.'

'It's too big for the letterbox.'

'Then leave it on the ground.'

'It's not safe on the ground.'

The dame sighs. 'You'd better come up then.'

The elevator is an old Otis, and its mirrored walls tell me I'm much the same as when I last looked – a broad-shouldered, hammer-fisted joker something over the six-foot mark in the old money, clad in green-striped daks, red-houndstooth jacket, and the sort of footwear they used to call 'correspondent's shoes' but which I call whitesides. My peepers are set in a face that looks like it's gone several rounds with a cage full of gorillas and they're staring hard-eyed out at a bleak world from under a yellow chequerboard fedora.

But it's not me I'm interested in, it's Annabel Franklin and when the Otis disgorges me I hightail it along a short hallway decorated with a mangy carpet towards a door that's book-ended with a garbage chute and an escape hatch. The number on the door reads pretty much like I expected it to read: 303.

The hatchway's shut so I give it a Mike Hammer.

The answer's a great deal of silence.

Chapter 3

ROOM 303

I'm all for the quiet life, which is why I've got no means of identification – no private inquiry licence, no driver's papers, no usurer's card, no phone except for the twenty or so dead-men's mobiles Rory palmed me, no email addresses apart from the ones I borrow from the unwary, no tax file number, and no real estate. None that anyone knows about, anyway.

My address might be fixed, but it's fixed only by a frayed, one-inch hempen hawser knotted to an anchor buried in the sands of an out-of-the-way hidey-hole in Sydney Harbour. The other end of the rope's attached to a tub that only just avoids joining the anchor because of a bilge pump and a lot of bailing. The tub's an old clinker-built ferry called the *Wooden No* – at least that's what I tell people who want to know more than can be good for anyone, most of all me.

'What's the name of your boat?' they ask.

I just say *Wooden No.*

Why do I need to stay under the radar? Because people are after me – crims; cops; an ex-wife; the tax man; jokers that for one reason or another either hate me or want money I haven't got; the odd identity thief; and Pandora.

Who's Pandora? Tell me the answer to that and we'll both know. All I can say is she's a killer with just one thought in the brainpan behind that horribly scarred face of hers, and that's to kill me. Pandora's the main reason I choose to go through life incognito. She's also the reason I nearly found myself dead on the cusp of the Handless Hood caper. But that's another story.

In this story I'm standing outside Annabel Franklin's apartment door just like I was told to do when I hear something.

And it's only after I've been listening too long that I realise what that something is. It's nothing.

When a dame's waiting for you, you expect to hear *some sort of noise*, even if it's only a coffee machine gurgling in the scullery, the flush of a water closet, or the barely-discernible purr dames make when they're applying their make-up. But right now the dust mites under my whitesides are making more noise than Annabel, and her silence can only mean one of two things – she's either not home, or she's dead.

The apartment door's a watermelon of a thing made of pastry flakes and bum fluff, with a lock that might have been snipped off the head of a premature neonate with sugar scissors. My hard-heft roll takes me along a hallway into a drawing room that's long since ceased to be used for drawing in and instead is your usual shrine to the computer age. There's a table propping up an AWA television, a TEAC hi-fi, a Compaq laptop saying it's got Windows 7, and the sort of printer you get for next to nothing from your local post office.

Television: Off and cold.

Hi-fi: Ditto.

Printer: Ready and waiting.

The laptop's got a dinky little sign on it saying words to the effect of: WHATEVER WAS ON THIS SCREEN IS CURRENTLY OFF IN LA-LA LAND, PRESS ANY KEY TO CONTINUE.

I do like it says but I don't hang around for the results. Instead, I haul out the Smith & Wesson Compact and check out the rest of the joint, in order to work out the silence.

The kitchen's one of those alcoves that even the most self-deluded of real-estate mohickeys would sticky-tape an *-ette* on the end of. It contains a cupboard that'd explode if you tried to cram anything bigger than a tea cup in it; a dinky single-plate floater-stove; a fridge that would require a cyclist's dose of hormones to qualify as anything more than an ice bucket; and a sink on which someone has left a knife.

The brass plaque on the half-open door next to the kitchen is in the shape of a lady's leg with the words *Salle de Bain* under it. Behind the door is the kind of scent Cleopatra might have worn to hang onto Egypt, a mix of Nile delta and rainforest with intimations of halcyon mist and desert mirages – but none of the odours you might describe as bodily.

Lime-green bathtub: Empty.

Lime-green hand basin: Wiped clean of all evidence of human occupancy.

Lavabo: Seat down and shining, a roll of lavatory wipes neatly hidden in the long blue skirts of a ballet dancer perched atop the cistern.

I hear a sound like a door opening and go into a crouch followed by a half-spin, gat at the more-than-ready. But it's only the laptop, its little bell advising anyone that cares to know it's finally come out of sleepy time and all anyone needs to do is press any key to continue. But there's one more room to check before I do that. In my experience, if you leave one more room to check, it's more than likely to jump out when you least expect it, and check you.

The sign on the door says *Couchez*.

I take it as an invitation, bang open the door and enter.

Pink carpet.

Padded pink chair with purple flowers on it.

Pink dressing table, complete with powder-pink brush-and-comb set.

Pink built-in and pink curtains opening onto a day that's far too nice for anyone to die in.

But tell that to the Fates, because the Fates are telling me – via the cerise-framed mirror in the built-in – that on the pink-quilted bed is the body of a beautiful dame who has died on this most beautiful of days. And I know for a fact when she died, because I was in her company no more than twenty minutes prior.

It wasn't a natural death. I can tell that by the look on Annabel's face, the fact that the clothes that hid little before are hiding even less now, and because the hole in the region of the heart could only have been made by the knife that the murderer left on the sink in the kitchenette.

Annabel saved my life but I've let someone take hers. I gave her one of my dead-men's phone numbers but it was either not enough or too much to stop someone killing her.

I lift the pink-quilted dressing gown from the foot of the bed and pull it over the body, being extra careful with the scars on the hands she got when she saved my life.

Suddenly I can't see too good and the Scene-of-Crime boys can read the cover-up any way they want to.

I get the hell out of the pink room.

Chapter 4

THE DAME PACKS A GAT

The Compaq's waiting so I do like it says and smack the tab marked ENTER and the screen coughs up . . . a list of names – no capitals and no punctuation, just a list of names and most of them badly spelt – like they were written by someone with only a couple of minutes to write them in.

While I'm waiting for the printout I run through the sequence of events that ended in Annabel's demise, like the private eyes used to do in those old James Cagney movies Aunt Rube used to screen on the dining-room wall of my childhood home, with Rube telling me: *Watch this and now this – all right, now tell me what might have happened after he died.*

I see Annabel hurrying away to her destination with death, taking the high road just like I told her to, the one that passes all the strip joints and the places selling genuine Australian mementos manufactured in The People's Refulgence of China, the road that was supposed to not have any shadows in it but did – just the one. And that one shadow followed Annabel from the scene of the crime with its hood up only a few paces behind her – because that's what shadows do. It bypassed the prostitutes with the too-short skirts and the cold sores, and the touts and the beggars and the druggies. It then worked its way along the mean streets after the dame with the ruby-red lips – because that's also what shadows do, particularly ones intent on killing people.

Annabel got herself in through the grille door – fumbling for her key to the security hatch – clicked open the lock and hurried inside, slamming the door fast because she sensed the Fates were fast closing in on her. She pressed the button in the Otis that would take her to the third floor, alone in the lift except for her fears, and the multiple images of the ashen-faced woman in the skimpy attire reflected back by all the mirrors around her.

The printer's making a noise like it's being strangled so I whack a few more buttons and it finally starts to produce the goods. At the same time the intercom crackles into life, followed by someone saying *Police here!* in the sort of voice that suggests they're not going to be there much longer.

I get myself fast into the kitchenette, lean down and smell the knife handle. All it tells me is the hand that wielded the weapon that killed Annabel Franklin was wearing a Mediflex surgical glove. I grab the printout, rip out the electric Fords and head for the hatchway, shoving the papyrus into my pocket, tucking the laptop under my armpit as I go. I'm too late to escape in the traditional manner, because as I get to the landing the lift-gates are already whanging shut like the steel-barred doors of a maximum-security prison and the grinding of the elevator gears are the machinations of the law.

A glance around the corridor reveals a little glass eye staring at me from the apartment at the other end, an arrow telling me the Otis is heading my way, a door with a green man on it indicating the exit, and the garbage chute. I chuck the glorified typewriter down the slippery slide, settle the fedora, and as the elevator shudders to a stop, step into the fire escape.

There are two types of fire escape – ones that are there for escaping fires by and ones that are there to die in. This one's the second type, with pot plants against the cracked-concrete walls, black bags of rubbish on the horizontals and mouldy food busy feeding an army of cockroaches. You'd be better off taking your chances with the fire.

A wardrobe blocks the downward passageway, but that's not the one I'm taking as I hurdle a pile of bins, my whitesides clickety-clacking on the steps as I hear the lift door opening below me.

The exit to the fourth floor is barricaded with a trundle bed, two side tables and an easy chair. Everything's easy but the chair as I scrabble my way over it, rip open the porthole on its rusty hinges, and dive out – only to find myself face to face with the voice in Apartment 403.

It belongs to a statuesque dame with eyes the colour of the sky on a midsummer's day, a handkerchief of a dress, and a body in the region of thirty-nine-twenty-four-thirty-six. And about where the thirty-nine's situated, the dame is fisting a gun – a Kirikkale MKE, to be exact, one of a truckload churned out in Turkey half a century ago, calibre either .32 or .38, depending upon your proclivities. If the signal pin tells me anything, it's that it means business.

'I've always wanted to get that door open.' The dame smiles as she waves the gat at me. 'So as a little reward for your efforts, Mr Postman, why don't you come in? After first handing over your Smith & W, of course.'

It looks a long way from rewarding as I sidle past the Kirikkale –

which is a little too much like the Walther PP as favoured by James Bond for my liking – to find myself in a mirror image of the joint I've just come from: brown carpet with more holes in it than carpet, a nice little chrome chair with a push handle and wheels on it, and wallpaper that looks like it's been clawed to death by a cat.

I check out the dame as she closes the door and ask the only question that's reasonable under the circumstances. 'What's with the wheelchair?'

'My father was a soldier who was involved in a number of unnecessary conflicts in the Middle East.' She's parked my Smith & Wesson but the Kirikkale stays on target. 'Unfortunately, he was shot by a fellow soldier while seated on the next bed but one cleaning a howitzer.'

They're always on the next bed but one and they're always shot by a fellow soldier.

'He was invalided home. And because no one bothered to check under the blankets, I inherited a military-issue handgun.'

I glance at the door with the frosted glass in it. 'So where is he now, this hero father of yours?'

'About where the person in the apartment below is, I expect.' She notes my raised eyebrow. 'Oh, yes, I heard it all, only I didn't know what it was at the time – the muted conversation, a scream, the thud of what I later worked out was a body hitting the floor, the dragging of the corpse to the bed, the clatter of a knife on the sink, and the sound of someone at a computer keyboard, who shortly afterwards vacated the premises. Followed by your belated appearance.'

'Is that all?'

'Isn't that enough?'

'So why didn't you do something?'

It's the dame's turn to raise an eyebrow. 'Sweetie, where have you been all your life? Where I come from, this is the Cross. And if a person does anything more than nothing in such situations in the Cross, there's the strong possibility they'll end up like my dearly-departed war-hero father – and the person in the apartment below.' She frowns. 'But what you haven't told me is how come you're here – a great lunk of a guy with a gun, busy pretending he's a postman when quite clearly you're not. How come you turned up out of the blue, tricking your way into my neighbour's apartment?'

I want to see her reaction so I tell her. 'Because someone just killed your neighbour's boyfriend.'

'That would be Tommy Tycho.'

'How did you know it was Tycho?'

'I didn't' – cool as whisky on the rocks – 'I just knew that was the name of the boyfriend.'

So she knows that much and she also knows enough for the information not to surprise her. In the silence that follows, I hear the cops rummaging about below.

'So did you call the police?'

She shrugs. 'Do I look like the sort of person who goes around lowering property prices?'

It's an invitation to look at what sort of person she is and what I see is a dame on the high side of tall, with beautiful eyes and even nicer lips, and the sort of figure a man could create a lifetime of dreams out of. She's dressed in clothes that wouldn't look out of place on a Parisian catwalk – loose black top, a tight skirt that's no longer than it ought to be, and high-heeled clogs that accentuate her legs: the sort of vision that could raise anything on a good day, even the dead. Only this isn't a good day.

I'm just about to answer in the negative when there's a hammering at the door. I don't have to be Samuel L. Spade to figure who it is and that the window and a dozen sheets knotted together are my only chance of escape.

But the dame wouldn't have a dozen sheets and besides, she's got other ideas. She jerks the Kirikkale at the wheelchair. 'Get in!' I don't do like she tells me so she does the logic. 'Look, Mr Postman, there happens to have been a murder and you just happened to be at – or at least unreasonably near – the scene of the crime, when you had no acceptable reason to be.' She slips my S&W into the back pocket of the chair. 'Going by what I see, even without a murder, the police will likely think you're very much a person of interest to them. You'd have to explain yourself. After that, I'd have to explain you. Which means we'd both be in all sorts of trouble. So get in.'

'Open up or we'll open up for you!'

'It's the chair or the cops, so you better do what I say.'

It'll never work but I do what she says. For one thing there's no alternative that springs to mind. For another, she's the one holding the equaliser.

'Wait!' she yells at the door. 'Now put this rug over your knees and look old.' I glance at the wig. 'Not that rug, you idiot, the blanket! The hairpiece goes on your head. All right, we're coming!'

The knocking stops and the dame's voice drops to a whisper as I hunch under the throwover like she told me to. 'Now the wig.' The rug's tresses are long and golden. The dame shrugs. 'All right, so daddy turned transvestite after he was invalided home. He was sick of pretending to be tough and so he became a girl. He told me it was his way of coping with the trauma.' She leans so close I can read the serial number on the Kirikkale. 'You know, despite pretty much everything else about you, you've got nice eyes.'

Then she parks her gat beside my S&W in the pocket of the chair and opens the door. There's a brigade waiting – enough cops to take San Quentin, sufficient blue-serge material to keep a Third World sweatshop in work for a year – dripping with walkie talkies and handcuffs and Tasers and truncheons, and fisting a glut of Glocks.

The dame wheels the chair straight at them. 'Could you bunch of unemployable cowboys get out of my way?' The fuzz hesitate. 'Look, I'll tell you this once and once only: I'm taking my mother out for some sunshine and if anyone lifts a finger to stop us, I'll sue the lot of you for the use of force in excess of requirements, got me?'

The constabulary falls back. I don't know if it's the threat or the dame's cleavage that does it, but one of the cops opens the Otis, while the more able rozzers rush to assist with the chair.

'Much obliged,' she tells them, as the lift doors shut in their collective faces.

Someone must have walkie talkied the situation to the forces at Ground Zero because, while we find a reception committee waiting in the foyer, instead of holding us for inquisition in the time-honoured manner of the fuzz, they tip their assault caps, see us onto the ramp, out into the paddock and home free.

'Where to now?' the dame asks.

I put two and two together and come up with Roarer's joint.

Chapter 5

THE FIGURE AT THE WINDOW

Rory kills people. At least that's what he used to do – before he went religious. Now he leads a peaceful coexistence in his once barely habitable hovel in Browntown, praying a lot and paving his way to Heaven with good intentions. I explain the situation to Annabel while parked in the wheelchair in the back of a taxi they custom-build to cart wheelchairs in, that looks like it's got its midships caught in a mangle.

Glancing in his rear-vision mirror, the cabbie interupts. Cabbies always interrupt. That's why they're cabbies. 'Bloody cripples.' He stares at me perched in the back of his chariot. 'No offence, lady, but that's what she is, there's no getting away from it.' He stares at me again. 'I mean, tell me this: can you use your legs?' He allows a break for what in some circles might pass as laughter. 'The answer's gotta be no. So we cop you. And by the time we factor in the hours spent loading and unloading your chairs and the fuel these things get through, plus the possibility of getting a hernia due to all the lifting and carrying, we –'

'Shut up,' the dame tells him.

The cabbie shuts up, and it's in that condition he unloads us outside Rory's place. I chuck the wig behind the fence.

'Hey, you're not a dame and you can walk,' the cabbie says.

'And, hey,' I say, 'you just scored yourself a wheelchair.'

The joker takes off before I change my mind, leaving us to turn my attention to Rory's hovel. The falling-down fence has been replaced with nice white palings, the pathway's got shiny new pavers in it, the lawn's been given a short back and sides, and there aren't any assassins lurking in the shrubbery – at least none that I can see.

Janet, the holy-roller who latched onto Roarer in the Handless Hood caper, opens the door wearing a brown housecoat to go with the brown hair and a smile that doesn't go with anything much. The moment she claps eyes on us her smile fades to yesterday. 'Rory!' she calls over her shoulder. 'Rory, my sugar petal, come quick. He's back.'

It's a line from somewhere and I don't like lines from anywhere. Lines are inclined to have hooks in them.

'It's all right,' I tell her. 'I'm not going to ask him to do any killing. We just need a temporary refuge.'

Rory appears – still built like a greyhound and still minus one leg, and to all intents and porpoises the crutch under his armpit still doubles as a rifle. But the difference is that he's togged out in a kangaroo-shoot, and instead of the killer he once was, he looks like a pacifist. The other thing he looks is at my companion.

'Hi, babe!'

Janet places a restraining hand on his crutch. 'I'm sorry, dear, but you're not meant to show familiarity towards members of the opposite sex. Under God's law, a husband shall not have any eyes for other women.'

I raise the eyebrow at Rory. 'Since when did you get hitched?'

Rory shifts on his crutch. 'I didn't. Janet's being anticipatory. But while it hasn't occurred yet, it's about to. And when it does, I want you to be best man.'

'If it requires me to write my name, you're going to have to find yourself another man.'

'Can you give me away, then?'

'I gave you away a long time ago, pal.'

Roarer looks appealing. It takes a lot for Roarer to look appealing. 'Will you at least come to the wedding?'

'When is it?'

He checks his chronometer. 'In fifty-five minutes' time.'

'Thanks for the notice.' I shrug. 'Okay, I'll do it. But in the meantime' – I glance about – 'would you mind letting us in off the rifle range?'

My companion holds out her hand. 'I'm Monica Best. You must be Rory.'

Rory takes hold of the hand like it's a lifeline. 'Yeah, that's me, the ex-killer.' He crutches backwards into the wallpaper. 'Welcome to the reformatory.'

The joint's unrecognisable. Maybe that's what makes me nervous, or maybe it's something in the innermost recesses of my mind and sideways onto my direct vision, something in the porphyry of my senses, the lurking idea that we're not alone, and that somebody, somewhere, is watching us. But the boys in blue waved us goodbye at the murder scene, there was no one of interest in the vicinity, and I checked up and down Macleay Street when we came out of Annabel's. Plus I'd swear that no one followed the cab. So why do I feel –

This is Browntown, so there's a bunch of killers down the road and a psychopath with a slice out of one ear contemplating mass murder by the mosque two torched hovels away, but no one looks to be after us in particular, so I shake my suspicions out of my brainpan, and lever myself into Rory's.

I don't like domestication, never have. I don't like to see Rory with his hair Brylcreemed back over his ferret skull, perched like a pimple on an anti-macassared couch, crutch-gun beside him like it's also been converted, sipping chamomile tea from a bone china teacup with his pinkie out, and smiling as though he actually *likes* people. While the dialogue follows its expected course, I let my peepers take a stroll around our immediate environs, thereby noting the following:

Christ on His Cross on the salmon-pink wall; an angel with half a wing propped in the fake fireplace; a Bible on the table next to Rory; and a plastic menagerie in a cowshed under the window. Through which I see a figure.

'Get down!'

Rory pulls his missus onto the pretty pink carpet and somehow – he's still quick on his one foot – gets Monica down, too. He's all nicely snuggled up on top of her, and I feel a pang of what might be a near-relation of jealousy as I crouch down under the *fenêtre* with my gat out, side-on to the drapes, while quartering the exterior. I've got the feeling – it's just a feeling – that the figure was dressed in black, or maybe it was the figure's shadow, a slim-pickings shadow with the outline of a throwing knife in its hand.

But all I can see now is a neat yard with plenty of concrete and a herbaceous border around the edges and trees that look like they've been bashed into submission with a flamethrower. I can't see a knife-wielding figure – not even the shadow of a shadow of one.

I pack the gat and straighten the fedora. 'Sorry. I thought I saw something.'

Chapter 6

KILLING FOR CHRIST

Rory's back on his foot and slicking down his hair, while eyeing me like one of us is following the wrong script, and it's not him. 'I saw something, too,' he says. 'A joker that might have been in the game a caper or two too long, a palooka that's copped one punch too many, a marksman using up the few remaining bullets he's got left in his magazine shooting at shadows.'

There's an answer to that, but I don't give it. Instead I keep to the itinerary. 'No one's safe here any more, Roarer.'

He gives what in polite circles might be described as a laugh as he crutches his way back to the couch beside the Bible. '*Safe?* Pal, what would you know about safe?' He parks himself. 'Look, since I got out of killer-mode I'm as safe as anyone can get. Want to know why? Because I got God on my side, Rain. You hear me, brother? And God looks after His children, His miracles to perform.'

Which makes about as much sense as the shadow.

'Roarer, I just saw Pandora. She must have been on dog watch here, waiting for me to show up.'

Roarer crosses himself. 'Like I said, Rain, I reckon you've had one spear-tackle too many, you –'

'I –'

Monica cuts across me, 'Who's Pandora?'

I owe her an explanation, so I give her the only one I got. 'Someone who's after me, a figure from the past. I don't even know what part of my past she's from, only that she wants to kill me. I also know if anyone gets in her way, she'll take them out, too.'

'But you must know . . .'

'Look, if I do know, that knowledge is buried deeper than logic in that Good Book of Roarer's. Meanwhile, we've got to get out of here.'

'We've also got to get to a wedding.'

Roarer and his missus-to-be exchange glances. You see this with people. Not content with exchanging bodily fluids, they also got to exchange glances.

'Roarer, if you've got something to say, say it, and say it quick. Because if I know one thing about Pandora, she'll be back. And she's not about to postpone the return visit till tomorrow.'

Rory's got the crutch in one hand and the Book in the other. 'Rain, mate, I been thinking . . .'

Bad sign.

I glance out the window.

Clouds.

Otherwise nothing.

At least nothing I'm aware of.

'Anyway, we – I mean me and Janet here – well, we're all signed up to the Church of the Latter-day Hillbillies.' He looks troubled. 'Think what you like, Rain, they just happen to be the New Religion – the way, the truth and the light.' He makes it sound like an insecticide. 'Anyway, signing up means I had to give 'em my house.'

I nod. 'Smart move, Roarer.'

'That's not all.' He takes a deep breath. 'The minister said if we wanted to be sure of getting to Heaven, we got to keep on shelling out. That means I got to find work.'

I'm starting to get the hologram, but I ask the question anyway. 'What kind of work?'

Rory does his one-shoe shuffle. 'There's only one line of employment I'm familiar with.'

'You mean: in order to get to Heaven, you got to go back to killing people?'

Rory looks uncomfortable. Then again, Rory always looks uncomfortable. Rory's an uncomfortable-looking kind of guy. 'Something like that.'

'It's not something like anything. You're either killing or you're not killing.'

He puts his foot down. 'Look, the concept's supported by the Book. *Life for life*, it says, *eye for eye, tooth for tooth, foot for foot. Exodus 28.*'

'But you've already given your foot and you've also taken out the joker that took it. What more can you do?' I glance at Janet. She's looking almost as confused as Rory's sounding. I turn back to Rory. 'Have you run this particular piece of logic past the Hillbillies?'

But if Roarer's run it past the Hillbillies, I'm not going to discover the fact this session, on account of suddenly Rory hurls his bone china teacup at the crucifix and he's down on his knee on the carpet. At first I think he's praying but then I see he's got the crutch up to one eyeball and he's loosing off a shot, followed by another, and on the reflex I grab Mae West in one paw and Rory's wife-to-be in the other and make for the doorway with Roarer bringing up the rear, his crutch switched to auto and still firing.

I yell to make myself heard over the fusillade. 'Where's the Caddie?'

Janet blinks behind her goggles. 'There's no Caddie any more, it belongs to the Church. We gave it to them as a down payment on the marriage and all we could afford in its place was a 121.'

As a getaway car a Mazda 121's about as useful as a Tonka Toy. I find it hiding in the Fibrolite garage like it's wet its pants. I shovel Rory's missus-to-be in the back and climb next to Mae West while Rory covers our rear.

And in our rear, lurking behind the shrubbery, standing so still it could be a shadow of the shrubbery, is a figure in black.

'We can't come back here in a hurry,' I tell anyone who's listening.

Chapter 7

TILL DEATH US DO PART

Where are we headed?'
'The leave-me-in-the-lurch, the cockies' perch, the church.
Me and Janet are getting married, remember?'

'What's the hurry?'

'We were supposed to be there an hour ago.'

'I mean what's all the rush in getting hitched? She in the family way
or something?'

Roarer shakes his head. 'God requires it of us.' His voice has dropped
to the level of his knee. 'We're supposed to be His holy messengers, yet
here we are living in mortal sin and anguish.'

The church is a church. A bunch of bricks in holy conformation, with a
lot of multi-coloured windows. There's gravestones, the usual Quasimodo
belltower, a garden, a parking lot, plus a not-so-usual lych-gate – corpse
gate, body hatch, call it what you like – and a fat man in a surplice ready
and waiting to join two more star-struck lovers in Holy Matrimony. We
find a Holy Sepulchre and a lot of empty pews. Apart from us and the
pews, there's an organ, an organ player and the preacher. The ceremony's
simple. I don't know what else it could be, with Roarer the principal
celebrant.

'Do you, Rory J. Smith, take Janet Q. Peters for your lawfully wedded
wife?'

Rory cranes around, frowning like he's about to exx somebody.
'What did he say?'

I hunch over the gat. 'He'd like to know if you want to marry the
dame.'

'Of course I want to marry the dame, that's why we're here, isn't it?'

'So tell *him* that.'

'Tell him what?'

'That you want to marry her.'

'But he already *knows* that.'

'Then tell him again.'

Roarer shakes his head and turns back to the preacher. 'Could you repeat the question?'

'Which question?'

'The one you just asked.'

'Do you, Rory Smith, take –?'

'So I can understand it.'

The preacher shrugs. 'Do you want to marry the dame?'

'That's why I'm –'

'So *I* can understand it.'

'Yeah, I do.'

'That's all I need to know.'

Janet's much quicker off the mark than Roarer – although that's never going to be the speed of a slug out of a Smith & Wesson – and before you can say *Sorry-pal-I-just-changed-my-mind-and-want-out*, Rory and Janet are hubby and missus. The organ grinder's all worked up over the Wedding Goosestep – the one by Mendelssohn, not the Wagner – and the chords are banging up into the upended-boat-frame ceiling of the holy house and dribbling down over the turn-turtle deck beams. Monica Best does signing duty in the sentencing book, and Roarer makes his mark with an X.

The preacher consults his barometer. 'If you leave now you'll still be in credit.'

Back in the bubble car, Janet asks, 'Where are we going if we can't go home?'

All I did was answer a distress call. Now I got Monica and Roarer and his missus, not to mention a debt of obligation to Annabel, which means tracking down whoever killed her – who may or may not also be the joker that took out Tommy Tycho.

'We got to get ourselves to a safe place. And on the way we got to swing by Castanet Close and pick up Imogene.'

Monica pricks up her fears. 'Who's Imogene?'

'My daughter.'

'I didn't know you were married.'

Am I imagining disappointment? 'I'm not. Me and the mother of my daughter might have parted company, but that doesn't make me divorced from the kid.'

'Why do we have to get her?'

'Because Pandora's next move — now that Roarer's joint is blown — will be to try and grab Imogene. I don't want the kid to be there when Pandora arrives.'

'But what can she do, this Pandora woman?'

I don't tell her. Just knowing is bad enough.

The villa I bequeathed to Salina in Castanet Close is crammed between another couple of shanties of a similar ilk. The silhouette of the black-cat mobile I made for Imogene still hangs in her bedroom window. Nosy Nora the neighbour is also hanging — over the side fence, hard up alongside the roller-coaster pathway to the front door of Salina's.

'They're not here,' she says.

'So where are they?'

A look of smug satisfaction crosses her face. 'Forgotten already, Mr Scutt? They've gone to the kid's ballet lessons, where do you think? They never miss a Saturday. And that's what I told her.'

'Told who?'

It's Nosy Nora's moment. 'Your wife's friend, of course, the one that called by just before you did, her old schoolfriend. I said that your ex-wife and your daughter were at the Dance Academy off William, that's what I told Salina's friend.'

The only trouble with that story is that Salina doesn't have any friends.

'Was the friend wearing black?'

'I thought you said you were interested in the kid. Now you —'

'Tell me, Nora.'

Nora shrugs. 'If it was any more black, I would of said it was mourning.'

Chapter 8

THE SECRETS BOX

It's still a nice day but the clouds over the rooftops of the hovels have suddenly got greyer, and the starlings fluttering around us have turned into crows.

I call Salina on dead-man's mobile No. 3.

'Who is it?'

I've taught Salina to be suspicious. Correction: *Proximity to me* has made Salina suspicious.

'Seamus Devine. We met on Facebook, remember?'

Pandora's not above tapping phonecalls. Come to think of it, in this day and age *no one's* above tapping phonecalls.

'Oh, it's you.'

I can hear the familiar tinkle of a piano in the background, and the *shuffle-shuffle-shuffle* of tiny feet on dusty floorboards.

'Yeah.' I choose my words careful. 'Looks like we require a termination.'

Shuffle-shuffle-shuffle. The piano's playing the black swan piece from Tchaikovsky.

'I thought everything was all right now.'

I take the breath. 'Yeah, I did, too, but I was wrong. A shadow's been discovered. So like I said, we require a termination.'

'Like now?'

'Like yesterday.'

There's a pause in which I can see the black swan leaping into the lake on her date with destiny. Then, wearily, 'Okay. Where?'

'The usual place,' I say and hang up.

I climb back into the conveyance. 'Souza's,' I tell Supergirl.

Souza's is an ice-cream parlour and it's the emergency rendezvous of the month. Next month's Terpsichore's. It goes alphabetical.

I find Imogene wrapping her laughing gear around a blood-red imitation-strawberry double bunger, while Salina looks like she's sucking a lemon. I do the headcount.

'Where are the twins?'

I had a couple of other kids – Scarlet and Rhett – until I found they'd been fathered by somebody else, since deceased.

Salina shrugs. 'After Clint copped it, the in-laws took them away. They said I was unfit to be a mother. And it's all your fault.' Everything's my fault, even when it isn't. 'You know, I thought when we got divorced I'd be shot of you.'

'No one's ever shot of anyone in this world, Sal.'

She steadies herself. 'So what's happened now?'

'Pandora's out to kill someone.'

'How do you know it's us?'

'It's always us.'

'So where are we going?'

'I told you, the safe house.'

'That flea pit!'

Years ago, I rescued an old biddy from the clutches of a murderer. Out of gratitude, she bequeathed me an island – or at least a shack on one. When I told her I didn't do shacks – or any other possessions, for that matter – by a complicated series of manoeuvres, masked by a shelf company in the Bahamas and dead-men's masquerades, she made the joint over to a trust fund that could never be traced to anyone, least of all me. It's no Taj Mahal, hence Salina's reference to flea pits.

She sighs. 'I suppose a flea pit's better than death.' She stares at the Tonka Toy. 'But one thing's for certain, we're not going in *that*.'

My turn to shrug. 'Sal, you got no choice. You don't have to worry about the overload because two of us are leaving.' I nod to Supergirl, who gets out of the Tonka Toy. 'Roarer will see you safe to your destination.'

Imogene ditches the cone. 'Can I come with you, Daddy?'

Imogene's seven, or maybe eleven, and she likes ice-cream. As a result she's a bit on the heavy side for a ballerina, but that doesn't stop me thinking it's no more than puppy fat and that one day she'll grow up to be a nicely-proportioned mastiff.

'Not today,' I tell her. 'Today you're escaping from the wicked witch.'

'Can you get my secrets box, then?'

'What secrets box?'

Imogene tells me what secrets box and where to find it and I park the information in my memory, alongside the image of Pandora.

'You lead an interesting life, Mr Scutt,' Monica says as we watch them drive away. 'Or maybe I should say Seamus Devine.'

That's when I should have got suspicious. But instead, all I do is shake my dumb head and say, 'It's neither.'

'All right, Mr Neether, what are we supposed to do now?'

Chapter 9

THE ROMANCE OF THE PRIVATE EYE

I was brought up to not trust people. Trust people and one day you'll find yourself chained to a piece of masonry with reinforcement sticking out of its corrugated sides, lying among the mud crabs and turtle soup and assorted body parts and the rest of Sydney's dirty little secrets at the bottom of what's laughingly known as this burg's safe and sparkling playground. But Monica Best is a beautiful dame, and rules go out the *fenêtre* with beautiful dames.

So after we swing by Castanet Close to pick up Imogene's box of tricks, we find ourselves at Maestro's, a classy little *nouvelle* eatery back at the Cross, my fedora on the table beside me, discussing a murder. That is, *nearly* discussing a murder.

'Before we go any further,' Monica says, 'I need to know a little more about you, Mr Postman.'

That's when she sits back, and when she sits back I notice a whole lot more about her than when she sits forward, and I don't know if that's good or bad, because the more I see of this dame, the more I want to see of her, but the more I see of her the harder it is to keep my mind on the stated objective.

'You see,' she goes on, 'all I know is that you happened to turn up at the scene of a crime at my block of apartments. I don't even know your real *name*, or even if you possess one.'

A waiter with tattoos goes on the hover. I order a pie and Monica orders everything. I decide to come clean, or as clean as anyone can when they're dirtier than they ought to be.

'Okay, I'm a PI – that's private detective in everyday expletives – but I don't blazon my name from the rooftops because the word *private* is part of the job description. Your turn.'

'Very well, Mr Smith. I'm the original can-can girl, unfortunately born in the wrong era. Daddy went to war leaving me to make my own way, only to find that my way wasn't everyone else's and by the time he came home an invalid, I was twenty-five, and no further ahead than when he left. After that, we moved into the apartment together, and shortly afterwards he died.'

There's something Monica Best is not telling me. But like the food in this joint, telling or not telling is not what we're here for.

'I need to know what you noticed this morning.' I take a bite out of the pie; it tastes expensive. 'Exactly what did you hear and when did you hear it?'

Monica shrugs. 'I slept late. In fact, I was still in bed when Annabel came home.'

I glance up from the pie. 'So you knew Annabel?'

She puts down her fork. 'You said *knew* . . .'

'That's because Annabel happens to be in the past tense. But I thought you already knew that.'

'*Knowing* is different from being told. Until you said she was dead I could pretend she wasn't.' She knuckles her eyes and takes a deep breath. 'I'm sorry, of course I know – I'm sorry, *knew* – Annabel. She was one of those beautiful people who will help anyone – a dog that's been hit by a car, a sick child, a crook. If anyone needed help, Annabel would always be there.'

I dole too much ketchup on the expensive *patisserie*. 'So tell me what you heard the morning of the murder.'

Old buildings have funny acoustics, she tells me, particularly ones like hers, with wooden floors instead of concrete. And in this particular building, if you knew what you were listening for, you could hear just about everything. Monica had been Annabel's neighbour for long enough to recognise the sound of her key in the lock, and because the apartment below had the same floorplan as her own, she could also trace her movements after she entered.

Annabel went into the kitchen.

'Not the bedroom?'

'I told you, I know Annabel's apartment like it was my own. She went into the kitchen and five minutes later someone else came to the door.'

'Which door?'

'First to the door outside, the one at street level where all the buttons are, then Annabel's.'

'After she buzzed in whoever it was?'

'She didn't buzz anyone in. I told you, he came to her door.'

'How did you know it was a *he*?'

'I suppose it could have been a woman,' she said, but she appeared doubtful. 'Anyway, after that came the scream.'

'And you didn't do anything about it?'

'Mr Smith, as I've already said, Macleay Street might be Potts Point for postal purposes, but whatever the euphemism, it's still the Cross. And in the Cross, you don't go *towards* a scream, you go *away* from it.'

'Even if it belonged to your beloved Annabel?'

'There were always screams from my beloved Annabel.'

'But you didn't think this particular scream might be different?'

For a second I have her attention. That's the romance of the private eye. It holds good right up to the moment you start asking too many questions. After that, it doesn't hold good any more.

'A third party doesn't present their credentials to women like Annabel every time they scream.' She gets to her feet. 'And if it was only sex she was screaming for, that's an even better reason not to drop in with a big smile on your face and a calling card. As I told you before, there was the scream, then typing, and after that the departure.'

I don't know where I went wrong. If I did, I wouldn't have gone there.

After Monica hits the high seas and the waiter with all the drawings on him delivers the pudding, I've got no choice but to drag out the list I culled from Annabel's printer, spread it out on the tablecloth, and eat what's in front of me.

Chapter 10

NOBODY LIKES A CORPSE

From what Monica said, the list is most likely a trap. But it's something, and right now something is what I'm most in need of. There are a lot of names.

Errol 'The Pig' Shadie.

Brutus Kariakis.

Percy Smith.

Richard Presto . . .

There's more of the same but while I'm working my way through the list I become conscious of an audience, and this audience has got a scent to it, and if you asked me to put a name to the scent, I'd call it *Too Nosy For Its Own Good*. I chose this eatery because it's near where Tommy Tycho copped it, but also because it's got cloths on the tables and I wanted to impress. I thought no one would recognise me here, on account of the tablecloths.

Wrong.

I put the eating on hold and roll to the ground. At the last moment I turn the roll into a double-twist so that by the time I'm back on my trotters I'm standing behind whoever it was at my elbow. I've got my gat in the space between his fifth and sixth ribs – or between the fifth and eighth dorsal vertebrae, however you want to play it – at about the place where life starts its lonely little journey to the mortuary.

Move the right way and no one notices anything but a little more action than usual, and by the time they think of checking the details, all they see is the waiter turning an ashen shade of jaundice, with a nattily-dressed customer standing behind and slightly to the left of him, giving him a pointer.

'And my pointer is to not look over people's shoulders.' I prod him to drive the pointer home. 'Now I'm going to pass the maître d' a C-note and tell him to keep the change while you are going to accompany me outside to give me much-needed directions to my destination, because

I'm a stranger in town.'

No one looks our way. This is the Cross.

'We'll start with a name.' I've got my hat and it's back where it likes to be and we're outside the café, all cuddled up to a telegraph pole, me and the waiter and the gat. 'And after the name we'll progress to the whys and the wherefores of your curiosity.'

'I wasn't up to anything, honest!'

'Funny kind of name.'

He takes the kind of breath that tells me he wants to keep living. 'It's John.'

'Okay, Johnny-boy. How about telling me what your game is.'

It's a fine day. That must be why he decides to tell the truth. It's nice to go on living on a fine day.

'I got a habit.'

'That'd be the habit of looking over other people's shoulders that you shouldn't look over.'

'No, a *habit* habit.'

'You mean you're a junkie.'

The kid's as thin as a hangman's rope and his eyes are a day-old corpse's. 'You had a list and I saw Bro's name on it so I thought –'

'You mean Mr Presto's?'

'Yeah.' The dead eyes refocus. 'I mean, yes, sir, that's what I mean. And it so happened I needed a – need a –'

'What you're saying is you need a fix and you thought I looked like a pusher. In addition to which I possessed a piece of paper with Brother Presto's name on it.'

'Yes, sir.'

I give him a prod with the gat. 'So what's with all the tatts? They make you feel big or something? Or maybe you get paid by someone to make you a walking advertisement for dragons.'

He shakes his head. 'Mates with a tattooist.'

I put away the gat. I must be getting edgy in my old age. Pandora makes me that that way and jokers looking over my shoulder make me even more so.

'See you round. And when I do, we never met, know what I'm saying?'

'Y-Yes, sir. I mean I can hear the words, but I can't even see who's saying them.'

Back on the boat I get the heebies. Heebies are those things that visit when you're least expecting them − grey, shapeless little metro-gnomes that don't go away when you tell them to and are impervious to anything but the passage of time. It's like the whole of my back story creeps up on me and whacks me over the head with its sordid details − the parents, the kids who bullied me at school, the failed relationships, Pandora and the rest of the jokers who are out to get me. Especially the jokers who are out to get me. Makes me realise how Tommy Tycho must have felt.

I park Imogene's tin box on the bunk she occupies because she'll be occupying it again, and climb into the dinghy bobbing in the Bay of Plenty. I don't have to do what I'm doing, no one's forcing me, and there's no Croesus-rich client running around waving fistfuls of moolah. So why am I doing this?

Harry Hopman's Hoop-la Parlour's open and I ask him for a caffeine hit. While I'm waiting for the muck to arrive I rescue a copy of *The Daily Terrorgraph* from the garbage bin and smooth it open to the spread.

DEATH OF A LADIES MAN

No apostrophe, and no apologies for the omission. Big fat, black capitals, leaving just enough room for the pictorial accompaniment − a headless body sprawled in the gutter, together with a story in the sort of prose that − if it wasn't for the subject − might be described as deathless:

There are those who say he had it coming.

Tommy Tycho, whose body was discovered yesterday sprawled headless and friendless in a Kings Cross gutter, might have been a ladies man − but that never made him anyone else's.

Tycho's death was what any respectable, law-abiding Australian might describe as inevitable. Because the whole of Sydney's underworld was gunning for Tycho.

Police say that because of this, the task of finding Tycho's killer is a more than daunting one.

In the words of Chief Inspector Janus Leytton, head of Operation John the Baptist, speaking exclusively to the Terrorgraph: 'Where do you start?'

Leytton shrugs a set of shoulders that have witnessed more crimes than Tycho possessed enemies.

'After all, every criminal and his dog were after Tycho. It'd be easier to begin with a list of people who liked him and go from there. But that would be a short list and comprise pretty much nothing but women.

'Because Tycho was a ladies man. What I'm saying is there are too many suspects for us to be confident of finding the killer inside anything under a century.'

Chapter 11

A CASE OF THE HEEBIES

While Tycho's death takes up most of the *Terrorgraph*'s first eleven pages, the other news of the day almost didn't occur. Like the two sentences on the disappearance of an unnamed backpacker in mysterious circumstances, or this little paragraph in a black-girdled box buried on page 17:

> The body of a young woman, Annabel Franklin, was discovered yesterday in her Potts Point apartment. No one was seen coming or going from the apartment but police are treating the death as suspicious. Any person or persons with information are requested to contact Kings Cross Police . . .

Straight out of the fuzz's PR file. The only thing that particular story tells anyone is that the cops are running dead on Annabel's demise, the same way they're running on the death of Tommy Tycho.

I'm just starting on another story headed *DUMMY RUN*, about a bunch of mannequins pinched from a window display in Myers department store, when someone says, 'So what do you know, Rainbow?'

I like Hopman. He's the sort of joker that looks like he's guilty of everything, yet is as innocent as an uncut lamb – old clothes, face with more lines in it than Central railway terminus, and eyes a thousand times sadder than a basset's.

'Too much and still not enough.' I lean back so Harry can deliver the mugful of slop described on his menu as coffee. 'I'm trying to work out if a guy's got a duty to the dead.'

Harry pulls out a chair and parks himself. His café operates out of an old garage in an expensive residential area and rush hour is six to seven

in the am when the tradies start. After that it's chat time. Harry doesn't
mind. He's a philosopher.

'Said guy being you, I take it?'

'That's the one.'

He shrugs and I get the profile – hunched shoulders, beak nose stuck
out like a bird's bill, and mouth down at the corners like a speed bump.
'Rainbow, mate, who else have people got a duty to, if not to the dead?
If you do a favour for the living it's like you expect the favour to be
returned.' His chin sinks into his shirt. 'And that makes it no favour at
all. In fact, it's little more than the usual quid pro quo of life.' He glances
across at me out of his sad eyes. 'So what's the deal?'

I tell him the story of how Annabel Franklin saved my life.

'And she killed this Pandora character?'

I shake my head and it feels like it's got feathers in it. No one kills
Pandora, I tell him; it's always the other way round.

'I'm in O'Leary's - you know, the speakeasy. Pandora was about to kill
me when this dame I'd never seen before turns out the lights. Literally.
She reaches up and squashes the bulb over her head with her bare hand.
Then she grabs me with the hand that hasn't been shredded and drags me
to safety.'

'Was she naked from the waist down?'

I do the frown. 'Harry, I'm serious. This really happened and, no,
for the record she wasn't naked from the waist down, or up, or sideways,
or any other way. This event really occurred. I never clapped eyes on her
before and yet she risks her life for me.'

'And what happened to Pandora?'

'She wings it.' I take a drink of the slush. 'Chucks a knife that misses
me by a fly's dick, then buggers off like a bat out of Hell. She's a one-hit
girl, Pandora, and if that one hit fails, she makes herself scarce until next
time.'

'You think there'll be a next time?'

I feel the heebies coming back. 'Like death follows life, Harry. Where
Pandora's concerned there's always a next time.'

Harry sinks lower in his chair, looking more like a hawk than ever.
Hawks are gentle creatures, in my opinion. They look bad, but are only
dangerous to lambs.

'So what happens then?'

I tell him about the phone call, the headless corpse, Annabel's demise,
and the dame called Monica.

'So I take it that, by some nefarious means or other, this Annabel dame finds herself dead because she phoned you regarding a potential murder.'

A black dog drifts by. Harry throws it a slice of bacon.

'You got it.'

Harry nods. 'Then I reckon you owe her one, all right, Rainbow. And I reckon you reckon the same as me. Meanwhile, what about this Monica?'

'What about her?'

'She could die, too, couldn't she?'

After I leave Harry's, I go straight to Mae West's, ringing her bell in the only way, et cetera and et cetera. 'It's me,' I say.

'What do you want now?' The voice is as cold as a refrigerated tomato.

'I want to apologise.'

'Because you need me?'

No. Because she needs my protection. But always tell 'em what they want to hear. 'That's part of it.'

Monica lets me into the building and this time I take the elevator straight to the fourth floor. The joint's the same as it always was. All that's missing is the wig and the chair and the happy greeting.

'What do you want?'

'I might have compromised you. In other words, you're in danger and I don't want another death in my overnight bag. I want you to join the rest of the entourage in the safe house until this is over.'

She thinks about it for a while and finally she shrugs and tells me *Yes*, in the only way, et cetera and et cetera.

But why do I sense that convincing her was too easy?

Chapter 12

THE WIDOW'S PIQUE

When a list of suspects comes your way out of the deep-blue azure during a murder investigation, there's two explanations – it's a trap or it's a trap. Accordingly, the first thing I do is pay a visit to a name that's not on the list, and that's the widow.

The background to Tommy Tycho is well known, but that doesn't mean I don't replay it in the back of the 399 omnibus on the way to the widow's. Tommy was a bastard. There's two ways of reading that, and you're welcome to both of them. His mother was a pro – and that doesn't mean she played tennis – while his father was a pole-punter, prepared to pay the requisite L-note for the privilege of spending seven minutes and thirty seconds with Tycho's mother-to-be with her clothes off, all of thirty-five years ago. Some 270 days later, give or take whatever there is to give or take in these situations, Baby Tycho was spat out into an unsuspecting world.

He grew up to be a good-looking bastard. An educated good-looking bastard, too – on account of after he was abandoned by his mother, he was taken in by a cuddle of Cistercian monks who taught him the classics: like how to shoot people in the foot and get away with it, as well as your basic Latin. Didn't do him much good – the looks or the Latin. Tommy came out of it figuring only one thing – and that was that the world owed him a living. Call it the Adonis Complex.

There are a lot of Mr Bigs in this town and every one has got his own calling card. The cards come in the form of hobbies you'd rather not know about, or mansions dripping with CC-TVs with watchdogs as big as panthers. Or it could just be the way they walk – a swagger like they got the world between their legs, and their sole purpose in life is to keep it there. But while there are a lot of Mr Bigs in Sydney, Tycho was never one of them. Tycho was a dough boy. In the free enterprise world of corruption, he found a nice little niche market in parasitism. On the underside of that mongrel known as White Collar Criminality, Tycho was an active and well-fed flea.

He lived on crime, but he was never really part of it. He fed off crooks, but never dined at the same table. And he prided himself on never getting done by the cops for anything – not twice, not once, not ever. Tommy not only lived off the Mr Bigs of this world – robbing them, blackmailing them and sleeping with their women – he wasn't above ripping off the little man, too: the shyster, the sharper and the spiv. As a result, he had more enemies in Sydney's underworld than your average contract killer has stiffs.

He had a girlfriend.

Let's call her Annabel.

He also had a wife.

Let's call her the widow.

I find her in a falling-down joint in Maroubra, just around the corner from a play gym, a Dulux paint parlour and a *patisserie*. It's the kind of hovel you wouldn't park a dog in – if you had any respect for the dog – with a fence that if it leant any more would be firewood, weeds sticking up from mashed-potato concrete like hair out of the skull of a leper, and walls that need another coat of paint, if for no other reason than to keep them upright.

There's a stench about most things these days, but the smell coming out of this joint is the sort on which a dead dog could be grafted, the kind of smell that if it was at a mausoleum you'd say it was where it belonged, a stink that if it was on your leg you'd have the offending member amputated, if only to ensure the gangrene didn't spread any further.

Crooks have got dolls and they got molls, but going by the face on the dame that raises the portcullis, Angela Tycho is neither. The story goes that when someone threatened to exx her on account of a stunt Tycho pulled, he just laughed and said go ahead and do it. It might have been a bluff or maybe it wasn't, but whatever it was, it worked.

Angela's face mightn't have been her fortune, but at least she didn't die from it. Her looks were her insurance then and they're still her insurance now, a little grey-haired potoroo wearing a torn plastic apron without any frills and a troubled look on her homely features that descends all the way to the dangle-down stockings around her ankles.

'Would you be from the police?'

I peer into a lounge room that's coloured puce-pink like the rest of the joint, with a view through the window of next door's toilet, and find that the smell just got that much stronger.

I wave away a fly. 'Yeah, the police is exactly where I'm from.'

She nods. 'I was wondering about your taking so long, particularly after handing him over. I expect you'd like to know where I was when my husband died.'

'I'm sorry, but it's something we got to do, Mrs Tycho.'

'My real name's Tychopoulos – Angie Tychopoulos. Tommy had the name changed to Tycho to further his career.'

'And what career might that have been?'

She looks surprised. 'Why, public relations, of course.' She seems to believe it, but that doesn't mean I got to. 'He did good works for people, a lot of it on a *pro bono* basis.' She glances at me. 'That means for nothing.'

I don't tell her I already know what it means. I'm supposed to be a cop and a cop wouldn't know *pro bono* from a professional pop singer.

'You see, my Tommy was more of a public benefactor than people gave him credit for. He was so good it was difficult to know how he ever made a living. But that was just one of the many reasons I had for loving him.'

She's trying to establish her love for her husband as an alibi, only it doesn't work that way.

'Look, Mrs Tycho, ma'am – I'm sorry, Tychopoulos – no one's saying you did anything.'

She clasps her hands and leans forward like she's doing callisthenics. 'That's right, because why would I kill Tommy?' Tears come to her eyes. 'Oh, he was so good to me, Tommy was, you wouldn't believe it. His life was such a struggle, one way or another, due to his unfortunate beginnings. But he always put first things first, and the first thing Tommy did was set me up in this lovely little home and see to all my needs.'

Second alibi: No grudges. But it still doesn't work that way.

She waves a skinny paw at her stinking surroundings. 'Oh, I know it isn't much to look at, but it's as good as Tommy could manage, given all his setbacks.'

If the joint was nicer than it is, I'd still say the widow lived in fairyland. But there are worse places than fairyland and if she wants to live there, she's welcome to it. Only I'm not after fairies, I'm after the troll that killed Annabel Franklin.

'And what setbacks might they be, apart from his beginnings?'

'All those people who for reasons best known to themselves, didn't –' She pauses. 'Look, I don't know if you're aware of it, Mr –'

'Smith, Detective Inspector Bert Smith. But just call me Inspector.'

'I'm sorry, Inspector. As I was saying, a lot of people seemed not to have liked my Tommy, for reasons best known to themselves. I never understood why, unless it was simply because he was too good – too good for his own good, really.' She shakes her head. 'People have never taken to saints, at least, not while they're alive. Look at Joan of Arc. I believe Tommy's very goodness made other people feel bad in comparison, so they hated him for it.'

Chapter 13

THE CORPSE IN THE KITCHEN

Itake notes. Only it's hard to focus on anything given the smell. 'And what else do you know, Mrs Tycho – sorry, Tychopoulos?'

'That Tommy would have been a great man if he'd lived.'

I write: *Delusional.* Then I stare through the smell at the Widow. 'Only he didn't live, did he?'

She takes a deep breath, which is more than I can do. 'He trusted people too much, Tommy did.' She stands. 'But, oh dear, I didn't offer you a cup of tea. What on earth would Tommy say?'

A lot more than he can now he's dead. I put the sort of expression on my dial-up that might be appropriate to the occasion. 'Look, Mrs – T – I didn't come here for cookies, as I'd say you got enough on your plate without adding biscuits. All I need to know is where you were on the morning in question. After that, I can get the hell out – I mean, leave you alone.'

She aims for a smile but misses and it comes out a grimace. 'Oh, that's easy. It's like asking people where they were when Oprah announced her weight loss or Lady Di told the world she'd been unfaithful to Prince Charles or they found Fergie sucking that horrible man's toes in her swimming costume. On the morning in question, I was at the butcher's buying scotch fillet for Tommy. I hadn't been to the butcher's for, oh, for ages, because meat's so expensive. I'm sure Mr Simms would remember my being there.'

I write: *Query meatmonger.* Then, 'One more question.' There's always one more question, even when there isn't. 'Given that it wasn't you that did the job on your late and much-lamented husband, who would you say killed him?'

She shakes her head. 'As I said, he had so many enemies . . .'

I get to my feet. I've got my nosewipe out and I'm clutching it to the *schnozz.* 'Well, thank you Mrs –' I've got to put the question – the smell's an elephant in the room and the place is humming with flies. 'Is there something dead around here?'

The dame smiles. It's the first real smile she's thrown me since I been in the joint, a glow like the dawn over distant hills, stars through clouds, the glimmer of what might have been but never was, on account of a miserable little, tricksy-dicksy, cheating loverboy by the name of Tommy Tycho.

'Why, yes, as a matter of fact there is, Inspector. I'm sorry I didn't show you before but I thought as a policeman you'd already know.'

Show me what? Know what? I recall what she said about the cops handing something over to her as I follow her along a hallway, where I pause long enough to get a lungful of life-giving air while helping myself to a piece of paper I find lying on the floor by the telephone. Then I move on. And all the while the smell's getting stronger and the flies more numerous, until I know I'm going to find myself in a cesspit, or dead from putrefaction, or both.

Just before the doorway, I stop. Even I've got my limits. 'Look, Mrs Tychopoulos . . .'

The smile's still there – if anything, it's even brighter – and she's pointing at something. 'No, *you* look, Inspector.'

So I take one more fateful pace that gets me to the kitchen, and what I see is something I've never seen before and never want to see again, even if it kills me. And that's a green kitchen chair in the middle of the floor, and seated in the chair like it belongs there, a corpse with a ring-a-ring-a-rosy of words in a necklace around its neck – which is headless.

I reel back. 'Jesus! It's Tycho!'

'Of course it's Tommy!' The widow's picked up a can of Mortein and is busy applying a liberal dose to the corpse. All it does is excite the flies. 'Who did you inspect it to be, Expector? I mean . . .'

But I know what she means, and what she means is: how come I don't know – if I'm from the rozzers like I say I am – that the widow was granted custody of her dead husband's body prior to burial, because:

1. The cause of death was as obvious as the nose on other people's faces.

2. No ID was necessary because of the tattoo around the neck.

3. The cops no longer required the stiff because they were running dead on the death of Tommy Tycho.

I still ask the question. 'What's he doing *here*?'

The dame shrugs. 'I believe in reincarnation. That's why he's here and –'

But I'm not hanging around for explanations. I head back to where I can breathe, drag open the front hatchway and stay alive. 'I know what reincarnation means. What I'm asking is how come they gave you the corpse?'

She shrugs. 'I just asked and the police seemed relieved to be rid of him. They said the cause of death was obvious and that Tommy was just taking up space. They even bent him into a sitting position for me.'

'What about their inquiries?'

She throws me a sweet expression. 'Don't you mean *your* inquiries, Inspector?' She doesn't wait for an answer. 'Tommy will be here for three days.' She nods to herself. 'Three days, after which comes the funeral.' She smiles. 'It's winter, so decomposition isn't as quick as it might be.' She takes a deep breath; it's nice that someone can. 'Meanwhile, I'm trying to find somebody to bury him. Everybody says there'll be trouble but why should there be trouble at a funeral? Do you happen to know of anyone who would bury Tommy, Inspector?'

I change the subject. 'I found a piece of paper in the hallway with a lot of stuff crossed out, leaving nothing but the word *Orange*.'

The dame's face goes mottled. 'Did you?'

'Yeah, I did.' I take the papyrus out of my pocket and uncrumple it. 'Look.' I prod at all the cross-outs that obliterate most of the writing, then at the only word left legible, the one at the bottom. 'See how it says *Orange*? Now I got to ask myself: why would a piece of paper be lying around with the word *Orange* on it?'

Her brow creases. 'What else have you helped yourself to, Inspector?' The brow uncreases, and the voice becomes the widow's again. 'Oh dear, I'm sorry if I seemed rude just then but please understand I've just lost my husband. I know that's no excuse for throwing wild accusations around, and after all you are from the police.' She nods, as if to herself. 'About the word Orange.' She glances around her. 'You see, I won't be able to stay here now that Tommy's gone. Because of his altruism, I'm broke. I'm going to have to sell up everything to survive. And of course I'm having the house painted and the colour I'm going to have it painted is –'

'Orange.'

It figures. Flea-puce to orange. I put on the fedora together with my just-born-yesterday look, the one with all the innocence in it. 'From memory, at the time of Tommy's demise you say you were at the baker's?'

She shakes her head. 'No, it was the butcher's. Mr Simms's, to be exact, on Anzac Parade.'

Chapter 14

THE CRONE IN THE QUEUE

Unlikely as it is that Tommy's widow could lift an elephant-gun – much less fire it without incurring more damage to herself than to the corpse – you're not much good in this game if you place your faith in the unlikely. So the next step is to check out the alibi she palmed me. When I do this, I discover the butcher's got blood on his hands. His mitts are dripping with the stuff but he wipes off the gore like it's no more than an afterthought, all the while eyeing me like I'm just another sausage, and therefore part of the food chain.

'Who'd you say you was?'

'I'm an inspector of police.'

He nods his butcher's head. 'Yeah, and I'm second cousin twice-removed of the Mona Lisa.' Simms places his fists on his display case and leans over them. 'Why don't you tell me what you want to know and I'll decide if I want to let you know it?'

I ignore the implications and read from my notebook like it's some kind of official document. 'I'm inquiring into the death of Tommy Tychopoulos, specifically, the whereabouts of his wife Angela on the morning in question.'

The butcher shakes his head and tries out a laugh that would look good on an orangutan. 'What, that little thing? Mate, if you reckon she had anything to do with her husband's murder then you lot must be an even greater bunch of mugs than the newspapers say you are. Sure, Tycho was bad to the bone, but Angie's the last person who'd duff him.'

'We still need to verify where she was on the morning in question. She says she was here.'

'That'd be yesterday. Yeah, she was here all right. For going on an hour she was here, if you really want to know.'

I tell him, yeah, I really want to know.

The butcher shrugs. 'Angie's the kind of lady who's always at the end of the queue. There must have been twenty customers come into my shop after she did and I guarantee she apologised to every one of them, before letting them in front of her. So she was here a bloody long time.'

'You sure it was her?'

Simms chucks me the sort of look that could only come from a butcher. 'As sure as I am that you're not a rozzer, mate.'

There are jokers that would call me paranoid. But when you been in this game as long as I have, you got a lot to be paranoid about. Apart from which, paranoid's the kind of insurance a private eye needs – if only to keep him alive for a period slightly longer than the lifespan of your average beetle.

So when I emerge out of the flesh-vendor's onto Anzac Parade and join the hodge-podge of animal life that calls itself humanity, I realise not only that Tommy's widow possesses a cast-iron alibi, but also that there's someone watching my every move – and I pay a lot of attention to that feeling.

Anzac Parade is the kind of thoroughfare people die on. It's named after a war – the second A and the C stand for Army and Corpse respectively – and this morning it's busy living up to its name, with traffic forcing its way through the roundabout, every second punter acting like they got nothing better to do than carry a grudge against the rest of their fellow travellers, and someone following me. I'm not concerned with the punters I can see, it's the ones I can't see that I'm worried about.

I scan the buildings across the goat track, but all I see is a dame doing her nails, a cat perched outside a white-anted window pretending to be asleep, and a kid staring bleak-eyed at an unpromising future. Otherwise, there's no more than a few tattered curtains and a whole lot of darkness. But I still get the hell out of there, and while I'm doing that I ask myself the following: Who would know I'm here? And who would take the trouble to follow me, once they knew?

The questions are almost as big as how the world began, so I catch a cab to White Bay then ride the 397 back to the city. I then take Shanks's pony to the Big Pond – also known as Sydney Harbour – and when I'm pretty certain I've shaken off my pursuer, I find a dinghy that no one's using and row to the remote inlet where I parked the *Wooden No*. There's no place like home, even when it's a boat.

I call Rory on dead-man's mobile No. 3.

'That you Rainbow?'

I sever the connection. Most of the time Roarer's brain's on auto-pilot and most of the time the auto-pilot's suffering a serious malfunction. I dig another mobile out of the bilge and try again.

'This – is – John – Smith.' I say it slow and deliberate. '*Smith*, got it? Smith as in packet of potato chips, the kind of dainties they hand around at the funerals of idiots whose fatal problem in life was they were terminally careless.'

There's a pause. 'Gotcha.' Another pause. 'Mr Smith, it is, then. So what can I do you for?'

I stay with the code. 'How's your family?'

Roarer stays stupid. 'Pal, you know as well as I do that I ain't got no family, apart from the new wife, and she's . . .'

I can hang up again or I can persevere. I persevere. 'Nice little homily, Mr *Daughter*.'

The usual pause. Sometimes I think Roarer's brain might have been amputated along with his leg. 'Oh, *that* family. Yeah, right, they're all good.'

'Have you had any visitors?'

'What have visitors got to do with the price of flounders?'

I think of Roarer tangling with the vicissitudes of life. One thing in his favour is he wouldn't notice most of them, they'd go over his head faster than a slug from a Steyr Bullpup.

'It's *code*,' I tell him.

'Oh, right, gotcha,' he says again. 'No, no one's bothered us. Everyone's – Look Mr – you know, Smith, or whatever you're calling yourself – can I go home?'

'You are home. For the foreseeable future, that's where you happen to be, unless you want to make a graveyard your home. On second thoughts, maybe we better have a little talk.'

'When?' Roarer sounds like he's at his wits' end. It hasn't taken long. Then again, we're talking about Roarer's wits.

'Sooner rather than later.'

'What's that supposed to mean? You got no idea what it's like here, it's a *jungle*. We got mosquitoes as big as cows and ticks the size of dogs and as for the fleas, Jesus wept! I swear I saw this *boa constrictor* yesterday, it was –'

I cut him off before he lets the snake out of the bag, the cat out of the closet, the whereabouts of his and Imogene's and the rest of the tribe's place of hiding to whoever might be listening, by way of association.

'Sooner rather than later' can only have one meaning. But one thing's for
certain, it's not now.

Chapter 15

DEATH COMES TO THE CLEANERS

I'm outside the dry cleaner's that acts as a front for Errol 'The Pig' Shadie aka the brothel king. There's enough silence to hear the footsteps approach, and also enough moonlight on this clear, cold night to see the flash of the knife. I roll to one side, tucking my knees up hard under me. I thrust myself into the first position before launching myself skywards, coming back down to Ground Zero as far from the blade as I can, while still keeping myself as close to upright as humanly possible.

My attacker is a small joker — long hair, loose clothes for easy movement, and dingo-headed — but still as sharp as a stiletto. At any moment he could do me, given the chance. Only I'm not giving him the chance because I don't particularly want to be done. I hurl myself onto both hands and cartwheel in the opposite direction to the one he thinks I'll be going in, namely *at* instead of *away from* him, my whitesides crunching into his portside malar, *en passant*. But he's a pro, I can tell that by the speed with which he regains his equipoise, squatting over his centre of gravity like he's been in this situation before, and shaking his head to clear a sightline, knife gripped between thumb and forefinger like he's got more than a passing idea of how to use it.

It's Saturday night at the movies, and lovers are strolling arm in arm within a rifle's length of us, but that's no use when you're dead, and if I don't keep my wits about me that's how I'll find myself, well before the projectionist turns up the lights at intermission.

The joker's wearing black and he's skinny and as a result an anorexic alley cat would make more of a target.

My next move could be my last.

I don't want my next move to be my last.

Accordingly, I put my next move on *Pause*.

A ship's hooter sounds in the Harbour and maybe I flinch or maybe he just expects me to, but it can't be coincidence that the instant the hooter goes off he makes his death leap, and I find him hovering above me like a fruit bat on steroids. I've got my arms out and fingers spread the way James Cagney did in – well, like a funambulist on a tightrope – but since I was robbed of my portside thumb, I'm not as balanced as I might be, and I stumble.

That's when the joker's onto me.

It's more luck than good managements but at the last nanosecond I manage to deflect the blade, hearing it rattle against my ship's anchor cufflink as I bring up the portside arm, and even in this twilight of the gods I see the look of surprise on his half-dog face, at the same instant as I catch a whiff of animal sweat in his nearside armpit as he goes by. It's the smell that tells me I've got a chance. When a skinny joker sweats on a cold night, it means he's nervous, and when he's nervous it means he's acknowledging the possibility of defeat. All I've got to do is realise that possibility for him.

He's behind me, and like any experienced assassin he expects me to mimic his movements as though we're executing a death dance. But I stay the way I am, facing the window of the dry cleaner's together with the reflection of my would-be killer behind me. That reflection tells me he reckons that all he's got to do after moving is sink the knife in.

Which is what he tries to do.

They generally do plate glass shatter-proof these days. It's in all the city's building regulations. But this is the Cross, and they do things differently here. The vitreous material is very much of the temporary variety – the same variety as my would-be killer turns out to be made of. The alarm goes off and stays going off. By the illumination of the little blue gizmo above the hatchway, I can see the blood leaking from the figure lying among all the glass-spattered clothes in the dry-cleaner's.

Any man's death diminishes me because I am involved in Mankind. And therefore never ask for whom the bell tolls, it tolls for thee.

Or words to that effect.

I kneel and take the skinny joker's head in my hands. 'You're going to be all right.'

'No, I'm fucked. What did you have to go and move for?'

'I wanted to stay alive.'

He frowns, like he's trying to come to grips with a thought that's rapidly drifting towards the utmost limits of its comprehension. 'What about me?' If I didn't know better I'd say there was an attempt at a smile. 'You selfish bastard.'

But there's a reason I spent too many hours outside a dry cleaner's. It's the head office for a string of brothels which means there's something

I got to know. 'Did your boss kill Tommy Tycho?'

The back-to-base siren's hooting like a tawny frogmouth that hasn't had a feed since downing a native marsupial a week ago, while the blood of my would-be assassin is soaking into my hands like cordial at a children's knees-up, and I'm starting to believe I'm never going to get an answer, when I see the hood's thin little lips move.

I lean closer. 'What did you say?'

Again the smile, only I can see now that it's not really a smile at all but the sort of expression you see on a dead man, otherwise known as a rictus. 'Tycho had evidence against my boss in an underage prostitution case but my boss didn't do the job because . . .' I lean closer. '. . . someone got in before him.'

He's making a big effort and in that effort I can see his childhood and also how that childhood might have been something very much like mine had I not had my Aunt Rube. What could anyone expect other than this kid'd turn out the way he did, somebody's miserable little would-be assassin lurking in dark alleys, failing to kill innocent people for a pittance?

'So why did you try and off me?' I ask.

'Because you was prying, wasn't you? What did you think Pig was gunna do, send you a welcome card?'

I lay the skinny hood's head down as gentle as I can – just as a white car with a black stripe and the word SECURITY along the side noses around the corner.

Chapter 16

THE MAN THAT DIDN'T BELIEVE

They're big and they've shaved their heads and there's two of them. They've relieved me of the gat so I go quiet, or as quiet as can be expected under the circumstances, which involve them pushing me around a bit after the security turkey makes himself scarce, before dragging me in through an Orb-steel door and up two flights of stairs, where they dump me before the Pig like a truffle.

He's propping up a leather-inlay desk. If he was any smaller he could be mistaken for a babe-in-arms, except his head isn't one you'd find on any mother's bundle of joy — a phyzog like a wild boar's, with dead blowflies for eyes, a snout, and a mouth that might have been put there by a madman with delirium tremens and a lino-cutter.

'Well, if it isn't Mister Rainbow.'

Just like I know Sydney's underworld, Sydney's underworld knows me. But if there's any respect to go with the knowledge, it isn't mutual.

'Before I have you properly seen to, would you mind telling me why you were snooping around?' It's a nice voice, with lots of cultured tones in it. But that doesn't make the message any sweeter.

'I have reason to believe –'

'No reason, please. And no beliefs, either.' He picks up my gat off the inlay where one of the goons dropped it along with my hat and waves it around the orifice. 'You see, this is a reason-and-belief free zone. So none of your bullshit, okay? All I want to know is why you're poking your snout where it isn't wanted.'

'You killed Tommy Tycho.'

Pig laughs. It's nice to see people laugh. Only I wouldn't categorise Pig as people. 'That creep!' He replaces my gat next to my fedora. 'Rainbow, those of us who have made a success of ourselves in this world don't have much time for the likes of pretty boys. And Tycho was a pretty boy, someone who got lucky and thought all he had to do was lie back and enjoy it. He was also a slug and I don't like slugs anywhere near my

257

flowers.' Pig might have been referring to his goons, only I doubt it. 'But I didn't kill him. I would have liked to, but I didn't.' He frowns. 'The word around the traps, Rainbow, is that the job was done by none other than you.'

'Nice theory.' I don't call him Pig but that doesn't mean I got to call him anything else. 'Only there's such a thing as motive. You had one – I didn't. He jammed your missus – I didn't. He was providing witnesses against you in a prostitution case – I wasn't. You hated him – I didn't. I just happened to find myself at the scene of the crime.'

Pig shakes his head. 'Not crime, Rainbow – *crimes*. There were two murders that day and you happened to be at both of them.'

It's my turn to shake the head. '*After* the event. In both cases. And again: I didn't have a motive.'

Pig leans forward. 'Oh, but they say you did, they say you most absolutely did. Because I hear you were sweet on the girl.'

I'm being fitted for something, and it's not a new pair of Y-fronts.

'You probably think I'm playing with you in much the way a cat plays with a mouse,' Pig goes on. 'But the fact is that, while I had every reason to want Tycho dead, I was at the Dentist's on the morning in question.'

I do the frown. 'Your choppers look okay to me.'

Act stupid and people given you answers to questions you didn't even ask.

'And you call yourself a detective. De*fect*ive, more like.' Pig stares at his goons until they remember to simulate laughter. 'I was referring to my friend Karl *Laughing Gas* Petrie. That's where I was on the morning in question, with my dear friend Karl, arranging a delivery of dollies for my girls.'

The answer to the question I didn't ask.

'Okay,' I say, 'so you were obtaining drugs for underage prostitutes. That's bad but it's not murder. Why not let me put you in the clear on the death rap?'

Pig aims for an expression of disbelief, but only manages an outer. 'I don't need you or anyone else to put me in the clear. You might be a detective but you're not the cops. As far as they're concerned, whoever put Tycho away did everyone a favour. Which, as we all know, is why the police are running dead on the issue.' He glances at me out of his beady eyes. 'Before I have you dealt with, would you mind telling me how you got the name Rainbow? It sounds like something you'd find in a showbag, no offence intended.'

I tell him no offence taken and also how I got the name – how my mum was a pregnant Nimbin hippy who dived into a dam when her waters broke, and when I bubbled to the surface a rainbow formed. It could have been worse: could have been an eclipse, I add, stalling the inevitable until I can work out a way of avoiding it altogether.

It's the goons' turn to laugh now, and my interlocutor joins in the general merriment and the atmosphere in the designer orifice is close to festive.

This is my chance, so I take it, placing my elbows in the region where the thugs are laughing, before turning on the half-step to put myself in the appropriate position when their heads come down. I haven't got two fists for nothing, and I'm busy deploying them to good advantage when a bullet whangs past my head. I crouch as Pig looses off a second slug out of my Holy Terror, stepping behind him and applying a half-Nelson before relieving him of my gat as the thugs get to their feet and come for me.

I twist Pig's trotter. 'Tell them to stay where they are or I'll break your *raison d'être*.'

Pig squeals. 'Stay where you are!'

The thugs stay where they are.

I tighten the hold. 'Now listen up. You wanted me taught a lesson and I'm very much inclined to return the favour. However, not having all the fine education you got, I won't, unless you force me to. Instead, I'm going to find out who killed Tycho if it kills me. And if it turns out to be you, I'll be back — not because I'm carrying a candle for Tycho but because of the other death that day. Got it?'

There's no answer so I shake his responses.

'I said, *got it*?'

'Yeah, I got it,' Pig grunts. 'But I didn't do it.'

'Then tell me who did.'

Pig's still got a squeak in him. 'I don't know. But if it was anyone, it would have been the Dentist. Tycho took a load of bo-diddlies off him and didn't pay for them. Consequently the Dentist don't like him.'

It could be true. Then again it could be a bunch of raspberries. I turn to go.

'Rainbow?'

'Yeah?'

Pig's cradling his twisted trotter. 'I believe Tycho hasn't been buried yet.'

'I thought you didn't believe anything.'

'As I said, I didn't kill him. But that doesn't mean I didn't *want* him dead. I'd like to go to his funeral, if only to pay my final disrespects.'

He chucks me a look that might be described as pleading, if it was on someone else. 'So could you organise that for me?'

I tell Pig I'll keep it in mind.

Chapter 17

BREAKFAST WITH RUBE

It's time to pay Aunt Rube a visit. Rube's presently out of the freezer: sometimes she's in and sometimes she's out, and at the moment she's back in the home she's always had, a rundown terrace in a rundown part of East Sydney. This is where she brought me up in the only way she knew how, after Dad dumped me on her when Mum blew her lolly on the fruit farm.

I take the alternative route, past the bespoke tailor's in Oxford Street that sells me a replacement for an outfit that's become too careworn to go unnoticed in public. I go for a nice yellow shirt with pink polka-dots, a bag of fruit in pale-green linen with silver and gold flecks in it, and a yellow fedora.

Rube's still Rube, a slight figure with short-cropped hair, all skin and ribs, but tough as Kraut steel when she needs to be. She's the hardest little number you'll ever come across – weight for age – this side of a kung-fu parlour in downtown Chinatown.

'You're looking well.' She glances up and down the boulevard before shutting the door. 'So what's she like?'

'She's got cornflower-blue eyes.'

I radioed ahead so Rube's already got the tomatoes, eggs and mushrooms humming on the back burner.

'*Has*, Rainbow, *has* – not *gott*. *Gott*'s German for God.' She sighs like she always does when she corrects me. 'But you always were a sucker for blue, weren't you? So, she a risk?'

I shrug as I sit. 'She can handle a gun and she can think fast.' Rube's one person that can make me see things just by asking questions. 'So, okay, I guess, all right, yeah . . .'

Rube shakes her head. 'Jesus, Rainbow, you and women. So what else are you involved in, apart from the eyes?'

With the daylight flickering through the small window lighting up the Willow Pattern on the dresser, I bring her up to speed.

'So to avenge this Annabel Franklin dame,' she says after I've finished my spiel, 'you're taking on a case that's going to pay as much as an also-ran at Randwick?'

'I got to do it, Rube.'

'Of course you *have* to, Rainbow. That's how you're made.' She sighs again and looks at me thoughtfully. 'And if anyone would know how you're made, I would, wouldn't I – seeing as I made you.' She composts herself. 'Is there anything I can do?'

'As it happens, Rube, yeah, there is.' I tell her the list of phone calls, calls I'd rather my name wasn't attached to.

'That all?'

I nod. 'Unless there's something about Tycho you know that I don't.'

Rube shakes her head. 'Only the fact that everyone hated him – but then the whole world knows that. And also the miraculous fact that he was clean. Because they never pinned anything on him, did they – apart from the toe tag they put on him after he died.'

I polish off the caffeine. 'Yeah, quick on his feet, was our Tommy.'

'You could say that. Then again you could say he wasn't quick enough.' She looks at me over my empty mug; it's the kind of look I'm used to, the look of a person that's taken care of you since you were a babe, the sort of look you can never escape from. 'Okay, I'll do the calls, Rainbow. But you'll have to do me a favour in return.'

I glance at her wary. 'Depends on the favour.'

'I want you to use Rory.'

'I'm using him as much as I can. He's looking after the kid in the safe house. Apart from which, he's found God and got married.'

'Didn't you tell me he was prepared to go back to killing in order to finance his beliefs? And can't your new-found flame look after Imogene? You've already told me she can handle herself.'

My turn to do the sigh. 'Okay, Rube.' I haul myself off the stool. 'Meanwhile, I better get moving or I won't get moving at all.' Rube suddenly looks smaller than I remember. 'But what about you?'

She shrugs. 'The day you need to care about me, Rainbow, I'll take a one-way boat trip to the Azores.'

Chapter 18

SAFE NO MORE

It's a breezy winter's morning with seagulls dipping their orange-red ice-breakers in the spindrift as I push off past the punters at the No Peer café. I scan the faces to see if there are any with murder in them, before parking myself low in the belly of the boat, taking hold of the tiller and setting sail in the opposite direction to the one that leads to the safe house. The tide's out and mud's in the ascendancy – greasy muck like the stuff they started the world with, a primaeval soup steaming off the shore of the bush-mangled island. I beach the skiff after going round the world to get there – and am just starting the long haul up the uneven steps into the jungle when someone starts taking pot shots at me.

I dive into the undergrowth, a tangle of blackberries, biddy bush and lantana. There's nothing natural about it, just as there's nothing normal about the gunfire. A second shot wings past my cakehole, followed by a third. The weapon's a .275 by the sound of it – and also by the sound of it, the safe house where I parked Imogene is safe no more. My heart goes into ragtime, the sort of beat Charlie Ellis was always after but could never find. Imogene's up there somewhere. And by the sound of the artillery, there's a good chance she'll never eat ice-cream again.

I resume the ascent, only a lot quicker this time, keeping away from the makeshift steps – and fighting the whips and tendrils of creepers at the same time as I'm fighting my fears. It could be whip birds, or it might be fairies. Except that whip birds and fairies don't ricochet past your skull and leave marks on rocks in passing.

A deep, dark, cantilevered cliff blocks my path and I've got to work my way around it. It's slippy-slide time, with the whitesides turning to one-tones and my heart to mush. Because somewhere among all this gunfire is my daughter.

The shooter's either Pandora or the killer that snuffed out Tycho and Annabel – unless it's no more than yet another random psychopath.

There's a direct line to the hut, but I don't take it. If someone's gunning for me, that's what they'll have their sights on. I have to get there sooner or later, but sooner or later's not now. Accordingly, I head for the high ground, leaving the Smith & Wesson nestled in the shoulder-holster as I hand-and-knee it past the ablution block, up around the dead-logs-for-charity section and the mosh pit where pioneers mined out naked dreams in the island's innocent past.

After that, it's around the remains of the dead kangaroo and the live red belly snake that appears out of its hole in the ground, angling away from the shack so I can come down on the bullet thrower from the high ground, climbing to my feet by the big smoky gum and hightailing it into the wilderness.

I could be a brush-tailed wallaby or a kangaroo.

Then again, I could be dead.

Another bullet gets airmailed my way, followed by another.

They're onto me, which means I got to switch tactics and take the alternative route, the one that takes me via the water tank I installed when the old dame first put this place my way more years ago than I care to remember, along in front of the wind-turbine and the nest of solar-plates, so I'll have the height advantage when I meet up with whoever's loosing off the musketry, as well as having the sun behind me, right where I want it to be.

Suddenly, there's a whole lot of silence, silence in which I can contemplate the panorama from the top of the mountain, the ins and outs of the Hawkesbury and the toy train trundling over the centipede bridge to nowhere, experiencing the cool breeze that tells me I better do something fast, or not bother doing it at all.

Movement below at 10 o'clock.

To hell with the noise, the gunfire can only mean one thing and that is that Roarer and the dame are putting up a fight. It might be Pandora or it might be the assassin, but two things are for certain – it's not a couple of Seventh Day Adventists spreading the good word, or the Avon Lady.

I haul out the equaliser and head south. My portside whiteside catches on a ficus root but I manage to change the fall into a tumble. I bring up an arm, lose my equilibrium, and slam into the water tank. A shot zings into the tank.

'Come out with your hands up or you won't be coming out at all!'

I recognise the dulcets.

'Roarer!'

'Rainbow!'

'Rory, you bloody idiot! Hold your fire!'

'It's not my fire,' he yells back, 'it's the kid's. What are you doing scaring the crap out of us?'

I shelve the gat and work my way back to reality.

They've been doing target practice – Roarer, Monica Best and Imogene. Don't worry about safe houses and forget about silence being golden, or even copper-coloured – the four of them have been busy whanging away at tin cans while Rory's dame and the ex are having a parley for two in the cowshed.

I herd the shooters back to the chateau.

'Did you bring my box, Daddy?'

I can't remember everything. 'Sorry, kid, I left it on the boat.'

The kid takes the information in her stride. 'Roarer says I'm shooting real good.'

'*Well*,' I tell her.

I sense the dame striding beside me stiffen.

'Is that all you can say – *Well*? Imogene's been so pleased with herself, hitting the Fourex cans at a hundred yards right in the middle of the exxes, and all you can say is *Well*?'

I pick my way through the minefield. 'I was talking about her grammar, not her accuracy.' Why do I feel like Aunt Rube all of a sudden? 'The kid said she was shooting good when she should of said *well*.' I pat the head that's bobbing along around about my Plimsoll line. 'Good work, Immo.'

'Thanks,' she tells me. 'Daddy?'

We're near the shack. Dark shadows lie under the rough-hewn pylons and the rickety structure stands atop them like the aftermath of an accident in a nuclear reactor.

'Yeah?'

'When can I learn more about sleuthing than just shooting at beer cans?'

I shrug. 'You're learning all the time, kid. And the name of today's lesson is: *No one's safe nowhere*.'

Mrs Rory doesn't want to be left alone, Roarer's sick of being holed up on the island, and Imogene's not going anywhere, so I agree to a change of venue – swapping the island for the boat, with Roarer in charge of logistics – while I leave with Monica. According to Roarer, she's got an eye like an eagle, and that kind of talent might come in handy where we're headed.

'I'll drop you back at your place,' I say to her. There's a nice breeze playing with her skirts as we wait at the station. I'm thinking about the past as well as fate and destiny, and in the process forget all about consistency. 'I got no right to expose you to any more danger.'

Monica's eyes rearrange themselves into silver bullets. 'What if I happen to like danger?'

The train arrives and we climb aboard.

'Everyone wants to be safe.'

'In that case, I'm not everyone.'

Any one of our fellow passengers could be after us – a short-handled knife tucked under their tresses, a sawn-off shottie stuffed down a trackie leg, or a homemade bomb nestled in their underpants.

A way out of the mess would be a one-way ticket to Bullamakanka under assumed identities. But there are two problems with that particular solution – it doesn't take Imogene into account, and there's still the debt I got to settle with Annabel. I glance at the dame as one of City Rail's built-in rock-and-roll curves launches me into her. I straighten myself quick.

'Okay, but you got to do what I tell you to, *when* I tell you.'

'Of course.' The expression on her dial-up's as innocent as a babe's.

So why don't I believe her?

Chapter 19

THE DAME UPSTAIRS

On the surface, Sydney is the destination of choice for the happy set, drawn by the sun, surf and playful sexuality. On the surface, nicely-behaved traffic works its way neat as toys along clean streets, sailboats scud sweet across an unsullied harbour, and in the wee hours of the morning fun-loving youngsters kick up sandalled feet in a happy and innocent playground of drug-free nightclubs.

If you want surface, subscribe to *The Sydney Morning Horrible*. The *Horrible* doesn't know shit from sewage, gang warfare from a spat in the playground, or road rage from a bout of post-cabbage flatulence. To the *Horrible* there's no underworld and the death of Tommy Tycho's nothing more than an annoying blip in the general Peter-Pan-and-Wendy run of things.

Accordingly, on Day Two after the death, the rag runs this reassuring paragraph on page numero due, the place where the blatt explains what it should have said but didn't, or could have said but forgot to, or tries to sidestep the next libel suit — its ultra-busy Centre of Correction:

CLARIFICATION

In some issues yesterday, we ran a picture of a headless body. We apologise if this picture offended anyone. Meanwhile, in connection with this story, Inspector Leytton, who is in charge of Operation John the Baptist, says that — contrary to rumours suggesting otherwise — police are pursuing their investigations with rigour. Police add that there is no evidence that the death of a young woman on the same morning had anything to do with the Tycho murder . . .

And Happy Fantasies, too, to Inspector Leytton. Because if this item confirms anything, it's that the cops are running deader than a flattened maggot in the deaths of both Tommy Tycho and the dame. Another thug's off the streets and they're grateful that someone did their dirty work for them. Call it collateral damage or call it unfortunate. But as Inspector Leytton might put it, *if you know anything that might help police with their inquiries — don't trouble us about it and we won't trouble you.*

We climb off the 412 six blocks early and trawl the rest of the way in our slippers. The walk gives me the chance to appreciate yet another of Monica Best's physical attributes. I'm six-foot-plus-something in my socks — the ones with the built-in air-conditioning in them — but the dame beside me doesn't have to look up to me to be on the level.

We've been back to Monica's place and picked up her work gear — a nice skirt, leopardskin tights, and a top that would have been tight on her when she was two — and I'm busy looking the other way when a thought strikes me. Like, where's all the tape — red, blue or otherwise? There's no crime scene, no blue and white ribbon strung all over the place like a cop's Christmas, and no short-arse rozzer hanging around with his hands behind his back singing he still calls Australia home while he waits for the relief shift. There's nothing at all to indicate a murder's been committed.

There's running dead and there's slamming an investigation into reverse. The cops aren't even pretending. Gives me food for thought, while the dame provides the dessert.

'How do I look?'

'Yeah,' I tell her.

'Is that all you can say — *Yeah*?'

On another dame I'd say the words were loaded, but on her they got a laugh attached — a full-hipped, throaty swagger of a laugh that's got me down on my knees on the floorboards and begging for more.

'Yeah,' I tell her again.

'I can see you're impressed.' She aims for a grimace but misses and comes up with a smile. 'Now if you'd just let me know where we're headed, I can accessorise accordingly.'

The joint's suddenly too small. Someone ought to open the windows.

'We're going to pay a visit to a joker called Petrie,' I say, and she frowns like she's just remembered something. 'Don't worry, you wouldn't know him. He's one of the city's bad men.'

Monica nods thoughtfully as she moves around her apartment, lithe as a cat in her leotards, the sort of creature you can appreciate evolution by, imagining her leaping about the jungle with the grace of a gazelle, the speed of an antelope, and the power of an anthropoid ape – while all she's doing is chucking a bunch of accessories into a side pocket of her anorak.

Before departing, we pay another visit to the floor below. Again, there's no sign of a crime scene. Annabel's door is closed, the fire escape's saying hello to a vacuum, and the seeing-eye in the door labelled 302 – the apartment at the other end of the hall from Annabel's – is unblinking.

I bang on the door anyway.

'Who is it?'

I stand aside from the peephole and motion Mary Poppins to come up with the necessary chit-chat.

'I'm from upstairs.'

The door's opened by a fat man wearing a white stick and shades.

Mary Poppins asks the question.

'Have the police been to see you?'

'Why would the police come to see me?'

'Because of – what happened.'

'What happened?'

It's clear he's the embodiment of the three chimpanzees – hears nothing, sees nothing, says even less.

'Nothing,' Monica tells him.

'I thought not,' says the blind man, and slams the door.

Chapter 20

INCIDENT IN A TOY SHOP

We're up near Central station and zeroing in on Hephzibah's, when Monica does something that sets my alarms jangling. She sidesteps a thug in a way that suggests she's done the same thing before, a slippy-slide, slow-dipping movement followed by an instant straighten up, like what just happened didn't, before resuming an even keel again – mast straight, sails furled, rock steady, like a beautiful yacht on a smooth sea in the dead-calm aftermath of a high wind.

I hear the echo of my aunt's last words on the subject: *Watch her.*

I shoot her a glance. 'How about providing some kind of back story? Apart, that is, from the bit about the mercenary father that went transvestite after losing the use of his legs.'

She shrugs. 'Private college.'

'After college.'

'Finishing school.'

'After finishing school.'

She looks across and our eyes meet. 'Shift work.'

'Meaning?'

'Security guard, debt collection, bodyguarding, chucking drunks out of clubs, that kind of thing.'

Oh, *that* kind of thing.

'You mean you bounced people?'

She nods. 'Like medicine balls.'

She had a hero soldier for a father and it got in her blood. It would account for all the nice movements. But I still got my doubts. In fact, I got even more doubts than I started with.

'This is dangerous territory we're entering – even for a hockey front forward, or whatever you were.'

Monica stops and does another shrug. It's a nice shrug, the finishing-school shoulders rising to form something like the apex of an eagle's wings, while the rest of the body stays as still as Venus's, statuesque in her shell as she rises from the vapours.

'Aren't you forgetting something?' The voice alone would finish anyone. 'Annabel happened to be my friend, too.'

Like a lot of businesses in Sydney, Hephzibah's is no more than a front. The sign under the canvas awning says they sell toys. But there are toys, and there are toys.

We enter and the stink of dope – not the opium-derivative variety, but the stuff you put on model aeroplanes to keep them airborne – hits me. It's the sort of stench that goes straight to your sinuses and stays there, then sets about eating you from the inside out, like a herd of starving piranhas. A father's amazing his kid by making a car move without the use of any noticeable devices, because the kid hasn't noticed his dad's standing on a button that activates the electronics. I see they've brought back Meccano.

Apart from father and son and the Meccano, there are two mothers and a granny, plus several more kids, as well as scale models of killer jets, military-style tanks that budding Himmlers can trash the lawn with, toy soldiers, a bunch of drones, swords that look like the real thing, too many gats – plus kites to make the joint look as innocent as a cubs' camp – and a shop assistant.

'Yes, sir?'

'I want to see the Dentist.'

'Maybe I can help.'

'And maybe you can't.'

'I mean this *Dentist* you're referring to might be a product we haven't heard of yet.' The kid's fiddling with his iPhone like he means to use it. 'If so, maybe we could try and chase it down. After all, we at Hephzibah's are always on the lookout for new products. Innovation equals expansion and expansion equals greater profits. And in the age of the Global Financial Crisis, greater profits are better than sex.'

If he knows what he's talking about, that makes one of him.

'Are you working at being thick, or were you born that way?' I don't want to hit him, he might break. 'Look, pal, get me Laughing Gas.'

He laughs. 'I think you've come to the wrong fun camp, Mister.'

That's when I step forward into him, and that's when the second assistant hauls up alongside. The second assistant's a meat in a black T-shirt that tells me he's kept up his membership in the City gym.

'Why don't you piss off?'

Unlike Monica, the meat hasn't been to finishing school. Accordingly, I don't have to give him the finishing school treatment.

'There's a lady present,' I say quietly. I take his arm and twist it enough to make liquorice out of it. 'Now tell me where I can find the Dentist and I'll let you go.'

There's a pulse hammering in the vicinity of the occipital. 'He ain't here.'

'It seems like you want to join him.'

Chapter 21

A VISIT TO THE DENTIST'S

Altercations aren't good for business, so the first assistant starts herding out the mamas and the papas and the rest of the impedimenta. He slams the not-so-innocent door behind them before making the necessary communication on his flapdoodle.

'The Dentist's on his way down,' he tells me.

I let the meat fall to the floor. 'No, he's not.' I haul out the gat. 'On account of we're on our way up.'

Monica's right behind me as I head for the mystery door, the one at the back of the play pen between the Hornby wind-ups and a scale model of a drone, reaching the steps just as the cavalry appears on the landing.

We duck under the stairs and Monica raises one beautiful eyebrow. 'Where are we?'

'This is organised crime *par excellence*,' I say to the tune of the musketry from above. 'This city's carved up like meat and potatoes, and it's not according to culinary taste. If Australia's a den of iniquity, then Sydney is Crime Central — some thugs control brothels, others weaponry, while others have got the mortgage on money laundering. Then you've got race fixing, politician bribing and crooked cops — this is the age of the specialist, after all.'

She still doesn't look as surprised as she might be.

'So what's this particular part of the scenery?'

'Dentist's a drug lord. You heard of a guy called Antonio Mokbel? Well, this guy makes Mokbel look like a choirboy. He controls most of this town's cocaine and amphetamines — ice, speed, juice, whatever you want to call it — and then some. Dentist's to drugs what Dame Joan Sutherland was to singing.'

They're coming for us.

'He's been hauled in several times, but it's only ever been for show. All he does is buy off another copper or judge or politician or offs yet another witness; whatever it takes to stay free.'

Why do I sense that the dame already knows what I'm telling her?

'Go on.'

'Ten years ago he was arrested for importing enough ephedrine to make a billion dollars' worth of ecstasy. Yeah, that's *b* for *bustido*. We're talking some not-so-minor country's entire Gross National Product.'

'Yet he's still at large?'

'He's more than at large, he's bigger than life – other people's.'

That's when the sky falls in. It's like one of those paintings with little men in them – lots of little men, as well as several big ones – down the stairs as well as from the general direction of the toy shop.

We don't go quiet, but we go. My head's playing *The Bells of St Mary's*, while a quick check of the dame reveals she hasn't fared much better, as they haul us up the steps into fairyland.

Shelves reach to the ceiling – and it's a high ceiling – shelves packed with boxes and bottles and little white packets with little smiley faces on them, and up and down the aisles run little forklift tractors without anyone driving them, stopping now and again to take down a palette of happy-haps before moving on again, while a non-stop chain-drive rattles around the periphery. It's Henry Ford's assembly line a century on.

If this joint's anything to go by, a billion dollar's worth of nasties would be no more than the tip of a very big iceberg. It's a highway to Hell, and that's where we find ourselves, shoved, prodded and kicked up another set of stairs into a big white room with a nice big, wide window opening onto bleak sunshine.

And in the centre of the room, a black chair.

Monica's on the floor and I'm in a dilemma.

I've been in enough dentist's rooms in my time to know that I'm inhabiting one now, a place full of grey metal cabinets with little grey metal drawers in them and an arc lamp hanging by a giant articulated arm from the centre of the ceiling, while a sweet little nurse in a white mask waits by the chair.

'Would you care to sit?' she murmurs from behind the mask.

'No,' I tell her.

Monica's writhing on the floor while around her stand a hurtful of hoods clutching too many machine-guns.

That's when the Dentist makes his appearance, and it's an appearance I don't like. He's got one of those faces you'd expect on a politician or an Emoticon, nice and round with little crinkles around the eyes, the sort that pretends it would never kill you, even if you didn't vote for it. Black hair done ordinary. But it's the threads that give him away. He's wearing a long white coat – the sort they put on shrinks in loony bins – like a kid playing dress-ups, with his sleeves rolled up and neat little feet perched in high-polished pumps poking out the bottom and delicate mitts with a pair of electric-blue Mediflex gloves on them. The kind of gloves favoured by sandwich hands, dentists and murderers. All round Mr Nice Guy.

But I Googie-egged him before we set out and nice guy he's not. Karl 'Laughing Gas' Petrie started life with the benefit of parents, but changed his status to orphan at age eleven, when he killed them. He came from the hard edge of town, the side that specialises in sudden death and general mayhem and too many unwanted pregnancies. His dad was a standover man who killed punters who stood up to being stood over, while his mum spent most of her life committing felony and extortion and being an accessory before, during and after the fact to a great many murders.

His was a childhood without toys.

It was on his mum's first night out of the slammer after her fourth stint in jail that he killed them – using skills inherited from both sides of the gene pool – shooting them with a sawn-off shottie that his daddy had given him for Christmas. After that, he torched the family home sweet home with a flame-thrower that his mother ditto, in order to make the affair look like little more than an unfortunate accident. They couldn't pin anything on him. For a start, no one believed he could have done it, he looked so nice.

And he hasn't looked back since – graduating to drugs before buying his own toyshop, plus a lot of important people – with the proceeds. Still got his own hair, to all intents and porpoises. Black hair, done ordinary.

He steps into the room and when he does, his army of goons steps aside respectfully.

On the floor, Monica groans and shuffles her hands in the pockets of her windcheater like she's having a bad dream, after which she rolls back and lies still again.

'So you're Mister Rainbow.' The Dentist adjusts his gloves. 'Pig said you might pay a visit, so I got it all ready for you.'

He looks nice, speaks even nicer. So why have I got this very bad feeling?

'I hope you enjoyed your inspection of our facitity.' He smiles, revealing a set of pearlies that any dentist would be proud of. But I've lived long enough not to trust nice enamel work. 'I understand you're under the delusion I might have killed someone.' Again the white teeth, simulating what he must think is a smile.

I come to bury Caesar, not to praise him.

'I'm not under the delusion that anyone killed anyone,' I say. 'I happen to know it for a fact, twice over. For a start, you had an excellent motive to kill Tommy Tycho.'

He gives me his dentist's smile, the one with all the teeth in it. 'Just like everyone else this town.'

'So where were you the day he copped it?'

The Dentist's smile turns into a dentist's laugh. Nice teeth, even right up the back where most people's are rotten. 'I was with Pig, although having the upper hand as I do' – he flaps his plastic-gloved mitts – 'I don't really have to tell you anything. But what I can say is that if I *could* have killed Tycho, believe me, I would have. The bastard took a lot of product from me and never paid for it.' The Dentist holds out his nicely-gloved hands, fingers spread. 'And no one – I repeat *no one* – does that kind of thing to Papa Petrie and gets away with it.'

He nudges Monica with his foot. She doesn't stir.

'As a result I find myself *personally* not all that unhappy at Tycho's passing. What I am unhappy about is that I didn't *personally* get to organise it.'

'Meaning you didn't do it?'

'You're dead right I didn't do it. And I've got no cause to lie, Rainbow, because after I've finished with you, you won't be in a position to use anything you know against anyone.'

He's moved so close I can smell his madness.

'But we're not here to talk about unhappiness, because they don't call me Laughing Gas for nothing.' With one nice, small hand, he indicates the chair. 'Please be seated, won't you?'

'No,' I tell him. 'You've answered my question, so now I can leave, along with the dame.'

Laughing Gas laughs and this time I figure it's a real laugh so I also figure that this time he's got something to laugh about.

I bend down to pick up the dame anyway.

That's when I see her eyes flicker and also that she's frowning at me, and not for the first time I figure she knows something I don't – and is prepared to do something about it.

I straighten, step back and find myself in the arms of the goons that aren't standing over the dame.

Chapter 22

THE TASTE OF PAIN

'Put him in the chair.'

They put me in the chair.

'Hold him down.'

The goons hold me down.

'Now knock out the dame.'

The thugs with the dame look up.

'What'll we use?'

'We've had a run on the Midazolam, so use the narcs.'

A shuffle from the figure on the floor.

'Which ones, boss?'

'Use your head.'

'I thought you told us to use the narcs.'

Something's not computing. Maybe it's a problem with the software, or maybe I just heard wrong.

'Why are you sedating the dame, when you intend operating on me?'

The Dentist does his thing with the teeth. 'All the more reason to sedate her and not you.'

That's when I struggle but it's no good because the goons have got hold of me – one on the legs, two on the arms, and another one holding my head – forcing me down into the banana lounge until the only thing I can move is my eyes.

The Dentist turns back to the goons. 'I've changed my mind, let's try the gas.'

The nurse bends over Monica and she's got a black rubber face mask in her little hands and from the mask hangs a long black tube – the sort with bend-wrinkles in it much like the wrinkles around Laughing Gas's eyes – and the black tube's attached to the inside of a black case. And while the goons are holding Monica, the nurse is fitting the mask over her face like she's intent on saving life, only I don't think saving lives is quite what she has in mind. There are a bunch of little black knobs on the case and the nurse starts fiddling with them. I hear the hiss of escaping gas.

'Nitrous oxide.' The Dentist's looking on with interest. 'The anaesthetic of choice in the nineteenth century, and amazingly still used now.' He frowns. 'Look, I'm sorry, nurse, I've changed my mind again. Let's use the narcotic.'

The nurse nods, puts away her box of tricks, and reaches for a syringe. At the same time, Monica writhes and fiddles some more. After which, the nurse inserts the syringe and she ceases to fiddle.

The Dentist leans over me, his kind eyes glinting. 'Now would you like an anaesthetic?'

'No.'

'That's excellent, because you aren't going to get one.'

That's when the goons tighten their hold and that's also when the Dentist forces something in my mouth, something made of plastic and steel with a ratchet attached to it, something that tastes the way pain always tastes – a mixture of tincture of iodine and mercury and fear – and with each turn of the ratchet, my mouth is forced open wider and –

The nurse shoves a suction hook down against my lower palate while I stare into a big plate-glass searchlight with the word BELMONT in the centre of it, like the bull's-eye in a very big target.

Only the light isn't the target, I am.

'Forceps.'

The dame palms the Dentist a pair of bent-ended pliers and I don't want to know what he's going to use them for so I try to focus on the light while he's probing. But his face is so close to mine that I can't see anything and I can't smell anything else but the ham and the anchovies followed by burnt toast he had for breakfast, and I can see the little green flecks in one of his eyes, and it looks very much like insanity.

That's when the pain starts.

He's got hold of a tooth in the jaws of his pliers – one of my right upper molars, I think – and he's tugging it like he wants to make a Jacobean chair leg, leaning into the job until the whole world of pain is concentrated in the back of my mouth like it's been inserted through a microscope backwards, and it's waterboarding, electro-voltaic shock, leg-breaking, fingernail-removal, eye-gouging – the works.

The hands of the goon gripping my face could double as snowshoes and he's got a knee in my ribs for extra purchase, when there's a crack, a wrenching snap like the world's been torn asunder, and the Dentist withdraws his fist, and out of the corner of my eye I see the wreckage of what was once my back tooth, a jagged lump of enamel with what might be tomato sauce adhering to it, only I know it's not sauce, it's blood, my blood, and I can taste its bitter-sweet saltiness as it fills my mouth so fast it threatens to choke me.

'Oh dear,' he says, inspecting the tooth. 'There wasn't a thing wrong with it.' He stands back. 'Shock has a curious effect on people, Mister Rainbow, but when you recover, you're going to do me a favour. Find out who killed Tycho, and I'll make sure I give him something for his trouble.'

If there's a logic in all that, it escapes me.

Just like my pearly white.

Chapter 23

IT PAYS TO ACCESSORISE

In my efforts to distract myself from the pain I think of two things:

One: That the steel arm that could hold a rhinoceros might be the key to our escape; and

Two: Roarer said something about *an eye for an eye and a tooth for a tooth*.

I try to work out how the two might go together, except my mind's dulling over, so I focus instead on the word BELMONT in the bull's-eye of the spotlight and tell myself that *Belmont* means *Beautiful mountain*, and I think, *Yeah, mountains are beautiful, they're there to prove yourself on, and also to teach you that what doesn't kill you only makes you stronger.*

That's when the vice closes over my next good tooth and I smell the baby-nappy smell of the Dentist's gloves and see his jaw clench along with the jaws of the extractor like he intends to *bite* the thing out of me without benefit of pliers, and I also note that one of his eyes has turned into a pinprick while the other stays standard, and sweat's beading on his forehead, while the flow of blood to my extremities is ceasing where the goons are gripping onto them . . .

. . . when suddenly the world explodes.

Belmont.

As the cataclysm gathers force, that's what I cling to, that one eye, a Cyclop's eye, an *eye-for-an-eye* eye – one pupil a maverick while the other's a piece of masonry – and I wonder how come I didn't notice it before, maybe it was because I had other things on my mind, like what's going to happen to Imogene when I'm no longer around, not to mention Monica, who all of a sudden is all over the place – a Catherine-wheel, a termagant, a Roman candle, a factory of fireworks into which someone has just dropped a match, causing the whole shebang to go skywards, the goons to slacken their hold, and the Dentist to jab himself with his forceps, as the dame's right instep collects him across the bridge of his bugle, the side of her left hand chops down on goon numero uno's *sterno-mastoid*, her right fist connects with the *solar plexus* of goon numero due, while the third goon cops a thump to the ribs that's going to require surgery if he's ever going to return to being upright.

I come out of the space where post-operative shock puts people and send the Dentist flying into the oxygen equipment, before giving the fourth goon a Liverpool kiss plus a whiteside into the gut.

But I forgot Nursery Girl.

By the time I unforget her she's no longer wearing a mask but a grimace, and she's got a gun in her mitt and standing nicely positioned between the chair and the spittoon, while me and Monica are between a ratchet and a hard face, the goons shaking their heads and the Dentist climbing to his feet with vengeance in his eyes, where before there had only been madness.

'How did you do that?' Monica standing in the middle of the floor with barely a hair out of place, looking like she might have come straight from a garden party, the sweetest of expressions on her beautiful visage, legs together, back straight, arms demure by her sides, wrists cocked.

'I went to finishing school.'

'I don't mean how you dealt with the thugs, I mean how you managed to counter the effects of the narcotic, how come you aren't comatose.'

'Moron.'

The goons are back on their feet, the assistant has swung the gun Monica's way, the Dentist's got vengeance at the forefront of his *cerebellum*, and all Monica can do is abuse them.

'Maybe you haven't heard of Naloxone.' She shrugs her shoulders. 'Naloxone hydrochloride is an opioid antagonist, which means it's an effective counter to the anaesthetic effects of narcotics. Naloxone starts to work in roughly a minute, after it's been administered intravenously.'

She's standing like Annie Gets Her Gun and I'm wondering what she's on about, considering Nursie's got the drop on her, while all the dame seems interested in is giving away trade secrets for nothing.

'As it happens, learning from Rainbow that we were paying you a visit – and being well aware of your tendencies – I armed myself with what I might require in the way of protection and when you kept changing your mind I had to keep selecting another antidote. You see . . .'

All eyes are on the hand that's emerging from the pocket of her windjacket, the one with the red-topped needle in it, and consequently no one's paying attention to the hand that's emerging from the other pocket, the one with the gun in it, the gun that she inherited from her mercenary daddy – along with the cold-hearted capacity to kill people.

It's a hip shot and she shoots the dental assistant in the leg and she sags down against the banana chair like she's suddenly tired of being a dental assistant, and all that goes with it.

'*That's* an anaesthetic.' Monica's smiling the sort of smile she must have learnt at finishing school. 'Ready to leave now, Rainbow?'

I shake my head. Partly to clear it, but also to indicate the negative. 'I need a minute with our friend here. I want to know who killed Tycho.'

'Brutus Kariakis is the person you're after,' murmurs the Dentist. 'He has access to all kinds of guns, including the type of weaponry that took out Tycho. And he's been gunning for Tycho ever since he relieved him of a cache of weapons intended for the Mafia, and bragged about it.'

'So why didn't you tell me that before?'

The Dentist holds out his hands. He's still wearing the Mediflex. 'You didn't ask me that before.'

I shake my head and turn to the dame. 'Ready now?'

She's got her head cocked and I hear what she's hearing, the sound of clodhoppers on the stairs, and they're not in three-four time, or any sort of time, they're a boiling surf at Bondi and they're on their way to dump us. I figure that's why the Dentist was so forthcoming about Kariakis, he's been stalling after calling up the boys in blue with his electronic gimmickry, the sort of trick fathers move toy cars with, the button on the floor by the chair.

'Wait.' The bastard still wants a favour. 'You gotta tell me – where and when's the funeral?'

It's the same thing Pig asked me, and no doubt for the same reason. But I put the question anyway. 'Why do you want to know?'

'Because I want to spit on Tycho's corpse and dance on his grave. I want to make sure the bastard's dead and see him buried. Is that too much to ask?'

'How do you know we're going to leave you alive?'

'Because I know you, Rainbow. I know that despite the way you dress, you got quality; despite the way you talk, you got style; and despite just about everything else about you, you got a sense of ethics. That's how I know you're not going to kill anyone.' The gendarmes are at the door. 'Now tell me: when and where are they burying Tycho?'

I shrug. 'Keep an eye on the *Wasted and Pasted* section of *The Daily Amoeba*, it's about the only thing the newspapers are good for.' I start for the window, Monica providing cover while whoever's outside is forcing the hatch. 'Or ask one of your friends on Facebook, if you've got any, or do a tweet or a blog or a corblimy.'

That's when the world explodes a second time.

283

Chapter 24

FLIGHT OF THE ANGELS

The thing about being anonymous is you can't allow yourself to get caught. Get caught and they got you – DNA, fingerprints, face scan, blood type, the works. You exist, and the moment you exist, it's game over. It's called identity theft. So when the rozzers bust down the door, I get the hell out. The alternative is to file my life in the history books.

I calculate there's a gross of them – that's twenty in the new money but I prefer *gross* – a clutch of state-sponsored racketeers wearing a faded sort of blue-grey nothingness, helmets pulled down over their eyes and wielding everything from hatchets to *Hail Maries* as they spill through the busted-down doorway looking for trouble. Monica's made herself scarce, and it's time I made myself that way, too.

The ceiling dangler that's been in the porphyry of my vision ever since I arrived takes centre stage, and all I can hope for is that when the time's ripe, it holds. Blavatsky taught me the flying fandango. Only she had a name for it: *Flight of the Angels*. It all comes back to me – the pad-pad of kids' padded toes in the big room, the stench of dust, and the sweet sounds of Tchaikovsky – as I drop to my haunches, one foot forward, one back, obtaining the requisite equipoise before applying full-thrust, my bodyweight centred on the springs of the gastrocs, quads and *breves digitora* as I launch myself skywards, fingers stretching for the high-point of the dangling arm, as the bastards-in-blue start to swarm.

I feel the robot-arm give as I grab it, a heart-sickening lurch as I give it a load it wasn't meant for – a 200-pound private detective – and the arm jerks down by the width of a broadsword, before the subsidiary anchor attaching it holds, and I complete my trajectory.

I've caught the rozzers off-guard.

There's a two-second response lag, two precious seconds during which the rozzers' well-drilled minds try to catch up with what their eyes are seeing, but by then it's too late – too late for them but not for me, as I let go and flip through the window, desperately seeking a safe landing outside.

There's got to be a reason for awnings, and as I plummet earthwards I find it, the shade above the toyshop door which is just enough to break my fall, before the canvas rips with a sound like a butcher's saw hacking through a steer's skull, and I find myself saying hello to the footpath.

'You all right?'

I'm alive, if that's what Monica means – my arms half-wrenched out of their sockets, a twisted ankle, a battered brain and a tooth missing, but you can't ask for perfect health in this game.

People are yelling.

'You better shelve the equaliser.'

The dame pockets the gat and the yelling stops.

'See you at the speakeasy,' I tell her.

It's only after I've travelled several blocks and the cold air's reminding me of the hole where the Dentist mined my grinder, that I remember telling another dame something very similar – *See you in five* – and a spasm shoots through me, because I get a premonition: Monica might be about to go the same way as Annabel.

Chapter 25

THE SHADOW IN THE CORNER

Detecting's a juggling act. A private eye's got to stay on the move while keeping several objectives in the air without fumbling. I keep my eye on the target, which is to locate the malefactor. Meanwhile I also got to keep alive, and keep Imogene that way. And at the same time, I got to put together all the awkward bits of a thousand-piece jigsaw, while keeping the rest of the act going with grace and fervour.

Dead-man's mobile *numero quinze* gets me Rube.

She's down by the waterfront.

In Sydney, there's waterfront and there's waterfront, most of it priced just within reach of a politician that's been extra-kind to the mining industry. Fortnum's is an eatery where you got to produce your bank balance just to get in the hatchway, a joint where the wait-persons wear hard-weave accents, vegetables are listed as an extra and they make a point of checking the silver before you leave.

'Can I help you, sir?' A thug in black roll-neck, skintights and a tuxedo, with eyes that look like they might have been rolled in a crap-game, is blocking my way. I don't like thugs blocking my way. Thugs blocking my way tell me someone's behind them, someone that's got money that rightly belongs to other people. They also remind me of my childhood.

'Yeah. You can help me by getting out of my way.'

The trouble with social niceties is that not everyone's in the mood to receive them.

'You got a reservation, smart guy?'

When jokers call me *smart guy*, I become what they say I am.

'Have you looked up the word *reservation* lately?' A look of uncertainty crosses the ugly mug. 'Because if you have, you'd know it's the power of absolution, of keeping your wafer after Mass, and – as a long shot – the land grant by which natives the world over can lie around in the mistaken belief that nothing's changed since their fathers were papooses.' I pause. 'So unless you got a meaning in commoner currency, pal, a reservation's not something I got on me right now.'

I flex the shoulders. Flexing the shoulders reveals the mother-of-pearl composite handle of the Taurus PT940 Special in the crossover holster, the one with the cock-and-lock safety catch, showing what I *do* happen to have on me at the moment, and that it might be worth paying attention to. It's a language the thug understands.

'That would be a table for one, sir?'

'That would be a table for none. I've come to see Rube.'

The look on the thug's face turns to one of respect. 'Who'll I say's here?'

'You'll say no one's here, pal, because that's who I am – no one – and I'm here in person, and in person I can tell her no one's here all by myself.'

Rube's seated by the window, her back to a harbour that's got no hint of what hides beneath – much like the look on her face as I pick my way between the lawyers, philanthropists, health care professionals, and politicians, as well as all the other thugs that represent the crème-de-la-crime of Sydney society, and therefore can afford to eat here.

'You have to make an entrance, don't you, Rainbow?' she says. 'How many times do I have to tell you that the secret of life is a low profile?'

'He got up my nose, Rube.'

'So what's a nose worth these days? A punch in the face? Your life? Somebody else's?'

I'm a kid again and Rube's my teacher, a dame that knows all the answers before anyone's asked her the question.

'I'm still learning, Rube.'

'We're all still learning, kid – the trick is to stay alive while we're doing it.' Something approaching a smile works its way around her mouth. 'Have you found the head man yet?'

I take the query at face value and tell her the state of play. After the food's delivered, it's Rube's turn to provide her take. 'It could still be any of them.' She stares out at the Harbour. 'Every one of those bastards had the motive and they also had the means.' She frowns. 'Even the Widow's not in the clear.'

'But she loved Tycho.'

'Don't wave your fork around, Rainbow.' Rube's not looking out the window any more; instead she's considering the possibilities. 'She *said* she loved him – there's a difference. Remember that before she became a widow she was a cheated wife. And cheated wives always have a motive.'

'But she said –'

The expression on Rube's face is the same one she had when I did a misstep at ballet, only older. 'What's she going to say, Rainbow – that she did it?'

'But she's got an alibi.'

'Only the innocent never have alibis.' She pushes her plate away. 'Now I'll tell you what I've done.'

Rube's checked out the bona fides of the bit players, the small fry in the ocean of evil – the whitebait and the yellowtail and the leatherjackets and the rest of the minnows that swim around the mussel-encrusted pylons of mainstream crime, until a shark comes along and they don't.

'And in following up the minor players,' she goes on, 'I'm discovering that every one of them possessed a motive.

'At the time of his death, Tommy Tycho was boffing the Lord Mayor's wife, taking bribes from Dorffmann the developer as well as the union Dorffmann was paying. He owed six-figure sums to Harold Park, the bookie, as well as High Steppin' Annie, the stooge. He was blackmailing a big-league people smuggler as well as a Roman Catholic paederast, and he reneged on a promise to get a Liberal politician preselected and consequently the politician had a contract out on him.' She shakes her head. 'Tycho wasn't what you'd call popular.'

Neither are we, going by a feeling I've just got, but I don't tell Rube that, because Rube would only tell me that feelings don't butter parsnips, it's facts that matter in this world.

'Meantime, I've checked where most of these jokers were at the time of Tycho's death and they either weren't in the vicinity or they're a damned sight cleverer than I'm prepared to give them credit for.' She frowns. 'But that doesn't mean peanuts. I'm halfway through the list and it's like trawling through sewers for ice that someone dropped down the S-bend. How long have we got?'

'Two days.'

'Two days!'

It's two days before the Widow buries Tycho, two more days that the corpse will sit rotting in her kitchen, after which – despite the fact that it's winter – even the Widow won't be able to stomach the stench.

'Yeah, that's all. By the time of that funeral I need to have all the facts. So, yeah, we got just the two days.'

I avoid looking at the face in the shadows in the far corner of the restaurant. It seems familiar, only I don't know where it's familiar from. It also seems dangerous, only I can't put my finger on why.

'Meanwhile, we got to exit this joint, Rube, like now, and via our respective *lavabos*.'

'Since when were you issuing orders around here, Rainbow?'

'Since I wanted you to stay alive, Rube.' I increase the decibels. 'I'm just going to the toilet, Aunt.'

Rube answers in an equally loud voice. 'I'll follow suit. My bladder isn't what it used to be.'

We get to our respective feet and depart, leaving Rube's bag and my fedora on the *tableau* behind us so that even a not-so-casual observer might imagine we'll be returning.

Except that after I enter the *Herren*, I depart by way of the *fenêtre*, leaving Rube to make her own arrangements. And the newt in the corner – when they finally realise what has happened – can make theirs.

Chapter 26

A DATE WITH DEATH

That afternoon, I meet Monica in a Kings Cross op shop, a joint that's seen better days, a down-at-the-heel hole-in-the-wall crammed with everyone else's mistakes, and smelling like King Tut's chamberpot.

'Why are we here?' she asks.

'Because no one gets murdered in Vinnies.' A little old lady with hair the colour of Paterson's curse is busy trying to flog a fake gold watch to a derelict. 'Vinnies is a lay-by to Heaven, the last refuge of the innocent, the place where guilt comes to die.' I try on a green-and-grey topcoat. 'Roarer's going stir-crazy. So what do you say?'

'It's a bit tight around the shoulders.'

'I'm talking about the boat not the coat. How about taking over dog-watch while Rory joins me for a stint?'

'Do I have a choice?'

I palm the blue lady a shekel. 'Yeah.' Monica's found a skirt that shows more leg than it should, but who's complaining? 'You can either do it, or you can do it.'

She hitches up the skirt to investigate something of interest on her inner thigh. 'Very well then.' She straightens, lowers the dress and smooths the hem, while the blue in her eyes has just got bluer. 'But only because you asked so nicely.'

The *Wooden No*'s where I left her, hidden under an overhanging pittosporum in a jagged-edged bay with others of its Ilkly Moor, her wraparound deck mucked with birdlime and the crack in her hull looking much like the Grand Tuxedo. She's groaning with every movement of the sea as the dinghy I borrowed from among the hundred or so on offer on the shore knocks against her like an afterthought.

'Ahoy there!'

290

Roarer's head pops out of the engine room, followed by Mrs Roarer and then Imogene.

'Daddy!' Imogene hurls herself over the gunwale. 'You're back!'

I disentangle myself from the kid and my emotions. 'Only for a moment, honey bunch. Just long enough to exchange Monica here for Uncle Rory prior to getting going again.' The kid's gripping something in one of her paws. 'What you got there, sweetheart?'

'My book. It was in that box you put on my bunk.'

'So what's in the book?'

'Important stuff that might help you one day, Daddy.'

Why does it hurt?

'Thanks, darling.'

'Can't you stay?' There's mist in her eyes. 'You could tell me about your case so I can write it in my book?'

I take the deep breath, but sometimes breaths just aren't deep enough.

'Only when it's safely in the *Solved* folder, sweetheart.' I ruffle her hair. 'Until then, Mum's the word.'

Imogene frowns. 'But Mummy's down in the bilge place, bailing.'

Salina's not looking too comfortable in her new environment. Then again Salina never looks comfortable in any environment.

'Aren't you done yet, Rainbow?' She's gripping the bucket, her hair's all over the shop, and her clothes look like they've just fought a losing battle with a mako. 'Hasn't this latest in a long string of emergencies finally drawn to a close, enabling us to return to what might laughingly be referred to as a home, but is Buckingham Palace compared to this – this' – she stares around at the rotten timbers, the broken bulwark and the swill – '*barge.*'

I got to get out of here. 'In a little while, Salina, I . . .'

'A little while!' She flings the bucket and it misses me by the width of a Gillette. It ricochets off the rusty fuel tank before coming to a rest by a leaking oil line. 'In – a – little – while!' She hunches into squat that would make a toad green. 'We're supposed to be divorced! I'm supposed to be shot of you! Nobody told me I'd be stuck with you forever! A divorce is a divorce, it's supposed to change everything, give a person a new life! Instead, all I've got is more of the same – only worse!'

It's meltdown time and I can't do meltdowns. I get up to go. 'Look, I'm relieving Roarer,' I tell whoever's in a position to hear me. 'You'll be pleased to know I'm leaving you another woman. You'll have a lot in common.'

'Are you saying that because we're women we'll get on like a – like a – a . . .?' She shakes her head. 'You're mad, Rainbow, you been through too much to be anything else. But why the hell do I have to be the one that suffers for it?' Her shoulders sag. 'Oh, just go, will you.'

I do what I'm told, and going by the sounds that follow me into the dinghy, Salina's found something else to throw to the four winds, and it's more than just caution.

'Home free!' Roarer's lying back in the bottom of the dinghy in the pale winter sunshine, his brain in neutral where it likes to be. 'You got no *concept* what it was like on that boat, Rain.' He parks his crutch-gun alongside the gunwale. 'It was hell on earth, man, like the Good Lord created the situation as a warning regarding eternal Damnation. They were at each other's throats like the servants of Satan.'

'They're just different personalities, Roarer.'

'They're exactly the same, if you ask me.'

'Sounds like you changed your mind about marriage.'

Roarer shakes his head, but it's a slow shake. 'Only if Salina moves in with us.'

We're hugging the shoreline to merge with the environment.

'So what do we do now?'

There'll never be a good time to tell him.

'We're going to see the Brute.'

Roarer's suddenly bolt upright, his one leg shivering out in front of him like an antenna. 'You got to be kidding. Why?'

'To accuse him of murdering Tommy Tycho.'

Roarer sinks back into the bottom of the boat. 'Yeah, right. Let me get this straight, Rain, or as straight as people can get anything when they're dealing with you.' He's been with Salina too long, his mind's turned. 'You're telling me we're *voluntarily* visiting the town's *mean*-man, after which, and again *voluntarily,* we're going to accuse him of murdering Tycho?'

I don't shrug. It only interrupts the rhythm of the oars. 'He's the last name on the list, Roarer, apart from the minnows, and Rube's taking care of them.'

'The last card in the pack, you mean.' Roarer throws up his arms; he looks like he's responding to a proselytiser. 'That hell boat you just rescued me from suddenly looks like a *sanctuary*. Don't you know that Brutus Kariakis deals ninety per cent of the illegal weaponry in the entire

Southern Hemisphere? That he's got more killers at his disposal than the entire Australian Defence Force? And that I'm a flea in his ointment, an annoyance he's wanted to give the flick to for *decades*?'

I shrug. It throws out the oaring but what can I do? 'I got to keep the faith, Roarer. You of all people ought to know that. A dame I owe my life to copped it on my account and I'm duty bound to find the perpetrator.'

'It's a misplaced sense of duty, if you ask me.'

'So do you want to bail?'

Roarer shakes his head. It's a slow shake and a sad shake. 'I guess I'm back in harness, Rain, and therefore I got to go where the reins lead me.' The pun wouldn't be deliberate. Roarer doesn't do puns. He's got his work cut out doing normal. 'And if I die in the doing of it, because I'm doing it for God's sake, it's going to provide me with a one-way ticket to Heaven.'

'You mightn't have to kill anyone, Roarer.'

But Roarer's stopped listening. Instead, he's cleaning his crutch, the one with all the rifling and the bullets in it, pulling down the stock, withdrawing the firing mechanism, sighting down the barrel, and when he talks, it's like he's talking to the gun.

'If it involves Karrybag, it involves killing.' He sights his crutch on a seagull. 'So, I got as much faith in that being the case as I got in God.'

Chapter 27

CLOSING IN ON A KILLER

There aren't too many shooting pits left in Sydney, and what there are have got so many regulations you're lucky to have time after the fulfilment of them to loose off a couple of rounds before the bell goes and it's time to pack away the gunnery and go home.

The Brute Shoot's different. It's private enterprise, meaning it's not what you'd call strictly legit, a shooting parlour courtesy of too many shish-kebabs to the local conciliators, housed in a facility that if it was any bigger, would qualify as a city. The only rule is you don't fire at each other — and even that's a rule that's there to be broken.

We approach careful and from the west. There's not much choice in either department, because the joint's built on a promontory jutting out into the Tasman, and the only approach you can make on a late afternoon on a winter's day is slow, and with the sun behind you.

'We could of notified him that we're coming.'

Something's happened to Rory since he found God, not all of it good.

'Think about it, Roarer.' I'm working my way through lantana that's as thick as thieves, with Roarer bringing up the rear. 'What do you reckon would happen if we called up Brute requesting visitation rights? *Oh, Mr Brute, look, me and Rory were wondering if we might trespass on your generosity and pay you a little visit.* You reckon he's going to tell us, *Sure, come on in,* and roll out the Axminster? You think he isn't going to *remember?*'

I wait to give Roarer time to catch up, in more ways than one.

'You talking about the Machine Gun Caper?' What else would I be talking about? 'For Christ's sakes, Rain, that was years ago! And all we did was stop him supplying a few rifles to a bunch of New Guinea headhunters opposed to a multinational corporation mining virgin rainforest. What's wrong with that?'

I consider what Roarer's just said, plus the hole in the ground that's materialised in front of us, complete with a six-foot-deep razor-trap in it.

'I'll tell you what's wrong with that, Roarer.' I work my way around the trap. 'For a start, it wasn't just a few rifles but ten thousand belt-fed machine guns, complete with a million rounds of ammunition. Not to mention the ten thousand spare barrels that went with it. Second, those ten thousand shooters translated into several million smackeroos. Think how many legislators Brute Force could have bought with that!'

Roarer whacks aside a native azalea. 'Rain, we performed a public service doing what we did. God would of –'

'We're not talking about God, we're talking about the antichrist. And we're also talking about our survival in the here and now, in the only life we can be sure of. We dudded Brute and now you're worried about an invitation. This isn't a garden party, Roarer, we're about to confront someone concerning a murder!'

The chain-wire barrier could double as a wombat fence, the mesh descending a fathom into the ground, and the whole affair electrified.

Roarer stares up into the stratosphere, which is about where the wire peters out. 'So how are we supposed to climb *that*?'

Roarer's negativity's one of the changes I've noticed in him since he found Christ, a tendency to look on the down-side of any given situation. Accordingly, I turn my back and haul out the pliers, the ones from Bunnings with the one-shot insulation designed to rot in harmony with the warranty. Always keep the receipt when you buy pliers from Bunnings.

'We're not climbing, we're cutting.' I start hacking. 'Look, I'm paying you good money for this and if you're going to earn your keep, you got to work for it. Pull the wire away after I cut it.'

There's a series of sparks and the shock waves send Roarer stumbling backwards into the lantana.

'You're supposed to be wearing gloves.'

'You might of told me!'

'I just did.'

Roarer's still whining like a tank with differential problems, but after we hack our way through the wire he gets into the swing of things. It's almost like being back with the old Roarer when he belts one of the two mastiffs that come at us after we get through, while I take care of the other one. They clear out, tails between their legs.

'That was easy.'

'We're not out of the woods yet.'

Roarer looks around him. 'But there's no –'

'It's just an expression, Roarer. All it means is that we're not there yet.'

'So why didn't you –'

Sometimes communicating with Rory can be like trying to do dialogue with a Martian.

'Don't worry about it, okay?'

'I wasn't worried about it until you started seeing trees that weren't there.'

God can't be too fussy if he's taking Rory.

'Just forget I said anything about trees and try to focus on the business in hand.'

We're in view of a building that could house a fleet of jumbos.

'What is it?'

'Keep your voice down.'

We're maintaining cover but we've still got to send a couple of support actors to La La Land and we'll come across a couple more members of Brute's army before we're through.

'It's the gun gallery, the place where Brutus invites punters to test the merchandise before buying, to which he also invites acquaintances for the odd angry shot.'

'I can't hear nothing.'

Rory's heart's in the right place. It's his brain that's gone walkabout.

'It'd be soundproof, Roarer.'

'I knew that.'

We're on the southern side, the sea a powder-puff of unreality to starboard, while a seagull's strutting its stuff along the cliff edge. And despite all the masonry and the padded walls and the sound batts I can still hear the soft Victa lawnmower putt-putt of variegated rifle fire, and the not-so-soft thuds as the slugs whang their way into the mounds.

I haul out the Smith & Wesson.

'Give me cover,' I tell Roarer. 'I'm going in.'

Chapter 28

ET TU, BRUTE?

The door opens as I edge my way towards the shooting house. A gat emerges, followed by the thug wielding it. The weaponry finds its way into the polar bear's armpit as he sets fire to a cigarette.

That's when I hit him. The crack over the skull has got to be the healthier option. I get myself inside — I find that I've just bought myself a one-way ticket to Fantasyland. There's a lot of shouting and the joint's lit up like a turtle on Stilnox. Ahead and slightly to the portside stretches a standful of shooters — a baker's dozen on the rough sum — wearing industrial-size bunny-muffs and goggles, and armed to the bicuspids with everything from Uzis to police-issue Glocks, to World War II .303s, and Vickers' medium machine guns.

Most of the metal they're firing is finding its way into targets trundling along the horizon in my peripherals but now and again something lethal ricochets off the bullet-proof glass and goes feral.

I quarter the joint. The cut-outs the punters are shooting at are in the shape of humans — life-sized figures wearing ties, zoot suits, fedoras, budgie smugglers, frocks, tracksuits, you name it — and while they appear to be walking or running or leaping or just mooching along, what they're really on is an assembly line to annihilation.

Daylight glimmers through holes in the silhouettes like twinkle-twinkles. I tear my peepers away from the ramifications. I'm looking for Brute. I don't see him. Brute's the kind of guy you normally see.

'Why, Mister Rainbow!'

The voice comes from behind, the place where my eyes aren't.

I do a spin-turn. The joker might be built like a smoke stack, but the voice hasn't descended to the fire box. It doesn't mean I don't pay attention to what the chimney's saying.

'Drop the Smith and Double-Yew for me, would you, there's a good chap.'

Brute – and I know it's Brute, we've crossed scimitars before – talks like a dame out of a music hall, a fluty sing-song kind of voice that's got the promise of a great deal of kindness in it, except that the Interdynamic KG9 converted to full automatic he's waving around says otherwise. He's looks like a former prime minister – the one that could have walked out of a Damon Runyon fantasy – and is togged out in what must be five thousand clams' worth of Ermenegildo pinstripe, no doubt with body armour underneath.

Equalisers are popping off all around me. Bullets are zinging. The floor manager's yelling. You could die of the echoes. I drop the gat.

'There's a good boy. Now let's get back to square one, shall we?'

That's when I see something I hadn't noticed before, and that is that the joint is set out like the sort of boardgame Aunt Rube would get me to play when I was a kid, to teach me how most people look at life. It's a boardgame with a difference. For a start, it's a dozen times the size of *Moronopoly*. And for a finish, the pretty-coloured properties haven't got a lot of nice-sounding names like MARYLEBONE STATION, BOW STREET, MAYFAIR and PARK LANE.

Instead they got titles like DEATH and DESTRUCTION, HODDLE STREET MASSACRE, THE END OF THE LINE and THE MORGUE.

'My little joke,' Brute says and prods me past a barred cell marked SOLITARY, while assorted signs read THE GIBBET, ELECTRIC CHAIR and THE SUICIDE OPTION. 'Like it?'

NO GO, NO CHANCE, NO PARKING and DEAD MAN'S CHEST. A rail station marked TERMINAL. Spaces labelled MADHOUSE and DEATHWATCH. The steel-framed door that closes behind us has got a sign on it reading: SQUARE ONE.

'Welcome to sanity.'

Silence, apart from the hiss and fart of a coffee maker followed by a, *Why, hello!* and after that: *How would sir like his coffee?*

The barista's wearing a bulge under his jacket and a fake smile.

'With plenty of caffeine in it.'

Brute shrugs his Ermenegildo shoulders. 'The usual for me, thanks, Bobby.'

He parks his death-dealing machinery on the tablecloth and looks at me out of eyes that could double as the business-end of a twin-barrelled shottie.

'Look, Rainbow, let's forget little problems like what you cost me in the matter of the machine guns that you quite unreasonably stopped me flogging to the cannibals — plus how you might have got here, and the damage you must have done on the way — and focus instead on the *Why*.' He shoots me what in some circles might pass for a smile. 'I do like focusing, don't you?'

I don't give him the benefit of a reply.

'Oh, dear, it looks like we might need some kind of ice breaker, doesn't it?'

That's when he goes all brisk on me, while I check out the camera at two o'clock high, and the barista.

'Let's start with the layout, shall we? If only to stop you getting any silly ideas. First, the camera you just noticed. It won't hurt to inform you that it's not a camera at all, but a rifle, a 7.62 M134, to be exact, complete with human heat sensor — as provided by an obliging Ministry of Defence — and it's got your temperature on it.'

I shift to starboard. The move's automatic, but so is the gun, its 7.62-gauge snout following me with all the magnanimity of a drone.

Brute smiles a smile that would look better on a corpse, as the barista deposits the coffee. 'This' — Brute waves at the bullet-proof window — 'is the biggest privately-owned firing range in the entire southern hemisphere, New Zealand included. Only Sheik Rhaman Taledi and the Taliban possess better.' I admire the scenery. 'That's where my clients try out the merchandise.'

He shoots me a glance — like most fruitcakes he's out to impress.

'I'm only telling you this because after I tell you, you're going to die.'

He doesn't look as upset as he might be.

'An interesting feature of this facility is that each shooting stand possesses an auxiliary firearm that looks very much like that gun you thought was a camera. Would you like to know why?'

I've already guessed why, but I don't tell the fruitcake that. I'd prefer to spend the time I got left working out how to increase the time I got left.

'It's to give the clients confidence in the product.' He sits back, the skin stretched over his frontal bone glimmering in the arc-lights, nose twitching. 'I've had those little babies programmed to take out the relevant target if a client misses, thereby giving the client the illusion that he hit it. It makes the weapon look good, at the same time making the buyer feel good about himself.' He frowns. 'But I see you're not impressed.'

I shrug. 'I'm not here to be impressed. I'm here regarding the death of Tommy Tycho.'

'Alas, poor Tycho, I knew him well.'

'It's quote, *Alas, poor Yorick, I knew him*, comma, *Horatio*, unquote, if you're trying to do the literary allusion.' I resist the urge to make a grab for the gat – judging by the coffee, the joker at the bar's more bullet-man than barista – and instead stay on song. 'Meanwhile, I believe you killed Tycho, or at least were responsible for his death. You had the means plus the motive. But what I'm really interested in, is if you also took out the dame.'

I get a Brutus-type smile for that. 'Rainbow, darling, you know I don't take out dames.'

Well, yeah, the whole world knows that and there's nothing wrong with not taking dames out per se. But I'm not interested in the Brute's sexuality, I just want to know who killed Annabel.

'However, I see what you're trying to say, and the answer is no, no and no.'

I correct him for the second time this session. 'I only asked you two questions, yet you've provided responses to three.'

For that I get a repeat of the smile. 'Yes, I know, dear, but the third *no* is in reply to your unasked third question. And that question is: *Are you going to allow me to live?* The answer to which, as I've already indicated, is – as in the other two cases – *no*.' Brute spreads his mitts, palm up, like he's somebody's saviour, instead of a slaughterman. 'How can I not kill you, Mister Rainbow? First, you trespass on my land. Second, you accuse me of a murder I'd like to have committed, but didn't. And third – most terrible crime of all – you correct my quotations.'

Chapter 29

A VIEW TO A DEATH

In fact, as I see it, the only thing you've done right' – he indicates the view through the bullet-proof glass, the marksmen and the not-so-marksmen firing at the targets outlined against the skyline – 'is that you've come to the right place to be killed.' He smiles the smile of a crackpot from a broken family, whose old man was sent down for killing a cop when he was ten, and whose mother was as crazy as sheet glass whanged by a volley from a machine gun.

'Given that you're going to have me put down' – one task at a time and the first task is to find out if he did it – 'would you mind answering one last question before you kill me?'

He shrugs. 'Why not? But as I've already told you, Rainbow, I didn't kill Tycho.' He takes a sip of his coffee and grimaces. 'Why do I employ that boy?'

'For the same reason you got the gun cameras – because he shoots straight.' I hunch the shoulders. 'But you haven't answered the question.'

'The question being . . .?'

'Who did it?'

'*Curiosity killed the cat* and you can't catch me out on that one.' The overhead lights illuminate his cheekbones, but they don't get any change out of the eyes. 'All right, while I have to confess I didn't do it – or even cause it to be done – I must say I wish I knew who did, because I'd give him a medal.'

To hear Brutus laugh is to hear vampires' wings whistling in the night, the rattle of shackles in the solitary cell of a condemned man, or the ground opening up under your feet in an earthquake.

'Because, you know, Rainbow, people like me might be bad, but Tycho was truly evil. Tycho made anything I might have done look like a wrist slap. He aided and abetted my competitors. He took part in collusive tendering. He put the story around that I was flogging second-rate weaponry. He –'

'You haven't answered my question.'

Brute shrugs and shoves away his barely-drunk coffee. It spills on the Interdynamic. It doesn't improve my chances of survival, but it's the answer to my question I'm concerned about.

'That's because I'm afraid I simply don't know the answer. All I know is that I'd like to attend the bastard's funeral. I want to gloat over his death and urinate on his grave. Above all, I want to make sure he's dead. And talking of death, Mister Rainbow, it's your turn to take a walk on the boardwalk. Without passing Go. Without even collecting two hundred.'

It's all sky and no horizon as I'm shoved, hands tied, out of Square One, past NO CARKING, and towards the killing zone. At a signal from Brute there's a cease fire. The troop of cut-outs trundle before me — a kid with a spear, an old gent wielding a walking cane, a crone on pogo-sticks, a lawyer with a portmanteau, somebody's mother, somebody's brother, someone else's aunt. Life-sized, two-dimensional human figures set before the wide, blue expanse of the Tasman.

'We've tried our best to simulate reality here.' Brutus is beside me, the ugly little Interdynamic slung over one shoulder, my Smith & Wesson in his hand. 'The shooters fire into the light instead of having it behind them, the targets are as real as the model people can make them — and of course there's the view.'

I know most of the shooters — in my business I got to — Rastus Nefarius, the Taliban warlord, armed with an Ingram; the Friesan Minister of Defence, General Dolas, fisting a well-oiled Uru Mekanika; Hayley Dools, the bookie, waving a nice little stainless-steel Anaconda; Inspector Moriarty from the Drug Squad, gripping a five-inch Taurus that wouldn't dent a mosquito — but the Narcs have only ever been about appearance; a trio of Triads; a biker; and a couple of contractors.

All here to buy guns, all armed with their weapon of choice, and all keen to try their weapon of choice on this real, live target that's suddenly been presented before them.

I check out Brute. 'Aren't you afraid they'll take a pot shot at you?'

He doesn't pause. 'Now why would they want to do that, Rainbow? I'm the good guy in this scenario, the benevolent uncle, their supplier, while you . . . Anyway, they're the most bloody awful shots. Apart from which, under the fancy clobber, I'm dressed head to toe in police-issue body armour.'

We've reached the silhouettes. It's the end of the boardgame. Next square: OBLIVION.

'Now because I'm such a sport, we'll play it like this. I'll leave your legs free and that way you can run any which way you like, and just as fast or slow as you are able.'

'Just like in real life.'

'There's no need to be bitter.' The mortician's features take on a hurt look. 'After all, you were trespassing, and our society doesn't take kindly to trespassers.'

A movement causes him to glance towards the door. 'Hello, what have we got here?'

I know what we've got here without even looking.

They've found Roarer and they're dragging him grumbling and kicking his one leg to join me among the targetry.

I chuck him a look with a fistful of slugs in it. 'You were my last chance, Roarer. What happened?'

They've taken away his crutch-gun, and he's teetering beside me, looking naked. 'When I saw Brute I thought you was a goner, so I went down on my knee and prayed to God.'

'Jesus, Roarer!'

Roarer nods like he's seen the connection – only it's the wrong one. 'But they must of seen me on their candid cameras, because they came at me from all directions. What else am I going to do but pray?'

'You could have tried shooting your way out of the situation, like you used to.'

But it's too late to be thinking of yesterday because it's today, and today's full of beautiful scenery, seagulls, and probable death.

The Brute stands back. 'You got a last request, Rainbow?'

I'm standing among the targets propping up Roarer, who's humming *Nearer My God To Thee* because he's seen the Titanic movie a few times too many, and the silhouettes are dancing past at their regulation sixty *pesetas* a minute, and we're about to join them. While no more than a hundred paces distant, the marksmen are licking their lips at the prospect of a duck shoot. The view's behind me. In front I can see the future, and it's not bright.

'Come along, Rainbow.' Brute looks disappointed. 'You must have one last request, everyone does.' He resembles a kid about to open his stocking on an otherwise lacklustre Christmas morning. 'Not even one last message for your little girl, what's her name – *Imagine*?'

He must have been a shrink in a past life, bringing up Imogene.

'No last request and no last message, either.' But mention of Imogene wakes me to the possibilities. 'Okay, I got an offer for you, and it's got two parts to it.'

There's no bullets yet but there's plenty of impatience. Rory hitches his psalm humming up an octave, while I keep talking, on account of there's nothing else to keep.

'First up you want to know who killed Tycho so you can give the guy a medal. And second up, you want to attend his funeral.' I pause to let those two pieces of intelligence sink in. 'Well, it just so happens I can make both your wishes come true.'

It's a long shot, but long shots can hit the target, you just got to pull the trigger at the right time and hope the wind doesn't drop. Meanwhile, up the other end of the firing range I sense the natives getting restless.

'Why should I believe you, Rainbow?'

I shrug. 'Why should anyone believe anyone? Why should a Yank believe the Stars and Stripes are forever or Roarer think that The Almighty's going to waste Godly time saving him, while the natives are dying in their millions in Eritrea?'

I let that sink in.

'Because people like to believe stuff, Brute – that's what makes them people.' I do the shrug of a man who likes to believe in stuff. 'It's called blind faith and what else has anyone got in this world? Leave me and Roarer alive and you got hope. Kill us and you got nothing.'

'Are you providing a guarantee with that?'

I nod the nod of a man who'll agree to anything. 'As good a guarantee as you give anyone you sell a weapon to.'

Chapter 30

COLOUR ME DEAD

So he lets us go just like that?' Roarer does incredulity better than anyone I know, and he's got a lot to be incredulous about. 'And all you gotta tell him is something he can read in the *Daily Muckraker* anyway?'

I don't look his way. I got my work cut out keeping an eye on the rear-vision. 'Roarer, the shyster was too busy chucking quotations at us to realise what I was up to. Apart from which, there's a price.'

I let that sink in. Give anyone long enough and there'll be at least a glimmer of understanding, even with Rory.

'You mean we got to slip him something?'

He's driving the little green car, the Mazda 121, the one that carries an introductory letter to the mortuary as an inbuilt option, along with the air-bags.

I shake the cerebellum. 'No, we got to go back.'

'Back where?'

Roarer would have made a nice inquisitor, if only he had a brain to go with the fervour.

'Back to the Widow's.'

'Why?'

I do the shrug. 'You'll see.' I frown as he makes it around a truck and I realise we just escaped death for the second time today, and by about the same margin. 'But first we got to swing by Rube's, closely followed by a visit to the colour shop.'

The penny – or whatever currency you want to deal in – dropped as I was being frog-marched around the *Moronopoly* board, a certainty that led to even greater certainty the more coloured squares we crossed. Colour me dead, or don't colour me at all.

'Can't you make this thing go any faster?'

'Is God a Christian?'

There's no answer to that so I don't try producing one.

'You got to stop spoiling me like this, Rainbow.' Rube's glance swings to Roarer. 'I thought you'd hung up your crutch.'

Brute handed it back when he let us go – along with the advice that Roarer's crutch is the day-before-yesterday's technology, and if Rory ever wants to upgrade, he knows where to come.

'I might of found God, Rube, but that don't mean I can't follow my vocation. It's in the Bible.'

'Oh, I'm sure everything's in the Bible, Rory. They've covered all bases, haven't they, their little mysteries to perform? But come in anyway.' She chucks the usual look up and down the broadwalk after which we follow her down the hall. 'How's the case coming along, Rainbow?'

'That's why we're here, to see how you're doing.'

She shrugs as she doles out the Kinkara, spilling a little on the table as she does so. 'I chased up all the little fish and they're all waggling their tails in clean water. At the time of the killings, some were in the cooler, some were committing other malefactions, and the rest had alibis you couldn't peel apart with a razor.' She settles the cosy around the teapot. 'It's starting to look like no one killed Tycho.'

After we toss things around without getting any further, and drink Rube's tea, we go back outside.

'Who owns the toy?'

'Roarer got it in exchange for the Caddie, which he donated to the God people.'

Rube nods thoughtfully. 'Someone's not stupid.'

Roarer smacks the steering wheel as we drive away. 'What did she mean by that? *Someone's not stupid.* She was having a crack at me, wasn't she? Saying I'm a dill while the Hillbillies are a pack of con merchants dudding me. What's wrong with Mazda 121s, anyway?'

I nod at the steering mechanism. 'You just snapped the rudder.' I check the rear-vision, after which I don't check the rear-vision. 'You got yourself a set of wheels with God as a built-in extra. How could anyone call that being dudded?'

I stare ahead, anywhere but behind us.

'Chuck a left here, if this thing can manage it. We need to stop by the paint shop.'

The vehicle that pulls into the kerb two car-lengths behind us is a late-model white Suburu Impreza with heavily-tinted windows. It's the sort of car you can't see into; that people drive when they're killers or cops or just real shy, take your pick. No one gets out of the Impreza and the windows are so black they don't even do reflections.

I bend down to the bubble car. 'Lock the doors, Roarer, and stay in your supercharged getaway car. And keep your crutch cocked.'

I stare straight ahead as I make my way along the boulevard.

Like most product in this world, what the paint shop sells is superficial, something to brighten your daily round with – a cover-up, a lick of balm to distract punters from the rough side of life, no more than a veneer designed to peel away at the first sign of trouble. Boxes of Spakfilla teeter, drop sheets and rollers and brushes hang out along the walls, along with a bunch of grey gasmasks that look like leftovers from yesterday's nightmare, and the guy coming from the counter doesn't look like the brightest patch on the colour chart.

'Do you want my advice, sir?'

He's long and he's rangy and he's got a bald spot, and what looks like purple paint on the bald spot.

I rearrange the Smith & Wesson. 'Why do you say that?'

'Well, you know, the clothes . . .'

'I'm after a colour chart.'

'Why do you want a colour chart?'

There's a car outside wearing wraps, a couple of crooks are waiting for me to break a promise, and several women are sitting vulnerable on a boat – and this turkey's making like he's Eddie McGuire in *Who Wants To Be A Dimwit*. But you learn self-control in this game. Lose that and you say goodbye to your right to keep on living. Accordingly, I don't lift the turkey up by the wattle and shake him. Instead I tell him an answer.

'It's to add a dash of colour to my otherwise lacklustre life, and also to lift my gun sights over and above the mundane level of hurting people.' I shoot him the hard look. 'What's it matter what I want it for?'

'I'm sorry, sir. What colour do you have in mind?'

'Orange.'

'Orange?'

'That's what I said – orange.'

'I'm afraid there's no such colour as orange, per se.' He ups the half-smile to three-quarters. 'So if you can't give me more of a clue than just *orange*, I'm not sure I can help.'

I'm running out of patience, not to mention time. 'Palm me a colour chart, pal.'

So he palms me a chart and when I open it, I see what he's telling me – there's no such colour as 'orange'. They got Cinder Glow and Citrus Combo and Outback Gold. They even got Orangeade. But they ain't got orange.

'You ain't got orange?'

Mr Paint shakes his brain. 'I'm sorry, sir. Like I said, we have Calendula, Sabre Sun, Coppersmith and Golden Koi, but there's no such colour as orange.'

I hear it coming in my head – a nursery rhyme – and I talk to frighten it away. 'What do you mean, *no such colour as orange?*'

'Multinational market research advises us that names like *orange* defy successful marketing. People don't buy ordinary any more. Ordinary died with the horse and buggy, lead paint and good manners. There's just no such colours as *red* or *yellow* or *blue* or – Heaven forbid – *orange*. We're not selling paint, sir, we're selling dreams – and the dreams people buy are the names.'

I got the nursery rhyme stuck in my brainpan and I also got what this joker's telling me, and together they don't make a pretty picture – whatever name you want to give it.

'It's not us,' he goes on, 'it's people. The paint company even gives us lectures on the subject. *You're not selling colours*, they tell us, *you're selling names – names like Golden Shower and Subtle Moonbeams and Shifting Sands and Sang Froid*. So I'm sorry, but basic orange has gone the way of the boomerang and vinyl records. If you want green you're out of luck. But we could do you *Robin Hood* or *Sheer Envy*. Now is there anything else?'

'Yeah, palm me one of them respirator things.'

The Impreza's still in place. I note the licence plate and text it to Rube via one of the dead-men's mobiles. Then I tell Roarer to get out of there, fast.

'This thing can't do fast.' He chucks a look at the respirator. 'What's that?'

'They probably call it *Several Shades of Grey*.' The Subaru's tight in behind us. 'Come on Roarer, step on it.'

'I am stepping on it, but it's like treading on a snail.'

Sometimes Roarer gets it right. I drag out the equaliser and haul down the *fenêtre*.

'So what's it for?'

'What gats are usually for.'

'Not the gun, the grey thing.'

We haven't got a chance in hell of losing the tail any other way so I shoot out the left front Dunlopillo and the Impreza swerves to port, mounts the kerb, and ceases following us. I pull my head in.

'It's for my own personal use and gratification, Roarer. Now shut up and chuck another left, then a right, then left again.' A check in the rear-vision shows that – for the moment anyway – we're in the clear. 'And if you can't go any faster, we can always drop into Hephzibah's and borrow a wind-up key.'

Chapter 31

VIEW TO A FUNERAL

The Widow's lost her taste for colour and is wearing black – black hat with a veil held up off it, black dress that covers everything but her hands, black stockings, black pump-ups, black look.

'Oh, I didn't expect to see you again, Inspector.' Her mood matches her garb. 'And this would be . . .?' She's looking at Rory.

'He's Short.' I figure I better elaborate. 'Detective Senior Constable Short.'

The Widow drops the veil, and if she's got an expression on her dial-up, I can no longer see it. 'I knew the police had changed the height restrictions but I didn't think they'd ever descend to . . . I'm sorry, it's the police force's business, not mine. Come in. And if you notice a smell, it's just some toilet fragrance I sprayed the place with, because my neighbour complained.'

It's hard to know what's worse – the pong that was here before, or the stuff she's overlaid it with. I drag Roarer in by the shoulder pad.

'What *is* it?' he whispers.

'It's Tycho,' I tell him. 'She's got him parked in the kitchen prior to burial.'

'But he's gone bad!'

'He was born bad, Roarer.'

'I'm sorry, what was that?' The Widow's got mourning rags over all the furniture and black crap covering the window, and as a result the joint possesses all the cheery ambience of a graveyard.

'Constable Short was inquiring as to the date of your late husband's interment.'

She hunches her shoulders under all the crappery. 'I'm afraid that's become something of a problem.' She leans forward on the couch. 'I've had a lot of people here, including the lovely folk from Bright Lady, and Cheapa Funerals, and they all say the same thing – Tommy's too hot to handle.'

'They were being metaphysical.'

The Widow stiffens like she's been starched. 'I don't see how that could be, Inspector, because that would imply Tommy was somehow . . .' She doesn't say how Tommy was somehow. 'No, I believe they were referring to the smell. I don't notice it, of course, because he's my darling Tommy and that's all that matters, head or no head.' She pauses. 'No, that's not all that matters. I want a Christian burial. Tommy deserves it.' She looks like she's frowning under the veil. 'Only I'm finding that true Christians are thin on the ground when it comes to headless burials.'

She's playing Roarer's tune.

He leans forward, hits the smell barrier, and rears back. 'You say you want to bury him?' His voice is nasal on account of he's clutching his nose. 'But no one will take him?'

'That's exactly what I'm saying. The last people suggested I call up a garbage truck, with one of those dumpster things they park in the gutter, and get a cherry picker and just throw him in the dumpster and cover him with builder's refuse and have him carted away to the tip.' The Widow's looking upset, even under the veil. 'But I couldn't do that, even if it were legal, which I very much doubt it is. But as I said before, people are starting to complain.' Her hands play tiddlies in her lap. 'Oh, what can I do?'

Rory adopts his beatific look, the one that says that with the help of God and a bit of money and the Hillbillies he's capable of just about anything. 'I reckon I know how and where you can bury your husband, Mrs Tycho.'

I hear the sound of a motor and figure the time that's elapsed since we last saw the car matches the time needed to change a shot-out tyre and get to the Widow's afterwards. I also figure I can follow Roarer's thought processes, which is about as difficult as tracking a rat over a corpse in broad daylight.

'I happen to belong to this church, see, and I know they'd be only too happy to conduct the funeral for you, for a little consideration. Do you happen to possess any funds?'

I can't see the Widow's face but by the set of the shoulders and the sudden straightening of the pigeon back I suspect she's offended.

'Nothing but the widow's mite.'

Roarer nods. 'They'll take that. It's in the Bible. *And there came a poor widow and she threw in two mites.* God's happy to take

anything you got, if that's all He can lay His hands on. My church will
bury your husband for you.'

'Oh, would they?' The Widow claps her hands. 'Would they really,
Constable Tiny?'

Roarer ignores the implication. 'I been to some of their funerals and
they put on a real good show. I'll arrange it all for you.'

The Widow claps her hands again. 'Oh, would you? And after he's
buried, would I be able to join this beautiful church of yours?'

Roarer must be on some sort of commission.

'Yeah, I can arrange that, too.'

Like they say, matters are coming to a head. Suddenly I got to get out
of there, and it's not just the smell. But first I got a couple of questions.

'You remember I found a piece of paper with a word on it, and you
said it was the colour you were painting the joint.'

'That's right, I did, didn't I?' She's got us to the hatchway and it's
like she's trying to push us out. 'In fact, I'll be painting the house right
after Tommy's taken care of, it will help in the marketing.' If she believes
that, she'll believe anything. 'That's the reason for the piece of paper you
found. I was working through possible colours.'

'And the colour – refresh my memory – was *lemon?*'

'Oh, certainly not, Inspector, it was *orange.*' The Widow seems to
have a burst of inspiration behind the mosquito netting. 'After all, orange
was our favourite colour.'

'I suppose you checked with the paint shop around the corner that
that's its name – *orange?*'

'Oh, yes . . .'

There's one more thing before we go. 'I need to pay my last respects
to Tommy.'

Roarer opts to stay where he is, while I slap on the mask, replace the
hat, and go in.

The body's still there and it still doesn't possess a head and despite the
cool weather and all the sprays – insect and toilet and maybe embalming
– and even with me wearing the mask, the remains of Tommy Tycho
still stink to high heaven. I do the visual. And on the greying flesh below
the Plimsoll line, just beneath where the head was blown off, I can still
make out the words *Populus vult decipi,* and I can also still remember how
the phrase translates from the Latin: 'The people wish to be deceived, so
deceive them'.

I complete the circuit, commit the rest to memory – which is the one
word, *decapitare* – before getting the hell out of Hell's Kitchen.

I tip the fedora. 'See you at the funeral.'

'What did you say?'

I take off the hat and the mask. 'I said, *We're going.*'

As I replace the fedora, instinct makes me drop on the turn, and the slug that takes out the hat and whangs into the architecture's a big one.

The kind of slug that, like Pig said, if it was in your garden you'd call in the cavalry.

Chapter 32

A GOOD DEAL OF DEATH

I haul out the equaliser and fire off a couple of shots as the Impreza accelerates away, its darkened windows sliding to the *rack-off* position and its tyres spitting fire. They're quick bunnies, Imprezas, unlike the Tonka Toy, and by the time I get a bead on the wheels, it's too late.

'Who was that?' Roarer's emerged on the stoop beside me, clutching his honker.

'I believe it's the joker that took out Lover Boy.'

'Lover Who?'

I could stick a fist in the aperture the slug made.

Same with Roarer's cakehole.

'Same kind of gat.' I'm talking to myself more than to Roarer. 'Same kind of slug.'

The Widow looks up the carriageway after the Impreza. 'Oh dear, do you think they'll be back?'

I shake the head and nod it all at the same time. 'Is the Pope a Protestant?'

The case is gathering momentum. I climb into the car. It's time to arrange someone's funeral.

'Next stop, the Killjoys.'

Roarer clashes the gears. 'It's the Hillbillies, for Christ's sake, Rain, the name of the church is the Hillbillies, and I don't find anything funny about getting the name wrong and poking fun at them all the time. They gave it that title so they'd attract the ordinary punter.'

A phone playing the theme song from *Spartacus* saves me from answering.

'The Subaru's hot.' It's Rube. 'Stolen from outside an early-morning eatery in Bridge Street where the cop that owns it was purchasing coffee and croissants, and it hasn't been seen since.'

If the road to Hell is paved with good intentions, the journey to the Church of the Latterday Hillbillies is a billycart ride. It's a great barn of a place set among rolling hills on the highest hill around – a bunch of tombstones, a garden landscaped to within an inch of its terrestrial life, and trees scissored into the shape of angels – all stained-glass *fenêtres* and crosses and flying mattresses and a roof as steep as current-day electricity charges.

The minister's tilling the graveyard. Rory crutches across the paddock to him, and I follow.

Rory goes all shy. 'Hi.'

They embrace. I wince. Roarer's supposed to be a killer, yet here he is doing the full-body thing with a minister. Roarer steps back from his embrasure.

'This is –'

'Smith.' I don't give him a chance to call me whatever it was he was going to call me. 'Mr Smith.'

The minister smiles the smile of the broad church, and I take a step back before he tries to do to me what he just did to Rory.

'Smith, did you say?' He looks from me to Roarer and back again as he drops his trident and raises his arms from the empty-hug position to the sort of gesture St Francis might have used when he was blessing unsuspecting animals. 'So you'd be brothers?'

It's my turn. 'In my world, Preacher, everyone's brothers.' I straighten the shoulders. Putting the gat on display isn't appropriate to the occasion. 'We're here about a funeral.'

'Yours or somebody else's?'

I don't laugh. Laughing only encourages them.

The preacher coughs. 'Yes, of course, certainly we do funerals.' He fingers the 38-carat gold cross on the 38-carat gold chain around his one-carrot neck while I hunch my body around the .38 in the shoulder holster. 'Would the deceased have been a believer?'

'Is that important?'

'It makes a difference to the emolument.'

'The moll I *what*?'

'The cost of the funeral.'

I'm back on song. 'What kind of a difference?'

'Non-believers cost more.'

So I tell him, '*Yeah, the body was a believer.*'

The minister's a pork pie of a man, long grey hair done in a horse's tail, fat figure all wrapped up in shorts, singlets and sincerity, but I got to believe he's a preacher on account of the cross.

'Right. Would you like the standard ceremony or the deluxe?'

'What's the difference?'

'About ten grand.'

I chuck Roarer a glance but the monopod doesn't look as perturbed as he might be.

'Am I still in the black?' he says.

The preacher looks down at his fork. 'I believe you're as black as anyone can get.' He coughs again. 'After all, you gave us your house and your car and all the money you had in the bank.' He inclines his head. 'So, yes, almost certainly, and without even looking at the books, I'd say you could afford the standard.'

I feel more nauseated than I did in the presence of the corpse.

Meanwhile, Roarer's still busy negotiating. 'How many Heavenly Credits do I get?'

'Let's see.' The shyster pretends to think. 'I'd say about seven.'

'And how many do I need to get to Heaven?'

'Ten should see you through.'

'Do we book him into a graveyard?'

The Preacher waves behind him. 'For a little extra we can bury him here.'

I shake my head as we make our way back to the Cyclops toy. 'Are these jokers on the level, Roarer? He's taken your house, the Caddie and all the money you got in the bank. Hand the bastard a shooter and he's a crime tsar.'

When Roarer shakes his head I can hear his brain rattle. 'You got it wrong, Rain. You haven't heard the bastard sing. Dames have been known to swoon. The most Highly Reverend Pentecost is truly blessed.'

'Yeah – a blessed shyster.'

In the rear-vision I notice him looking after us as we leave, like he's afraid we might deface one of his death stones on the way, or tear up one of the angels.

But that's not what I'm looking at.

Behind the preacher I can see the snout of a vehicle that's more than familiar, the bonnet of Rory's pink Caddie, parked halfway between the church and the mansion behind it.

But that's not what I'm interested in, either.

I'm more interested in what's humming in the greenery.
It's not bees.
It's the Impreza.

Chapter 33

THE HOLE IN THE HARBOUR

I'm a juggling man. But unlike the jokers you see with their fedoras upturned, an emaciated canine beside them and a forced smile on their dial-up, I'm not throwing rubber bouncies in the air, I'm juggling lives. A lot of jokers have got a lot of reasons for following us. To the crime bosses I've been paying visits to, you can add the myriad of smaller fry that Rube's been checking up on. After that, you can factor in the cops, the crims I've crossed over the years, people I owe money to, and jokers that just don't like my face – not to mention the bastard that took out Tycho and Annabel.

Added to that, there's always Pandora.

And . . .

Winter's why the body in the Widow's kitchen hasn't turned completely putrid, but it's not the reason my blood suddenly goes colder than a corpse in a mortuary.

'Step on it,' I tell Roarer.

'I am stepping on it.'

'Then step on it some more.'

'Rain, these babies might go slow, but the upside is they're dirt cheap on fuel.'

'And seeing that the Right Reverend Dolittle's ripped you off so bad, you got to save on fuel, right?'

'Why've you got to go on about it all the time?'

Darkness is looming and the tide's receding when we get to the pontoon. I'm starting to wonder if my tide – as well as that of everyone else near and dear to me – is about to go on the ebb as well.

We've managed to lose the Subaru but I haven't lost the feeling we're in more trouble than a drunken nun at a christening.

We commandeer a dinghy that's still got its bung in and I phone Rube on one of the untraceable mobiles. 'I want you to check out the dame.'

'Got a name?'

It's then I realise I got nothing on the dame but suspicions. 'I got a name but I suspect it isn't the right one.'

'So give us a lead.'

'We got an address, the joint above you-know-who's place, and an address always comes complete with a name – like an owner or a renter or someone with a mortgage. From that point, we can get a handle on the dame. The address, in code, is as follows.'

Talking of addresses, I gave the preacher the address of the Widow so they can attend to the details – decide on the songs and the sentiments to be expressed and the rest of it – and we've swung by the Widow's and told her to expect a visitation and now we're on the way to the *Wooden No*, where I got no idea in the wide blue yonder what awaits us.

I realise I don't know Monica Best from a box of socks.

She turns up in the apartment above that of the dead dame.

Fortuitous.

She's got a gun.

More fortuitous.

And apart from all the lucky strikes above, she turns out to be more than handy with said gun, as athletic as any Olympian, and a more than willing participant in the various nefarious activities I employ her in. And I've left her in charge of the kid.

Like Rube said, it's the eyes. Show me a beautiful dame and my brains go out the window. Give her a pair of peepers to go with the beauty and I'd murder my mother for her. All right, so that's not going to happen, because I've never possessed a mother, but –

We round the first cove.

Roarer's rowing and I'm perched on the pointy end of the coracle with my gat out, scanning the horizon like Ozymandias – and I wish I didn't think that, because as soon as I think that, the words of the poem pirouette in my skull like a murderous fairy:

'My name is Ozymandias, king of kings: Look on my works, ye Mighty, and despair. Nothing beside remains. Round the decay of that colossal wreck . . .'

'Faster, Roarer, faster!'

'I'm rowing as fast as I can!'

I could call Salina, but that would only alert Jezebel that we're coming.

Theory 1: She killed Tycho.

Cancel that theory, as she was in her apartment at the time.

Theory 2: She killed Annabel.

Put that particular theory on hold.

Meanwhile she's got Imogene.

It's a long row, longer on account of my suspicions, tacking in and out among the bird-limed hulks that clutter the byways and why-bays of Sydney Harbour, and all the rats and fleas and barnacles and other creeping low life accompanying them, reflecting the ups and downs of their owners' misfortunes — 60-foot Halvorsens, twin-engine Gypsies, broken-masted windjammers and tattered-hulled tubs, cats with one keel in the grave and the other in Davy Jones's locker, and ocean goers that look like they couldn't even handle the Harbour on a nice day.

And buried among them, the *Wooden No*.

I've spent half my life hiding that tub from danger, only to invite danger on board, along with the kid. I shove Roarer aside and take over the rowing. It doesn't make us go any faster but at least it gives me something to do, the in-and-out rhythm of the oars hauling me ever deeper into Hopeland, and I'd give Roarer's God everything I haven't got and then some, in return for whatever He can do to save Imogene.

We've got around the fifth promontory, heading north-by-east.

'It's all right, Immo, we're coming.'

'What did you say?'

I shrug myself back into the oars. 'Nothing.'

'You said something.' I can't see Rory because he's in the bow and I'm rowing, but I can feel his eyes casing my back so I clam up. 'You're not praying by any chance are you, Rainbow?'

I tell him to shut up and after that I paddle faster.

The voyage takes forty-seven minutes twenty by my chronometer, but a century might have passed by the time we round Cape Hopeless — where at low tide you can still see the tip of the masts of the schooner it's named after — and find ourselves face to face with where the *Wooden No* was.

Was.

I stare around.

Nothing.

A few white-topped wavelets, the ragged reflection of a lighthouse, the bent shadow of a straggly-gum, a spectrum-smear of oil on the surface of the water.

But apart from that, nothing.

Then I spot it, rocking gently, and my brainpan lurches along with it, amid all the muck and grime of not-so-distant memory, a little girl gathering her treasures about her the way an old dame clutches her skirts when the wind lifts — toys, a rusty bobbin, the book she's writing . . .

Like a drowning man, I'm lying on my stomach in the crap room at Saturnalia's, and the kid's fussing over her box of goodies like she's busy collecting knick-knacks for a jumble stall. Puts me in mind of Pandora's box of tricks, Imogene's tin of goodies – an old Arnott's biscuit tin with a silly looking parrot on the lid, balanced unsteadily on one claw while the other's clutching a Milk Arrowroot.

'No point hiding stuff where no one can see it, sweetheart. You want to keep everything above board in this world, and your hands on top of the table.'

Imogene hunches her narrow shoulders inside the fairy-floss skirt, and when she shakes her head, the purple-and-yellow clasp holding the ponytail rattles like a machine gun. 'But Daddy, if I've learnt one thing from you, that's just what I *shouldn't* do.'

'Shouldn't what?'

'Tell everyone everything.'

'So what should you do?'

She deepens the voice, and does a fair imitation of a certain private detective. 'Don't tell nobody nothin'.'

She's good, I'll give the kid that, like I'd give her a lot of things if I had them. No one's pushing her around, not even her paterfamilias.

'I still don't recall teaching you anything about tin boxes with parrots on them, kid.'

A nod of the head, machine-gun rattle of the hair gripper. 'But you *did*. You always said that nothing's permanent. *Nothing's forever, kid*, you told me.' Again the voice. '*And you better believe it*. So I've been putting everything in my box – my best doll, the rat skeleton, the book I'm writing . . .'

'Oh, yeah, the book.'

'That's right, Daddy, there are some things I want to keep forever . . .'

Chapter 34

LADY GO NAKED

The water's icy, chilling my blood along with the thought that this might be all that's left of the kid — a parrot-topped box bobbing among the waves, with water dribbling off the beak of the bird like angel's tears.

I get back to the boat and with trembling hands prise open the lid which has been sealed with plasticine, fishing through the contents, like I'm scrabbling through betting discards well after the last race has been run.

And this is what I find:

A fairy picture.

A ferret's skull.

Assorted miscellanea.

The book.

The ink smears as I flicker through the pages, until I come across what I'm looking for:

'I'm writting this in my cabin where the man in the mask locked me, using the light of my lady detective's torch to write by.

He came for us at midnight but I couldn't see his face because of the mask. The lady tried to save us with her gun but the mask man grabbed me and held me in front of him and told her to drop it or else, so she did.

Then he put mummy and Janet and the lady with the gun in the aft cabin and me in my cabin in the proud where

I'm writing this and when I heard him start the motor and felt the boat move I knew what I had to do so I'm putting this in the tin box and after that I'll put Blue-Tack around the edges so water can't get inside and throw it out the porthole and hope that sum-one finds it.

I figger we're heading east . . .'

Man in a mask . . . lady tried to save us . . . heading east . . .

It's like a message from the grave. Only there ain't going to be any graves, not where Immo's concerned, not if I've got anything to do with it.

'We got to borrow a boat.'

'We already borrowed a boat.'

'Not a tinnie, Roarer, a big one, one with a donk in it, a stink boat, a launch. We're going to need power, and a lot of it.'

It takes a while but we eventually find one – a metal launch called *It's a Steel* tucked away next to its tombstone buoy in this watery graveyard, an Island Gypsy with just enough in the battery to start the 135, an engine capable of producing eight knots on a good night, although this night's shaping to be anything but good.

We come across the *Wooden No* up by the quarantine station, out near the open seas, and one step short of the Harbour floor – almost on the rocks, because whoever brought her here cut the cable and left her to scuttle herself before they departed.

It's started to rain and the seas are up and Janet's down on her housemaids on the outer deck praying to God Almighty, while Sal's screaming, someone – it must be the kid – is trying to start the engine, and Monica has discarded what remained of her modesty and is poised on the prow ready to leap into the briny, wearing a greasy hempen line around her waist, and little else worthy of mention.

Past the mist of rain, Imogene appears in the stern, wet hair plastered over her face, and waving. A yellow-and-black buoy is near enough to be useful and I can see that's what Monica's aiming for. But I'm looking anywhere but at Monica, yelling to Roarer to shove the *Steel* into reverse before tossing a jury-rigged anchor over the portside to Imogene.

'Grab it, Immo!'

The storm's increased and so has the urgency.

The tiny figure scrabbles for the lifeline.

'I've got it, Daddy! But it's too heavy!'

Roarer's got the *Steel* treading water, but the *Wooden No* looks like the water's about to tread her. She's heading for the rocks. Monica's stroking out among the choppy waves, but she can't make it to the buoy, breaching like a mermaid before turning back as I hear the jury-anchor rattling out of Imogene's hands along the deck on its way to uselessness as the *Wooden No* lurches towards the shore, rocks clawing out towards the old tub with Imogene on it.

Imogene and –

'You okay, Salina?'

'Piss off, Rainbow!'

That accounts for Salina, while Janet's still praying and I can see the cable coiling around Imogene's legs ready to take her over the side of the *Wooden No* along with the anchor.

Monica's drawing abreast of me as I launch myself over the great divide – *phalanges* reaching into air to curl around the *Wooden No*'s railing – as the hull crunches into the rocks.

It's the end of the line. Up Whatever-creek without an outboard, fists gripping the railing of the *Wooden No* as she lurches further rockwards, legs flailing helplessly in the water behind me.

Sorry, Immo.

Who had much more faith in her father than he was worth.

But that's when I feel a pair of vice-like hands clasp my uncles and I know whose hands they are. I force myself not to visualise what's attached to them as Roarer increases the tempo of the *Steel*'s engine while chucking it into reverse, and every atom of my anatomy from my *trapezia* to my superficial transverse ligaments screams with the strain.

I can feel my knuckles crack as they attempt to drag themselves loose from their sockets, along with the *humera*, the *radia*, and the *ulnae*. The two vessels are joined and once one of them's on the rocks we're all gone, lost forever in the torment of the seas and the hungry jaws of the sharks, with nothing remaining but the odd head, a foot, an arm, and a box of biscuits with a parrot on the lid.

I force my mind into reverse, along with the purloined boat's engine. I'm strong enough to hold the *Wooden No* and it looks like Monica's strong enough to hang onto me. But will can only go so far. After that, it rapidly becomes *won't*.

I feel my fingers slipping and Monica's grip loosening, while the sea around us has turned into a battering ram, and the boats I'm slung between the wheels of a rack.

'I've got it, Daddy!'

As the boats lurch on the cusp of certain disaster, I see the small figure snarl the anchor around the stern capstan, a determined little figure with what looks like blood all over its determined little features.

I yell at Roarer. 'Go for it! Give it all you got! More power!'

Roarer puts the stolen craft into overdrive – an ear-splitting roar that drowns even the wind – and the lurch as the strain takes charge of the boats tears my uncles out of Monica's grasp and I see the stern of the *Wooden No* spin towards the rocks before rearing upwards like Janet's God has decided to ditch the Ethiopians, arresting the tub within death's breath of its date with Destiny.

The *Wooden No*'s bow takes a dive as the cable that Imogene managed to snarl in the capstan twangs taut under me, flinging me skyward, and the last thing I see before I smack back down into the shark-infested seas is a small, pale face leaning over the side of the tub, staring worriedly down at me from a busted railing.

Chapter 35

DEAD MEN DO TELL TALES

S o who did it?'
The wind's subsided and with it the seas, and we're back in the comforting embrace of the Harbour. We've untangled the jury-anchor from the *Wooden No* and found safe anchorage after re-parking *It's a Steel* back where the owner can find her.

Salina's settled as much as she's ever going to settle and Janet's stopped praying and Rory's doing a one-legged strut like he's just saved the world. Imogene's checking the contents of her parrot box to make sure none of her past's gone missing, and Monica's wrung the last of the Harbour out of her clobber and got respectable.

Sparks fly in the early dawn light as she runs her fingers through her hair. 'I think it was some rich kid with too much time on his hands.' She has another go. 'I mean he didn't kill us outright.'

'You still would have been dead.'

She frowns. I can see she blames herself. 'He had Imogene. Anything could have happened. I did what he told me to do.'

'Did you get your gat back?'

She nods her electric hair. 'He didn't care about the gun. As I said, he struck me as a Hooray Henry who wouldn't know his *glutea maxima* from his *humora* – with a mask on. Look, I know you came looking for us because you were suspicious of me and quite frankly I don't blame you.' A breeze is whispering among the black trees on the shore. 'You find me in a place I shouldn't be, carrying a gun I shouldn't be carrying, and capable of acts I shouldn't be capable of.' Her peepers on me are like the caress of the breeze. 'You have a right to your suspicions – you're a detective, after all. But I think you realise now you can trust me.'

I drag myself out of the pull of her ambience and climb to my feet, stretched joints cracking like automatic rifle fire. 'Lady, I don't have to trust nobody.'

'Except, Mister Rainbow, I strongly suspect that in my case you already do.'

We're moving in tight formation along the boulevard – Roarer, Monica and me – and our way takes us past familiar territory. The crime scene's been cleaned up. The coppers have gone – taking their blue-and-white tape and trestle horses with them – and the blood's been mopped up so nice that an innocent bystander might imagine it never existed. The window of the dry cleaner's has been replaced.

There's no one outside Monica's apartment block, but I didn't expect there to be, while the wheelchair ramp's still *in situ* and the security grille's still in place. The little green buttons that give the residents the opportunity to attract or repel boarders are still all present and correct, and yet . . .

I shrug off the and-yets. Ours not to reason why, ours but to see the case to its conclusion.

We get ourselves to Lulu's.

Tattooists are the Leonardo da Vincis of the 21st century, creating works of art in impossible-to-get-to places. There are plenty up the Cross, but Lulu was the pin man I was after. But I'm too late.

Some jokers warrant a place in the *Horrible*'s *Cark it, Park it and Mark it* department, the section up the back near the comics they call the *Obituaries*. But not Lulu. He was lowlife and the *Horrible* doesn't recognise lowlife; it's too busy with more serious issues like the *Recipe of the Week*, celebrity divorce settlements and what socialite's on drugs. Accordingly, for the finer details on the passing of the tattooist, I've got to rely on Aunt Rube.

'He was fed a shiv.'

'His head wasn't blown off?'

'Use your brain, Rainbow, if you still possess one after that dame's been at it. If you're looking for a similar modus operandi to the one used on Tommy Tycho, you're forgetting that Annabel Franklin was dispatched in much the same way that Lulu was.'

There's a crackle over the wire, but we're both using dead-men's terror-phones, so the dialogue's as safe as such things can be – until the time when it's not.

'The perpetrator was looking for a death, not trying to create a pattern. He didn't blow anyone's head off on the boat. We're not looking at the means now, we're looking at the end.'

'When did Lulu cop it?'

'All I know is it was after closing time.'

So the ink slinger's was shut when it happened, just like it is now. But that's no guarantee nobody's home. While Roarer and Monica keep their eye on the locale, I consider the façade. The cops have come and gone. There's a piece of tape on the door, a ladies' hairdresser specialising in Brazilians on one side, and a strip joint on the other. Photographs depicting the late Master's work litter the window – flying horses leap over beautiful corpses, wreaths of elaborate floral arrangements decorate the corpses of dogs, and there are the usual dragons, skulls, guns, knives, scimitars and Memories of Mother.

I hammer on the door. No answer. I kick at the door. Still no answer.

The hatchway finally gives to the shoulder and I make my way in, closely followed by Monica, Roarer and the alarm system, gat at the ever-ready.

You seen one tattoo parlour, you seen them all. Pretty pictures line the walls and more pretty pictures grace the books on the window seat, the ones with black covers on them. I flip through the tomes looking for a clue, but all I find is more memories of mothers when I'd like to forget my own, plus dragons and snakes and wild animals, and more dames – all in more or less the state they were born in, only older. The lingering pork belly burning smell reminds me how portraits make their way onto people's skin, while the faint sweet-and-sour stench of blood, and the police artist's outline on the floor, reminds me why we're here.

The police artist was no Leonardo, but the drawing he's done is enough to tell me the corpse still possessed a head when it got that way. Like Rube said, it wasn't a modus operandi the killer was after, just another death.

At the back of the studio I find a nice big chrome machine with a needle hanging off it, followed by a sink, a couch – and the inevitable door to the little dark room out the back.

The room's got a lavatory in it.

It also contains a kid.

The lavatory doesn't tell me a thing.

Neither does the kid.

I recognise him by the pink-and-white tracksuit and the tatts, together with the marks on his skinny white arms, the skinny joker I first met in the vicinity of the corpse in the gutter, and after that in the eating house with the tablecloths. The drug-addled number who thought I could get him methamphetamines just on the strength of the way I dress. The kid that let himself into this joint when he heard of his master's death, shooting up afterwards on whatever he could find, plus uncut grief.

'Who's this joker when he's at home?'

I remove the tourniquet and the needle. He doesn't wake. 'I'd say he's already at home.'

Monica slaps the kid's face and the pinpoint eyes flicker.

I shove her aside and lean over him. 'Where did your boyfriend Lulu keep his books?'

They all keep records. No one thinks they do, everyone imagines it's all nice and anonymous, that when they get *I LOVE JOE* inscribed on their fanny no one will ever know. Except, of course, for Joe – plus all the boyfriends and girlfriends that come after. But the tattoo merchants have got to be ready for the health people when they pay a visit. Then there's the Goods and Services Tax, along with every other mercenary in this town that wants a piece of the action.

'What books?' He's got his weight on one needle-tracked paw and he's rubbing his slapped cheek with the other, pretending all the while he's as silly as he looks – at the same time as he's imagining I'm going to fall for it.

'Your boyfriend's book, stupid. The records. The book with all the names in it, including the chart of your own pilgrim's progress.'

The kid looks like he's set on remaining intransigent. But that's before Roarer taps him with his crutch. He cringes, and says exactly what you'd imagine he'd say, which is, 'Don't hit me!' His squinty eyes clear as he recognises me. 'Hey, it's you! Look, man, I'll tell you what you want to know if you'll give me some – I don't care what, just give me anything!'

'I'll give you something all right if you don't tell me what I want to know.' I haul back the footwear. 'Where's the book?'

At first I think he's shaking his wasted head but then I realise he's pointing it and that's when I shelve the gat and rip up the square of blue-and-white lino he's shaking his head at and haul up the floorboard. Eventually I find it, an exercise book not unlike Imogene's, except that, unlike my daughter's, this one contains a lot of names, dates and illustrations. I leaf through until I find what I'm after, the reason Lulu was exxed before he told anyone what he knew.

Only whoever exxed Lulu overlooked one important fact. And that is that dead men do tell tales. It's just a matter of finding the book they tell them in.

Chapter 36

HERE COMES A CHOPPER . . .

The tattooist's phone's still functioning, which is more than the tattooist is.

'It's No-Name here.' Rube knows who it is and I got no time for the niceties. 'I need a check done – description and form of one Percy James Gardener-with-an-e.'

Nothing fazes Rube. 'By the sound of things you need the information yesterday.'

'Make it the day before.'

When I hang up, I check out my companions. Roarer's nervous and Monica's even more beautiful than when I last looked – the paint shop bloke would probably describe her cheek colour as *Dawn Gloss* – but the pallor on the junkie's face has turned to junket, so I call in the mercenaries.

'St Vincent's Casualty? I got you a client. Details as follow: junkie; male of the species; age sixteen, going on a hundred; currently hugging the floorboards in Lulu's Pin Parlour.' I give the address. 'Temperature 39, sweating like an oil pump, and inflamed trackline suggests serious infection. Prognosis: If you can't do the ambulance in five, make it a hearse.'

'Your name, sir?'

They always want your name. They reckon it's for the records. Tell that to the snoops.

'Look, pal, having a name won't keep this kid alive, while shutting up and getting on with the job just might.'

We're out in the nice, clean ambience of Bayswater Road – pollution reading in the vicinity of ten out of ten – and the mean streets are humming with the kind of action that, if this was a compost heap, would turn fresh cabbages into mulch in a microsecond.

'Do you think he did it?'

I stall for time. 'Do I think who did what?'

'Do you think the person who killed Tycho and Annabel also killed the tattooist?'

We're walking fast, because we got a lot to walk fast for – the ambulance is already screaming around the corner. Tomorrow we got a funeral to attend, and if we hang around breathing this air much longer, that funeral might just turn out to be ours. The tail's swapped the white Impreza with tinted windows for a pale-green Mercedes, also with tinted windows. I know it's him – not because I can see him but because of the way he drives, with oversteer-and-correction to the left like he's holding a gun in the right – and he's lingering on the corner of Victoria and Bent like he's in two minds about continuing the tail – or executing us on the spot and getting it over with.

There's an alley to my right and I head for it. It's the kind of alley that in this part of the world can turn into a dead-end – the kind of dead-end you don't come out of except in a body bag, the sort of place they flog filched flat-screen televisions, hot DVDs, and purloined grave-digging equipment – and the pale-green Merc is coming our way like the driver's suddenly not in two minds any longer.

I barrel Roarer and Monica into a fast food franchise just as machine-gun Charlie lets loose with a fusillade.

The blatts are right – there's too much violence in the Cross and the sooner they do something about it the better. Meanwhile innocent bystanders like us just have to do the best we can under the circumstances.

A random voice asks, 'Do you want fries with that?'

Another volley rat-tats into the window as Monica cranes for a glimpse of the perpetrator.

'Those dark windows – I can't see anything!'

'You're not supposed to. Get down!'

I shove Monica under a table and work my way out of the shattered doorway just as the Mercedes swings into another laneway. I jam on the hat, haul out the gat, and chuck the hoofs into overdrive. I head off after the Mercedes – past the shoeshine parlour and the real estate con merchant's and yet another strip joint – until I find myself deep in the shadows of Temporary Lane, where I come across the Mercedes in a too-close-encounter with a garbo.

'Idiot!'

I can't see the shooter but I see the results. It's Greta Garbo's famous last words as the gunman unloads him into the great rubbish tip in the sky.

After which the shooter makes himself even scarcer than he was before.

The good thing about tin cans is that not even madmen are going to steal them. The bad thing is that they do five miles per honorarium – which is *why* madmen don't steal them – and that's what we're doing as we head along South Dowling towards the autobahn.

Dead-man's mobile numero dix does a ring-a-ling.

'I got the information you requested.' Rube's voice is calm. 'The name belongs to a person they call the Backpacker. Backpacker's never done time. Repeat, *never done time.* So there's nothing on him locally, nothing with Interpol, nothing anywhere. Apart from any tattoo he might now possess – he's clean. Last seen gunning for our mutual friend over a woman. Physical as follows.'

For *our mutual friend* read Tommy Tycho, and the more Rube talks the more I know I'm in possession of enough facts to bust this case wide open.

'I got one last chore for you,' I tell her. The connection crackles. 'Shoot.'

So I shoot and what I shoot is a request to send out invitations to a funeral.

'Deal me date, place and time of funeral – plus the name of the corpse. In code, of course.'

I tell her what she wants to know and after I shelve the communicator I throw a shooftee in the rear-vision and what I see is pretty much what I expect to see, and that is the poky nose of what I know is yet another stolen vehicle – this time a black BMW – going nice and slow like it's a family and the family dog, looking forward to a nice Sunday picnic on a weekday. Except I can't see either the family or the dog. Because, one, they don't exist but also because, two, the windows are painted – in a shade that the paint people would probably call *Cutout Delight.*

'Scar on face,' Rube advised me, 'physical as follows . . .'

There's a kids' show on the Tonka's wireless and it's playing one of those all time favourites:

'Oranges and lemons, say the bells of St Clements.
'When will you pay me? say the bells of Old Bailey.
'When I grow rich, say the bells of Shoreditch.
'Here comes a candle to light you to bed,
'And here comes a chopper . . .'

Chapter 37

... TO CHOP OFF YOUR HEAD

I've spent a bad night going over the scenario, and I'm still going over the scenario as we head for the hills.

Orange, the Widow told me – she was going to paint the joint orange.

Monica senses my urgency. 'Can't this thing go any faster?'

I shrug the shoulders that are supporting the Heckler. 'If this thing went any faster, I'd join Roarer in believing in miracles. Slugs can't fly.'

'If they come out of the business end of an equaliser, they can.'

Why does this dame continue to surprise me? Aunt Rube would have the answer to that. *Because you're in love*, she'd say. *And it's a well-known fact, little recorded, that when jokers are in love, they don't see with the eyes of ordinary men, but with eyes that have a large part of a mortuary in them.*

I glance in the rear-vision. Monica's in it. So is our follower's latest conveyance, a black Beamer.

'Where did you learn to talk like that?'

'From my dad, for a start.'

'And for a finish?'

'I've spent more time with you than could possibly be healthy for a growing girl.'

It's two-fifty-five in the post-meridian. Happy Hour's slated for three. I hear them doing the warm-up as we approach.

The Widow showed me the menu, which is how I know they selected Brahms' *Voluntary and Fugue*, to be followed by *Nearer My God To Thee*, and after that *Just a Closer Walk with Whosit*, *The Holy Thingummy*, *A Walk in the Park with the Old Boy*, the *Ave* – always the *Ave* – plus *How Great* et cetera, with a grand finale of *Give Me That Old Time Religion*. Toe-tapping favourites that are always going to knock ditties like *Oranges and Lemons* into a gum tree.

When Rube sent out the invites, everyone came running. The car park's standing-room only – with black duco in the ascendant – as Roarer eases the Tonka towards the church on the hill, with the BMW following. Because there's no room at the inn, I get Roarer to poke the 121 around the corner of the prayer house next to the Caddie, while me and the dame make our way towards the church, leaving Roarer beside the Caddie like a lovestruck Romeo.

The corpse gate – also known as a lych gate – is a bunch of stone and lattice and fairy weed perched a couple of body lengths from the western entry to the praying house. It's the place where they park the coffin until the mourners are ready to take receipt of it, a place of repose. But I got no time for repose.

I turn to Roarer. 'You coming?'

'I'll join youse in a tick.'

That leaves just me and Monica – plus whoever's going to follow us out of the Beamer. I check the gat's in place and start in on the approach.

It's a nice church if you happen to like churches – a lot of expensive windows and baa-relief over a foe-gothic doorway saying: *GIVE YOUR ALL TO GOD AND YOU'LL BE RICHLY REWARDED.*

I pretend to retie the whitesides while I check out the interior. In the smoky light, made that way by all the *fenêtres*, a black-garbed congregation is staring at a bunch of organ tubes staring right back at them – unseen eyes behind dark slits, an elongated army of Ned Kellys. The piano player's knocking out the voluntary and fugue but I'm not hearing church music – only the echoes of the song I heard on the Tonka's wireless, and its ramifications.

Oranges and . . .

Hamstring Harry's got pole position on account of the leg, and strung out beside him in no particular order are the distinctive forms of Howard 'Fast One' Hardie, the starting price bookie; king of the smoky poker parlour, Quick Draw Pete Davelo; Jackie the Pimp; Moses Johnstone, the slow drugs maestro; usurer Jock McAddock; plus a bunch of hairstyles lined up in the back pew generally belonging to the two-wheeler set – cats' tails, possums' tails, beavers and plaits . . .

Don't ask me why, but I've got a funny feeling as me and Monica get ourselves along an aisle that's crowded on both sides by the assembled thuggery, while the organ pumper belts out *Nearer My God To Thee* – any closer and we'd be humping tombstones.

They're the names on the list — names I gave Rube plus the ones I checked out personal and then some — all names that possessed larger-than-death-sized motives for exxing Lover Boy.

We come to bury Tycho, not to praise him.

Fixer Murdoch. Flame-haired Annie 'Six-Gun' Tenschyle — pronounced Tan-schoolie, if you know what's good for you. Sensitive Sam, the homicidal maniac. Pete Scissorhands.

People that Tommy Tycho at some point in his non-illustrious career crossed several times, in a way that most people only manage once.

Genuflecting Jennie, Stan the Man, Hieroglyphics Bosch the forger, Hitman Harry 'The Hedgerow' Harvey, a bunch of killers known as The Goon Show, Lightfingers Whitman, a lug that's got a reputation for turning people into stone, the Concrete-Mixer, Prostitute Pete . . .

All persons that for one reason or another wanted to see the arse end of Tommy Tycho.

The light softens the scene like a halo as me and Monica make our way to the altar in the embrace of music that's as soft as the fudge my grandmother used to make, and about as good for anyone's health. The organ grinder could be playing *Hymn to a Massacre.* You can touch the glory, see the heavenly light, hear the celestial music, *taste* the incense. But the smell of the hate that permeates the place trumps all.

Chapter 38

THE UNLOVED ONE

The hate's as tangible as the sandstone steps under the gothic archway, dark as the rafters looming overhead, hard as a bullet, and deep as the grave beneath the tombstone awaiting the contents of the hearse. Which right this moment is pulling up outside. All heads jerk around at the sound of it. The Dentist. Karrybag. Pig. And in the far corner of the front pew, her face in shadow, someone I'd prefer never to see again this side of Hell – Pandora.

It's more like Dante's central circle of the nether-life than a church, more a collection of the archangel Azrael's followers than a congregation, Fate instead of a funeral. All covered in ethereal light, the kind of colour that generally accompanies an inferno.

The preacher appears out of the door to the chancel. He's exchanged his gravedigger's gear for his preacher's canonicals and his arms are raised like bats' wings. Me and Monica sidle in beside the Widow, turning just in time to see four black-clad goons under the pointy doorway, a coffin teetering on their over-developed *trapezia* as the organ grinder swings into the strains of *The Death March*.

Even through the rosewood lid I can smell it, the pong of the decomposing body that's been parked too long in the kitchen at the Widow's joint, a stench that no one in their right mind would voluntarily suspirate. Except that very few here gathered could be described as being in their right mind.

All eyes are fixed on the coffin and all minds on the dead man inside it – the corpse of the bastard that took their women, dobbed them into the fuzz, and nicked their ill-gotten gains from under their schnozzes. And never got done for any of it. Who managed to slip through the interstices of the law, and who right now looks like he's in process of escaping his victims' individual and collective fury forever.

As the rosewood coffin with brass trimmings reaches the halfway mark – little more than an eight-legged silhouette, a giant spider – a figure appears in the doorway behind it, wreathed in black. It's poised like it's on a fleeting visit, like it's only come to see the body into the grave before departing – an anonymous figure: black cloak reaching from the top of its head right down to the church step, hands hidden within loose sleeves, and something concealed in the folds of the cloak. It's like an avenging angel, but it's also like it's not here – on account of no one, with the exception of me, is paying it any attention.

Instead, all eyes are on the coffin, borne aloft by the corpse-carriers. Who carefully lower the box onto the plinth in front of the preacher before turning to face the congregation.

The main man raises his arms. 'Praise be to all of us gathered here together.'

'Amen!'

'Lest our light be dimmed before our time, let us each and every one of us be prepared to be taken at any moment.'

'Amen!'

'Light of light, heart of hearts, soul of souls.'

'Amen, amen, amen!'

The preacher's eyes linger on the gathering. 'Welcome.' His face is full of benevolence. 'Before burial, a short commercial break.' He smiles. 'I just want to say that the Hillbilly Church is a fine new establishment and in it we worship God Almighty in a fine new way. No matter what your sins, the Hillbilly Church is the way to salvation. Even after you die, under the auspices of the Hillbilly Church, you can expect to go on living. All it takes is a little bit of giving.'

Impatience accompanies his words.

'Get on with it, mate, we're here to see the bastard buried!'

'Very well. But first, is there anyone here present who would like to say a eulogy?'

At this point the figure at the back of the church, poised for flight, hesitates.

Pig clambers to his trotters and turns in his pew hole to eyeball his brothers. 'Yeah, I would.' It isn't in the script, but that doesn't stop it happening. 'This bastard dudded me good, the way he dudded everyone else here.' He's forgotten his expensive education and instead is saying what he thinks. It doesn't make what he says any prettier. 'He robbed me of money but worst of all he stole my self-respect. I hated the bastard then, and I hate him now. I don't get many happy days in my life, but this is one of them.'

He resumes his seat and after that it's the Dentist's turn, then Karrybag's. But it's when Psycho Harrigan gets to his feet – Psycho Harrigan with the scar on his schnozz that Tycho brought about, courtesy of a whip – that the script takes a turn for the worse. Unlike the rest, Psycho's thinking outside the box.

'How do we know there's even a body in there?' he says. The seed's been planted and there's a general murmur of assent. 'All right, let's say there is a body. Anyone got a bit of paper that says it's Tycho's?'

There's action in the doorway, but there's more action in the church. The Widow's got to her feet and is about-facing the doubters. Silence falls over the congregation.

'For those that aren't aware of the fact, I'm the Widow Tycho.' She's no longer the person who gave up her place at the butcher's. 'If anyone knows my husband, it's me. Haven't I been his loving spouse since I was a girl? Haven't I lived with his corpse for three days? Didn't I personally see it into the coffin?'

'What about the ID?' someone shouts.

The Widow nods her head. 'All right, there aren't any fingerprints to identify him by. But that's only because Tommy never did anything wrong and never did time or was even arrested. So there's no head on the body. There's still the tattoo that says people like to be deceived and that Tommy's deceived them.' She glares around. 'It's got to be him. Who else could it be?'

It's a big speech, but after that it's my turn. I don't like public speaking, never have. I'm more a fist-and-gun man than a mouthpiece. But sometimes you got to do it, and this is one of those times. So I climb to my feet and face the music. The organ grinder stops as I turn. I'm still facing the music. Most of these crims know me and most of the crims that know me don't like me, because I'm on the other side of the ledger from the column most of them occupy. But I got their attention. The only movement comes from the doorway as the cloaked figure makes what appear to be minor adjustments to its cloak. But that's before there's another movement beside the figure.

'I realise,' I begin, 'that to all present, time is a precious commodity. Life might not be, but time is.' I send my eyes on a tour of the pews. 'But there's someone not present.'

'Yeah, Tycho.'

The observation raises a laugh, but I'm not interested in laughs. I haul out the book I found at the tattooists. 'This is the records from Lulu's Pin

Parlour. You all knew Lulu.' I open the book. It's a nice exercise book in the old style with a green cover, the sort that's got a little white patch on the front to put your name and address in. The space is blank but the pages aren't. I got one eye on the book and the other on the doorway.

'I draw your attention to the following entry.' If anyone knows what's coming they don't show it. 'The entry concerns someone known to most of you by the moniker Percy James Gardener.' I keep my voice casual. 'Some of you knew him as the Backpacker, a small-time gambler that was part-time innocent backpacker, but like most of you here present was actually a full-time rogue.'

I got their attention. The doorway hasn't.

'All his life, just like Tycho, Gardener managed to evade the law. He existed on the edge of crime, but that didn't mean he was apart from it. Recently, just like the rest of you, he was gunning for Tycho. But can anyone see him here?' There's a general shaking of heads. 'That's because two things happened to prevent him. One, Tycho crossed one person too many, and so for the first time in Tycho's life, Sydney got too hot for him. And, two, Gardener crossed Tycho.'

'So what happened?' a voice up the back yells.

I let them have it between the eyes. 'Nothing. At least not to Tycho. No one killed Tycho. Instead, Tycho killed Gardener. After warning his girlfriend he was in danger, he drugged Gardener and took him to Lulu's, where he got the pin man to write an inscription on the Backpacker's neck.

'After that, with the help of a random space cadet, he took Gardener down the road and blew his head off. No head and no recorded prints meant there was means of identification. Apart from the tattoo, which told everyone who wanted to know that the body belonged to Tycho.'

It takes a while for it all to sink in but when it does it leads to the inevitable question.

'So who's in the coffin?'

I let them work it out for themselves.

'It's gotta be Gardener!'

That leaves something else to work out.

'SO WHERE'S TYCHO?'

I don't nod towards the back of the praying house because if I do, the figure in black with Roarer riding shotgun — and thereby stopping it either drawing its gun or escaping — is going to die of more bullets than anyone has ever died of before. I nod to Roarer to get Tycho the hell away. But I'm mistaken regarding two things.

One: I've overestimated Roarer's brainpower.

And two: I've underestimated the power of hate.

These non-mourners are here to witness the funeral of Tommy Tycho and no one – repeat, no one – is going to deprive them of it.

'That's him up the back!'

Chapter 39

THE DEATH OF A LADIES' MAN

I don't know what I thought was going to happen on this nice winter's day in this nicest of all praying establishments. But it turns out everyone in the congregation is packing a shooter, and suddenly they're waving them around. There's Benellis and Berettas and Frommers and Rugers and Heckler & Kochs, even the odd Hotchkiss – commonly known as *The Hotchkiss of death*. The air that's tinted courtesy of the church windows becomes as full of lead as a hole in the ground belonging to Mount Isa Mines or BHP Billiton. It gives a whole new meaning to the word *leadlight*.

Tommy Tycho thought he was safe. He's been following us – even taking the odd potshot, as well as threatening the lives of everyone on the *Wooden No* – because he was determined to see his last con out to the end. He wanted to attend his own funeral. His wish is in process of being granted.

Roarer's made himself scarce, while the preacher's yelling and the Widow's trying to push past Monica only she can't because Monica's got hold of her arm. Monica's not about to let go in a hurry, even as the pointy-topped windows come down around our lugs and the figure in the doorway – Mediflex-gloved hands clutching its elephant gun – jerks about like a man possessed.

Only he's not a man possessed, he's just Tommy Tycho, who's miraculously come to life again, and I'm certain of that fact because – when his arms come up and the cloak of anonymity finally falls away – I can see the ring-a-ring-a-rosy conformation of the infamous tattoo around his neck. The tattoo that says everyone in the joint except Tycho is an idiot. But that's not what the new script says. Because when Tycho's reborn it's only for the briefest of seconds. And after those briefest of seconds he's nothing more than a lifeless body clutching a gun under the caption above the doorway that says GIVE YOUR ALL TO GOD AND YOU'LL BE RICHLY REWARDED – why does it look like *retarded* – his body, his hopes and the new head he's grown full of sweetmeats.

I turn and gesture to the organ grinder. He nods back at me and begins hammering out the next item on the menu – *Just a Closer Walk With Thee*. Roarer meanwhile reappears and slams a couple of slugs out of his crutch rifle into the chandelier to get everyone's attention.

In the silence, I take up the refrain. *'Jesus grant it is my plee-ee-ea.'*

Voice played a big part in Aunt Rube's curriculum – how to use it, how to throw it, how to play it – and it's like the congregation suddenly remembers where they are, as a couple of willing and ready volunteers drag the newly-minted corpse of Tommy Tycho up the aisle, past the wreckage of the light attachment and the remnants of the windows, and dump it on the already-occupied coffin. The gats find their way back into their respective hidey-holes and the hymn books come out as the piano player leads the way into the chorus, and one by one the voices of the celebrants climb into the music alongside.

Everyone seems happy, or as happy as they'll ever be, and they're settling into the singing real nice, and to settle them still further, I give them *Ave Maria* in the original Latin, the way it should be sung:

Ave Maria, gratia plena/ Dominus tecum/ Benedicta Tu in mulieribus/ Et benedictus fructus ventris.

It shuts them up for a while, and after I reckon it's safe, with the clergyman shivering like he's in a paroxysm of disbelief, and the organist still hammering away and the little Ned Kelly masks in the organ pipes giving with the chords like they're loving every minute of it, the congregation raises its collective voice to heaven, and segue into everyone's all-time favourite, taking the organist along for the ride:

'Lord my God, when I in awesome wonder . . .'

I give Roarer the nod and he underarms the crutch that doubles as a gat and hops up the aisle. While the congregation is otherwise employed, we escort the Widow to the door to the chancel. The congregation's too involved with the hymn singing to notice.

'I see the stars,
'I hear the rolling thunder
'Thy power throughout the universe displayed . . .'

The criminal element of Sydney is right in the swing of it now. They're back in their miserable childhoods peering into some dim-lit crevices of their souls, while I'm still giving with the big brassies as I head out after the others.

'Then sings my soul, my Saviour God to Thee
'How great Thou art, How great Thou art . . .'

I don't wait to see what happens after that. Wait to see what happens after that and I've got to face more music than I care to face right now, namely a bunch of heavily-armed hoods that might suddenly remember they don't like me all that much, not to mention the avenger in black at the far end of the front row, who of all those assembled would have little or no interest in Tommy Tycho – only in me, and the possibility of making a trifecta of the occasion: Pandora.

Roarer's already in the vestry while Monica is following with the Widow. I bring up the rear as we head for the interstice between a kirk and a hard place, the church and the McMansion, the place where the Caddie's ready for the getaway.

'She got enough gas in her?'

Roarer's waving a length of garden hose and nodding towards the car park as he climbs in behind the wheel. 'Those babies won't be going anywhere in a hurry, but we will.'

'What about you, Roarer?' I glance back at the church. 'You reckon you're going to make it to heaven after this little lot?'

'After what little lot?'

'Oh, you know, being ultimately responsible for the death of Tommy Tycho – I mean if you hadn't been there he could have escaped – plus sacrilege, blasphemy, impiety, profanity, desecration and probably simony, not to mention robbing the church of a car.'

Roarer shrugs. 'I reckon I've given the church more than it ever gave me. Apart from which, all those potential sign ups has got to put me back in the black.'

Roarer's maths produces a silence that's broken only by the flap of the wings of God's starlings and the buzz of God's bees. Add to that the syncopated bellow of a bunch of crooks demanding the return of that old-time religion while the bullet-spattered corpse of Tommy Tycho – the man who was already dead but has just died some more – lies atop the coffin of his victim.

I always find something moving about a second passing.

The Caddie takes off past the tombstones and all the de-fuelled getaway cars – including the stolen Beamer. We say goodbye to the nice little church with its windows all shot up – plus the roar of Sydney's crème de la crime yelling *Gimme That Old-time Religion* like it's some kind of stick-up. But I'd prefer that we moved just that little bit faster, to make sure we get out of here in a different manner to the one Tycho did.

'Step on it!' I tell Roarer.

We're not in the Tonka car, so he steps on it.

Chapter 40

NEVER TRUST A DAME

Me and Monica are in the speakeasy and we got the *Daily Terrorgraph* spread out between us. Monica's perched on the other side of the tableau and she's still got blue eyes and she's also still more beautiful than she's got any right to be.

'So how did you know?' she asks.

I shrug. It settles the gat. 'I first got suspicious when I was handed that list of suspects – free, gratis and for nothing.'

'Suspicious of what?'

'Of lists in general and the death of Tommy Tycho in particular.'

'Why?'

'I knew Tycho.'

'And after that?'

I put on my Jimmy Cagney look, the one where he grapefruits the dame. Only I haven't got a grapefruit, so all I'm left with is the look. 'I'm the one asking the questions. And my first question is: who are you? And don't tell me you're the daughter of a war veteran in the habit of smuggling military-issue weapons out of Afghanistan, because even the Australian army doesn't arm people with anachronistic bangers made in Turkey sixty years ago.' I hunch the shoulders. 'So how did you really come by the gat?'

It's Monica's turn to shrug. 'The way anyone gets anything – at a price and on the black market. It saves a lot of paperwork, and you don't have to pay the Goods and Services Tax.'

That answers some of the question. I ask the rest of it. 'Having figured the gun, I also figured there wasn't a war hero father who also happened to be – so help me – a cross-dressing, depressive transsexual. So I return to my original question: who are you, how come the apartment – and what's with the wheelchair I donated to the cabbie?'

When Rube checked who owned Monica's apartment, she came up with a lot of mumbo jumbo about holding companies and straw men and third parties and John Does – and nothing at all about who actually held the title to it.

She sighs. 'The apartment – like most things in this town – belongs to an insurance company, and so do I. Insurance companies are like banks – they own property the way people like you and I own debts. The apartment belonged to a workers' compensation fraudster and the wheelchair was part of the fraud. The fraudster got a jail term while the company got the apartment, and its contents.'

'Plus you?'

'Yes, you might say they got me, too. Like you, Mister Rainbow, I started out as a private investigator. Except that somewhere along the line I sold out. I now investigate insurance fraud.' She plays with her whisky sour. 'It's big business, insurance fraud. Again just like the banks, my company avoids unnecessary payouts. They've been onto the Tychopouloses ever since a new salesman inadvertently gave them a cheap rate on Tommy – remember, he was relatively young and he was also clean – with the wife as sole beneficiary. We knew they were up to something, only we didn't know what. So the company set me up in the apartment they'd come into possession of, situated just above that of Tycho's girlfriend.'

Annabel Franklin. The dame I owed a debt to. Who called me in thinking I could help, after her lover said someone was out to kill him. Information that Annabel was supposed to take to the police but came to me with instead.

'But then three things happened. One: someone got their head blown off. Two: Annabel was murdered. And three: you turn up on my doorstep like an avenging angel.' She tries a smile. It comes out a grimace. 'Requiring me to keep a close eye on you, because you were going to do my dirty work for me – exposing the Tycho scam at the same time as you were looking for Annabel's killer.' She reaches across the table and her hand lights on mine like a death wish. 'I'm sorry, but it's my job.'

I shift the fist and the wish list falls on the tableau.

'So you're a P.I. that found the easy way out, making sure the little man goes on losing while the big boys keep rolling in clover. And meanwhile you been in the game so long you carry your own insurance – in the form of Naloxone and Flumazenil, plus any other accessories that might save you from the depredations of strangers.'

The nickelodeon's on playback and the tune it's playing is *Wooden Heart*. Elvis is busy telling the world to treat him nice, treat him good, treat him like it really should, while Monica Best looks at me with what a casual bystander might take to be sadness. The beautiful peepers are still blue, only now there's an emptiness in them, like a cloud's just covered the sun and a cold winter's day just got that much colder.

'But, please,' she begs, 'tell me how you knew.'

'Knew what?'

She waves a beautiful hand at the story in the *Terror* that's telling anyone who cares to know that the cops have cracked the mystery of who killed Tommy Tycho, that it's out of the *Cold Case* basket and into the one marked *Too Easy*. The rag also reports that there was a funeral, and that a number of colourful Sydney identities were present, and that it was a moving occasion – moving, that is, in that Loverboy Tycho was finally moved to his final resting place.

She takes a deep breath. 'How you knew that the corpse in the kitchen wasn't Tycho's. How you knew . . .' She fidgets. 'I'm sorry but I need this information in order to make out a report for my employers.'

I've got nothing to gain by withholding the information, only more sadness than I already got. 'Everyone was keen for that corpse to belong to Tommy Tycho – so keen they conveniently ignored facts that were staring them in the face. And the facts staring them in the face were that the tattoo was the sole identifier. There was no head and no one had ever taken Tycho's dabs, leaving nothing but the tattoo. A tag around the neck of a goose saying it's a duck don't make it a duck.'

Chapter 41

ORANGES AND LEMONS

Tycho was a worm and a dobber,' I continue, 'a sneak and a creep, a phantom in a world of ghosts. He was quicker on his tootsies than Cassius Clay and never got caught for so much as non-payment of fare on the 339 to Clovelly.'

'So when did you realise he wasn't the corpse?' Monica asks.

'I happen to know Latin. And when I looked at the neck at the Widow's I knew the inscription didn't conform to the original. It was meant to read: *Populus vult decipi decipiatur* – "The people wish to be deceived, so deceive them". A neat little quote for someone that spent the whole of his life on the con.' I shrug. 'But the last word on the neck of the corpse in the kitchen wasn't *decipiatur* but *decapitare* – no longer "so let them" but "let's do a beheading". Someone had altered the lyrics. The ink slinger wouldn't have known Latin from lantana, which meant the person who did the switch must have been Tycho. Tattoos aren't like Words for Windows, where you hit *Delete* and everything trundles off to *Recycle*. If you want to alter a tattoo, you got to find yourself a new canvas. Which meant the new words had to have been on somebody else's cutaneous tissue. It turned out to be Tycho's last joke.'

She nods. It's the sort of nod that et cetera and et cetera.

'You gave me a clue when you told me that no one buzzed to gain entry to Annabel's apartment. A lover's always got the key to the apartment of his *inamorata*. After Tycho killed Annabel, he just had time before I rocked up to type into her computer a list of persons that hated him enough to kill him, a nice little bunch of red herrings designed to send the cops on a wild-goose chase, if they were in the business of chasing. All I needed to do after that was identify the corpse. When Tycho realised that, he did away with the tattooist. When Lulu copped it, I knew why. And after the junkie – the kid who helped Tycho set up the rube for the shooting – pointed me to the book, I knew who belonged to the new canvas. For Tycho, the beauty about Gardener was that – like Tycho himself – he had no form. Like Tycho, there were no records to link his fingerprints to. Knowing the cops would run dead on the case, all Tycho had to do was put the identifier around Gardener's neck and ever so carefully blow his head off.'

'You've explained why he killed Gardener and the tattooist, but why Annabel? Annabel did nothing wrong apart from coming to you. And that's not enough to kill anyone for.'

'Think about it. There was a deal between a man afraid for his life, and his wronged wife. For once, this wronged wife had the upper hand. Sure she was getting a cut of the insurance but she wanted more: she wanted the girlfriend dead.'

Monica frowns. It's a beautiful frown. 'You said there was a final clue.'

This is the bit I like, the bit that puts the final coat of gloss on the case. 'There's no paint colour that goes by the name *orange*.'

'Meaning?'

'At the Merry Widow's I came across a piece of paper with a lot of crossing-out on it and right down the bottom the word *orange*. When I asked the Widow what it meant, she fed me some story about the joint needing painting.' I shrug. 'Two problems with that. One, if you're trying to flog real estate in this town, you don't paint it orange. And two, no such hue exists in any paint company's repertoire. So the Widow's not-so-white lie tied her into the jig. And the rest, as they say, is history.'

Monica looks up from her note taking. 'So what – in context – did the word *orange* mean?'

I kick the record player and the xylophone switches to something with *heartbreak* in it. 'To qualify for a payout from your insurance company, the Tychos had to "prove" the corpse was Tommy's. The fingerprints didn't matter because neither Tommy nor Gardener possessed any – at least not as far as anyone was concerned. The big identifier, therefore, was the tattoo around the neck, and the major counter identifier was the head. That meant Tycho had to blow off the head – while at the same time leaving the tattoo. Accordingly, Tycho and his missus came up with the idea of the elephant gun. After that, all they had to do was experiment with distance – how far the gun had to be in order to take off the head nice and clean, while not affecting the tattoo. Hoping all the while – because it would be that much easier – that Tommy could do it from a distance.

'They experimented with shop dummies, their theft being duly recorded in the newspapers. They tried several paces away, a couple of paces away, and at arm's length – until finally they accepted the inevitable:

that Tycho would have to get right up close and personal if he was going to remove the head yet still leave the tattoo in place.'

'And that distance would have been 0-range,' she says.

Monica's voice is soft and sweet but it's her famous last words as far as this defective's concerned. I've paid my debt to Annabel, and I never did have a debt to this dame, unless it's the age-old debt that anyone suffering from blind, abject love owes to the object of his infatuation, after she says the only interest she ever had in you was 'professional'.

Accordingly, I grab my fedora and place it on my head. 'One more question,' I ask. 'Does the Widow get to keep the dough?'

Monica looks up at me and I see that her eyes are no longer beautiful but calculating. 'We'll find some way out of it. We always do.'

With that, I leave the speakeasy, nodding to the kid behind the bar as I enter a world that's got a sky the colour of the dame's eyes when I finally realised she doesn't care for me all that much.

Roarer's behind the wheel of the Caddie, ready to take me to where I should be a lot more than I am. Because I'm not just a private detective, I'm also a dad. And the six- or is it ten-year-old that makes me that way is waiting for me to get on with the long-overdue business of fathering.

Chapter 42

SAVE THE LAST DANCE FOR ME

'One step, two step – higher, higher, that's better – three!' Madame Blavatsky cries. 'Imogene Scutt, concentrate! Pay attention to the music, and what it's telling you!'

There aren't too many dance academies left in Sydney. Come to think of it, there's not too much of anything left in Sydney. Not after the wreckers have been at work and all the extortion and rackety by-play that goes by the name of progress has torn down anything that really matters. Not after the great god Dough-Re-Me has nodded from on high and his disciples have put their hands in other people's pockets to pay the dues.

Dance academies are soul and soul has been excised from this burg. All that's left are millions of punters glued to their idiot boxes, ten thousand ant-brown corpses baking on Bondi Beach, a couple of hundred empty minds in parliament house and the hollow uniforms of the fuzz in their ivory towers pretending to do their dirty work for them.

Correction: there are fragments of soul, the barest silhouette, and it comes courtesy of the likes of Madame Blavatsky. She's striding around the dance floor, her great leotarded form towering over the littlies in ballet pumps – my daughter among them.

'No jewellery, Mary-Jane,' she bellows, 'how many times do I have to tell you? Get rid of those silly dingly-danglies at once, they interfere with your movement!'

The kids struggle to get their leg-warmered legs over the impossibly high barre that runs around the mirrored wall of this great, grey, cavernous room.

'One step, two step, three: that's better!'

Some pirouette – if they're able – their faces set sturdy to the music as the tinkle-tankle of the piano in the corner interprets Tchaikovsky like he's never been interpreted before – a sort of ballet in ragtime.

'No, no, no! Stop, stop, stop!'

When I was a kid, Aunt Rube brought me to Madame Blavatsky's to pick up the moves, to learn how to pirouette and come back to earth in a perfect arabesque – in other words how to leap and duck and side dive, the rudiments of the rhythm of movement, especially the *cruciate-ligament pas-de-seul*, the basic step of survival.

'You're moving like a herd of bloody elephants,' Madame Blavatsky says. 'Has anyone here seen an elephant in a tutu?' She allows the titter before cancelling it abruptly with a glance as sharp as a stiletto. 'No? Well, I have.' She waves an arm that's got more grace in it than any prima ballerina in the *Ballet Russe.* 'I've seen it *here.*' She stamps her foot and the earth moves. 'Yes, this is where I've seen it, here and now, as performed by the whole bloody pack of you, in my – *my*, mind you – academy of dance.'

She glares around at the minuscule miscreants. 'And what does it tell me you've learnt? Nothing. What can you do? Play rugby league football probably, because you certainly can't dance.' She steps back, all two hundred pounds of her light as a feather, and that's when the graceful arm comes out again, first to indicate the piano player, and then to give the Noddy to me.

When you're in Madame Blavatsky's, you do what Madame Blavatsky tells you to do. And right now Madame Blavatsky's telling me to dance – whitesides and all – so, after parking the hat and the gat, that's what I do.

What the kids should be seeing is what Madame Blavatsky has just described to them – a bull elephant dancing. But that's not what's before them. As the music of Stravinsky scorches the heights of the ceiling and ricochets off the mirrored wall and echoes through the mean streets outside that right now are turning to blood-dusk, my X-rated musculature responds to the magic of the muse.

There's no bull elephant in the room.

Just Robert Murray Helpmann. Or maybe Rudolf Khametovich Nureyev. The kids sense the wind in the trees, the magic when incredulity flaps its awkward wings and beats a hasty retreat. They see what happens when a miracle occurs and a great lumpy beast of a private detective takes flight in a dusty dance parlour in inner-city Darlinghurst. Finally, they hear the sound when that private detective's bulk lands on the floorboards with the merest whisper of a suspicion, and not even the tiniest mote of dust is disturbed.

The music stops and I bow and return to my place next to Madame Blavatsky.

'That's how it's done.' The grand dame glares at her charges yet again. 'That's poetry and that's what I want from you – perfect stanzas, beautiful couplets and the most eloquent of imagery.' She nods in my direction like

Eugene Goossens acknowledging the tour-de-force of a principal danseur after a performance worthy of an angel. 'Thank you, Mr Smith, thank you, pianist.' Then she turns back to her downcast flock of fledglings. 'Now, dance, damn you, dance!'

We're making our way back through the mean streets, the kid with stars in her eyes and me with a hole in my cakehole where my back tooth ought to be.

'Do you think any of the others have a father like me?'

Her mitt in mine feels like a wasp.

'I doubt it.'

'Do you think they're jealous?'

I shake my head. 'I doubt that, too, sweetheart. In fact, I doubt it a very great deal.'

Because in reality I'm a thug, not the kind of dad who rolls around on the floor with his daughter and knows what her exam results are and remembers her birthday. What kid in her right mind's going to be jealous of that? But you got to take the rough with the smooth in this world and Immo takes the rough with the rougher and still comes up smiling. I like that in a kid.

Come to think of it, I like that in anyone.

Salina's waiting in the doorway of the dump I bequeathed her after we got ourselves unmarried and I went to live on a boat. The look on her dial-up says it all.

'I suppose I ought to be grateful for small mercies, Rainbow. Specifically, that you brought my little girl home in one piece.' She holds out her arms like she's taking delivery of a decrepit pound puppy. 'Come to me, darling.' The kid comes to her and Salina embraces her, all the while glaring at me like I'm some kind of criminal. 'So what happens now?'

'What always happens, Sal. I dump Imogene with you and then I go back to the boat. After a while, I get a phone call and after that I go out into the big, wide, dangerous world and take yet another tilt at the windmill.'

Sal's not the type to waste valuable time on allusions, literary or otherwise. 'We're still not safe, are we?' The house is behind her but the rest of her life's still in front. 'I mean, all those horrible people you're surrounded with are never going to go away, are they?'

'If you're talking about Tommy Tycho, he's dead and buried. If you're referring to Pandora, it's not you and the kid she's after, it's me. Meanwhile, the rest of the evildoers have more important things on their minds – like prostitution, drugs, extortion and murder.' I check the fedora. There's a bullet hole in the crown I didn't notice before. 'However . . .'

There's always an *however*.

Salina hugs Immo close and kisses the top of her head. When she looks up her eyes are shining. 'Things aren't going to get any better, are they?'

'Yeah, sure they are, Sal. They'll get a whole lot better – you can rely on it.' I jam the fedora with the hole in it on my skull and turn away, on account of my eyes might have acquired a bit of a gleam in them, too. 'Only you can also rely on the very great probability that first they're going to get a whole lot worse.'

C.S. Boag

MISTER RAINBOW

in the Case of the Horses for Corpses

For Jane and Julia

Chapter 1

MARKS INCONSISTENT WITH

It's early morning in the city – derelict time – and all around are greasy figures under greasier blankets. They clog Sydney's interstices, the gaps between too much money and mere survival, the crooks and nannies of that bleakest of wastelands between death wish and harsh reality. Wherever you look you'll find them – under concrete overpasses, in hidden corners of parks and shop doorways, behind trees; most of them alive, although you wouldn't know it.

I'm jogging past Central station when I see the van, and after that – but only because I'm looking – a woman moving silently among the shapeless shapes like a nurse in a war zone. She cuts a small figure in old joggers and an even older tracksuit – bending, tending, caressing, assessing, leaving or carrying, before moving on – fluttering over her charges like a heart that won't stop, willing them to survive. As long as I've known her, Annie's cared for lost souls, toiling among the city's destitute, lugging some into her van and carting them to refuges, or taking others to the morgue. Plenty of charities do the same, but Annie's the only one I know does it freelance.

'Hi Annie.'

She straightens and turns. 'Rainbow.' Nice eyes, set wide. 'What brings you here?'

'I was on my way to Bondi for an early-morning arm-over when I spotted Gertrude.' Gertrude is Annie's battered splitscreen Kombi. Down the side is written ANNIES VAN in multi-coloured lettering, together with a few too many flowers.

With the toe of my whiteside I nudge a figure slumped in a rose bed. 'Reckon they're worth it?'

Annie wipes her face with the back of her hand. 'Someone's got to do something.'

I frown over the figure I just toed. 'This one's gone.'

'It happens. People bash them. Or they just stop breathing.'

I bend down and pull back the blanket. The clothes are clean. So is the body. 'So it's the boot, the brick, the broken bottle – or nothing at all?'

'No shades of grey round here.'

I take a closer look at the body. Odd. 'This wasn't a regular street death. The marks are inconsistent with passing away quietly in the night – or a violent death due to boot, broken bottle or brick.'

'What do you mean?'

'See here. Little cuts, bruises, a few burns. And that's all. If he wasn't dead, I'd describe this corpse as well-dressed, well-fed and happy.'

Annie looks away. She also looks troubled. 'This isn't the first. There was another one. I don't know what's going on. The weather hasn't been too bad, there hasn't been an epidemic ...'

I peer closer. The bloke's young-ish. Nice complexion for a corpse, so not a drinker; fingertips clean, so he didn't smoke himself to death; and no track marks to indicate drugs. 'Look.' I point to his arms. 'And there and there again. What could be cigarette burns, but aren't. A couple of bruises, but small ones, not the kind that might have been made by a ham fist, or a length of pipe. Weals to the wrists – and I don't mean cartwheels. A missing fingernail.'

'Exactly like the other one.' I wait for her to go on. She'll go on if there's anything to go on about, and keep quiet if there's not. She's sharp, Annie – nice but sharp – and doesn't miss a trick unless she has to. 'Usually I can help them, Rainbow, but not these ones.'

'The other was male, too?'

She looks at me in surprise. 'Now you mention it – yes.'

'When?'

'Few weeks ago. What are we going to do, Rain?'

'Sorry, but I got enough on my front gate without worrying about this.' Like a swim at Bondi, followed by a date with my daughter, Imogene – the daughter that my ex, Salina, has been threatening to take away. 'The cops'll sort it out.'

Annie shakes her head. 'Rainbow, we both know the police won't sort out anything. To them, they're just derelicts. No political strength, no family, no friends. They're road bumps on the highway to nowhere. Couldn't you –'

'Annie, I care, okay? But right now there are other things I care about more.'

She nods and bends over her next patient, a pink-grey mess in the dull grey dawn, huddled deep in a cavernous declivity of a warped and twisted

Moreton Bay fig. I point to the sign on the side of the van. 'You need an apostrophe, Annie,' I tell her. She doesn't reply.

Time to resume my jog. As I do, I catch sight of a shapely blonde in leopardskin leotards. She doesn't belong here. But then, who does?

Chapter 2

CASINO ROYALE

An hour or so later, I've had my swim – five kilometres up and down Australia's most famous stretch of surf and sand – concentrating on keeping my head underwater for three minutes at a time in order to increase lung power, but also to avoid thinking about Annie and her corpse. Not to mention the blonde in the leopardskin leotards. After which I take Imogene on her long-overdue outing to the pictures.

The call comes in on dead-man's mobile No. 3, just as me and the kid are decanting ourselves from the movie house. It's a dame. I don't recognise the voice, only the panic in it.

'We have to save him, Rainbow!' Mostly they give you too much information, but right now there isn't enough to blow your nose on. 'The devils have him in their thrall,' she continues. 'It's as if he can't see left or right as they drag him into the pit. He's not like this at heart. Underneath, he's a decent man, we both know that. It was the – accident.'

Next to me, Imogene's fiddling. In my experience, kids are always fiddling with something – if it's not electronic gimmickry, it's your heart.

'What accident?' I ask.

The panic leaves the voice and is replaced by surprise. 'Surely you remember?' Cultured tones under the surprise, tones that take me smack-bang back in time into the presence of a gorgeous twenty-year-old with a face so beautiful that a joker required shades just to be in its presence. And that memory conjures up another memory – of a soggy afternoon at Royal Randwick and a three-year-old galloper veering out of control across a packed field, with its rider ending up under the hooves of too many horses.

Yeah, I remember all right.

I also remember the jockey that ended up under all those horses.

It's the connection I don't remember.

'Is it always like that, Daddy?' Imogene's eleven, or maybe she's fourteen, and apart from electronic gimmickry, she likes asking questions.

'Hold that thought.' I put my mitt over the cellar-phone and turn my attention to the kid. 'Is what always like what, sweetheart?'

She glances at the punters emerging from the movie house before turning her peepers back to me. 'Is gambling really like *Casino Royale*? Are casinos places of luxury, with beautiful chandeliers and aristocratic ladies dressed in silk, and dealers wearing silver armbands and waistcoats with cards on them, and men in tuxedos winning millions, and people driving beautiful cars?'

I tell the kid no, it's not at all like that, before going back to the voice on the phone.

'Rainbow, are you still there?' She doesn't wait for a response. 'They're after him.'

'Who's after who?'

'The shysters, the racketeers, the hoons – I don't know what you call them – the gambling people, the ones he owes all the money to.' There's the sound of a deep, shuddering breath at the other end of the Telefunken, after which she says, 'He can't stop and I didn't know who to turn to. I hope you don't mind, I got your number from your Aunt Rube.'

Rube's the aunt cum private detective who took me in when Dad dumped me after Mum topped herself. Aunt Rube raised me on ballet, old Jimmy Cagney movies, and the principles of detecting.

'So take your friend to Gamblers Anonymous.'

'I did, but it turned out to be just another opportunity for him to gamble. You know how they sit around listening to each other's stories? Well, Cyril turned it into a – a – I mean, well, he – opened a book on how long the gamblers' resolutions not to gamble would last, and soon everyone was betting on it. In the end, even the facilitator was having a flutter.'

At least I got a name.

'So where is he now, this Cyril of yours?'

'There's someone following us, Daddy.'

I put the voice on hold again while I look at where Imogene's looking. And where Imogene's looking is the following:

1. Posters featuring giant monkeys, maniacs carrying weapons, and a bunch of beautiful dames trussed wild-eyed to lampposts;

2. The crumbling pillars of the rerun movie house; and

3. Only part-hidden behind one of the pillars, that shapely blonde in

leopardskin leotards.

Rule numero uno for a tail is never to wear leopardskin leotards.

And rule numero uno for the tail-ee is to work out how come you got a tail.

There's Pandora, the woman in black, the dame that's always there. But this ain't Pandora. There's all the people in the world who hate me, but something tells me this isn't one of them. And there's the figure I saw when I was checking out the corpses at Central. Coincidence?

I don't do coincidence.

So why is someone on the follow?

There's no reason I can see, unless she just likes the colour of my hat.

Chapter 3

A VOICE FROM THE PAST

There's always somebody following somebody else, Immo,' I say, slipping into my fatherly reassurance routine. 'It's the way of the world – it's called stalking. And if we can see this particular stalker, it means she's a rank amateur, and therefore not worth worrying about …'

'What did you say?'

I remember the Telefunken. 'Sorry, I wasn't talking to you.' I nod to Imogene, while readdressing myself to the phone. 'Meanwhile, my question is: where's the pelican now?'

'What?'

'This Cyril character.'

There's a sound like a receiver banging against something hard, which tells me either that the dame's in distress, or in a public telephone booth, or both. 'He's busy throwing away what little money we have – not to mention a great deal of money we don't have – trying to win back enough to repay what he's already lost.'

I strain to hear past the emotion – while keeping a weather eye on the dame in the leopardskin leotards only half-hiding her curves behind the pillory.

'We're two months behind in the rent,' the woman goes on. 'He lost our car in a bet with a man who came to turn off the gas, over nothing more than a couple of cockroaches that happened to be crossing the sink at the time. And without my knowledge or consent, he pawned a diamond necklace belonging to my great great grandmother – not to mention a pair of priceless Paspaley pearl earrings I'd kept from my modelling days. Meanwhile, we haven't had a decent feed for months. He –'

'Look, I'm really sorry, lady, but I gotta go.'

'Rainbow, if I don't get Cyril back now, he'll be lost forever.'

The trouble with life is it's got history in it. And part of my history contains a dame that once upon a time rescued me from the depredations of a busted marriage and the equally unfriendly floor of a speakeasy. I take a deep breath. 'Okay, okay. So where is this —?'

The kid answers the question meant for the dame. 'She's still behind that post over there, watching us.'

'Sorry, Immo, I was talking to the dame. And not that one — the one on the phone.' I aim my dulcets back into the dulcimer. 'Sorry, I missed the last bit — where is he?'

'He's at the betting joint.'

'Which particular betting joint would that be?'

'The one that spells R-A-T-S backwards. Please, Rainbow, can't you rescue him — if only for old times' sake?'

Old times have a lot to answer for. 'Look, lady —'

'Will you stop calling me *lady*. My name's Angela Golightly.'

The Angel that was. My angel of mercy. The dame that took me in and got me back up to speed, after which we did the mutual-parting trick, and after a suitable interval Angel took up with her jockey, after which —

'Yeah, well, look, I got my daughter with me, see, and —'

'Oh, yes, I remember. *Imagine*, wasn't it? She was a real sweetie.'

Imagine must have been how Angela saw the kid at the time, the kid she would have preferred not to exist.

'Im-*oh*-gene.'

'Oh, of course — Im-oh-gene.'

There's too much information going back and forth for comfort — but I'll replace the dead-man's mobile with another one, courtesy of my little mate Rory. And after that, no-one will be able to tie me to the Angel dame, or her to me, or the kid to either of us, and I'll be home — or what passes for home these days — free. Me and Angela Golightly will be nothing more than ships that once-upon-a-turbulent-sea, happened to pass in the night.

'Give her my love, Rainbow.'

'Yeah, I'll do that.'

'What would the little darling have been then? Three? Six? Your Imagine must be quite the grown-up now. Which means you could take her to the casino, couldn't you? The whole thing would only take a minute. Then you and Imagine could both go back to doing whatever it was you were doing before I so rudely interrupted.'

'I'm not taking my daughter to a casino.'

'Please? For me?'

I glance at the kid, who's playing with whatever she's playing with. 'I —'

'It'll only take a moment.'

What's a moment, compared to a lifetime? I take another deep breath. 'Okay, Angel, I'll get your husband back for you.' I adjust to work mode. 'What's he look like now?' Once he was a handsome pocket jockey, but then there was the accident.

'He looks like too many horses ran over him.' It's a clever reply, but she must figure she owes me more than a clever reply, because she adds, 'Aside from which, he'll be with Lord Haw-Haw.'

I rack the grey matter. 'This Lord Haw-Haw joker – he a gambler, too?'

This brings a laugh from the other end, and the laughter's sad enough to tear my heart out. 'Oh, Rainbow, Lord Haw-Haw's not a person, it's a – a horse.'

I frown. 'What do you mean, a *horse*?'

Chapter 4

ABANDON HATS, ALL YOUSE THAT ENTER HERE

There's a pause while Angel reins in the chuckle. 'Just what I said – Lord Haw-Haw's a horse.'

I struggle to come to terms with what she's telling me.

'Not a *real* horse – just one of those cuddly toys that people give babies. We bought it when we were trying to – when we hoped we might … But then there was the accident and Cyril's legs were so badly hurt he could never ride again. Also he couldn't, you know – I mean, well, we were never going to have a family after the accident. So instead of being something for the baby, Lord Haw-Haw became *Cyril's* cuddly toy.'

Two beats of silence, then, 'It doesn't *mean* anything, but Cyril took to carrying Lord Haw-Haw with him wherever he went. It was sort of – company for him. And he insists that he brings him luck.' Another mirthless attempt at a laugh from the other end. 'That's what he *says*. Which is all very well, except that Cyril and luck have become, well, estranged. Only it's more than that, a lot more. You see, Cyril's a – well, a depressive. Blame the accident, blame his misfortune, blame me – but somehow Haw-Haw seems to – well, buck him up when he's down. It's as if he *needs* that thing with him to – survive. Does that make sense to you?'

I do another deep breath, the one with the three-minute underwater survival potential in it. 'As much sense as anything does in this world, Angel.'

After I click off, I check out the figure failing to hide its curves behind the faux pilaster in the foyer. She's of medium height, and with no standout characteristics apart from the obvious. So – except for the leopardskin leotards that tend to distract attention towards instead of away from her –

she'd answer to the description of the perfect follower.

The kid glances up from her gizmo. 'Are we going home now, Daddy?'

Home is an old tub parked in Sydney Harbour, a once-upon-a-time ferry with a smashed-in bow and a wraparound pedestrian mall. I call her the *Wooden No* – as in *Where do you live? Wooden No.* But that's not what Immo's talking about. Her home's where the mother, Salina, is, the narrow-gutted scrap of real estate on Castanet Close where we used to play happy families – before I realised I was playing to an empty house, and a memory.

'We got a detour to make first, sweetheart.'

The kid nods. 'Mummy says your whole life is nothing more than a series of detours.'

I'm careful not to reply with anything that might be considered defamatory. 'People could say that of anyone, kid.'

Imogene suddenly goes thoughtful. 'Mummy's going through one of those detours now. She met a man she calls Mr Perfect – although she says that after you anyone would seem perfect. I haven't met him yet, but she says he's got a lot of money, which is another – But don't worry, Daddy, I'm keeping tabs on him.'

I glance down at her. 'How are you doing that?'

She waves the gizmo at me. 'Like this.' She flicks a switch.

'Yeah.' My voice emerges out of the technology. *'Well, look, I got my daughter with me, see, and –'*

Pause.

'Im-oh-gene.'

Longer pause, long enough for me to see where this is going.

'Yeah, sure.'

Another pause.

'I'm not taking my daughter to a casino.'

Pause.

'I –'

Pause.

'Okay, Angel, I'll get your husband back for you ...'

The kid switches her recorder off, and a look like a purring cat takes over her dial-up. 'Like you always say, Daddy, a person's gotta do what a person's gotta do.' She shakes her head as she files the recording studio in a poche in her jeans. 'And you just promised someone that you'd take me to a casino, so you can't get out of it. I've got you on record.' She shakes her fourteen- or is it forty-year-old head. 'After *Casino Royale*, I want to see the real thing. All that glamour and sophistication.' I go pale. 'Oh, don't worry, I won't tell Mummy. Plus I can keep an eye on that woman who's following us.'

I glance around. The old crowd of movie goers has been replaced by a new crowd of movie goers, but there's no sign of the dame not well enough hidden behind a pillar, fake or otherwise. 'What woman?'

But the kid's moved on, too. She's been to the movie and now she wants to experience the reality. She tugs at my jacket. It's still got sand in the pockets from the swim at Bondi. 'Come on, Daddy, stop jumping at shadows and take your daughter to the casino.'

In Sydney town, it's not what you know, but how much money you got when you know it. It's a way of thinking that grows no cherries, in my opinion, but it's still the raison d'être of most of the inhabitants of this burg. Everyone wants a slice of bacon and most punters believe that places like the casino are where it's served. Wrong. The casino's where people go to get poor, the place where punters part company with whatever they had to begin with, and go into hock for the rest.

There's a lot of pathways to gambling and there are plenty of entrances to the Star. I take the mechanical steps, followed by the black-and-gold stairway to Hell, and the kid follows. Too much fake marble, too many fake flowers, too much false hope, and too much security.

'Where do you think you're going?' He's wearing a purple tie with a couple of dice doing the tango on it, he's waving a wand like the Fairy Godmother on steroids, and he must be hard of hearing because there's a curly black wire sprouting out of one of his ears.

'We're about to enter your establishment.'

'Not wearing that hat you're not.'

'Why, don't you like the colour?'

'The colour's fine, pal, it's the hat I don't like – not to mention the insect life under it.' The goon waves his weapon sniffer at the wall beside him. 'Like the sign says, for people that can read, we got dress rules, and those rules say that your headwear's illegal.' He then produces a cackle as spontaneous as the 700-year-old misquote he's about to hand me. 'So, in the words of the bard: *Abandon hats, all youse that enter here.*'

Never trust jokers that misquote Dante. 'The Devil can cite scripture for his purpose,' I reply.

The goon frowns. 'What did you just say?'

Chapter 5

CASINO NORMALE

I'm just trying to maintain the status quote.' I chuck the hat down the golden stairway and it fetches up on a fake aspidistra. 'Satisfied now?'

But the goon's wagging his head as well as his metal detector, at the same time as he's talking to his tie, the purple one with the matching pair of dice on it. 'Yeah, Joe? Look, I got a danger man here. Yeah, you got the cameras on him? The one with the orange-check promissory note, the two-tone footwear, and the kid.' He nods at the tie without taking his eyes off the object in question, me. 'Gotcha.' He hangs up his tie, and waves me back to oblivion. 'You can't come in, anyway, on account of the age limit.'

'Since when was there a limit on age?'

'Since the Devil invented gambling.'

I'm Mr Anonymous. Which means I haven't got a driver's licence, a credit card, or a permit for the gun that I left on the boat in order to be with the kid. Accordingly, I haven't got proof of anything, even if I wanted to prove it.

'Look, pal,' I say, 'use your eyes, if not your brain. I'm forty-something. How can that be the wrong age to lose money?'

He sets his feet apart on the fake marble floor, while his knuckles whiten on the wand. 'I'm not talking about you, wise guy.' He waves his wand at Imogene. 'I'm talking about the kid. If she's under eighteen – and my guess is she's way under – then she can't come in.'

I don't know how old Imogene is, but I'm pretty sure she's not eighteen yet. It doesn't stop me arguing the toss, or the tosser – take your pick. 'Afraid she'll take your money?'

'No, I'm afraid she can't come in, period.'

'So what am I supposed to do with her? Check her into the cloak room?'

That's when the goon turns into something he wasn't five minutes ago. 'No, you can try being a proper father, and keep her away from places of evil.'

The kid's busy excavating the fedora from the faux greenery when I return.

'The man up there says we gotta go,' I say.

When she straightens, she's frowning. 'But, Daddy, you promised you'd get that lady's husband back for her.'

I shrug the jacket that hasn't got a gat in it. 'So now I can't.'

'But you promised.'

'Some promises just can't be kept, Immo.'

'That's not what you tell me.' She gestures around. 'Besides, I'm safe here.'

I quarter the environs. A bunch of fancy stores, the aforementioned fake flowers, too many punters arriving to donut too much dough-re-you to the richest men in Australia, and a couple of garbage bins at the foot of the stairs. I remember Little Orphan Annie and the corpse at Central.

'Sweetheart, this is Sydney, which means you're not safe anywhere.'

Imogene gets that look, the one that says I'm messing with forces I don't understand. 'Daddy, thanks to you, I know how to look after myself. Anyway, it's broad daylight and this is a public thoroughfare. And you won't be long – you're just going in to rescue that lady's husband.' She holds up the recorder. 'Besides, while I'm waiting, I can practise being a detective.'

I think a lot of things, but mostly I think of what my ex-wife Salina would say if she found out I'd abandoned her daughter at the Gates of Hell – and weigh that against a debt I've got to a memory. 'Look, I'm sorry, Immo, but I can't.'

The kid's planted her feet firmly on the ground, like she's pretty certain I can. 'You've got to let me. If you don't, I'll end up being dependent on you forever.'

I take a deep breath racked with uncertainty. 'Well, if you're sure …'

Imogene takes hold of my sleeve with the hand that hasn't got the hat in it. 'Sure I'm sure. If you keep me wrapped up in cotton wool I'll never become what I *want* to become. How can I become a real-life detective if you … I'll just wait on the bottom step until you come out, all right? And don't worry, I'll be as safe as – as the *Wooden No.*'

As an analogy it could have done with a bit of fine-tuning. But I hand over my blade and shrug myself out of the jacket and turn it inside out, so it's no longer orange any more but black. I then make my way up yet another staircase that leads to the gambling parlour. At the top, I pause, turn and look down. The knife's no longer visible and Immo's gripping

the gizmo she records people with, along with my hat, and she must have
sensed me looking because she glances up. She seems a lot smaller than
I'd like her to be, but I tell myself it's just the perspective. I give her the
thumbs-up and she juggles the recorder into the hat and gives me the
thumbs-up back – together with that reassuring smile of hers.

So. I've altered my profile. No hat, different-coloured coat and, above
all, no kid. Also I'm facing a different Cerberus with a wired-up lug hole.
No doubt he's been told to watch out for a weirdo, but I'm a different
kind of weirdo to the one he's been told to watch out for, so he waves me
through.

If you've seen one of these joints, whether it's Monaco, Nevada, Atlantic
City, Baden-Baden, or Hobart – the things spawn like maggots on a
dead dog – you've seen them all. The aim is to relieve punters of their
livelihood, while giving back less than nothing in return.

Music plays and security pretends not to be security, while down-
at-heel derros and round-shouldered crones perch on flick-back stools
in front of rows of poke-your-heart-outs bearing monikers like Crazy
Harry, Blonde with a Wand and Yours for the Asking. There were no
pokies in *Casino Royale*, but *Casino Royale* this ain't. This is the real world.
And what counts in the real world is not how things look or feel, but what
brings in the most cash to the big boys. And what brings in the readies
in these places is the extra oxygen they put in the air-conditioning to
make people feel more like gambling; the absence of clocks and windows
to remove unnecessary distractions; while the constant clink of bottles
against glasses says they got the all important alcohol angle covered as
well. There's no pearls and no evening dresses. At the Rats, you got
gambling stripped to its barest inessentials. There's only one winner, and
that's the jokers running it.

I check out the CCTV cameras as I pass a geezer manning a Big Six
– Money Wheel, Wheel of Fortune, call it what you will. With an eighty-
to-one chance of a payout it's the biggest rip off since the postage stamp.

Chapter 6

DOWN AMONG THE GAMBLERS

Looking for something, big boy?' She's got cherry-red lips, a drinks tray and cleavage like the bum crack on an overweight labourer.

I hunch the shoulders. 'Yeah, I'm looking for a friend.'

She leans forward. She should have checked the frock was shrink-proof before she wore it. 'Aren't we all?'

'Not that kind of friend. I'm looking for a gimp with a limp.'

She throws her weight on one hip, which does interesting things to her cleavage, and the drinks tray looks like it's only kept level with gimbals. 'I can do limp.'

At a nearby table a bloke of Middle Eastern appearance is being taken to the cleaners, the House dealing him a pair of jokers only lightly disguised as drink waiters. The muscle's barely apparent as he's shuffled away to the little room under the stairs, where the House turns public embarrassments private.

'It's not the limp I'm after,' I tell the dame, 'but the guy wearing it.'

'Oh, so you're one of *those*.'

'I'm not one of anything, lady, unless it's one of a kind.'

The fake marble floor under my whitesides is unforgiving, and so is the look the dame shoots me as the music they dish out along with the extra oxygen segues into *Ain't She Sweet*. At the next table, a geezer in a wheelchair gets dealt another losing hand and the man behind the croupier behind the cards checks his little screen to ensure the House is raking off as much as it can, without breaking any obscenity laws.

I'm minding my own business, counting CCTV cameras – twenty-three or thereabouts – when a weightlifter appears by my side.

'Can I help you, sir?'

I keep the arms loose and hanging forward – a la James Cagney in *Public Enemy*, plus every other movie he ever appeared in – ready for anything that might come my way. 'What's with this joint? All of a sudden everyone wants to help me.'

The weightlifter is wearing a suit, but that's not enough to make him civilised. 'It's just that I don't see you gambling, sir.'

'I don't see *you* down among the hard balls, either.'

He tenses. 'I'm not paid to gamble, as I only bet on certainties. And for my money, it's a certainty that you spell trouble.'

I got a job to do, and it doesn't include offloading thugs into poker machines. Not only that, Imogene's waiting outside. 'Sorry, pal, I'm looking for the McDonald's.'

'The what?'

'You know, the place where they take your hard-earned, smile too much, and ask if you want chips with that.'

'Just like I thought, a wise guy.'

'But not wise enough not to lose, buster.' I start towards the money cage, slow enough not to trigger any alarm bells in the bloke's head, but fast enough not to give him time to work out what I just said.

Steaming's when a punter chucks everything he's got into the ring to make good his losses. That's exactly what Cyril Golightly's up to when I finally locate him. He's in the company of a bunch of other shills and is hunched over a scratch pile of poker chips clutching a moth-eaten beast of a blue-and-white toy horse. It's awful – a crazy-eyed, leering-toothed thing about the size and build of an overweight chihuahua.

'Would you care to join us, sir?' asks the dealer.

The chair next to Cyril looks lonely, so I roll it out and keep it company. I check out my neighbour. Once he was an acquaintance but now he's a gambler, with eyes for nothing but the mirage of the big win. He's slouched in his low roller's seat, head barely visible above the table, hugging his ugly furball and looking at his cards like a kid peeking at something he shouldn't through a walk-up-and-bend-down keyhole.

I check out my cartes-de-sejour while I consider my next move. Imogene's outside and she can't stay outside forever, security's circling, and I got to work out a way of removing Cyril without overexciting the gendarmes.

'Are you playing, sir?' the dealer asks again. 'Or are you just here for the ambience?'

It comes out *ambulance*. I dribble out a couple of McDonald's chips while cocking an eyebrow at Cyril. The music keeps playing and the oxygen keeps pumping and the one-armed bandits keep doing their ding-a-ling thing, and the dealer continues to lead the card players by the nose on their roundabout to nowhere.

I talk out of the side of my moosh. 'I'm getting you out of here, Cyril.'

I receive a glance from the ex-hoop, but it's like a grimace from his horse – a look with no recognition in it: two greasy eyeballs in a pair of streaky bowls of soup, lips as tight as a billionaire's wallet, and an expression on his phyzog that says he reckons he could be another James Bond, and that it matters.

'I know nothing but the value of my cards and of silence, mate, so leave me alone.'

I shake the noggin. 'Come on, mate, don't you remember me? I'm –'

The automated voice interposes. 'Are you playing, sir? Or perhaps you'd like to start a sewing circle.'

After half-a-dozen hands, my pile of tiddly-winks has halved. The shuffle machine continues to deal out more hope slips, and a sign on the green-baize table says we can attempt to control our barely-controllable urge to gamble by contacting a nice person on the following number.

'Look, Cyril ...' But I'm talking to the toy horse.

'Excuse me.' He turns to the muscle behind the dealer, otherwise known as the Ladderman. 'This person's disrupting my play, and I find myself wondering if he's a stooge of the management.'

The Ladderman exchanges glances with the pit boss, following which he moves around the table. 'I'm sorry, sir, but we thought he was a friend of yours.'

Cyril shakes his head. 'I wouldn't know him from Saddam.'

The pit boss leans over my shoulder. 'In that case, I'm afraid I'm going to have to ask you to leave. Or change seats. Or perhaps tables. Nothing personal, but Mr Golightly objects to your being here.'

I go into Phase One. 'I'd prefer to stay where I am.'

The muscle leans so close that I can smell his eau-de-colon. 'And we'd prefer that you didn't.' I sense the fist tighten on my rollie chair. 'So if you don't mind ...'

'But I do.'

Phase Two.

The grip tightens. 'Then I'm going to have to ask you to leave.'

'You and whose army?'

Which moves us nicely and naturally into Phase Three.

Chapter 7

THE DEAD MAN'S HAND

Aunt Rube always said that if there was a God, She'd only help those who help themselves. But no-one's helping Cyril, so it's up to me.

I straighten suddenly so that my parietal bone comes into contact with the ape's mandible. At the same time, I slap the wheelie chair into reverse, simultaneously slamming my foot against the bar of the table so the back of the chair rams into the thug's fruit and vegetables, reducing him to a very active part of the pattern on the Axminster, after which I grab hold of Cyril and his donkey.

'Okay, high roller, I'm removing you from your palace of dreams.'

No-one's looking our way, if you don't count the twenty-three CCTV cameras, a thousand and one gamblers, twenty meetya maids, and security. Meanwhile, Dean Martin's crooning *White Christmas* over the Tannoy.

With his free mitt Cyril's clutching anything he can get his hands on. 'No, you're not!' He tightens his grip on the chair and the horse. 'I'm staying where I am!'

When jockeys come into the straight, they get themselves high up out of the saddle and lean forward into fresh air. That's just what Cyril does when I yank the pew out from under him – leaning well forward with his bum out, feet twisted around the chrome-plated foot rails of his chair like they're stirrups, while clinging onto the cream-coloured lip of the green baize like it's reins. The only difference is that his horse is in his armpit instead of under him.

'Don't be Cyril, stupid!'

The cavalry moves in. Jokers that were posing as drink waiters and dames that were pretending to be dames suddenly reveal themselves to be neither. Cyril's collar comes off, and when his cards scatter I see that they're bulls and eights – otherwise known as the dead man's hand because legend has it some poor bastard went down in a hail of bullets holding it. But Cyril's not going to die. Not right now. Not if I can help it.

'Come on, mate, if only for Angela's sake.'

'Who's Angela?'

The horse finds its way into Cyril's other armpit, and his shirt buttons mix it with the chips, while his feet and fists lock harder onto the table's protuberances.

Something's got to give and it's the table.

An alarm bell starts ringing. Cyril's got the horse tucked under his arm, and I've got Cyril tucked under mine, as I get the three of us onto the next available table, from where it's only a short hop onto a poker machine, at which point we're nicely within reach of a low-flying chandelier.

Gamblers' ultimate aim is to beat the system that's beating them and suddenly it looks like they got the chance to do just that. A couple of security turn into birds and go flying. Poker faces take to the carpet. Chips find their way into punters' pockets. I take to the air and take Cyril and his piebald mate with me. The chandelier carries us to the next bank of pokies. A sign warns anyone that cares to read it that in case of malfunction the management regrets that there'll be no payouts. We land on Sweet Queen and the machine malfunctions. It pays out. Never trust the signs in a casino. Heavies appear on the walkway and on the double but there's not much they can do. I convey Cyril on a falling fruit machine to ground zero, get him into a fireman's bend, and head for the departure lounge.

By this stage the joint's in automatic lockdown, but the main entrance features no more than a real security guard and another fake bunch of flowers. I offload Cyril into the flowers, take out the security guard, and after that it's slippy-slide time down the moving staircase to freedom ...

... but no Imogene.

Cyril is struggling. 'I got to get back to the table!'

I clout him over the head and he quietens down. Now I have to lug him as well as the toy horse, but at least he's no longer struggling. I resume my search for the kid. This is where I left her, at the bottom of the stairs, minding my hat and her recorder, as well as her own business. Only she isn't here now.

Possibility numero uno: She left of her own accord. A possibility not even worth considering. Imogene's too smart for that.

Possibility numero duo: A cop, playing it by the book, asks the kid, Where's yer father? At which point Imogene screams the kind of scream that only she can scream, because I've taught her to take shameless advantage of people who play it by the book. Only I didn't hear any screams, which means it wasn't a cop. Which is a bastard, because I can do cops.

Possibility numero trio: She's been abducted by a person or persons unknown.

Chapter 8

HELL HATH NO FURY

A cop's coming our way. I toss him a reassuring smile and receive a reassuring smile in return. I backload Cyril and make for the rubbish bin by the escalators. I peer inside. Half a McDonald's quarter-pounder. Two empty cigarette packs. My fedora with something grey and metallic nestling inside it.

'Excuse me, sir.' The cop's playing it by the book.

I do the same and nod at Cyril. 'He's had one too many, officer.'

The cop considers his options and can't find any. 'I see. Well, good luck with that.'

The horse is under one arm and Cyril's over the other while I reach down into the bin and grab my fedora and what's in it. I then heft Cyril and his toy horse into safer keeping, put the whitesides into gallop mode, and head for the hills.

Normally, I'd deliver my charge to his place of residence, but this isn't normally, because Immo's still missing. So I offload Cyril, shut him the hell up again, grab the recorder out of the hat, slap it into reverse, press STOP, and, after that, PLAY.

The gizmo produces a familiar voice. '... *there are around eleven persons of Middle Eastern appearance going up the centre staircase. Dead ahead, a goon, 190 centimetres, beefy, grey suit. To the right, a kid nagging his mum. Further south, two women, then a cop. Women and cop speak. I sense a camaraderie here. What's that all about? Sorry, Daddy, that's conjecture. Cop leaves. Women looking my way. I hand them a smile, the one that says I haven't been dumped outside a casino by my uncaring father — that's a joke, Daddy — but am here of my own accord. Looks like they'll leave me alone ...*'

Cyril moves. I switch off the machine, clout him again, then switch it back on.

'Correction. Women returning. Description: first, what you'd describe as beautiful. Blue eyes. Just your type, Daddy. Second: middle-aged, bit frumpy, brown hair, and the kind of eyes you don't mess with …'

This is followed by a voice a couple of paces away that's not playful – and not Imogene's. *'Where's your father then, darling? Playing the pokies, is he?'* Scrabbling sounds. *'Come on, you can tell your Aunt Phoebe.'*

I hear the kid muttering she can do anything but.

Then the same voice again. *'So where do you live, darling?'*

After which, Imogene's voice returns. *'Aunt Phoebe what?'*

No opportunity wasted. Immo's angling for a name while the dame's still in unsuspecting mode.

'Why, Aunt Phoebe Riesling, darling.'

The kid, sotto voce, *'The Riesling woman's grabbing for my hand, the one without the hat and recorder in it.'* Sound of struggle, of shoe soles scuffling for a foothold. *'Could you leave me alone, please? I promise I'm all right.'*

Another voice, also female, only firmer this time, more decisive. *'And I can promise you that you're not.'*

We've taken a cab to the boulevard around the corner from Salina's place in Castanet Close. Cyril – aka the root cause of all my problems – is leaning against me cuddling his pony. My ex is home. I pretend nothing untoward's happened, and hand her the recorder.

'Can you return that to Imogene for me, Sal?'

She looks down at the gizmo like it's a scorpion. 'Jesus, Rainbow.'

'I take it she's here. In case you didn't realise it, I arranged with Imogene to make her own way home, in order to teach her self-reliance.'

'Bullshit!' Sal's eyes flash, her nostrils flare like a lollied-up thoroughbred's, and she waves my knife about in my face like it's got blood on it. 'Can you believe I found Imogene with this? That was after a couple of women brought her home, telling me it was my duty to stop my husband gambling. My husband! My duty! Do you have any idea how I felt when they said that?'

I don't want to know how she felt when they said anything, but I can't tell Salina that. Apart from which, she's going to tell me anyway.

'I felt an anger towards you greater than any I have ever felt before. In fact, I wanted to kill you. Here were these two women lecturing me on the duties of motherhood and what made it worse was they were right.' Gasp of indrawn breath like she's coming up from the depths of a very deep sea. 'It's hard to believe I married you, Rainbow, and then had a kid by you. The horrible thing is that unmarrying you didn't do anything to correct a pretty well unbearable situation.'

'Look, Sal, it won't happen again. The situation was beyond my control. I —'

Sal shakes her head. Hell hath no fury like a woman shaking her head. 'You're dead right it won't happen again.' She takes in the mess of humanity hugging its toy horse by my side, and just as quickly takes it out again. 'And do you know why, Rain-bloody-bow? Because I'm taking my daughter away, that's why. And do you want to know something else? You couldn't stop me if you tried. And you couldn't stop me for the very simple reason that you don't exist.' There's a lot of hand waving. 'Non-persons can't take people to court, non-persons can't have people arrested, non-persons have no recourse to the law, non-persons —'

'Look, Sal —'

'No, you look, Rainbow. And when you do, you'll see a future without your daughter in it.'

'Well, that was a success.'

I'd clout Cyril over the head again but that would only temporarily alleviate my feelings, as well as rendering him senseless, meaning I'd have to lug him and his stupid horse home to his missus.

I chuck him a frown. 'What's with the toy, anyway, mate?'

He hugs the thing closer, as if afraid that I might try to yank it off him. 'It brings me luck.'

'If it's bringing you luck, mate, you'd be in a bloody bad way without it.'

Chapter 9

ANGEL

She was the sort of dame that stopped traffic just by sashaying down the boulevard. A mannequin? Give me a break. Mannequins wear clothes. In Angel's case, the clothes wore her. She soared on golden wings in an Olympian stratosphere, far above anything they cared to garb her in – be it Giotto, Givenchy or Gutter. She was a ballet, a song, a poem, a dream.

It wasn't just that she was beautiful – any dame can be beautiful. No, Angel was like her name says. And that's what she was to me, an angel that put the word 'hope' back in my lexicon. Through a blood-red haze from the floor of the speakeasy at a time when I wasn't feeling too good, the vision took something off and mopped my face with it.

After which she took me home, where she took off some more.

At the time, home for Angela Pendlebury-Hart was the kind of apartment you read about in dime novels. She was a classy model. Her pad took up the entire top rung of the highest piece of real estate in Sydney, with the kind of view most jokers only have courtesy of Google Earth. I get vertigo just thinking about it. Angel was a high flier, while I didn't have a head for heights. But ours was one of those affairs that – while it was never going to have staying power – lasts a lifetime. We were still mates after we split. Even after she hooked up with Cyril, at the time a jockey worth putting the farm on. Even after she married him. Even after my own horse and carriage crashed and I went to live on the *Wooden No*, while Angela Golightly – née Pendlebury-Hart – continued on her heady journey through the stratosphere.

Or so I thought.

I'm sure as hell thinking it no longer as Wobblefoot, with Lord Haw-Haw leering under his arm, reins up at a hole in the wall bearing a sign some wag has doctored to read 'TOiLET'. It's one of a ragged string of bulldoze jobs in inner-west Camperdown adjoining the murder and mayhem of Parramatta Road.

'Hi Rainbow.'

If it wasn't for the voice – plus the faint glimmer of the bangle that's hanging from the micro-thin wrist – I'd say it wasn't the same dame, while in the dim light of the decrepit tenement I'm willing myself to think otherwise. But it's not enough to be willing. The joint's horrible, the smell is worse, and the woman crumpled against the paint-peeling wall bears as much resemblance to the beauty I once knew as a wireframe dressmaker's dummy to a flesh-and-blood model. Gone is the fluidity, the sex appeal and the looks. In its place is a haggard scarecrow garbed in rags, thin as a mass murderer's alibi, and with eyes as sunken as her hopes. If it wasn't for the voice … It's the voice on the phone, the one that rang when me and Imogene were leaving the movie house, the kind of voice you want to close your eyes and drift off to sleep on.

'Hi Rainbow,' she says again, like she's afraid I mightn't have heard her the first time.

I shake my thoughts out of a beautiful past and back to a bleak reality. 'Hi – Ange.' That's when I drop the glossy-white lie. White lies are cheap – something like my feelings right now towards her husband. 'You haven't changed a bit.'

She aims for a smile, misses, and comes up with a tragedienne's grimace, at the same time brushing a cobweb of hair out of one eye with a hand as substantial as a whisper. 'You never were a good liar.' She turns away. 'But thanks for rescuing Cyril.'

The useless bastard perched beside her is as lopsided as Angel's grin. He's gripping onto his stupid horse with one hand and scratching his backside with the other, while the traffic thunders by outside like malevolent Destiny.

I make a lunge for the bright side of this scenario, and come up with the jewellery. 'I see you still got the blingle-bangle.'

She grimaces again. 'Rainbow, I'd die before I'd part with it.' When she raises her coathanger arm, a stray patch of light catches the bauble. 'Whenever I'm in danger of forgetting who I am – or rather, who I used to be – I look at this bangle. I find it somehow – comforting.'

I want to say something but there's nothing to say. I want to stay, but I can only take so much. 'Well, nice to see you again, Ange.' I glance at Cyril and his toy horse. I ought to say what you say at such times – *Look after her* – but the words stick in my throat. Instead, I return my attention to his victim. 'I'll always be there for you, chickadee.' After that, I turn and head for what passes for a door in this joint. I've paid my dues to the past. Now it's time to do something about the present.

But the beautiful voice stops me. 'Do you mean that, Rainbow?'

I pause. My knuckles whiten on the door handle. 'Do I mean what?'

'That you'll always be there for me.'

I take a deep breath. It's got the scent of mould and of something rotten in it, as well as more than a hint of a shared past. But I'm still inside the hovel, looking at the door, like just looking might get me out of here. 'Of course I mean it.' Only right now I'm wishing I didn't, because I know what's coming next.

'Then would you save Cyril for me?'

'I just saved Cyril for you.'

'I don't mean just now, I mean from gambling. From – himself.'

When I let go of the door handle, it's like I'm letting go of Imogene. And when I turn around, it's like I'm saying that the letting-go might be permanent. In the gloom, Angel is gripping the spare mitt of the useless husband who's clutching his toy horse, like a drowning woman clutching the waterlogged flotsam of a boat that sank to the bottom of the ocean of life long ago.

My mouth goes dry. 'Do you want to spell that out for me, Ange?'

Chapter 10

RIDING FOR A FALL

So she spells it out for me. 'Cyril and I – well, as you know, we were both pretty successful in our own right. I was doing well with the modelling, while Cyril was a top jockey, riding for the best stables, and winning every race that mattered. So, separately, we enjoyed a great deal of *material* success.'

Now for the *immaterial* success.

'But we both knew there was more to life than money. And when we met, we recognised something in each other.' She looks down at Cyril and clearly sees something I can't. 'And that was that we – we were both somehow different from all that. We –'

'Ange, you lost me when you started using words of more than one syllable.' Every moment here is a lifetime away from my daughter. 'Why don't you get to the point?'

She takes a deep breath. Once, that breath would have set me quivering, but now it's little more than a harsh wind in a bleak field.

'Most A-Listers have a level of social awareness that goes no deeper than their bank accounts. When Cyril and I met, we weren't like that. So we got together, and shortly after that, we got married – well, you know all that, Rainbow: after all, you came to the wedding.'

I nod. I was there when the preacher asked if anyone present saw cause why Cyril and Angel shouldn't get hitched, and said nothing.

'But then Cyril had the accident and then, of course, the big payout. And so I abandoned my career to look after him.'

There's still time. I can still crawl out of this warren of no return and set about trying to claw back my daughter. But instead all I do is murmur, 'Still, with all that love floating around, if you were in some sort of race to happiness, the bookies would have had you as odds-on favourites to be first over the line.'

Angel shakes her head. 'The favourites don't always take home the marbles, Rainbow, you know that. Besides which, after the accident, our race seemed to be fixed. Cyril's legs were ruined, which meant he could never race again. He had the big payout, but he also had a lot of time on his hands. And, of course, he wanted to look after me. So ...'

There's more – much more. I can see that by the way the three of them – the dame, the ex-jockey, and his toy horse – are propping each other up.

'So Cyril took to gambling. In the beginning, he won. He knew jockeys, he knew horses and he knew form. Above all, he knew the system. But then the horses stopped running true to the system and he began losing – badly. He branched out and lost even more badly. He owed people money. Then along came Cameron.'

I take the fateful step back into the gloom. 'Cameron?'

Cyril disentangles himself from his missus and, still hugging his evil-looking toy, limps away.

Suddenly, Angel doesn't know what to do with her hands. 'Cameron's –' She waves the hands she doesn't know what to do with at the threadbare carpet, the crappy sink, and a future that's there in name only. 'Sorry, I'm being neglectful. Can I get you a – a ...'

Cyril breaks in. 'If you're going to suggest a cup of tea, we haven't got any – cups *or* tea.'

'... a glass of something, then.'

'There's no something, either.'

'What about water?'

'Don't you remember? They turned off the water – along with the gas.'

Angel manages a rueful smile. 'Then at least we won't be able to kill ourselves by sticking our heads in the oven.'

So it's that bad. Bad enough for me to come away from the exit, bad enough for me to venture back across the threadbare carpet and put my hand on Angel's shoulder. Bad enough even to pretend it can ever come right again.

'Tell me about Cameron, Ange.'

Cameron, she tells me, is the Mr Clean of racing. On the one hand, you got corruption, and on the other you got Cameron. I know a bit about him. I remember a marriage, a divorce, and an estrangement from a sister.

'Cyril was riding for him the day of the ... Anyway, Cameron paid for Cyril's surgery and the prosthesis and the term in rehab. He said he didn't want anything in return but Cyril felt obligated. Which was one of the reasons he started gambling. Cameron –'

I rein her in. 'Tell me about the – accident.' She's got me stumbling over the nomenclature now.

She nods in the half-light, and in the half-light the bangle on her wrist glimmers and I can pretend she still looks halfway like the woman she once was. 'It was Cyril's first ride on Lord Haw-Haw. I believe the horse was slated to become the next Phar Lap. Anyway, Cameron instructed Cyril to ride to win – although Cyril doubted that the horse could.'

'How come?'

Cyril answers out of the shadows. 'On his previous three outings, Lord Haw-Haw came last. It was like he had, well, even more lead in his saddlebags than the handicap he usually had to carry. You'd think his previous riders were a bunch of apprentices, when in reality they were veterans. It was a miracle there was never an inquiry. Lord Haw-Haw should have won every race he was entered in. But the day I rode him, he was rated so low no-one bothered putting money on him – nobody except Cameron. Believe it or not, the magnificent Lord Haw-Haw was a rank outsider, with a starting price of fifty to one. Only Cameron had faith in him, and stood to make a mint if he won.'

It's a long speech, as long as Cyril can manage. He leans against the dame, clutching his toy horse so tightly it looks like its eyes are going to pop.

Angel takes up the baton. 'Except that, as we all know' – she shudders – 'Lord Haw-Haw didn't win.'

I remember, but I let her go on. It stops me thinking about Imogene.

'Cameron, Lord Haw-Haw's owner, a man who never lost on anything, was sure that Lord Haw-Haw was going to win. His last minute instructions to Cyril were to go for it. Cyril was to position the horse in third place until they came into the straight, after which he was to come down on the outside and win. That's what Cameron said, *ride to win*.'

Chapter 11

THE YELLOW CROSS

Angel shrugs her shoulders. 'Cameron wasn't – isn't – a man to bet against his own horse. It wasn't surprising, then, that he instructed Cyril to win. Except that –'

Even in the gritty light, I can see the anguish in her face. But beyond that, I see her bouncing up and down in the connections stand, the eyes of the other punters not on the race but on her, splendid in her frock and fascinator, eyes agleam with anticipation because she knows her husband is going to win. Instead of which –

'At the turn, Cyril was nicely tucked into third. He wasn't botoxed-in, or even in any danger of it, but riding sweetly with Lord Haw-Haw striding out ...'

Cyril nods. 'He had it in him. You can feel it when it's like that. There's a sensation under you like – like –'

Angel pats his arm. 'Go ahead, darling, you can say it – like a good woman. That's what you used to say to me. *You're just like a good horse, darling.*' She turns back to me. 'I always took it as a compliment. After all, Cyril is – or rather, was – a great jockey.'

Cyril scratches himself again; he's close to tears as the dame comes into the straight and says how, with 200 metres to go, and with the jockeys all standing in their saddles, Cyril takes a tumble, Lord Haw-Haw goes down with him, and the entire field ...

'It was my fault. I fell. How come a first-rate jockey falls? It was ...'

How it looks to Angel from up in the stands is that every horse is trampling her man into the turf after his mount rolls off him. How horse and rider are still lying prone as the rest of the field thunders across the finish line.

'The upshot being that Cameron did his dough.' Angel hugs herself. 'Cameron had told Cyril to win and he put a lot of money on the nose. So it couldn't have been Cameron.' A faraway look comes into her eyes. 'Anyway, he's not like that.'

That's when I figure there's something she's not telling me. I don't like it when there's something somebody's not telling me. Especially a client. Especially a non-paying one.

'It sounds like this Cameron meant a whole lot more to you than someone your husband once rode for.'

Angel's complexion turns a shade of raspberry. It's the sort of inner-glow that derives from heat, or lust, or simply the embarrassment that comes with guilt. 'I – he – we ...'

Cyril's voice is savage. 'The bastard seduced her. It was Angel's way of paying off my debts. After things started going wrong, I developed the recklessness of the loser.' His mouth twists like he's got a shiff in his guts. 'But Cameron came to our rescue. So, yeah, I guess I owed him.'

Angel's knitting her hands together like she's making a jumper. 'He was so nice to us. He said it didn't matter. He said that he could afford to bail us out. But I told him I didn't like being in debt. So he said why not cut out the debt by – nothing sordid – but one thing led to another. I was still – pretty then, and looked a lot younger than my years.'

'And the debt?'

'The debt seemed to disappear into thin air after we started – going out.'

'How convenient.'

'When we – made love – it was only ever going to be a one-off.' She's having difficulty breathing. 'The trouble was that just as Cyril's gambling became a habit, so did my arrangement with Cameron. Then one day Cyril came to ask Cameron for money to put on a sure thing and discovered us ...'

I glance at Cyril lurking in the shadows. It's not hard to guess how he reacted. 'What happened then?'

'I realised that my love for Cyril was great enough for me to let him go on getting into debt, but not enough for me to go on sleeping with Cameron to get him out of it.'

'So what happened to the gambling debts?'

'They were – amalgamated.'

I feel like I'm in a place of the condemned. If we were in the Dark Ages, this would be a domicile of the Doomed. In the Year of the Plague, the joint would have a yellow cross on the door.

'Going back, you said quote, unquote: *Cameron seemed to think Lord*

Haw-Haw would win. What did you mean by that?'

'I meant that – for possibly the first time in his life – Cameron hadn't been in control.'

'One last question, and this one's for you, Cyril. Who went down first – you or the horse?'

Cyril scratches himself as he ponders the question. 'It was me,' he says at last. 'I went down first.'

I go to squeeze Angel's arm but find little more in my fingers than skin and bone. 'Try and keep him out of the clutches of the nasties, okay, Ange?'

I let her go and the dame nods. There's something like hope in her sunken eyes, or maybe it's just the darkness. 'I'll try.'

I'm no betting man, but I'd lay good money against her chances.

Chapter 12

THE GAMBOLLING MAN

I manage to lose the dame in the leopardskin leotards (I figure it's not Pandora, Pandora wears black) by cutting through the traffic, darting behind a 327 omnibus, turning a high-flying leap into a three-spin roll, and finally banging through the mob halfway between Books on King and a cut-price shoe shop.

On the other side of the Harbour, at the counter of the empty caff under a sign saying *TWO-UP COFFEE – THE ODDS ARE IT'S GREAT*, Harry Hopman's looking even wiser than usual. But the hand carrying the muck that passes for coffee in his establishment is shaking. Harry always shakes. He says it's with merriment, only he hasn't got much to be merry about.

'How are they hanging, Harry?'

'By a thread.' He drops the mess of caffeine in front of me. 'But on the bright side, I could be dead tomorrow.' He chucks me a glance. 'How about you?'

I debate whether to try the coffee. Enjoying Harry's company doesn't mean I got to die doing it. 'Depends which side you're on.' I shrug. 'I just scored another non-paying customer and I'm in danger of losing Imogene. Otherwise everything's great. But I'm not here to complain.'

'No, you're here for my excellent coffee.'

'That, too.' I take a sip to show there's no ill feeling, but immediately wish I hadn't. 'Tell me, what do you know about the current state of horseracing?'

Harry used to be a bookie. 'Ask me something I don't know.' He wipes his nose on his apron and seats himself. 'In a word, once upon a time it was corrupt. Since then, only the names have changed.'

'What form does corruption take now?'

He spreads his hands and looks at me like I was born tomorrow. 'Mate, your question should read: *What form doesn't it take?*' The sunlight picks out the life scars on his face. 'Trainers manipulate form, bookies bribe anyone that'll take their money, jockeys bet on horses they're racing against, stewards turn a blind eye to obstruction, and every other day a new drug's invented that doesn't show up on a swab.'

Harry's entitled to feel bitter. His missus left him for a female impersonator, his only kid's a junkie, and he lost his bookie's ticket for refusing to agree to a fix.

'Nice coffee, Harry.'

'Thanks, Rain.'

'Nice, too, the way the clouds form themselves into shapes. See that one over there to the left, there, above that mansion, the one with all the curlicues on it? Looks like a pig's snout.'

Harry doesn't look up. 'So what's your question?'

I come down out of the clouds and back to Harry. His coffee's crap but that doesn't mean his advice is. 'I want to know what – if any – organisation is involved. These race fixers you're referring to – are they freelancers or is there some kind of logic to it – mafia, triads, bikers?'

Harry wipes his face like he's using his beard as a pumice. His five-o'clock shadow comes into contention five minutes after he shaves. 'Those groups you mention are into everything. This is the age of non-discrimination. This is a free-enterprise society meaning corruption is freely open to all.'

I feel the table. It's solid, but the answer isn't. 'You haven't answered my question.'

After Harry lost his bookie's ticket, he wasn't worth a brass razoo. A miracle payout on one of my jobs helped get him this hole-in-the-wall café. It's not worth anything, either, but that's the way he likes it. In a sad kind of way, he's a happy man. He examines his fingernails. They're dirty. 'You know the biggest beneficiary of gambling in this state? The government. On the one hand, they say we shouldn't do it, and on the other they're running TABs and lotteries and getting massive rake-offs from everything from pokies to scratchies. Not to mention sport.'

'So government equals corruption?'

Harry shrugs. 'I'm saying, seek and ye shall find. Because in the end, it depends what you're looking for.'

I lean back. The clouds still resemble pigs. 'Come on, mate. I'm looking for an answer to a conundrum. Let's try another tack. What do you know about a racing identity called Cameron?'

'Justin Cameron? The guy that owns racecourses?'

'Mate, no-one owns racecourses in this country.'

Harry picks up a copy of *The Daily Terrorgraph* that looks like it was mauled by a pack of dingoes. He riffles past stories about footballers throwing games in return for sex and cricket players throwing away sex in return for a game of cricket, and comes to a spread of a tall, smiley-faced gent in front of a Rolls-Royce and a racetrack. The headline reads:

FOR CAM THE MAN, LIFE IN THE FAST LANE IS NOTHING MORE THAN A GAMBOL

Harry waves the rag like he's just dropped a handline in a puddle and come up with a five-pound flounder. 'This one does.' He pauses for breath.

'Last year, this rag ran a story on a guy that spent $10 million on a Formula One racetrack on the NSW Central Coast – five kilometres of road on five hectares of land.' Harry smacks the paper. 'Justin Cameron is to racehorses what that bloke is to F1.'

I check out the photograph. This is the joker Angel was talking about. He's tall – close to my height. Except that, unlike me, he's got what you'd call class – pressed shirt, nice cravat, beautifully-tailored threads – and a smile that looks like it was put there by a surgeon. But it's the way he's standing that really impresses. Photographs usually diminish people but this guy diminishes the photograph. He's not smiling at the camera, the camera's smiling at him. And the Rolls-Royce by the racetrack looks like a toy.

'Impressive.'

Harry shoots me a glance. 'I know what you're thinking, Rain – that's he's not exactly your shot of vodka. That doesn't make him any worse than anyone else. Get a load of this.'

Harry shows me another picture, this time accompanied by a bunch of statistics, under the heading:

ROYAL CAM-WICK

Circumference of Track, 2224 metres

Width of Track, 30 metres

Length of Straight, 410 metres

Width of Straight at Winning Post, 18 metres

Everything everyone doesn't need to know about Randwick Racecourse, and then some. So the man owns a track just like Randwick, so what? I plonk down the mug. 'What do you put in this coffee, Harry? Toadstools?'

'It's state of the art, Rainbow. Just like Cam the Man's track.'

'Yeah, and just as likely to give you the trots.' But I'm not here to do a commentary on the coffee. 'Tell me what else you know about him.'

Chapter 13

THE SKELETON AT THE TABLE

Harry parks himself back in his seat and squints into the clouds.

That's why he serves crook coffee. It's to keep the customers away, so he can sit and squint into the clouds. What I don't know is what drives Justin Cameron.

'Well, he's a big man.'

'I can tell that just by looking at the photo. How about telling me something I don't know?'

Harry drops his head between his shoulders. I call it his bird-of-prey look, only anyone less like a bird of prey would be harder to pick than a winner at Randwick. 'We both know about losers, Rain. Losers are your day-to-day everyman. It's a word that carries plenty of connotations but means nothing. Everyone's a loser in my book and there's nothing wrong with that. Losers are just the people that admit it.'

'Only this joker doesn't?'

He shakes his head. If everyone's a loser, Harry's a winner among losers. Everything's gone wrong in his life – family, fortune and reputation – but somehow he always comes up smoking daisies. 'No, Cameron wins and that's his problem. He doesn't have to buy politicians, they fawn over him without his paying them a sou. He knows racing backwards. And – until recently, anyway – he always backed winners.'

I forget the coffee. I forget Imogene and the fact I'm on the cusp of losing her. I even forget the shadow that's flitting among the trees down the road.

'What do you mean – *until recently*?'

'Just what I said, *until recently*.'

'How recently?'

'About two years recently.'

'Cameron's been losing for two years?' I tap the blatt. 'He doesn't look like he's losing here.'

'The *Terrorgraph* specialises in old photos.'

'Okay, so tell me how come he's losing. Is it the Global Financial Casuistry? His investments going bad? Cards not falling the way they should?'

'None of the above. Cameron's a specialist. He only does racing, and then only one kind of racing. Not the doggies, not the trots – not even camels or cane toads. He's Justin Cameron and with him it's just gallopers.' Harry shrugs. 'Hence the beautiful, turfed racetrack you see on the table before you.'

'So what happened?'

Harry gazes at me out of eyes that go back to the beginning of time. 'My guess is that something leapt out of his past at him. Some folk call it karma.'

I feel my skull contract. 'Why do you think that?'

Harry shrugs. 'Because there's no other explanation for his misfortune.'

I bring myself back to the main line. The clouds have turned back into clouds, and I remind myself that the only reality you can rely on in this world is the facts. 'So tell me about the beautiful, turfed racetrack.'

Harry raises an eyebrow. 'What's there to tell? It's on a slab of land carved out of rainforest south of Sydney. And like the newspaper says, it's built along exactly the same lines as Randwick – same size, same dimensions, same layout. I suppose Cameron organises private races on it. No law against that. A little something for the man who has everything.'

'And?'

'And what?'

'There's always an and.'

Harry climbs to his feet, revealing the fact that he's in about the same physical condition as a thousand-year-old mummy. 'You're the detective, Rain. I'm just an ordinary, everyday barista. Show me a field of horses and all I see is the colour of the silks on the jockeys riding them. To me and to the rest of the world, Justin Cameron's exactly what he appears to be – a winner.'

I decline a second cup of coffee. To accept might put me in the same physical state as Harry. So I stand, jam on the chapeau, kick the chair back under the table and chuck a final glance at the blatt. Down in the bottom right-hand corner, I notice an ad for some bunch going by the name MRS GRUNDY, featuring a skeleton crouched at a card table with – standing apart and looking on – a beautiful dame with a concerned smile on her dial-up and a comic-strip word bubble coming out of her mouth:

Gambling a problem?

Why not pay us a visit?

Followed by an address, a website and a telephone number.

My way back to the *Wooden No* leads past the kid. Today, tomorrow and forever, my way back to anywhere is going to lead past the kid. I knock on the door of the joint on Castanet Close and Salina answers.

'What are you doing here?' Her fingers tighten on the door knob.

'I just wanted to see the kid.'

'Well, you can't see the kid.'

'I need to remind her that I exist.'

'And I want to remind her that you don't.'

Maybe I'm imagining the movement in the hallway. 'Is there someone there with you?'

'Yes, my daughter, Imogene.'

'Anyone else?'

'Like everything in my life from now on, Rainbow, that's for me to know and you not to find out.'

I turn away.

It's the kid that matters, my feelings don't butter parsnips.

I got to find a distraction.

I got a name for the distraction.

Justin Cameron.

Chapter 14

DEATH BY OVERSIGHT

The tail's still in place, a dame in colourful leotards – sometimes patterned, sometimes plain, but always colourful – behind trees, in shop doorways, lurking on the other side of cars, half-merging with the crowd, but never quite making it. She's an inept follower. Which is why I don't try to double back on her. Why bother? She's easy to see, easier still to lose. She's been with me, on and off, since I first stumbled on that stiff at Central. Since then, another body has been found with the same tell-tale marks: slight contusions, cuts, burns and abrasions. According to the news reports – paragraphs that are no more than fillers – the fuzz aren't too interested, filing the corpses under 'Death by Societal Oversight', and leaving it to people like Annie to dispose of the remains.

I shake the dame that's following me at Pimlico's, heading through the billiard room, out through the end window – the one with the rock 'n' roll lock on half-cock and the cut-price surround – and down the side alley. After that, I get myself to Rube's.

'It's been a while, Rainbow.'

'Sorry, Aunt. I've been busy.'

She's cased me through the peephole and now she's standing in the doorway of her Darlinghurst down-at-heel, checking right and left along the boulevard like she always does, scrawny as a bug-empty stocking, but still capable of taking on the world.

'No need for excuses.'

There's barely enough of her to throw a shadow as she precedes me down the hall.

'I could lose Imogene, Rube.'

We're in her kitchen, a place full of blue china and memories.

She shrugs. 'Everyone loses their kids at some point. If you bet against that, you'd put your life savings on a grass seed in a whirlwind.'

'I haven't got any life savings.'

'It's just an expression.'

'Right.' Rube's coffee is better than Harry's. Then again, mud's better than Harry's. 'So what do I do?'

'Focus on the job. From what you're telling me, Sal's found herself a fella. Let the dust settle. The kid can work out how it goes from here.'

'What if he's dangerous?'

Rube inclines her head. 'Your ex-wife can look after herself.'

'I'm not worried about Sal.'

'Then ditto the kid.'

For once I reckon Rube's only half-right. It could be because I'm jumping at shadows. Then again, it could be because Rube's only half-right. I down my mug of caffeine and watch my past dance around the walls – ballet, ethics, music, detection methods, James Cagney movies, escapology.

'You're too close to the action, Rainbow. With everything in this life, you got to ignore the bones and consider the skeleton. Just because the occipital's a long way from the tarsus doesn't mean ...'

Rube's voice trails off and after I've used her computer, so do I.

I don't need a sniffer dog to locate Phoebe Riesling because, one: the name of her current employer's familiar; two: she's not trying to hide from anyone; and three: the joint where she works is in sunny Newtown, just around the corner from Cyril's. I find Phoebe at her desk in the front room of a yellow-painted terrace.

'I'd like to speak with your boss.'

She chucks me a glance out of the hard eyes, says she'll be with me shortly, then goes back to whatever she was doing before I showed up, leaving me to check out my surroundings.

Cramped reception room that feels even more cramped on account of all the signs in it. *MRS GRUNDY INC.* reads the plaque over the yellow door behind the dame. And underneath:

We're not concerned with being what we're not, and not afraid to be what we are.

After I've given up trying to work out that little gem, I discover it's open slather on epigrams.

Give away gambling, not your money

Family first, last and always
Trust in God, not man
Tobacco or not tobacco — hardly a question
Drink for Thirst, Don't Thirst for Drink
And more obscurely:
We might live in a yellow submarine, but that doesn't mean we have to go down with the others

Posters cover every available inch of space. Shots of happy families, pictures of sad ones. Crosses for stubbies of beer and ticks for what look like bottles of Vichy water. Brisk walks are in, wild parties out. Hard work's favoured. So is neck-to-knee swimwear. All very interesting, but after five minutes of wallowing in holy water I'm done.

'Have you pressed any buttons yet, lady?'

Phoebe Riesling shakes her coif. 'I said I'd be with you shortly. So in the meantime, would you mind taking a seat? You're making me nervous.'

'Yeah, I would mind as a matter of fact. I also mind standing around doing nothing but read *Aesop's Fables*.' I nod at the door behind her. 'You got a boss tucked away in there somewhere. Get her for me.'

'All in good time.'

I shake my head. 'No, all in bad time, lady.' I move a step closer.

She frowns. 'Really, this is most improper.'

'Life's most improper, get used to it. What you did with my kid was most improper. And if you don't find your boss for me in a hurry, I'll most improperly bust down that door behind you and most improperly find her myself.'

Chapter 15

MRS GRUNDY SAYS

When Phoebe's boss appears, she's sporting a nice hairdo, nice white, sensible, surgical-type footwear, white gloves, white frock and stockings – and the sort of face that's usually worn by a shop window dummy or a nun: perfect, composed and flawless.

'I believe you have a problem.'

Under the hairdo, the peepers coolly take me apart. I take my own eyes for a return tour of the signs on the walls, before bringing them back to the dame at the door.

'We need to talk.'

She manages the kind of smile that's not going to do permanent damage to the flawless complexion, but does a lot of damage to me. She glances at her colleague behind the desk. 'Thank you for notifying me, Miss Riesling, you did the right thing.' A curt nod is thrown in my direction. 'Follow me.'

I keep my mind on what Rube told me while I follow the dame. Keep your eye on the big picture. So I keep my eye on the big picture, and the big picture tells me that under the white gloves and all her get-up and go-for-it, this dame's really something. After that, I try to forget the beautiful calves, the promise of fine strength in the lithe body under all the starched whiteness, and the wasp waist.

'Please sit.'

I remove my fedora and sit as she pirouettes easily and calmly on her sensible shoes before leaning back and pressing the appropriate part of her anatomy against the edge of her desk. At the same time she crosses her arms and fixes me with eyes of the same cold blue as the water at Bondi this morning. 'I don't believe we've met, Mr er –'

'You don't believe right. The name's Brown, John Brown.'

'Fancy that.' It's like she was expecting an invention and what I just gave her was pretty much what she expected. 'Why are you here, Mr Brown?'

Her room's much like the one outside – minimal furniture, a window that looks onto a brick wall, and possessing about as much ambience as a mausoleum.

'And maybe you could, too,' I say. 'Like, for starters, what's with the "Grundy" caper?'

She eases herself off the desk and for a moment I get the wildest of fancies she's going to hurl herself at me. But it proves to be no more than a sad case of the wistfuls, because instead, she dusts imaginary dust off her gloves, moves back behind her desk, and sits, and there are still no creases in the perfect complexion when she smiles.

'It's just a little fancy of mine, Mr Brown. Mrs Grundy was a character in a play by someone named Morton called *Speed the Plough*.'

Speed the Plough did the rounds of theatres in Merrie Olde Englande something like two hundred years ago. I know the story but I need to see where this is going, so I let her tell me.

'Mrs Grundy was the neighbour everyone worries about. People would ask: *What will Mrs Grundy say?* Of course, Mrs Grundy was a figure of fun – that's what she became, anyway – but I believe she represents everything that's good in this world. Mrs Grundy is *morality.*'

So now we got a morality play on our hands.

'When I was setting up my organisation and looking for a name, I decided to adopt hers. Because just like Mrs Grundy, we stand for what's good in this world, and we're not afraid to admit it.'

'So you became Mrs Grundy.'

'I suppose it sounds silly, but, yes, that's who I became.' She cuts across my thoughts. 'Look, I know what you're thinking – that Grundies are no more than people who don't mind their own business.' She shrugs. 'But don't you think, Mr – Brown – that sometimes other people's business needs minding? If only for their own good?'

'Yeah, like, for instance, when my daughter was minding her own business and you and your colleague decided to abduct her.'

The dame frowns. 'Do refresh my memory, please. Exactly what business was your daughter minding, and where?'

I do the pause most people do before they come out with half-truths. 'She was at Darling Harbour, in the city.'

She caresses her throat with one of her gloved hands. 'Whereabouts at Darling Harbour, in the city?' She has a pen in her hand and she's writing with it, and her body – at least what I can see of it above the desk – has a kind of hard-edged wiriness about it. The clothing doesn't do her justice. Then again, maybe I'm not doing her justice.

'The northern end.'

'That would have been on the steps outside the casino?'

She's got me on the back foot. I don't like being on the back foot. 'Look, she just happened to be waiting for me.'

'And how old is this this daughter of yours who just happened to be waiting for you?'

'She's – I –'

She strokes her beautiful throat with her white-gloved hand. 'I see. So you don't even know the age of this much-loved daughter of yours. And I suppose you were just visiting old friends in the Star.' The gloved hand stops its stroking and returns to the desktop alongside the other one with the pen. 'Mr Brown, let's stop pussy-footing around, shall we? Gambling is bad enough without also leaving your child at the mercy of an uncertain populace.'

After forcing my way in here, I had no chance of winning this dame's affections. Now I got even less. I take a deep breath – the kind I usually take before putting my head under water. 'My daughter was in no danger, except from people like you. Now, as a direct result of your actions – taking her back to her mother, thereby implying that I'm a bad father – I'm probably going to lose her on a more or less permanent basis.'

She puts down her pen, stands, and moves across to the window that overlooks the brick wall. 'But if you're a gambler, Mr Brown, don't you think you deserve to lose your child?'

'Yeah, except I'm not a gambler. I was rescuing someone who was. So it looks like I might be in the same business as you.'

'I see.'

'I don't think you do.' I hunch the shoulders, then I unhunch them. 'You think you got all the answers, when in actual fact, you're part of the problem.'

She turns and faces me. 'All right, you've made your point.' The voice is suddenly gentle and I'm suddenly in love again. 'Exactly what do you want me to do?'

'I want you to pay a visit to my ex-wife and tell her you acted prematurely. That her – our – kid wasn't abandoned, that you and your colleague only thought she was. That you're convinced I wasn't neglectful, and nor was I gambling. That you made an honest mistake, and that you're of the honest opinion that me and the kid shouldn't have to pay for it.'

She comes up close to where I'm sitting, and this time when she smiles, it looks like it might almost be real. 'I'd be more than happy to revisit your ex-wife, Mr Brown,' she purrs. 'And let me add that I'm genuinely sorry for any inconvenience Miss Riesling and I might have caused. We take our work very seriously. As a result we sometimes get a little carried away.'

I got one last question. Always ask the last question. 'What is your work exactly?'

She moves away, like somehow it's safer, and maybe she's right. 'Clearly you don't read the women's magazines.' She's back behind the desk. 'In a nutshell, I run a well-known and highly-respected charity set up to help people with problems, particularly in the area of gambling. And to help me, I employ what are generally known as *fallen women* ...'

Chapter 16

WHERE THERE'S SMOKE ...

I think outside the square – and beyond the room – to Phoebe Riesling in the foyer. It makes sense. Something bad can sometimes lead to good.

I nod. 'I understand – *the harlot's cry* I believe the poet called it, something to do with *the whore and the gambler* ...'

'Oh, for goodness' sake, Mr Whatever-your-name-is, I'm not using fallen women in that sense. The women who work for me aren't ex-whatever they're called these days – sex-workers. No, I'm talking about women who have been irrevocably hurt, usually in their own homes. Women who have had the ground cut out from under them by – some person or other. Women who – I give those women a chance to be –'

'I get the picture.'

She recovers her equipoise. 'Let's just say I find such women make excellent assistants. And before you ask how we manage to keep ourselves in such luxury, as far as the running costs of our organisation are concerned, benefactors make donations, while others pay us to help rescue their loved ones from whatever their problem might be.' She throws me a look out of her Bondi-blue eyes. 'Perhaps there's something you'd like to contribute, Mr Brown?'

She's right.

There is.

But I slip her a ten-spot instead.

The joker that ducks into the government-run Totalisator Agency Betting place – all right, the TAB – just as I emerge from the Grundy pad looks familiar. So does the figure that follows the joker in, a black-clad male in cowboy boots known around the traps as Bat Masterson – or just plain Batty. Bat's an enforcer, a thug sent out by persons to whom the debts are owed to collect. Call him a commission agent. Call him dangerous.

A siren sounds in the distance, so it must be lunchtime, and the TAB's in full swing so it must be Thursday, the day when punters are handed the dole and can't wait for the chance to hand it straight back to the people that gave it to them. This is the inner city. Once, it was prostitutes, razor gangs and bent police, but now it's mostly gambling, and the cops stay home and do the paperwork, because gambling's legal. The barred-window terraces could be cells, the four-wheel-drives outside look all set for a tour of duty in Afghanistan, and the sirens are echoing in company with the unmistakeable smell of smoke as I ease myself into the betting parlour.

There are two figures at the grilled window, while the face with the fake smile on the television screen perched among all the racing ads is introducing the next race at Royal Randwick.

'*The track favours the cleanskins, so the smart money's on The Mole.*'

Cyril's clutching his pony and I get close enough to the action to realise that Bat Masterson goes through life without benefit of deodorant.

Cyril shoves a sheaf of notes through the grille. 'A hundred on The Mole.'

Batty shoves Cyril aside and palms the dough-re-me. 'This gentleman's not betting today,' he advises the grille.

'I would have thought that was for the gentleman to decide,' the grille replies.

'And I would of thought you'd shut your cakehole.'

The grille purses its mouth and Cyril shrugs. 'I guess I'm not betting today.'

Batty's got one hand on Cyril's shoulder. 'I want everything you've got,' he snarls, 'and then some.'

'I haven't got anything!'

'Why don't I believe that?'

'The money's not mine.'

'You're dead right it's not yours.' The rest of the punters keep their heads down as the thug shovels Cyril past the television towards the exit. 'And neither is your life if you don't pay me the rest of what you owe us.'

'Look, I'll pay you, I promise.'

'I don't do promises.'

The television goes into overdrive. '*... but The Mole's come nowhere! The favourite ...*'

Batty spins on his heels. 'Turn that off.'

'I'm sorry, but the television's on automatic,' says the grille.

'And so am I.' Batty punches the TV and the screen goes black. He turns back to Cyril. 'Hand over the dough, Cyril, or you're next.'

Another siren sounds and Batty flinches. I think he realises the jig might be up and that today he's going to have to leave empty-handed. He lets go and on his way out gives me a bad look.

I grab Cyril.

'Hey, you're hurting me!'

'Stop struggling or I'll hurt you some more. Now move it.'

We get ourselves into a side lane where the smell of smoke has just got even stronger.

'Handy, isn't it – having a betting parlour just around the corner from the hovel you've reduced Angel to.' I give him a shake; I feel like giving him a lot more. 'So what was that all about?'

Cyril hugs his toy horse. 'It was a cop car.'

'I'm not talking about the sirens, I'm talking about the joker in the Roy Orbison outfit. He work for the people you owe the money to?'

'One of them.'

'So how many are there?'

'Heaps.'

When I shake him, it's the horse's teeth that rattle. 'How much do you owe the people that Batty works for?'

'By my reckoning, nothing. The horse they told me would win just came last. How can that be owing anyone?'

'You're using the wrong logic, pal. If a bloke like that says you owe him, then you owe him, and if you want to stay alive, you pay him.'

Cyril's shoulders slump even lower. 'I can't afford to pay no one nothing.'

The smell of smoke keeps getting stronger. 'Then you can't afford to stay alive.'

Chapter 17

... THERE'S MURDER

If I'd been concentrating on the big picture instead of rescuing Cyril, I'd have known who the sirens belonged to. As we turn into Cyril's street, punters up and down the boulevard are gaping at the action and hoses are all over the carriageway.

Lord Haw-Haw grimaces as Cyril tightens his grip on him. 'Jeez, if it's not one thing it's another!'

I resist strangling him. 'Wrong, pal.' I haul him out of the way of a fireman. 'This is not another thing because what just happened is all part of the same thing. And that thing is that you're an inveterate gambler wallowing in his own misery. That's the reason you got no funding, the heavies are onto you, you're living in a hole, and it just burnt down. It's also why I'm in danger of losing my daughter.' A thought hits me. 'Where is she?'

'Who, your daughter?'

I tear my eyes away from the remains of the shack and fix them on Cyril. 'No, you idiot, Angel!' I shake him. 'Was she at home?'

Cyril does his bent-shouldered shrug, and the toy horse shrugs with him. 'How would I know?'

'She's your wife!'

Something seems to stir in his memory, but nothing moves in what's left of the hovel. 'I seem to remember something about her going to the pawn shop on King Street. Something about a bangle.'

The hovel's a wreck, the firies have finished putting away their hoses because there's nothing left to play them on, and the wet ashes glimmer like lost hope in the wan sunlight. I cast my eyes around the smoking cinders, fear in my heart. There's a broken cup, a charred table leg, a burnt sack of rubbish, a blackened shoe. I turn away and am confronted by the wreckage of the joker beside me.

'Cyril, do you even care?'

A cop car cruises by and I drag him into the crowd and out of the squaddie's sightline. This place is too hot for comfort. Aside from which, I suddenly – make that urgently – need to determine the last-known whereabouts of Angela Golightly.

'So where's this pawn shop?'

Hope springs eternal in Cyril's eyes. 'Why, you got something to flog?'

The pawn shop's a pawn shop – dusty guitars chained in the doorway like mangy kelpies, its next-door neighbour a brothel, and too full of the proceeds of crime for comfort.

A hairball adjusting the scenery frowns at Cyril's mangy horse. 'Youse can both piss off and take your shitty toy with you.'

You can't reason with usurers. I chuck a glance around the shop. 'We're looking for a woman.'

'Next door.'

'A specific woman.'

'Like I said, brothel's next door.'

I haul out the gat.

Hairball backs off. 'Just kidding.' He gets behind the counter. I watch the hands. He sees me watching the hands and keeps them away from the alarm bell, fingers spread like he's drying nailpolish. 'What's she look like, this woman you're after?'

'Brunette. Tall, blue eyes, skinny. Once beautiful, but that was before she fell victim to a husband that gambles.'

The usurer looks at Cyril. They know each other. 'This the husband?'

I put away the gat. 'Yeah.'

'And the woman's five-nine, whippet-thin, and answers to the name of Angela Golightly?'

I tell him *Yeah* again.

'Sorry, mate, ain't seen her since the day before yesterday.'

The firies and the crowd have dispersed. Where the hovel once stood there's nothing but a sodden pile of ashes, a bunch of witches' hats, a few lengths of red tape, the blackened remains of a sign that once read 'TOiLET' and a great deal of sadness. No cops. I suppose it was only a hovel.

I make my way into the sadness and the whitesides turn monochrome. The decay has been replaced by burnt decay. I see a patch of threadbare carpet that somehow escaped the inferno, the collapsed remains of a kitchen sink that a couple of cockroaches once raced on, a charred shoe and what was once a petrol can.

Then I see the bangle. It's the one I gave a once-beautiful dame for saving me from post-marriage desuetude, a band of 32-carat gold with no strings attached that was tight on her arm when I gave it to her, but loose as a mug punter's morals when I saw it last time.

But that was last time.

At first I think it's just the smoke seeping up out of the wreckage that's getting in the way of my vision. Because everything's gone hazy — the brow-beaten walls, the charred rafters, the fallen-in, corrugated-tin roof and the still-smouldering remains of a once-beautiful dame.

I pick up the bracelet and get the hell out of there.

Chapter 18

THE MATCHSTICK MAN

In the street, Cyril's hunched in the gutter clutching Lord Haw-Haw. There's soot all over his face and his mumbling sounds like a snake slithering over charred stubble after a grass fire.

I drag him away from the ashes, the witches' hats, and Angel. 'That was your wife in there – or what was left of her after you and the conflagration had their way.'

He cringes as if expecting a beating. I don't do the physical, I hit him with the truth instead. 'Fact number one: she's dead. I wish it was you in her place, but the sad reality is that it isn't.'

I shake off the bad thoughts, recalling the remains of the petrol can in what used to be the hovel's doorway. 'Fact number two: it was murder. Some matchstick man wanted to kill you but got your missus instead. It seems that your miserable life might have been saved by the thug in the betting parlour, rendering you too late for your own funeral, but dumping Angel in the coffin instead.'

I stop, turn and face Cyril and what's left of his conscience. 'And fact number three is I'm going to find out who did it, starting with your mate at the TAB. He could have been on the same team as the matchstick man, and it was all nothing but a monumental cock-up, a case of the right hand not knowing what the wrong hand was doing.'

Cyril's eyes glaze. I don't know if he's worked out he's a widower, or just thinking about the next race.

'So who's Bat Masterson work for? Who was into you for money?'

'I – I don't know. Jeez.' Tears spring to his eyes and his mouth quivers. 'It could have been – anyone.' He shakes his head. 'I owe so many people. I know it sounds bad, but it seems like there wasn't anyone I didn't owe money to.' His frown is shared by his toy horse as he squeezes it. 'But why would anyone want to kill me? I was going to make a – a killing. And they'd all get their money back. They'd get nothing from me dead.'

That's when a new thought strikes me. 'Did anyone want to kill

Angel?'

Cyril stares at me. 'Who'd want to kill Angela?' His eyes brim. 'She was a — a — a —'

I shake him. 'Keep it together, Cyril, you owe it to her. Tell me the name of your major creditor.'

Cyril shakes his head. It's like it's all finally got to him. 'Jesus, I feel — down.' His feet shuffle on the footpath and if his shoulders were any more bowed he wouldn't possess any. He sags back into the gutter like a sack of suet, parking the horse on the kerb beside him. 'I feel like topping myself.'

'Well, would you delay the process until we find out who killed your missus? After which, you can do what you like as far as I'm concerned, as long as it doesn't involve killing anyone else.'

He frowns. 'Hey, wait a minute, I remember now. I amalgamated all my debts.'

'Who to?'

He shakes his head. 'I — I don't know. Someone approached me one day and said they'd amalgamate my debts and I said okay.'

'People don't just —'

He shakes his head again. 'This one did. And I agreed. I mean, why not? If someone's silly enough to —'

'Was it by any chance Cameron?'

'No, like I said before, Cameron was losing, too. My fall was part of it.'

'Part of what?'

'Jesus, all these questions! How do you expect me to know?'

'Okay, okay. Back to Cameron: where do I find him?'

'Probably at his club.'

'And which club might that be?'

'They call it the Residence, but it's by invitation only.'

I dump Cyril at O'Leary's — the speakeasy that doesn't exist on Patterson — slipping Hank the barman my last fifty to keep an eye on him, in case he decides to honour his threat. I then make my way to Club Privilege. The joint's on Castlereagh Street in an edifice thrown up in Queen Victoria's time to make Sydney look like an integral part of the Empire — all sandstone and marble and Corinthian columns — and while it takes twenty minutes to get there, it takes a whole lot longer to get past the flunky in the highly-polished doorway.

'I'm sorry, sir, but you can't come in dressed like that.'

I'm wearing the candy-coloured coat teamed with the red tie, green strides, whitesides, and the all-purpose fedora, and the gat's not apparent – even if you were looking for it.

'Dressed like what?'

'We have a dress code, sir, and in about a hundred and one ways you don't even begin to conform to it.'

'I'd prefer we not get hung up over wardrobes.'

'A lot of us would prefer a whole lot of things in this life, sir, but it doesn't mean we get them.'

Chapter 19

A MATTER OF GILT

Out on the street, a Rolls-Royce Silver Spoon disgorges a dame wearing what looks like a close-knit family of dead wombats. She waltzes up the staircase without being challenged over the marsupials, and a joker in a top hat and green livery bows so low he almost licks her Gucci-clad hoofs. This woman is alive, while Angela's as dead as egalitarianism.

I try a different tack. 'I'm here to see one of your members.'

The flunky's got the courage of his connections. 'I'm sorry, sir, but I very much doubt if any of our members would *know* someone like you.'

I square the shoulders. 'They mightn't know me, but they'll know what I'm here for.'

'I very much doubt that, too.'

'It concerns the death of a mutual friend.'

'So go advertise it in the newspapers.'

'I'm not handing out invitations to a funeral.'

A bunch of tourists has noticed the altercation and is busy bringing out the cameras. I don't like cameras, never have. I hunch my back to them.

'I'm coming in.'

'Not if I can help it.'

'You can't help it.'

I'm out of the firing line and into the foyer, where I find an expensive carpet, a lot of chandeliers and too much mahogany.

The goon's followed me and lays a heavy hand on my shoulder. 'This is as far as you get without giving me a name.'

'I don't give my name to nobody.'

'I'm referring to the name of a member.'

I give him the name of a member.

The name excites the minion. 'I'm sorry, sir, no-one sees Mr Cameron.'

'Tell Mr Cameron the death I'm inquiring about is that of Angela

Golightly.'

'I could tell him that, sir, but I don't see ...'

'So go tell him, and don't bother looking.'

A bellboy in a performing monkey's hat shows me to a room that's as dark as a murderer's thoughts. The walls are designer green, the only lighting's by way of sconces, and the rest of the darkness comes courtesy of an expensive Axminster.

'I don't believe we've met.'

We're both on the upside of six feet, but after that, any resemblance is purely illusory. Justin Cameron is dressed in the sort of gear only a great deal of money can buy and an expression that would be at home on the dial-up of Pope Francis. In contrast I'm dressed by Vinnies and possess a face crafted by too many maulings.

'The name's Black.'

'Black by name, black by nature, eh?' There's no handshake, and little else by way of welcome. 'Well, Mr Black, I can't say it's nice meeting you because that would be dishonest of me. For a start, I don't know who or what you are.' He examines me through his aristocratic eyes. 'In fact, I don't even know why I agreed to let you in.'

'She's dead.'

I'm watching the face, but the darkness and the breeding prevent me seeing anything worth seeing.

'My good man, I don't believe we're – how might your sort of person put it? – reading from the same form guide.'

'Look, pal, I know for a fact that Angela Golightly was a friend of yours. I also know she's just died a gruesome and unjustified death.'

Cameron's features start to make sense in the gloom, and the sense they're making is that he's halfway listening. It's a start.

'By the time she was burned to death, Angela was so malnourished as a result of her husband's gambling it was a wonder there was anything left to burn.' I drag the bangle out of my poche. It glimmers dully in the dull light. 'She was wearing this at the time. It was all there was left of her.'

The bauble shows obvious signs of the fire and Cameron shows even more obvious signs of recognising it. Finally some emotion creeps into the Easter Island features. His fine hands cover his face, and his voice is a whisper. 'My God ...'

The dame wearing the family of wombats waltzes in. 'Oh, there you are.' She glances at me. 'I was looking all over … And this would be?'

Cameron doesn't look at her. 'Be quiet, dear, and go away, will you?'

Mrs Cameron – it's got to be Mrs Cameron – obliges, like she was never there in the first place.

I home in on the remorse, chagrin, mourning – call it what you will. 'Someone killed her.'

'How do you know that?'

'I don't have to be Sherlock Holmes to know a torch job when I see one.'

'A torch job?'

'Someone lit the fire deliberate, Cameron. And Angel was home at the time.'

'But why would anyone want to kill her?'

'Because her husband's a compulsive gambler and deep in debt.' I pause. 'I figured you might be the one holding the promissory notes.'

Cameron shakes his head. 'I – I tried to help.'

'By seducing Angela and afterwards waiving a few debts owed by the husband you cuckolded. It's a good thing you were trying.'

'You don't understand.' He's right. I don't. 'Why kill Angela?'

'Whoever did it was after her husband and they just happened to hit the wrong target. Torches aren't known as people of great and unerring discernment.' I watch him up close and personal while I say it – my rods and cones have adjusted to the twilight – to determine if the distress is genuine.

He takes his hands off his face. The distress really is genuine.

'And what's your interest in all this?'

'I'm an ordinary, everyday gumshoe, a nosy parker, a private eye who – like you – happens to have once been a lover of Miss Golightly's. And being what I am, I'm going to find out who murdered her.'

Chapter 20

A NICE LITTLE SHORT-CUT

I remember what I've learned about Justin Cameron, then I forget it, because it's always better to start with a clean slate.

He looks at me sharply. 'Why should I know anything?'

'Because her husband, Cyril Golightly, used to ride for you – until the accident. You seduced Angela Golightly. Following on from which, you're a big potato in the racing world. That all adds up to your being a prime suspect.'

I haven't been invited to sit in one of the buttoned-down leather couches. I haven't even been invited to sit.

'That doesn't mean I killed her. Your evidence is hardly what you people might call damning.'

'Circumstantial will do to start with. I won't ask where you were at the time of Miss Golightly's death. Going by your hands, I'd say you're not the kind of person to get them dirty torching a tenement. But that doesn't mean you wouldn't pay someone else to do it for you.'

He winces. There are a lot of ways of reacting when you're guilty, and wincing isn't one of them. 'Look, Mr – Black, I feel just as strongly about this – murder as you apparently do. Miss Golightly was a beautiful woman, in all senses of the word. And now that I know of her – passing – I will be paying for her funeral.' He considers me for a moment, but only for a moment. 'I would also like to retain your services in the matter, in the hope you might be able to discover the identity of the killer.'

'Why would you want to do that?'

'Because I didn't do it, and I would like to know who did.'

'Or you did do it, and in hiring me, hope to convince the world that you didn't.'

'Except that I'd say that the world's not all that interested. Oh, people will eventually discover she's dead. And because she used to be someone, there'll be the usual kerfuffle in the tabloid press. But our lovely libel laws will keep them away. And the police are very careful with people like me.'

He straightens the flapdoodles on the pockets of his expensive jacket. 'Do you want the job, or not?'

'I'm already doing the job. The question is do I want to take your money in order to do it.'

Cameron nods, but only slightly, like it's more of an effort than it's worth. 'Your principles are noteworthy, Mr Black, but princi*pal's* always more persuasive in these matters, I've found. Among the corrupt, money is a nice little short-cut to the finishing line. I'm in no way corrupt, but I suggest you're much more likely to solve a case when you possess the wherewithal to solve it.' He reaches into the breast pocket of his expensive jacket and withdraws a wad.

I grab the moolah and tuck it away. 'You've convinced me.'

'Very well. Someone's dudding me. Someone's fixing the races.'

I remember what Harry Hopman told me about corruption. 'Come on, pal, all races are fixed.'

Cameron makes the sort of gesture you can't buy in an opportunity shop. 'That's a hackneyed concept, if you don't mind my saying so. It may have been true once, but it's not so now. At least it wasn't until someone started it all up again a couple of years ago.'

'What do you mean — *it all*?'

'I mean, *changing the pattern* — altering the way races are run. Winners suddenly stopped being winners.'

'You mean the horses you were confident were going to win, stopped winning?'

He chucks me an aristocratic look, the kind that frowns on innuendos. 'There was nothing untoward in my knowledge. I'm an intelligent man. I simply apply that intelligence to racing.'

I move onto the next race on the card. 'Okay. Got any idea who's doing the fixing?'

'No idea. Only that once upon a time I could win.' He glances at me in the expensive gloom. 'But now I can't.'

I hunch the shoulders. 'All right, question one: how are races fixed?' I know the answer but I want it from the horse's mouth, or as near as I can get without being bitten.

'How long's a whip? For a start, there's dermorphin — otherwise known as frog juice, because somehow or other these scientific johnnies get the stuff out of frogs. Then there's etorphine — they call it elephant juice, or cobra venom ...' He makes a gesture. 'It's a long list, because there are many ways. For instance, there are the painkillers, like the opioid analgesic butorphanol. Am I going too fast for you?'

'Not as fast as some of those ponies must go.'

'That's just the doping. There are plenty of other ways. Standover riders threaten the jockeys. And some aren't above taking a bit on the side to lose. I believe the going rate at the moment is a hundred grand – depending on what's at stake. It buys a jockey a lot of diuretics.'

'Diuretics?'

Cameron nods. 'Passing water is a tried-and-true method for losing weight.'

I cut across him. 'Well, thanks for the ancient history, but you still haven't answered my question. How are they doing it now?'

He spreads his hands. 'That's just it. I don't know. You see, it varies. For instance, take that jockey –'

'Cyril Golightly?'

Cameron nods. 'He was a good little jockey. I'd tell him to win, and he'd win. Yet on the day of the accident, he simply – fell off his horse. We had to have the animal destroyed and, as I recall, the jockey wasn't worth much afterwards, either.' He considers me for a moment before continuing. 'Similar things have happened a few times since, but not on a regular basis, you understand. The people involved vary their – how would you put it – modus operandi.'

'So it's horses for courses?'

'If you want to put it that way, yes, it's horses for courses. All I know is that when I'm most certain of a winner something happens that makes the race turn out otherwise. I find it most – annoying. You see, Mr Black, while I don't need to win, I don't appreciate not doing so.'

I lean forward. I've got the money. All I got to do now is earn it. 'All right. Who would want to stop you winning?'

'I'd tell you if I knew, I really would.'

I nod. They like to see you nod. It makes them think there's an outside chance you believe what they're saying. 'Okay, I'll do it the hard way. Who stands to benefit if you go under? Or, another possibility: who hates you enough to want you to take a dive? And who knows, we might come up with a name that's comfortable in both camps.'

'Mr Black, again, if I knew that, I wouldn't be coming to you; I'd go straight to the police.'

'But you didn't come to me, remember? I came to you. How about telling me why someone might hate you enough and also how someone might benefit by your losing – and leave it to me to put a face on the figure.'

It's like greasing rust. However much you add to the bearings, the wheels still don't want to turn. But after a while the axle always gives up the unequal struggle and breaks.

'I really don't know.'

'Okay, last question: what gives with the track?'

'What track?'

'Your faux course, the racetrack as big as Randwick, your private peccadillo.'

He shakes his big shakeroo. 'Sorry, but that's out of bounds, to you and everyone else. I had to talk to that bloody newspaper about it because it was spotted on Google Earth, until I had it unspotted. But that's irrelevant to your inquiry. This is about the death of Angela Golightly and I'm buying your services to solve that particular matter. No-one visits my track, except by invitation, even if that someone happens to be helping me out of a —'

'Fix?'

Cameron shrugs. 'Your word, not mine, Mr Black.'

I stand and hold out my paw.

'More money? But I've already —'

It's not more money I want. 'I thought a handshake would be in order.'

People like Cameron don't like getting their mitts dirty, but after a while, in a bizarre hand-over gesture, he takes my right with his left, and produces the sort of shake a dead fish would be proud of.

The speakeasy looks like a bomb hit it. Tables are upended, there are broken bottles all over the joint and Hank the barman's wrestling with the nickelodeon, which is reclining on its side by the GENTS.

'Where's Cyril?'

Hank shrugs the straps of his pink singlet back on his waxed shoulders and straightens. 'With any luck, the bastard's has gone to the Devil and taken his stupid toy with him.'

I could ask what happened, or I could help Hank pick up his music box. I help with the music box. Hank's wearing Chanel Number 9 and a cross expression on his dial-up.

'Here's fifty, look after Cyril for a moment, there's a good lad.' A curl breaks free as he shakes his head. He tucks it back into place along with the others. 'Christ, Rainbow, you may as well have asked me to babysit a wild bull.'

A wild bull? Cyril?

Hank heads behind the bar where he finds a broom and starts in on a round of sweeping. 'That boyfriend of yours is severely manic depressive – and you left me holding the manic part. He had too much to drink and after that he wanted to bet on – well, anything, really. He wanted to bet on who'd walk through the door next, and when no-one would bet on that –'

'He just lost someone close to him.'

Hank exchanges the broom for a long-handled cleaning scoop. 'Rain, everyone loses someone close to them, but they don't go around creating mayhem over it.' He shoves bits of broken glass in a garbage bin and slams down the lid. 'You know what he did when no-one would take his bet? He called them a bunch of wankers. So Hair-Trigger Hoffman – who'd just walked through the door – started breaking bottles – which happened to include a 2005 Grange that was just there for show. Then Harry the Wolf upended a table. Crazy Jane got in on the act and that's when the cops showed up.'

I slip Hank a couple of the crisp green bills Cameron gave me, after which I palm him another couple. Grange doesn't come cheap, not to mention hurt feelings.

'On the bright side,' I say, 'it looks like all the baddies have gone home.'

Hank tucks the money into his jockstrap. 'Everyone except Cyril.'

I glance around. 'You mean he's still here?' I palm Hank another C-note. 'What happened?'

'The cops tasered him. He's in one of the cubicles.'

Sure enough, Hop-along's locked in a stall, still hugging his horse. I push his head into the bowl and press flush.

'Wake up, mate, we got work to do.'

At the serried-eyed time of eventide, Kings Cross is like a madman with the pills wearing off – quiet for the moment, but you know what's ahead so you get yourself elsewhere. Money or no money, Justin Cameron's still suspect number one.

'You used to ride for Cameron,' I say to Cyril. 'Therefore you'd know the location of his racecourse.'

Sometimes people are stupid and sometimes they just play stupid. 'What racecourse?'

I stay on track. '*Cameron's* racecourse. The private track where he trains his string of thoroughbreds. The track he had built along the exact same lines as Randwick.'

Cyril's collar is torn, what hair he's got left looks like the rats have been at it, and his toy horse looks like it's gone ten rounds with a crazed orangutan.

'She's gone.'

'I know she's gone.'

'It's all right for you.'

I drag Cyril to his feet and the rest of his collar comes off in my hands.

'Listen, you' – with difficulty I avoid the obvious epithet – 'it's not all right for me, got it? It's not all right for anyone except the bastard that killed her. It's –' I pause in the peroration. Cyril didn't do anything deliberate. 'Okay, it's not all right for you, either. But the difference between you and the rest of the world is that you get depressed while the rest of the world –'

But he's stopped listening, so I feed him something to start him again. 'Where's Cameron's track?'

He gives me one of his funny looks. It tells me that while he knows where Cameron's track is, he also knows something else.

Chapter 21

THE DARK HORSE

Annie's back at Central. Gertrude's all booted-up and Annie's leaning over the usual dirty figure huddled under the usual dirty blanket.

'Annie, any more unexplained corpses?'

She straightens. 'Nice to see you again, Rain.'

'Cyril, this is Annie, she helps people.' I note her practised eye take in the shambling wreck by my side. 'Annie, this is Cyril, he used to be a jockey but now he's a useless gambler.'

'Hi Cyril.' Annie nods briefly in Cyril's direction before turning back to me, her face soft in the moonlight. 'Yeah, there's been another since – since last time ...' She shakes her head. 'Same sort of thing – bruises, scratches, tiny burns, other marks not consistent with – you know. I told the police but they weren't all that interested.'

'Male?'

'Yep.'

'Where'd you find him?'

'Behind those cars there.'

I keep my voice casual. 'Blanket over the corpse?'

She shakes her head. 'Not even nearby.' She hugs herself. 'What do the marks mean?'

I glance at the cars Annie indicated – they're a thrown crow from the station entrance – then back at the slight figure before me. 'More than they should and less than I'd like them to. You been checking the pockets?' She shakes her head. 'Okay, if you get the chance, check 'em. Meanwhile, I got a few things on my plate right now. Maybe afterwards, I – you know, we ...'

She huddles herself. 'How's Immo doing?'

I met Annie a few years back while disarming an identity-stealing gang preying on the destitute. After that we hooked up now and again, and now and again she babysat Imogene while I was out on a case. These days she's a friend in need, always there when anyone needs her.

'She's – fine.' It'll be light in a couple of hours. After that it'll be too late to do what me and Cyril have got to do. 'You ever come across the Grundy organisation in your travels?'

Annie nods, briefly. 'They do good work. People have said …'

'What do you say?'

'They do good work. They stop people gambling.'

'Do you know the dame in charge, one Paris Witherspoon?'

Annie nods again. 'Yeah, she's beautiful.' Suspicion clouds her eyes. 'Why, have you met her?'

I shrug. 'I came across her in the line of business, and like you say –'

Annie frowns. 'Just make sure you just keep your line of business businesslike, Rain.'

As we head along the concourse towards platform 13, Cyril wavers between mournfulness and mourning. 'I'm sorry about the bar, but the bastards wouldn't bet with me. I told them they were being un-Australian but that just made things worse.'

'Where did you say this racetrack is?'

He tells me where the track is and I check arrivals and departures.

'We'll just make it.' I hustle him along. 'Mate, there are other things in life besides gambling, you know.'

The little man hobbling beside me shakes his head, and the bug-eyed horse he's carrying shakes its head along with him. 'Not for me there isn't. Not since the accident. And now my beloved's gone, my reason for living's gone with her. Gambling's my way of coping.'

I don't want to be a death-watch beetle. Mum took herself and my sister out via a fire-wheel when I was a kid, meaning I've had enough of suicide to last me a lifetime. Unlike Annie, I'm no babysitter.

'Cyril, forget gambling. And you're too long in the bo-diddly to be carting a cuddly toy everywhere, too.' The horse's head's just about off and half its tail's missing. 'You been putting so much work into hugging that thing, it's falling apart.'

But like the story Rube used to tell me about the wind trying to blow a joker's coat off, when I try to huff-and-puff these two apart, all that happens is that Cyril just hugs the mangy thing closer.

'Lord Haw-Haw's not an *it*, he's a *he*.' Cyril strokes its ears. 'Also, I've booked him in for a repair job. He'll be all right after that.'

I shrug. 'It's a pity they can't do the same thing with humans.'

Cyril puts up a last bit of a fight before we get on the train, like he's just remembered something, and the something he's just remembered isn't pleasant. But I push him into the carriage, climb in after him, and slam the door after us both.

'Look, I got better things to do with my time than to wet nurse a thumb-sucking gambler. But it just so happens I owe a favour to Angel, and it also happens that you're part of that favour.'

He tries to get up but I pull him down.

'Hey, you're hurting me!'

'So maybe you want to be hurt. In the meantime, you're going to show me this racetrack of Cameron's, and after that I'm going to take steps to cure you.'

'Cure me of what?'

'We'll start with the gambling.'

Even as I tell Cyril that, the shadows fall all around me. The shadow of my mother killing herself. The shadow of Imogene. The shadow of Angela. And the not-so-elusive shadow that appeared on the edge of my consciousness after I saw the first corpse, the one that was flitting around behind Annie, which was one of the reasons I had to get away from her, the shadow which might or might not have accompanied us onto the train.

'How do I know I can trust you?' he whines.

'Don't you realise you got no choice? Your legs are stuffed, you lost your wife and you're in debt, big time. I'm your dark horse, and for my money you got nothing left but to put your last dime on me.' I gesture out at platform 13. 'What I'm saying is you can find an ex gratia copy of *The Sydney Morning Horrible* and shamble off to the nearest piece of parkland and crawl under the newspaper and die in the next heavy frost – or by the same nefarious means that the others are dying from – or you can come with me.'

'I suppose I got no choice,' he says.

'You suppose right.'

A voice over the loudspeaker tells us our train is about to fart. Public transport's shelling out several million Pelaco collars teaching their employees how to speak.

Until then, our train is about to fart.

Chapter 22

SEE HOW THEY RUN

We get out. There's a lot of shadows. They might be people. Then again, they might be shadows.

'Are you sure you know what you're doing?'

I've got Cyril by the sleeve and he can keep up or he can fall by the wayside.

'You sound like you want certainties,' I tell him. 'When are you going to learn there are no certainties in this world, apart from death?'

We've been followed from the station, and it's not by a guard wanting to fine us for fare evasion.

'Can't you slow down a bit?'

I stop and ease my hold of his sleeve. He smells of unwashed toy, desperation and mothballs.

'Do we have to do this? It's just a racecourse.'

'Listen up and listen good, because this is the first and last time I'm going to say it.' I've never liked the smell of mothballs. 'I got problems of my own I should be attending to. But first I'm going to find out who killed Angel.'

Between Annie's corpses, Cyril's debts, a man called Cameron, and the death of Angela Golightly, I'm thinking there's got to be a link. Like Rube says, there's always a link.

Cyril clutches his horse and a last straw. 'But it's a lost cause. I've lost Angela and whatever you do can never bring her back. I'll just go on betting, I know I will.'

I take a deep breath. It's got the flavour of gumtrees and danger in it. 'We'll see about that, Cyril.'

Never Neverland isn't what I expected, but fairytales rarely are. At least the shadows have gone, and in their place is the following:

One racetrack, complete with barrier docks.

Four arc-lights.

A viewing platform.

A handful of horses, complete with jockeys.

And a familiar figure.

'So, all right, you've seen it,' Cyril says. 'Now can we go home?'

'What's eating you, Cyril? I know you must of rode trackwork here but that can't be enough to give you the heebies. Is it the memory of your fall?'

'What if we get caught?'

'Pal, you're already caught – in a web of your own making. And one of the objects of this exercise is to get you uncaught. So shut up and hang close and there's an outside chance you'll survive.'

As we draw nearer, I quarter the ponies lined up to race, as well as the person that looks familiar.

'Do you recognise the horses?'

'All of them.'

I hand Cyril a scratcher, as well as something to scratch on. 'So write them down – all of them.'

The breath of the night air is in my nostrils as I watch the beautiful creatures run, and I'm reminded yet again – if anyone ever needs reminding – of the sport's allure. The track bursts into a kaleidoscope of colour. The horses are coming into the first turn, tails streaming because the farmer's wife hasn't lopped them off yet, the jockeys crouched low over the withers as they settle into their stride, wearing all the colours of the rainbow, and then some.

On the second turn, number three begins his run, a fine, tall bay with a white slash marking his face, nostrils flaring in the moonlight, flanks quivering, neck muscles straining, a faint sheen of sweat glistening on his neck.

'Want a bet, Rainbow?'

I tell Cyril no and the horses finish, then immediately form up again, as a familiar, aristocratic voice wafts over the night air. 'That was very nice, boys and girls. Let's see if we can replicate it, shall we?'

I get a nudge from Cyril. 'I'm on three this time, all right? I know the horse. He's by far the best over this distance and Jerry's up. A tenner straight – okay?'

I don't bother replying. Number two's holding as they thunder past, muscles bunched, sinews glistening, all the jockeys out of the saddle, leaning up and forward like they're floating on air.

Just like Cyril said, number three makes a dash in the final straight, coming up on the outside like it owns the race, legs flailing like an out-of-control automaton.

But it's number one that ends up winning.

Chapter 23

DEALING WITH CYRIL

We've made our way back to the station and I've made up my mind about Justin Cameron. But first I got to deal with Cyril. I glance down as he clambers gratefully back on the train.

'You all right?'

'A bit depressed but other than that …'

I find us seats in another graffiti-covered carriage.

'You can't go through your life depressed.'

'Why not?'

'Because that's not much of a life, that's why not.'

The little man shrugs. 'I remembered, watching those nags, that I'll never ride again. It was never so clear to me as it was tonight. And that's why I gamble.'

'Correction – that's why you used to gamble. Because from now on, you're not going to gamble any more.'

'Why, what are you going to do?'

'It's not what I'm going to do. It's what someone else is going to do.'

'What?'

I'm standing on Rory's front porch. Cyril's dawdling by the front gate, hugging his horse and looking furtively up and down the street.

'I said I want you to cold turkey Cyril.'

Roarer frowns. 'What do you mean, *cold turkey Cyril*?'

Rory's a killer. That was before he found religion. Now he just asks questions.

'Just like I say. People take drugs, you cold turkey them. Stop them taking drugs and they cease to feel the need. The same with drink. Well, Cyril here's a gambler. I need you to keep him off gambling until he loses the urge. I'm offering you a chance to win some of those Heavenly

Credits of yours. I can also pay you real money.' I hand him a sheaf of Cameron's dough-re-you.

'Jesus, Rain.'

'Exactly. Tell Cyril he'll have to go to church if he doesn't stop gambling. Tell him you'll break his arm if he even considers a flutter. Tell him you'll kill him if he rings up a betting parlour.'

'But I don't kill any more.'

'Yeah, but Cyril doesn't know that.'

Cyril comes up behind me, looking like the wreck of the Hesperus. The bits of bush hanging off him don't do anything to soften the image. 'What doesn't Cyril know?'

'That I'm leaving you here with my mate Rory.'

Cyril sizes up the killer. 'What if I don't want to be left here with your mate Rory?'

'You haven't got a say in the matter. You're staying, and that's final.'

'But I want to get Lord Haw-Haw – fixed.'

'So get him fixed.'

'I've got to take him to the shop.'

'So take him to the shop.'

Cyril glances at Rory. 'But will he let me?'

'Of course he'll let you.' I glance at Rory. 'You okay with that, Roarer?'

'Am I okay with what?'

I stay patient. 'Will you take Cyril here to the shop where he can leave his toy horse for fixing while you're keeping him in a gambling-free environment?'

Rory raises his eyes to heaven. 'Why don't you look after him?'

'Because I'm busy.'

'So why doesn't someone else – Hey, what about that bunch that fixes gamblers? Mrs Grinder's, or whatever they are. I saw her on telly. She's –'

'It's Grundy's.'

'Yeah, them.'

I check out Cyril. He's talking to his horse. I come back to Roarer. 'Let's just say they're a last resort.'

I hand Roarer another hundred to help him to be the second-last resort.

'Hello?' Soft modulated tones, the sort you'd like to take to bed with you, full of the promises of Heaven. 'Is that you, Mr Brown?'

I don't hang up and throw away the phone. I'm Mr Brown, or Red or Yellow or Green — any colour the voice wants me to be. 'Why, who's that?'

But I know who it is. It's Cleopatra, Diana the Huntress, Elle Macpherson and Venus de Milo all rolled up into one, the answer to every man's dreams. I just want to hear her say it, with that deep-throated chuckle, the sort that —

'Why, it's Paris, of course — Paris Witherspoon.' Two beats. 'Known to all the world as Mrs Grundy.'

I try to keep my response as cool as an undertaker's storage box. 'What can I do for you?'

The answer's melodious. 'Oh, Mr Brown, as the late US president John F. Kennedy once said: *It's not what your country can do for you, it's what you can do for your country.*'

'Meaning?'

'Meaning I've got some good news for you. Could we meet somewhere?'

We can meet any place, but in the end we settle for the Mystic's, the one overlooking the Harbour.

The longer I live in this burg, the more I realise it's not all it seems. There's a chasm between the soft dreams it promises and the hard reality it ends up palming you. It's like everyone wants Sydney to be nice, and goes into denial when it's not. Headless bodies and bodyless heads. A nice little calling card that turns out to be a .45 slug in the back. People leaving buildings via the forty-fourth-storey window. Houses going up in smoke. Politicians on billionaires' row. More corpses on the mean streets with unexplained and inexplicable marks on them, which the cops do nothing about. And I'm still being followed.

Chapter 24

THE LATEST FROM PARIS

Say *Sydney* fast enough and it comes out *Sinny*. Say *Mystic* fast enough and it seems like it's *misty*, and that the clientele are here for the good of their health. I know better, but Mrs Grundy doesn't. Which is why I find her sitting under a sign saying 'Teahouse of the August Moon' surrounded by signs astrological, imagining she's where she belongs, which is probably somewhere between the Botanical Gardens and Noddy Land.

'Why, Mr Brown!'

Well, I know why, only I don't tell her that. Tell her that and she'll depart from my life forever, clutching her modesty in both beautiful hands, and screaming electric blue manslaughter.

'Sowaddayawan?' He's big and he's missing most of the digits on his paws, which is how I recognise him, despite the daisy light penguin suit – the hands, and the gap-toothed leer. Man Mountain is on parole between murders. I tell him I'll have a chai.

'Chai what?'

It could be the beginning of a riddle, only I'm not playing. 'I've just changed my mind, I'll have a bottle of water with the top on.'

The dame smiles her sweet smile. 'And for me a cup of chamomile tea, thank you.'

After writing down his life's history in longhand, the criminal leaves and the dame smiles her non-face-cracking smile. 'So how is it that you know the waiter?'

I don't have to disillusion her straight away. 'We met, socially.' All right, so the segue into another subject is clumsy. 'What's your organisation do again?'

The soft light forms an aura around her head.

'As I told you, Mr Brown, we cure gamblers. Horseracing gamblers mostly, because right now horseracing seems to have become even less predictable than usual, thereby creating a more than usual number of – victims.'

'Big organisation, is it?'

The coif stays in place as she nods. So does the nice expression. 'There are twenty-one of us in Mrs Grundy's, all women. Women who need help, in one way or another, but who also find affirmation in helping others.'

'And who pays for all this — affirmation?'

Mrs Grundy spreads her beautiful hands. 'As I've also already told you, people are very kind. Wealthy relatives pay us to look after their loved ones. As well, we receive generous donations.' She shoots a glance around the room. 'Oh, isn't this just the loveliest place?'

'It's a place.'

'The Harbour looks beautiful.'

'It's a harbour.' I do the pause. 'You had some news.'

Looking at her is like looking at the sun without wearing shades. She's wearing a white, floppy, tight-around-the-neck number that gives the merest hint at what lies beneath. Beautiful hair tortured into a bun atop an expressionless but beautiful face. Slim neck, long as a swan's. Eyes that —

'Here's yer order then.' The thug takes his thumb out of the chamomile, dumps it on the tableau along with the Evian, and shuffles off to do harm to others.

When the dame leans forward, the piecrust edge of the table presses into her shapeless clothes, and makes a shape out of them. I look away.

'I do have some good news, Mr Brown. Excellent news, in fact.' She sips her chamomile, and the shape in the shapeless clothes on the other side of the piecrust table makes itself comfortable, while the tea makes her lips so shiny the reflection brings tears to my eyes.

I chuck her a napkin. 'The mouth.'

'What about the mouth?'

'You might wipe it for me.'

Paris Witherspoon wipes it for me, and I can hear the rasp of the cloth while she does the wiping. 'Is that better?'

I ignore the question. 'You had some news.'

'Oh, yes.' She sits back, which makes matters better, but it also makes them much worse. 'And the news is that I've been to see your Salina.'

Sweet Jesus. 'And?'

'And I believe I've fixed the little problem regarding your daughter.'

'That's' — I envisage the scene, then I don't envisage the scene — 'Yeah, well, thanks for that.' It was a long shot, borne of desperation, the way most long shots are. And like most long shots, the chances always were that I was on a loser to nothing in the shooting of it.

'Don't thank me,' she says. 'Just thank your lucky stars that Salina was amenable.'

'Are you sure it was Salina?'

Paris Witherspoon nods brightly over her chamomile. 'A fine, upstanding lady with a decided manner and direct gaze?' That's one way of describing my ex. 'Yes? Well, after I explained matters to her, she said she believed that Miss Riesling and I had done the right thing in returning the child. She added that she thought that you were at best well-meaning, which is wonderful, isn't it?'

What was the name of the kid that always looked on the bright side? Pollyanna? Yeah, well, this dame makes Pollyanna look like a pessimist.

'And what did she say I was at worst?'

'Oh, we needn't go into that. What matters is she said that what was a potential disaster had turned out all right in the end.'

'She called it that?'

Pollyanna nods. 'Or words to that effect. Anyway, I just wanted to say that everything's fine on the ex-wife front.'

I hunt for an alternative subject and the words are out before I can stop them. 'You might be able to help me on another front.'

Chapter 25

AT THE GATES OF HELL

When I've finished telling Paris no more than she needs to know, she leans back on a cushion that's awash with astrology signs, her face as readable as a Patrick White novel. 'And what precisely do you want from me, Mr Brown?'

'Just a name. You look after punters, bettors who have lost and lost again because someone keeps dudding them. Well, one or more of your dud punters must have dropped a clue as to the identity of the person or persons who dudded them. Most of your clientele are horse gamblers. So who's putting the fix into the ponies, who's screwing the races? All I need is a name.'

Paris Witherspoon looks at her watch – a big dangly thing on her firm wrist – and straight after that she gets up from her cushion. A hard wind has been waiting for just this moment and her shapeless clothes cease to be shapeless. 'I'm sorry, Mr Brown, but I – have an appointment.'

I get to my feet, too. It brings us too close for comfort, but I'm not here for comfort. 'Just a name. Look, no-one's going to get hurt – at least no-one that shouldn't.'

She takes a breath so deep she could do a five-minute dive with it. 'I'm afraid the only name that comes to mind on the spur of the moment ... Do you know, Mr Brown, I've never really known what that expression means? Is it something that jockeys do, in order to make their mounts go faster?'

'You're thinking of whips, not spurs.'

'So why don't they call it the *whip* of the moment?'

'I guess that spur in this context means cusp, from the Latin *cuspis*, meaning point. But that's beside the *cuspis*; you were about to give me a name.'

Pollyanna frowns. She still looks beautiful. 'One name does keep coming up during the treatment of our clientele – you know, they keep mentioning it – but I can never make head nor tail of it.'

434

The huge waiter sidles up beside us. Pollyanna doesn't let it stop her talking.

'It – it sounds more like a geometrical shape than the name of a human being.' She pauses, then comes out with it. 'The name is – Pentagon.' She reaches out and her hand's got the same feel to it as the name. 'But, please, you must promise me, Mr Brown, no hurt must come to this – Pentagon person.'

'Only if he tries to hurt me.'

After I leave the caff, I check out the Harbour. Politicians want to stick a heliport in the middle of it. That's all right for politicians. They don't live in the real world. But neither, it seems, does Mrs Grundy.

I ring Imogene on dead-man's mobile No. 3. It's almost out of credit. So am I.

'That you, sweetheart?'

'No, it's me, Salina, and I thought I told you to stop ringing.'

'Come on, Sal, she's my daughter.'

'That's why I want you to stop ringing her.'

'Didn't the dame – Mrs Grundy – explain things to you?'

'Your girlfriend, you mean? That oh-so-sweet-and-innocent beauty with the over-large mammaries and the cornflower-blue eyes? The one that's supposed to run some do-gooder organisation or other to help problem gamblers? Give me a break, Rainbow.'

Salina does the Salina pause.

'In fact, don't give me anything, because I'm no longer a willing recipient. Yes, sure, the dame, as you call her, fed me some preposterous story about your inadvertently leaving Imogene on the steps of a casino while you tried to save someone from a lifetime of depredation. But do you know something? I think she actually wanted me to disbelieve her.'

'What the hell would she want to do that for?' I ask.

'Why don't you tell me? After all, you're the one with the answers. Meanwhile, and I'm telling you this for the last time – Stop. Calling. Imogene. Otherwise the consequences, at least as far as you're concerned, will be dire.'

I detect a new note of confidence in Salina's voice, the kind of confidence a gambler gets when he finds no-one's fixing the races any more, or that your ex-wife acquires after she finds herself a new boyfriend.

'Yeah, but ...'

The phone dies a sudden death. I chuck it in the Harbour, the one with all the little white triangles in it.

Work, Rube told me. *When such moments as these slam you in the face, lose yourself in work. There's always something to do, so get on and do it.*

The advice is like a spar floating on the surface of the sea after your boat's sunk, but I got no choice, so I grab it.

A look of relief lights Rory's dial-up when he opens his front door in response to my rat-a-tat-tat on the portcullis.

'I take it you've come to pick up Creepy Man. The missus was just saying –'

'You take it wrong, Roarer, because I haven't come to pick up anything – other than a new dead-man's mobile phone and some information.'

The downcast look on Roarer's face would look good on a whipped dog. 'It's just that the missus was saying –'

'Well, she was saying wrong. What do you know about a joker called Pentagon?' Rory goes to close the door but I get there first and jam my foot in it. 'Look, I'll handle Cyril, Roarer. Just give me the requisite information.'

So Roarer gives me the requisite information, looking to right and left and above and behind him as he does so. They call him Pentagon, he tells me, because that's the act he's best known for – pent-*agonising* people. It's the shape that's left over after he lops off his victims' head, arms and legs and chucks what's left into the sea.

'But why does he do it?'

'Because he's not a nice person.'

'Come on, Roarer.'

'No, you come on, Rainbow. You can't mix it with people like Pentagon. He's big-scale drugs, and he protects his empire like Sir Boris at the Gates of Hell.'

'Cerberus.'

'Whatever.'

'I'm told he's also into gambling.'

Roarer frowns. 'In that case, I been out of the game too long. Because as long as I been killing, Pentagon's been drugs.' He adds a codicil. 'Meanwhile, the missus told me to tell you that we've had this Cyril of yours too long. We left his horse thing to get fixed, and now he's whining about missing it. If you don't collect him soon, she's going to chuck him onto the street.'

'Tell her patience is the key to Heaven. Meanwhile, where do I find this Pentagon?'

'On his boat.'

Chapter 26

THE BELLY OF THE BEAST

The boats are the size of tankers. They're moored where tankers are usually moored – in a bay called La Perouse just around the corner from Port Botany. La Perouse was named after the French navigator that landed on a pristine beach way back in 1788. These days it's where people park their containers and all the other corruption that attends the smuggling game, until they come up with something more permanent.

I'm dressed for the occasion: T-shirt, sneakers and jeans, with a knife in a shin-scabbard under the jeans. I exit the cab and make my way to the wharf.

'Well, if it ain't Mister Rainbow.'

He hasn't got a cup of chamomile tea in one de-fingered paw and a bottle of Evian in the other, but he's still big and he's still got trouble expressing himself, and he's still Man Mountain.

'You sure get around, Mount.'

He shrugs his mountainous shoulders. 'A little bird warned me you might be coming after a pal of mine.'

Ballet is like riding a bike, you never forget the basic pas de deux. So I do the half-step to the right – watching the man mountain shiver along its fault lines – after which I bend to the left, following up with the goose-step from Bach's *Jeun Homme et La Mort*, with me in the part of La Mort. Man Mountain loses his equilibrium so I find it for him, pointing him at the ground as he goes past, after which I back-end him into a stanchion. He staggers to his feet.

'No-one mucks with Mountain!'

But he's had one too many dim sims, too many potatoes, and too much KFC. He's a walking memorial to the fast food industry, a joker that's always said *Yes* to the eternal question: *Would you like fries with that?* He comes at me like an Intercity Express, and when I do the pas seul he ends up a train wreck, a mass of blue-singleted flesh among all the McDonald's wrappers that have preceded him. I drag his head up by the leash.

'Which boat belongs to Pentagon?'

'Go to –'

I thump him in the region of his last meal. 'Which boat?'

'That one.'

The tub could double as the *Queen Mary*. It's a four-decker carrying more funnels than an extended family of arachnids – white superstructure, mauve and black hull, sturdy scrabble-ladders. I leave Mountain trying to work out the meaning of life, find myself a rowboat that no-one's using, and start rowing.

It takes ten minutes getting through the filthy water and I'm still no closer to the *Queen Mary*'s hull. A jumbo from nearby Kingsford-Smith airport chops the sea into sandpaper as it lumbers skyward, while the joker in the singlet back on the wharf has woken up and is waving his arms about like a windmill. The thing about rowing backwards is you can't see what you're aimed at, only what's behind. And what's behind the joker semaphoring is …

Pandora's so much with me that she's become almost a companion animal, a slinking black panther rarely more than a death breath away. But the figure behind the pile of ropes behind the joker waving isn't Pandora. The figure detaches itself and slips behind a stanchion. When you expect to see something, you see what you expect to see. I expected to see Pandora, the dame in black that has pursued me ever since my mother died, so that's what I see as I plough my way away from the jetty. Only it's not black, it's blue, and it's not Pandora, it's someone else. Mountain's still waving but now he's got his mobile phone out. My sightline's momentarily obscured by a hawser attached to a buoy, and when I can see anything again, the figure's gone.

I quarter the wharf.

Nothing.

Containers, cars, tanks, cranes, ropes, but otherwise nothing. Nothing, at least, that I can put my finger on.

So I keep rowing, because there's nothing else to keep.

The boat's like the Great Wall of China, a giant, rearing behemoth of a thing rising sheer from the surface of the water, formidable above, rippling black below, with grapple ropes hanging from it. I grab one and start grappling.

If Cyril was around he'd place bets on a certainty – odds-on for Rainbow to get caught. The sisal's as thick as Roarer, two hand-grips' diameter, the thickness of Mountain's forearm. I straddle and haul, straddle and haul, straddle and – I'm halfway up when Mountain takes a pot-shot at me from the wharf. The bullet sings like Joan Sutherland off the hull by my head. It's only a .22, but even a pinprick can kill if it's going fast enough. I kick away hard, but not hard enough, and after I let go the ladder I crack my head against the *Queen Mary*'s hull.

Then I go down.

A good part of my time with Aunt Rube was spent doing swimming lessons, day after day at the Boy Charlton pool, followed by deep-sea diving off the Heads. *What about sharks!* I'd ask through teeth chattering like a machine-gun. *Deal with it,* Rube would say, and push me off the cliff. Since then, I've kept up the long Bondi swims, and as a result, I know my way around water. It doesn't make drowning any easier.

The rescue launch has got two outboards, and the guy at the tiller's got a sense of humour. He's also got a gun. 'Nice day for a dip.' The tiller-man waves his gat as another thug drags me aboard. 'What were you doing down there – solo synchronised swimming?'

He's more intent on his humour than on an exchange of worthwhile information, but after a while he settles down, and after a while longer a maintenance board's lowered and I'm hauled up onto the ship's deck. There I find a welcoming party about as welcoming as the Great Plague of London.

'So what's your story?' He's a thug and he's accompanied by other thugs.

'I fell in.'

'Yeah, and I'm the Shah of Persia. We got someone here wants to meet you.'

Chapter 27

THE SPECIALIST

The hands are a long way from gentle and the deck's the size of a Boeing runway.

'Who's the someone?'

'That's for us to know and you to be amazed at. So shut up.'

So I shut up. After being dragged along a kilometre or so of deck, I find myself on the floor of a stateroom that could double as the Banquet Hall in Versailles. It contains a table, a chair, and a big, fat bastard with a tablecloth around his neck enjoying a banquet.

He wipes a set of lips that could double as sausages. 'Who's this?'

'We fished him out of the bay, boss. Mountain told us to expect him. He said −'

'I don't care what Mountain said.' The big bloke's got a chicken leg in his greasy paw and hasn't taken his eyes off me since I was dragged in. 'You from the tax office?'

I tell him no, but the information doesn't compute.

'Mountain said he −'

'I thought I told you to shut up.' He still doesn't take his fish eyes off me. 'Don't you people ever give up?' He waves an arm at his surroundings. 'So I got some, so I'm lucky. Why should honest citizens have to pay tax on lucky?'

I try to get to my feet but I'm palmed back off them by the thugs. 'Because you're not honest and I'm not from the tax office.'

'You all say that. You expect us to tell the truth, but you lie like crazy. I've had a gutful of your single standards.'

I make the necessary correction. 'It's double standards. The tax office has *double* standards.'

The smart's wasted on my host. 'Whatever. Anything to declare, tax man, before my boys chuck you back in the drink?'

We could talk about global warming or the state of the economy, but something tells me Pentagon's not all that interested in social philosophy, so I come straight to the point. 'I'm not tax and I've got standards and they're not double. I'm a detective and I'm looking for a killer.'

Pentagon laughs so hard he breaks wind. 'You come to the right place then.'

I persevere. 'Not just any killer – someone that's in the habit of fixing races, who also torched a terrace in Camperdown, and took out a friend of mine in the process.'

'And you think it was me?'

'If your name's Pentagon, you're in the ballpark.'

He stops laughing. 'This friend of yours that ended up dead. Did he by any chance end up minus his legs, his arms and his head?'

'It wasn't a him it was a her. And no, she just ended up incinerated.'

'I don't do incinerations. Come to think of it, I don't do inquisitions, either. Which means you just ran out of time.' He nods to his goons. 'Feed him to the sharks.'

'Just one last question.'

'If it doesn't have to do with the menu – mine or the sharks' – I don't want to hear it.'

'You'll want to hear this one.'

'Okay, try me.'

'Why bother fixing races?' I nod at the stateroom around me. 'It looks like you already got enough. Why branch out into gambling?'

'Sounds like two questions to me, when you promised me just one. Which proves what I said about your standards, Mr Tax Man. But the answer to both is, yeah, sure, I enjoy a flutter – but only for my laundry. You know what that is, don't you?' He wipes his face and grins a sickly grin. 'I reckon even a moron like you can see I don't need to fix races for that.' He waves his fist. 'Take him away.'

'You're saying you gamble, and yet you don't fix races?'

'Mate, where did you come from – outer space? I don't have to bother myself with any of that.'

'So what do you bother yourself with?'

He contemplates me over a forkful of fish eggs. 'I'm a businessman in import/export – and laundry.' He smirks at his goons. 'Which means I can put dirty money on as many horses as I want in the same race, or buy up half the tickets in the two-dollar lottery, or just send my associates out to buy up every Scratchie in the newsagent's.' He lifts his mammoth shoulders and then sets them down again. 'I put in a million, and take a quarter of a million out. You might call it bad accounting. I call it natural shrinkage.'

He chucks me a glare. 'Meanwhile, you've just taken away my appetite by reminding me of the injustice of man to man.' He waves to his goons. 'Chuck the bastard overboard. Now.' He rips the napkin away from his neck, shoves his fists on the table, and heaves himself upright. 'And I'm coming out on deck to make sure you do it right.'

Chapter 28

SWIMMING WITH CONCRETE

Three of Pentagon's thugs hold me in the ankles-wrists-neck position while another one chains a lump of concrete in the shape of a cross to my leg.

'I'm religious, see?' Pentagon's standing over me. 'Besides which, a cross is the best shape, design-wise. It gives you something to tie the chain around. Plus the ends of the cross act like the flukes of an anchor – they dig themselves into the seabed, along with anything that happens to be attached.'

I estimate the sinker weighs in the vicinity of 50 kilos, just under a hundredweight in the old money, about the same as my Aunt Rube. As much as I like Rube, I don't fancy my chances at the bottom of the ocean with her strapped to my ankle.

'They'll know it was you, Pentagon.' Even from where I'm lying, held with my mug to the deck by the thugs, I can see that he's not too worried about the possibility.

'No-one of any consequence saw you arrive and no-one's going to see you go. And we're leaving, so when they discover what's left of you, we'll no longer be here. Apart from which, this isn't my style. If the sharks leave anything after they've finished with you, it'll be no more than a skeleton chained to a cross.' He places an iron-toed boot against my groin. 'You can keep all that in mind while you're busy drowning, Mr Tax Man.'

They haven't bothered pulling up the legs of my jeans and the knot they're employing is chain-over-chain. I tense the gastrocs. Pentagon's boot presses harder against my groin like I was hoping it would, making it look natural when I bring up the leg they're working on.

'Hey, boss, every time you do that, the bastard moves. It makes it hard to tie the chain.'

'So hold him tighter.'

'We are holding him tighter.'

By the time they've finished, I'm not going anywhere but over the side.

Perhaps I am a postman.
No, I think I am a tram.
I'm feeling rather funny and I don't know what I am
But round about
And round about
And round about I go …

This is what goes through your mind while a dead weight drags you too many fathoms into the wilderness, the poem that Aunt Rube used to murmur as she lowered me into the sea to practise escapology a la Erich Weiss – aka escapologist Harry Houdini – causing me to wonder funny things as I go down, like if Rube has ever been in love, and if so, when, with whom or what, and how.

I must ask her some time, after I get out of this.

If I get out of this.

Houdini specialised in chains. He knew how an escape artist could benefit by struggling while the tethers were being affixed, knew how to –

But round about and round about …

I've trained myself to go at least three minutes underwater, and I got maybe two and half left, as well as slightly more buoyancy than the concrete weight, which is why the weight goes first and I come afterwards, down to the depths of the bay as I struggle to pull my trouser leg up out of the tangle of chain.

I think I am a Traveller escaping from a Bear …

The trouser leg's tangled in the links and it's taking both my hands and all my concentration to get it free, working on touch alone, because the darkness of the ocean coupled with the speed of my descent makes seeing what I'm doing next to impossible.

No thumb on left hand – the handless hood saw to that – leaving me only four digits on that mitt, and two minutes and fifteen seconds on the chronometer accompanying it, to untangle the knot that was put together by a thug distracted by my attempts to deflect the iron-toed boot of Pentagon.

The knot that's over the trouser leg.

Which in turn is over the knife in the scabbard strapped to my ankle.

Houdini on chains: A chain is only as secure as the precautions you took when the people chaining you were securing it. More from Houdini:

Mess up the links, and you got yourself an escape route.

Call it a chain reaction.

I got three things going for me.

One: getting Pentagon to put the boot in fouled up the chain, so that while it might have looked secure when they were done, it wasn't.

Two: the knife under the trouser leg bulked up the calf they tied it over.

And three: I want to survive.

I'm in the belly of the bay and I got less than two minutes. It's taken that long to work the leg of the jeans up. But the links are still cocked, because …

I can feel the problem now that I've dragged the trouser leg away.

The links have hooked themselves under the hilt of the knife.

Which means that what I planned to be my lifeline might turn out in the end to be my death line.

Through the waters I vaguely sense the throb of the ship's engines, but I got more important things to deal with than engines. Like holding my breath, and at the same time getting something under the chain links to lever them outwards.

The knife's out of the question.

The knife's stuck.

The knife's part of the problem.

I hit the seabed, taking my weight on my elbows. I'm at the bottom of Botany Bay with my options fast disappearing. I need to breathe. My hands are an all-but-dead man's, clawing into the sand, right one flailing, left one – the one minus a thumb – touching –

Sydney's seashore is a garbage tip, its continental shelf no more than a slippy-slide for detritus – plastic bottles, bags, tin cans, refrigerators, bits of cars, body parts …

Left fist closing over –

Sharks take off people's arms, legs and heads much like Pentagon does, afterwards ejecting various bits and pieces and leaving it to smaller fish to deal with the remains. The bone my hand closes over has been chewed clean. I identify it by touch as a rib, one of the lower five that isn't attached to the human sternum. Which means there's a point to it − if there's ever a point to unnecessary death.

Thirty seconds of life remaining.

I get the point of the rib under the chain link and lever with it, but my strength's ebbing. I'm using the knife hasp as a fulcrum under the bone, the point of which is under the chain, but it's − not − going − to − be − any − good ...

The rib slips, bites into my shin, and slips from my hand.

I scrabble for it in the mud, find it, jiggle it and get it under the twisted link again. This time I try to bring it up at more of an angle. Break a leg, they tell ballet dancers before a performance. It's meant to bring them luck.

It'd bring me luck.

It'd hurt a great deal, but it might bring me luck.

Chapter 29

DEATH ISN'T MEANT TO BE EASY

I've got no more than twenty seconds' worth of air left in my lungs. And that's pushing it.

Time to draw up my will. Make that will power. Time to draw up my will power. *Idiot! Think, concentrate, focus.* There's nothing to leave anyone anyway. Not even anything for Imogene. But she'll make her own way, when she's old enough.

Trouble is, she's not old enough yet, nowhere near, nowhere …

With one final effort, I give it everything I've got, and then some. I'm in the roly-poly position, head down, feet up, hand heaving.

I feel the rib bend.

Then it snaps.

What's left of the rib jags into my shin like a spear. At the same time, there's a loosening of the chain. There's still hope, however slender.

Now – if – only – I – can – free – the – scabbard …

If only I –

Stuff the absence of the thumb. I'm using it as an excuse. The buckle on the scabbard won't come undone. Water's hardened up the leather. So un-harden it, fool, make it work! The missing thumb doesn't make it easy, but someone once said that death wasn't meant to be easy. Use your fingers, get that greasy tip of leather back through the buckle. Don't try to ease it, no time. *Push, for God's sake, push!*

Ten seconds.

Harder!

Scabbard out.

Chain links suddenly loose.

But there's still no guarantee that I'm home free.

Five seconds.

I'm out of my concrete boot, but only if I can remove the shoe. I try to toe it away, get the wrong one off, but find the shoe I need to remove has water-glued itself to the sock.

With my last failing strength, I push harder.
Shoe –
Finally –
Off.

My sight clouds and it's not just because of the murkiness of the water.
A weight's been lifted, and as a result I feel light-headed. Therefore, it's
logical, isn't it, that I can stay down here buried in this cushiony-cushion
of the seabed, with nothing to worry about, and oblivion to comfort me.

But that's only what I think.

What I know – and know suddenly for a life-giving fact – is that my
head's suddenly out of the water and I'm taking in deep lungfuls of air, air
that says I'm not going to die after all, air that says that at long last I can
breathe again. Even if it's air filled with diesel fumes. I tread water with
my shoeless feet, taking in breath after breath of the stinking air while
trying to focus.

Pentagon's boat has got a whole lot smaller, heading for the horizon,
engines throbbing in syncopation with my head. My lungs are burning,
yet somehow still functioning. No limbs broken. Stinging sensation in the
left leg, due to the wound to the shin.

I got to get out of the water.

It's a long swim and a slow crawl down memory lane, every painful stroke
dragged out of somewhere I didn't know existed. Once I smack into a
slime-covered buoy, know it's a shark come to claim me, but keep on
swimming anyway.

A boat rows over the top of me, like I'm nothing more than a rotten
plank or floating plankton. I keep swimming right through that, too.

Half an hour, an hour, who knows? All I know is that in the time
it takes for the behemoth boat to become a smoking black funnel on the
horizon, I finally drag myself onto the shore.

'Jesus! What happened?'

It's the middle of the night and I'm on my knees and Roarer's standing on his doorstep. I know it's Roarer because I can only see the one leg. I also know it's him because I can hear his missus, Janet.

'Be careful, Rory! It might be someone out of your past come to get you!'

'It's all right, sweetpea.'

'What do you mean it's all right, honeybunch?'

'I'm okay, sweetness. It's only Rainbow.'

Pause. Then, 'He can't stay, do you hear me? That man can't possibly _'

Roarer's shrug is the shrug of a man who's lost everything he ever had, when he never had all that much in the first place, and when he talks, it's in a whisper. 'Best we go into the kitchen, mate.' His look takes in the mud and the blood as he helps me to my shoeless feet. 'It's got a washable floor.'

Chapter 30

OBJAY DART

I roll up my trouser leg and take off the shin-scabbard while Roarer fetches a bowl of lukewarm water and a few rags from the sink. After that he parks himself on a stool and keeps watch on the doorway, like he's afraid the Virgin Mary might turn up.

'So how's Cyril?' I ask by way of conversation. 'Giving you much trouble?'

Roarer glances at the doorway again. 'Doesn't give me anything else. He keeps saying I can trust him, and then he tries to escape. He says the last thing on his mind is going back to gambling, all he wants is his freedom.'

I mop at the wound. 'Do you believe him, about the gambling?'

'He offered me an even-money bet that he had it beat.'

'What else?'

Roarer shrugs. 'He drinks a lot and gets depressed even more.'

Me and Roarer have always been good at silence. Sometimes it's because we're on a job and we got to be silent, or be dead. Other times –

'Ever think something's missing, Rain?' Roarer shakes his head. 'I thought God and marriage would do it, only it hasn't worked out that way. I miss the old life. In fact –'

'Rory, is that man still there?' comes Janet's voice from the other room.

Roarer tries a grin only it doesn't work out that way, either, and when he raises his voice to reply to his hugs and kisses, he doesn't even sound like the old Roarer. 'Won't be long, dear.'

He lowers his voice to conspiracy level. 'In fact, if I was a betting man, I'd say I was on a loser to nothing. Most of me pension goes to the Church of the Latter Day Gooseberries, and the missus takes everything else. I think I'd feel guilty going back to my chosen profession.' He shakes his head. 'Mate, what am I going to do?'

'I dunno. Meanwhile, getting back to Cyril ...'

Roarer scratches his cheek, the one with the scar on it. He looks uncomfortable. 'Yeah, well, Cyril was pining for his toy horse, only the jokers that he took it to say the work's going to take longer than expected.' Scratching his face seems to have reminded him of something. 'Don't know if you noticed, but Cyril kept scratching himself. Well, it got so bad, I took him to a doctor. I thought it might be saddle sores.'

'What did the doctor do?'

'He got Cyril to pull down his strides and after that he made him lie face down on one of those bed things doctors have got. Then he put some stuff on where Cyril's been scratching and gouged around for a bit with a shiff. Finally, he said *Ah!* like he'd discovered the meaning of life, and tweezered something out of Cyril's left cheek.'

'You stayed there watching while all this was going on?'

'You told me to keep an eye on him.'

I think about that, then immediately stop. 'What was the something the doctor dug out?'

'It looked like some kind of needle.'

'A needle?'

'The doc said it might be a dart and got all serious on me. Wanted to know where it came from, see? He said he was going to the police over it.' Roarer notices the glance. 'It's all right, Rain, I told him I'd kill him if he did.'

'You what!'

'I got him out of the Yellow Pages, the advertisement said client confidentiality was assured.' I'm still staring at him. 'Look, it's okay, I didn't kill him. But he got the message. He's not going to nobody over nothing. Also I made him hand over the dart.'

'So where is it?'

Roarer climbs onto his foot and hops across the linoleum to the nicely-painted kitchen cupboards where he pulls open a drawer. After he's scratched around for a bit, he comes up with something that looks like no dart I ever seen before — a shiny, tubular projectile measuring about half an inch long, with tiny built-in fins of the same material on the tail, inverted.

'Where the hell did this come from?'

'I told you — out of Cyril's bum.'

'I mean before that.'

Roarer shrugs again. 'The doc didn't go into details, Cyril was moaning and I just wanted to get the hell out of there. So we got the hell out of there.'

'Where is he now?'
'Who, the doc?'
'No, Cyril.'
'Roar-eee?'
'He's asleep behind locked doors and I ain't going to wake him for no-one.'

Roarer's lying. I know that because whenever he lies, he scratches the leg that isn't there and all he ends up with is splinters. My bet is he's dumped Cyril on the Grundy dame.

Chapter 31

DEATH DOESN'T TAKE A HOLIDAY

It's morning, which means there's another unexplained corpse littering life's canvas in the inner city, and Little Orphan Annie's busy cleaning the brushes.

'How's it going, Annie?'

She looks up from a pile of blankets. 'These poor people …'

Annie feels things too much. She's thirty-something but looks fifty – trackie pants smeared with gunk, hair all over the joint, and her eyes tell me that she's been crying.

'Another one same as the others. With those same marks.'

'Did you check their pockets?'

She nods and produces a few crumpled scraps of paper.

'Betting receipts?'

She nods again.

'Anything else?'

The nod changes to a shake. 'It was as though the bodies had been wiped clean. I only found those' – she indicates the crumpled papers in my hand – 'because you told me to look. They were scrunched up in their pockets. They what you were expecting?'

'Only in retrospect.' I pocket the betting slips. 'Annie, you done good. You also need a holiday.'

She shakes her head and looks around at her bleak surroundings. 'Death doesn't take a holiday, Rain, so how can I?'

The dame's got red hair and a fake smile. I can handle the hair. It doesn't mean I got to like the smile.

'You're new here, aren't you?'

She touches the coif. 'I've been on other duties. So, yes, this is my first day in the office. I haven't even blogged on yet. But before I do that,

454

perhaps you could tell me how I can help you?'

'Where's Prudence Shoehorn?'

'Do you mean Phoebe Riesling?'

'Yeah, that's the one.'

'She left.'

'I'm her cousin and was going to surprise her on her birthday.'

'Oh, I see. Well,' she whispers, 'Phoebe got – retrenched. For being a little too – over-enthusiastic.'

'How could that be a problem?' The posters in the office are still in place, and so is the lack of ambience. 'Or maybe my question should be: how can someone get over-enthusiastic in this business?'

'There's business and there's business.' The redhead narrows her ee-whys, like she's suddenly smells a rat. 'But you haven't told me why you're really here.'

'Do you happen to know why your Mrs Grundy sent me on a wild gooseberry chase, and nearly ended up getting me killed?'

'On a who? Nearly ended up getting what?'

'A joker called Pentagon, a joker I find has got nothing to do with anything I'm interested in right now, apart from his own nefarious trade, nearly pentagoned me. Do you know why?'

'No, I don't. Now I'm really sorry, Mr-whoever-you-are, but I must blog on.'

'It's log in, lady. And don't let me stop you doing what you got to do. But while you're doing it, you might try multi-tasking and tell me where I can find your boss.'

'She's working out.'

That would explain all the curves. 'Could you tell me where your Mrs Grundy's doing this working out?'

She shakes her head. 'I'm sorry but that comes under the heading of client confidentiality.'

'But she's not a client.'

'No, but you might turn out to be.' She turns back to her computer. 'Meanwhile, I have to – sorry, what was it? – bog in.'

I position myself. 'While you're doing that, maybe you could give me an answer to another question.'

The dame doesn't look up, because she's busy reading from a sheet of paper on the tableau beside her. 'That depends on the question.'

'Where can I find Cyril Golightly?'

I can see her lips moving as she works the keys. She keeps reading, nice and slow. And also she keeps typing, nice and slow. 'Real name?'

'That is his real name.'

It's like the guy at the internet bofferteria already knows that everyone's a fraud, so he's not going to waste anyone's time putting too much effort into his questions. 'Wadayawan?'

'You happen to have a spare ordinateur?'

He doesn't look up. 'Yeah.'

'Mind telling me which one?'

'Numero nineteen, smartarse.'

I type *mrsgrundy@etcetera* followed by the password I found out by the twenty-first century equivalent of holding an inverted tumbler against a hotel room wall while simultaneously peering through a keyhole. And after I key in *Golightly, Cyril*, there's the information that Mrs Grundy's minion was trying to protect me from.

You could call it client confidentiality.

Or you could call it enlightening.

Chapter 32

YOU DON'T SMILE FOR PASSPORTS

Subject Cyril Golightly arrived in the care of a male, aged approximately 35 years, with one leg, who gave his name as Smith. It was noted in passing that 'Smith' suffers a number of what appear to be serious pathological problems that could manifest in ultimate harm to others, at the same time as he professed a strong belief in a Higher Being. NB re 'Smith': future client?

Assessment of Subject Golightly: Male, aged 37, slight physical build, a situation worsened by injuries to his legs, caused, we were advised, by a fall from a racehorse. Golightly possesses many of the traits of the problem gambler, including low self-esteem.

Outcome: While initially Subject Golightly refused to self-commit, he changed his mind on being advised that while undergoing treatment he would have ready access to excellent facilities. After being so advised, Subject Golightly proved more than willing.

Recommendation: Two weeks in the Yellow House.

Approved.

Committed.

I log out of *mrsgrundy@etcetera* and do the Wikipiddlier and Googlemania. Press reports prove to be the usual fluff. Dames' magazines run glossies of Paris Witherspoon, together with a fuzzy-faced bunch of what look

457

like nurses snapped against a backdrop of bush that all but hides a long, two-storeyed, yellow-painted building, while the news blatts are more hard-edged, and even include one or two names. Mrs Grundy comes up in print just like she did in the not-so-skin-and-bones, smelling like a geranium – a bona fide Mother Teresa with her feet on the ground, head in the clouds, and her hand on her heart swearing allegiance to love and goodness towards all humankind forever.

A typical report, courtesy of that hard-edged news magazine, *Mothers Weakly*:

EXCLUSIVE

'There is so much evil in the world,' Grundy tells this reporter, sadness etched on her beautiful brow. 'To tell the honest truth, I like to think that we're like Florence Nightingale and her wonderful nurses in that terrible war men fought in the Crimea 150 years ago. That is, no more than a group of ordinary women doing our little bit fighting the evil that man does.'

Paris Witherspoon – or Mrs Grundy as she prefers to be known – is beautiful. But at a time when simply being beautiful is too often sufficient for women to obtain fame and fortune, Mrs Grundy turns out to be much more than just a pretty face.

Had she less depth and compassion, she might have become just another Cate Blanchett or Nicole Kidman or Julia Gillard. Granted, she possesses cupid's-bow lips and blue eyes in a flawless complexion, but while her body would vie with that of Elle Macpherson, her soul is that of a saint.

Mrs Grundy – the organisation – is devoted to people who have gambling problems. Applying what she calls a

So everything in the garden's lovely. So why do I suddenly –?

I look for the expected photo attributions.

There are none.

Which means that the photographs were supplied by Grundy's
Inc. Also no address for the big, two-storeyed yellow-painted building.
Repeat: *No address.*

Maybe that's why I –

I'm bailing out the boat when a dead-man's mobile in the bilge breaks the
silence.

'It's me, Imogene.'

I picture the kid clutching the other end of the terror-phone,
whispering, and my heart splits along its ready-made faultline. 'Nice to
hear your voice, Immo. How's things?'

'I think she's serious, Daddy.'

I know what she's talking about, but I ask anyway. 'Who's she, doll?

And what's she serious about?'

'Mummy. And she's serious about taking me away. She told me not to say anything but I had to. There's this man and it's like he's got her hypnotised.'

'Make sure you do the surveill, sweetheart.'

'I am doing the surveill, Daddy, but they're playing it close.'

'Then make sure you play it closer.' I look at the water seeping between the water boards, the place where the rot's set in. 'Where's she taking you?'

'She won't say. But I had to see a doctor and get a passport.' I hear the catch in the breath. 'When the passport people asked, Mummy said there was no father, and I wasn't allowed to smile. I don't like not smiling.' Another pause. 'Daddy?'

'Yeah?'

'I don't want to go. Can you talk to her?'

I think about what Salina told me, and then I don't think about what Salina told me.

'I —'

'Someone's coming down the corridor, Daddy, sorry. Bye.'

'I don't know what you're doing about it, Black, but it's still happening.' The big man that's usually got a self-satisfied smile on his dial-up looks a long way from self-satisfied. 'If anything, I'd say the situation has worsened.'

'So just how has it worsened?'

'How far can I trust you?'

I'm uncomfortable but I got a lot to be uncomfortable about. We're back in the rich man's refuge and we've got some drinks and the chair's soft. But my kid's about to be taken away from me, the tail's still in place, and I'm still a long way from discovering who killed Angela Golightly. I shrug. 'About as far as I can trust you. But neither of us has got much choice in the matter.'

He takes one of those breaths that jokers take when they're several rungs above you on the pecking ladder, breaths that tend to terminate in a polite little shudder. 'Look, I'm a very important person. I'm not exaggerating when I say that I move in exclusive circles. Just acknowledging that I know someone like you could be a problem. I'm on the boards of a number of blue-chip companies. As such, I provide a great deal of

credibility to racing.'
    'Thanks for the curriculum vitae, but I'm afraid the job's taken.'

Chapter 33

THE TWIST IN THE TAIL

He perseveres. People like Justin Cameron always persevere. It's what makes them people like Justin Cameron.

'Look, granted I enjoy a flutter. Call it a perquisite of who and what I am. And if I win, one can put it down either to a deep and impenetrable knowledge of horseflesh, or the prerogative of the natural-born winner.' He leans forward in the button-down Chesterfield and the wall sconce turns the whisky in his glass to gold. 'But someone's been interfering with that winning streak, and I want to know whom.'

I guzzle my beer and don't bother wiping the scum off my face afterwards. 'Who.'

'I'm sorry?'

'It should be who not whom. The rest of the sentence is understood. What you want to know is who's doing the interfering, not whom. It's in the nominative.'

He gives me his boardroom stare, the one that's just this side of ignoring whoever happens to be at the other end of it. I dispense with the grammar lesson.

'I got a name – you needn't know from where, but the name's Pentagon. I went to see him, but it turns out he's not the one doing the fixing. I also nearly got myself killed, but I'm not asking for danger money. The fact is I find myself up a blind alley without the benefit of a companion animal.' I fix him with one of my stares. Normally it works, but with Cameron I might as well be chucking fairy dust. 'Is there something you're not telling me, Cameron? Like the name of a person or persons that might have it in for you?'

'No. But I did receive this letter, courtesy of the club.'

He palms me a piece of paper. His name and the name of his club have been cobbled together using characters cut out of multifarious headings in newspapers. He has committed it to memory.

'It says I'm finally going to "cop" what's been coming to me for a long time during the races at Randwick today.'

I hand him back the note. 'So don't be at the races at Randwick today.'

He inspects the gold in his glass. 'The trouble with that advice is I have to be there. It's a massive promotional exercise. The day is in honour of a sheikh who's all set for a big win and as a result is going to make a sizeable donation. He will be in attendance. And apart from any other consideration, I do not bow to threats.'

'You realise the sheikh might cop it, too?'

Cameron swills down the rest of the gold then nods. 'That's a risk I'm prepared to take.'

'Then it looks like it might be a sheikh-down to me.'

He stares at me over his empty glass. 'Was that meant to be a joke, Mr Black? Because if it was, it was in extremely poor taste.'

I shrug. '*I'm* in extremely poor taste, Cameron. But I thought we'd already established that.'

The news-vendor relieves me of a ten-pointer and I take possession of the latest copy of the rag they put out with the day's races in them. It gives all the names of all the jockeys in all the races and I got a handful of them, courtesy of the list Cyril jotted down at Cameron's racetrack. I also got the jockeys' colours, and the number of horses in the relevant race. It's race five at Randwick which kicks off at four o'clock. Hard surface. I check the time now. It's two-thirty. That means I got just ninety minuets. Take away thirty-five for the taxi ride to the racecourse, and that leaves —

Four rings on dead-man's mobile No. 9. It's Cyril.

'Is that you, Mister Rainbow?'

The voice sounds weak, like its possessor thought he'd just gone through Hell, only to discover that's he's not even crossed the Acheron yet.

'You okay?'

'Far from it.'

I've worked out why, but I ask anyway.

'I think you already know why.'

'Yeah, but I need a confirm.'

While the precious seconds tick away, he gives me a confirm. And the confirm is that he doesn't like the way the Grundy organisation's treating him.

I'm back at Central, the place where they're finding the bodies, the place where all the clues are, a metropolis within a metropolis. There's a big clock in the concourse dangling low over the passing populace like the blade swinging lower and lower over the joker in the pit in that story by Edgar Allan Poe. Weary backpackers, innocent greybeards, drunks, druggies, policemen, and –

I turn my attention back to the phone.

'They started in the normal way.'

'Who started in what normal way?'

'The Brady Bunch. The Grundy Mob. You know, like Alcoholics Anonymous or Weight Busters, where everyone sits around on plastic chairs and admits what terrible people they've been to their friends and family, and after that take vows never to do what they were doing again, and later they keep the rest of the sinners informed of their progress.'

'Like they haven't had a bottle of Glenfiddich or a McDonald's burger for a week, kind of thing?'

'Kind of thing. Except this is to do with gambling, not eating or drinking.'

It's the same dame and she's paying a lot more attention to the arrivals screen than is necessary. It's as though there's something beyond the names and numbers that she's having difficulty seeing – like my reflection. She's wearing a figure-hugging orange T-shirt and red jeans and she looks like she knows how to handle herself, standing on the balls of her sneaker-clad feet like she's –

Our eyes meet and immediately she starts moving away, a lithe figure walking slow, then hurrying, mixing it with the other shadows under the clock, while all the time angling her way towards the escalators.

Chapter 34

FOLLOWING THE FOLLOWER

Iswitch my peepers to departures. In the reflective perspex I can see her departing, snatching the odd glance in my direction over her shoulder, slowing, gathering speed, then slowing again.

'Just one more question, Cyril,' I say into the phone. 'You met a dame called Phoebe Riesling?'

'Her!'

'Yeah, her.'

'Haven't seen her since — Well, to cut a long story short, they got rid of her. At least they got rid of her out of here. That doesn't mean she mightn't still be working for them in some other capacity. Someone said she was over-enthusiastic.' Just like the dame in the orifice said. 'Look, Mister Rainbow?'

'What?'

'Can you get me out of here? And when you do, can you bring my horse with you?'

I'm still watching the dame in the leotards. 'Lord Haw-Haw?'

'What other horse is there?'

She's doubled-back and is moving again down the concourse of non-elegance. 'Maybe I can and maybe I can't.' She's stopped by the blatt seller's. 'On the off chance I can, where is it?'

'Where's what?'

'The address of the place you're at, followed by that of the horse-fixer.'

Cyril tells me he hasn't got a clue where he is, that he believes that not knowing where he is is all part of what someone's told him is a disorientation process. But he tells me the address of the joint where he left Lord Haw-Haw.

'But wait, there's more,' he gasps.

The dame in the red jeans has reached the escalators, and this time I can tell by her movements that she's not going to come back. I start after her, leaping a drunk sleeping it off under the clock and an old woman eating a mango by the coffee vendor's, heading for what I last saw of the dame, a red derriere making itself scarce.

'So tell me.'

But Cyril doesn't tell me. Instead there's a muffled cry, followed by a scuffle and a click and the line goes dead.

I park the phone, jam on the fedora, rebuckle the shoulder holster, and hurtle down the escalator after the dame in the red jeans.

I do the sidle-shift and the hip-swivel and the half-sidestep as I make the descent, taking care not to dislodge anyone off their travelling shoes, at the same time as I'm keeping an eye on the dame. There's no uncertainty about her progress. She knows where she's going and I like it that way because I want to know where she's going. We're out in the street. You can't assume the person you're tailing isn't going to suddenly stop and turn-turtle you, so I keep a block behind her.

I'm too close to the finish to risk blowing it now, hugging the terrace-line, ducking into doorways, keeping as low a profile as a six-foot-something private detective can keep, going into a crouch whenever she does the sudden stop-and-turn, and coming out of it as soon as she starts moving again.

She's perched on the corner of Horowitz and Cranberry, an egret-slim figure, long-necked and aware, legs slightly apart, one foot poised on tippy-toe, head up like she's sniffing out all the possibilities before making the turn.

Suddenly, she's gone. There's a bunch of buildings on one side, while on the other there's nothing but parkland. I do the pause. It's hot and the sweat's rolling off me in rivulets. No dame. Entwined lovers, pissing dog, pub, assorted shops, big double-doors to a warehouse. But no dame.

It's getting too close to the time I need to be leaving for Royal Randwick. Too late for public transitory to be of any use, so I make the call.

'I need a lift to Randwick Racecourse. Pick-up in twenty.' I check out the warehouse doors – they're big, no-nonsense affairs – the dame must have gone inside. Then I picture Little Orphan Annie next to her van, with her hair awry, at the other end of phone.

'Tell me where you are,' she says.

I give her the address where Cyril left the horse and also the address of the warehouse. And I add that when she gets here, to make sure she comes in careful.

After that, I close off the connecting link, shrug the gat into the easy-draw position, straighten the fedora, and go in.

You never know what you'll find when you go in, but you go in all the same. It's the nature of the beast, the way you get to the crux of a case — you make sure the equaliser's at the ready, and you go in.

Only this time, it's not so easy. The warehouse doors are heavy-duty, with steel reinforcement over the original wood, and what look like vestiges of sound-padding around the edges. There's no-one in the vicinity. People sense when there's trouble. It goes back to when they lived in caves.

I stand back, drag out the gat and blam the lock. I push the doors open and the stench of sweat and Vaseline and vacant dust and darkness mingled with the stench of smouldering candles and burnt gunpowder hits my nostrils as I enter.

Chapter 35

A FLY IN THE OINTMENT

It's another one of those sub-sets of Sydney town, one that I take care not to go anywhere near in the normal course of things. Except this isn't the normal course of things. Because in the normal course of things, terror doesn't lie around every corner, Cyril isn't pleading for mercy, old warehouse doors aren't reinforced and insulated, and I don't find myself in the bowels of a torture house.

No sign of the dame in the red duds, not even the faintest echo of her.

I'm in an unfurnished entrance hall, lit only by wall candles, ten paces sideways, by four to the next set of doors. Doors that look much like the ones I just shot open, except for the lack of locks.

The radioactive indices of my chronometer tell me I got forty minutes before the race starts, twenty to find out what I came here to find out, and after that get to the racecourse, in order to prevent –

The candles waver in their sconces. I remember something of Shakespeare's that Aunt Rube drilled into me, that play where Macbeth and his missus dissed a king and as a result the dame can't sleep, just keeps rabbiting on about candles.

And all our yesterdays have lighted fools
The way to dusty death
But what's it mean, Rube? I asked her.

It means you got to learn from your mistakes, kid. You know, Shakespeare could have been the world's first private detective. If the playwriting thing hadn't worked out, I mean.

I shelve the gat, take hold of the handles of the doors in front of me, twist, and push them open.

'*Welcome to my parlour,* said the spider to the fly.' She's wearing figure-hugging yellow lycra – the kind they employ slave labour in Third World countries to stitch together using crap thread – her figure's so wasp-waisted not even the figure-hugging lycra can contract to it, and she's standing by a wheel with chains hanging off it. She's also holding what looks like a stockwhip. 'You're aware of the literary allusion, I imagine?'

I shrug. 'I take it you mean the one that goes: *Will you walk into my parlour? said a spider to a fly.* Lady, you just stuffed up a good quote.'

Paris Witherspoon goes for the big laugh but comes up with a twisted grimace instead. Once upon an age ago, Mrs Grundy was a beautiful dame. But that was when she was all dressed in white and everyone thought –

'You men act as though you're in control when really – It never occurred to you, did it, that I meant you to be here? Because I didn't want you to be somewhere else? That I wanted you to be aware of the tail I had on you from day one, so that when I wanted you to follow her, I could just twitch the line, and you'd be hooked.'

I splay my hands. It flexes the finger joints. After that, I shrug again. It eases the shoulder muscles. 'And did it never occur to you that I might have been aware of your reverse-tail ruse from the start?'

A glare of hate takes the place of the twisted grimace and a flick of the wrist makes the whip writhe. 'Well, there's only one fact that counts right now, and that is that I've got you at my mercy.'

That's when she touches a lever on the Wheel of Fortune and the padded doors swing shut behind me.

I quickly case the joint. Big clock on the wall in front of me. Ceiling, walls, and no doubt the floorboards, insulated against sound. Handcuffs hanging from the wall. Ropes with neck-sized running loops dangle from industrial-strength rafters, and on the opposite side of the room from the doors that have just been locked, wooden shutters cover what I assess to be a loading dock to nowhere.

I'm reading a sign on the wall that reads *A chain's only as strong as its weakest link* when the whip snakes out and my gat leaps from its shoulder holster and skids across the floor, while blood seeps from a cut that's suddenly appeared on my hand.

'Just in case you were thinking of using that symbol of male superiority men like you try to scare people with.' She flicks a brittle tongue over her lips, moves away from the post and begins circling me, her lycra-clad feet scuffling across the floorboards like lizards, the only wrinkles in her figure-clutching outfit the ones around her waist, the slightest bubbling of superfluous lycra that I park in my memory bank, along with the yellow Post-It reminder that I want to survive.

'I can't let you out of here alive, you know, Mister Rainbow.' Her voice is as soft as the sound her feet are making. 'Oh, yes, I know who you are. I had you checked out long ago.'

I got to keep her talking. 'You go to a lot of trouble just to keep something like this going.'

'Oh, but there's more. And you know there's more, don't you? Except that you were never completely sure what that "more" was, were you? And if it hadn't been for the over-enthusiasm of our Phoebe, you would never have suspected anything at all.'

'Where is she now?'

'Surely you know that, too. Only you're not quite sure what she's up to, are you? You've worked out the where and the when but not the how, which is why you're here now. You thought you'd get the how from me, but instead you're going to get the what-for.'

'Come on, Paris, why don't you tell me who and where she is, and who or what you're protecting her from.' I wave a hand at the surrounds. 'After you do that, who knows? None of this might be necessary.'

But all I get in return is the mad laugh, too mad for Paris Witherspoon's own good, and far too mad for mine. I circle away from her towards the clock that's telling me I got even less time than I thought I had.

The whip snakes out and I feel my throat suddenly go cold.

'That's just a little bite from my cat, a taste of things to come,' Paris says. 'You see, before I kill you I'm going to teach you not to be such a bad boy.'

'Like you've been teaching Cyril Golightly.' And then the big one. 'And just like you taught Angela.'

The whip snakes out again, a hole appears in my upper sleeve, and the coat starts to go two-tone — red blood on yellow fabric — and the smile on Paris' face widens.

'That kind of treatment does Cyril and his sort good.' She's behind me now. 'After all, they like the pain. And after his treatment, Cyril's never going to gamble again, I can assure you of that.'

Then she tries to deal with the second part of the accusation.

'You must understand that Angela was a weak sister. After I took over Cyril's debts — yes, I had to neutralise him in some way, he was getting in the way of our program — I tried to get Angela to join our organisation. But the stupid woman wouldn't, even though she had suffered along with the rest of us. Instead, she tried to warn her little man — the person who had all but destroyed her — what we were doing. And when he wouldn't listen, she contacted you.' She gives that time to sink in, but she's too late. It sank in long ago. 'Angela wasn't on the side of the real angels, you see, so she had to go. She had herself to blame. We sisters need to stick together to survive.'

The snick to my upper arm stings but I don't flinch. 'And I don't need to ask what's in it for you, Paris. Because other people's pain is just so much dogfeed to you.'

She's creeping around behind me to my right side.

'Oh, yes, I get a kick out of this, don't worry about that.' Twitch of the lips as she circles, flick of the whip to my right knee, causing the skin over the patella to open like a flower. 'This place — the entire organisation, in fact — is how we get our own back on — because all men are —'

Got to keep her talking, find out —

'All men are what?'

'Just ...'

The whip snakes out again, and the words come with each stroke, like they're forced to emerge by all the exertion.

'... like ...'

Harsher whiplash this time, one that digs deep into my groin, a fraction of an inch to the left of my femoral artery.

'... Uncle Ronnie.'

She's in front of me now and her sweat has darkened the yellow lycra at her armpits.

On the off chance that I'm getting out of here alive, I need more information. 'You might answer one last question before you kill me, Paris. If you happen to know the answer, that is.'

Chapter 36

THE COUP DE GRASS

You want to know what happened to Uncle Ronnie?' Her eyes well with tears. 'I tried to kill him, that's what happened to Uncle Ronnie. He'd been doing it for years, but Mother would never believe it, so I decided to – take matters into my own hands. He'd come to spend Christmas with us – his then-wife had left him, probably because she knew what he was, and he was alone this Christmas.'

She shudders, and instead of a madwoman in yellow stretch, I see the little girl she once was.

'One day when he was out, I went into his room and found a pile of – magazines. And among the magazines was some sort of anatomy book. I studied it until I knew it by heart. Then on Christmas Eve, I took Mum's red-handled paring knife to bed with me, so I'd have a nice little present all ready for Uncle Ronnie when he roamed through the house to –'

Her lips quiver. I keep my tone mild.

'But the knife was too small, wasn't it? And you were too weak. Apart from which, despite all your study of anatomy, you didn't realise how hard it would be to actually kill someone. Then, anyway.' I press for the information I'm after. 'But you managed to scare him, didn't you, and maybe even to mark him. Did you go for his face?'

She shakes her head. 'If only.' She waves the whip. 'But I still got him – on the hand.'

I know, but I still ask. 'Which hand?'

I say it fast because I want the information while she's still in the mood to provide it.

'I got him in his right hand – diagonally across the palm.'

'At which point he went screaming into the night.'

She allows herself a smile at the thought. 'He didn't even stay for Christmas. He left a brief note, and there was blood on it. Mum was – stupefied. I didn't enlighten them as to what had happened. Maybe I should have. Maybe that would have ...'

I don't let her slow down. I remember the report referring to Cyril's admission to –

'So what's with the Yellow House? And where is it?'

She smiles. 'The answer to your first question is it's my little joke. Do you know what Uncle Ronnie used to say whenever he did it? He'd say – and he'd sort of laugh when he said it – *You can yell out, but nobody's going to hear you.*' A look of triumph spreads across her dial-up. 'So when he screamed when I stabbed him, do you know what I whispered back at him?'

'Yeah, you told him words to the effect that: *You can yell out, but nobody's going to hear you.*'

She smiles to herself, no doubt seeing again the tormentor gripping his clothes with one hand while nursing the other as he fled the room.

'It always sounded as though he was saying "Yell Ow. You can yell Ow, but nobody's going to hear you." Of course, we couldn't make head or tail of it. It was just meaningless words. Just like we couldn't make sense of what he did.' She winces, pauses, regathers herself and the whip. She takes a deep breath, and the lycra wrinkles and stretches. 'So that's what I called my healing place when I finally set it up – The Yell-Ow House. *THE YELLOW HOUSE.* Nice touch, isn't it?'

'Nice answer, too,' I tell her. 'Only it's not the answer to the question I asked. At least, not the second part.'

So she tells me where the Yellow House is. Then she wishes she hadn't.

'What makes you think I'm going to wait around letting you ask questions, much less provide the answers to them?'

'Because it's been a secret for too long. Also you like to spin out the pain, don't you, Paris? It's your way of avenging yourself on the world.'

'On a man's world. So what's your question, dead man?"

'How were you doing it?'

'Doing what?'

'Well, for some reason you targeted Justin Cameron. Maybe it was because he was the tallest poppy you could find. How have you been screwing his certainties, killing his chances of winning?'

'That'd be telling.'

'So tell me.'

'I suppose I may as well, seeing you'll soon be dead, anyway.'

So she tells me. There were numerous ways, all of them aimed at stopping the particular horse that Cameron had arranged to win. There were the usual methods – drugs, bribing jockeys, threats. And the unusual methods.

'Like tormenting me over my daughter.' Then assuring me she'd squared matters with Salina, when the reality was exactly the opposite. Which is a good part of the reason why –

'So what's your latest method?'

'We've been using snipers. We position them in a high point at the racecourse and they long-range a dart into the relevant horse at the relevant time from a distance. We've experimented with different – concoctions.' She smiles at the thought. 'Our first attempt was with Lord Haw-Haw. Because it was our first attempt, we neglected to allow for the fact that jockeys tend to rise out of their saddles when they come into the straight, and we – scored a behind. Little Cyril Golightly's behind, to be exact.' She flicks the whip. 'But still – same result: the horse lost. And with the building works going on at Royal Randwick – they're putting in a new grandstand – you could say we're at an all-time high in our endeavours.'

'Meaning?'

Paris Witherspoon's face clouds. 'Meaning I've already told you too much. He's going to get it. At last he's going to get it. And there's nothing you or anyone else can do about it.'

She draws back the whip and a sad look replaces the cloudy one.

'You know, I've rather come to like you. It's such a pity it has to end like this. I don't think you're just out for what you can get.' She takes a deep breath. 'But I can't possibly leave you alive now, can I? Not after telling you so much. We're ready for the coup de grace at the racecourse. And now I have to put you out to grass, too.'

She flicks back the whip.

'So goodbye forever and forever and forever, Mr Rainbow.'

It's a child's voice, like a kid saying goodnight to her Mum before cuddling up to her favourite toy, all soft and sleepy like she's got no control over what she's about to do next. Which in the kid's case would have been going to sleep, but in Paris Witherspoon's case is killing me. She's got her back to the whipping-post and she's in the full-death position – legs apart, hair down, head up, eyes glinting, whip hand out. The clock on the wall tells me I got eight minutes to be out of here. That is, if I'm ever going to –

'Aren't you going to beg?' The question takes me by surprise, when it shouldn't. 'They all beg, so why don't you?'

Chapter 37

TROUBLE WITH LYCRA

'm past begging, Paris. From an early age, I've been in pretty much the same place as you. The difference is, I've resolved it in other ways.'

I think of the bully boys in the playground, before Aunt Rube pulled me out of school and taught me how to survive.

'I mightn't have had an Uncle Ronnie, but that doesn't mean I haven't been in dark places. So I know half the fun for the people that put you in such places is hearing you scream. As a result, I'm not going to beg; I won't give you the satisfaction.'

A look of uncertainty crosses her face. It only lasts a nanosecond, but it's enough. I've established a link with my tormentor. They don't like that. Nor do they like their victims turning on them, which means she's got another cause to be upset as I launch myself across the torture-chamber at her, keeping to my right, the side with the lash in it, because that's the safer option.

With the whipping-post behind her, and me crowding in on her from her left, she hasn't got room to swing a cat in. But the cat still snakes at me, Paris's cut-down cat o' nine tails. I roll myself in a tight ball, clutching my shins, head between my knees, but the razor-snake snaps at my right ear – I hear the scream and the crack of it, the sting as it threatens to do to me what the knife did to Uncle Ronnie – but I'm past and behind the whipping-post as she turns.

She goes into the full crouch and I see her eyes glint and her thighs tense as I feint to the right before coming at her from the other side, hands out for a grip on something – anything to get her off-balance – and finding lycra. Lycra's a second skin that clings so tight that mostly there's nothing to get a purchase on. It's a bunch of tiny filaments that can stretch many times its length. Which means that even if I manage to get a fistful of it, it will be something like grabbing the rubber band of a slingshot.

It doesn't stop me trying.

Nothing to get a grip on now except hope, but there's not going to

475

be a second chance, so I get my hooks into the place where the stuff's bubbling around her waist – the skein of second skin – and hang on like grim death.

There's nothing else to hang on to.

Waist not, want not.

When lycra's put together it's only as strong as its seams. And these seams are weak.

Paris Witherspoon is like a snake sloughing in a quiet corner of the bush at the start of summer, her spandex peeling open like a banana – at the points where it's been sewn together.

There are sights men shouldn't see, and this is one of them – Paris Witherspoon, a woman of eye-glazing beauty, stripped to her bare essentials, feet apart and crouching as she circles, snarling.

There's no pretence now, because there's nothing left to pretend about.

The outer doors might be shot out, but the inner doors are snapped-to and my gun's on the floor by the escape hatch and there's no way I can go for the knife. So I keep my eyes on the whip and my body in tandem with Paris' – a pas deluxe to the death – her and my legs apart like his-and-her towels. We're both in the full-crouch position, arms out from our sides, moving as though an invisible cord links our hands, feet and bodies, her past and my past, as well as both our futures.

The clock on the wall gives me three minutes, four at best.

We've done a forty-five degree turn when I go into the leap. What throws her is that she expects me to leap at her. Instead, I hurl myself backwards, throwing myself into a handstand and arching my back like the acrobat in *Les Sylphides*, and holding it just long enough for Paris to think she's won. That's when she drops the whip and comes for me, teeth bared, fingers clawing the air. Hate's good in an opponent. It gets in the way of their judgment.

Bending my elbows, I launch myself rafter-wards. Fear and anger have got the better of her. She lands sprawling, but spins as I come for her, throwing herself sideways, at the same time bringing her leg around, straight-kneed, collecting me where I never want to be collected, and I go down.

I'm on my back and she's leaning over me, snarling and clawing for my eyes, mouth, ears, hair. I grapple for her wrists but they're slippery. Nails rake my face as her hands seek for my throat. I try to break free, but suddenly and inexplicably she's too strong.

Then I realise it's not her strength but my own weakness. My vision starts to fade. I relax my hold. My arms weaken and fall away. I feel her fingers tighten around my throat.

I can't see the clock any longer and there's no time any more, just the blood-red vista of the ceiling of the torture chamber, Paris Witherspoon straddling me, her once-beautiful face close to mine, sucking in breath like she's drawing sustenance as my weakened fingers claw at the floorboards, and my fingers close on –

I expected nothing but dust and splinters, nothing to provide anything that might go by the name of hope. And true to my expectations, my fingers close on – nothing.

I'm seconds from infinity. Death has me in her arms. Time to say my goodbyes. But I've only got one, it's all I've got breath and time for.

Goodbye – Imogene – I'm – sorry – that – I – failed – you – I –

'Die, Uncle!'

There's an injustice here. I'm nobody's uncle. My only sister's dead. My mother killed her just like this woman's killing me now. Meantime, Imogene's alive while I –

I've got thirty seconds.

After which, there's no time at all.

Chapter 38

PIPPED AT THE POST

That's when I hear the sound of splintering wood and clanging metal, and through the haze of death I see the locked and sealed doors smack inwards, and in their place –

It's not possible. I'm dying and as a result I'm seeing things.

Not angels and whipcord beauty and clouds floating in a haze of song or my past life, but a careering, drunken bull bar and attached to it the snout of an old van, a split-screen Kombi with shards of timber all over its split screen and what looks like a brand-new scar on its left cheek, and behind the wheel a white, white face and a set of fists white-knuckling the steering wheel, black eyes staring into the gloom as the bull bar comes up hard against the whipping-post, there's a terrible scream, and then everything –

Stops –

Dead.

There should be bleak blackness, emptiness. The world should have stopped. There is no life after death. So why am I hearing my heart thud and a woman's voice calling my name, as though across the echoing depths of a canyon?

'Rainbow! Answer me!'

Aunt Rube tried to get me to imagine death. It was part of her training. *See it for the nothing it is, so that you know exactly what you're avoiding. It's nothing. And if death is nothing, then it's nothing to fear, is it?*

It's nothing.

So why should there be a voice in it?

Or sirens, great, wailing, howling, caterwauling sounds, the sirens that drag sailors to a watery grave.

'Rainbow! We've got to get out of here, the police are coming!'

It's that last that does it. Eyes opening, sleepy-time eyes, eyes full of the muck of childhood blinking in the harsh light of a torch held by a torturer. To see –

The bleak interior of the torture chamber. All the necessary accoutrements – spinning-wheel, whips, chains, ropes, spikes. And a lifeless body, blood yellowing on its beautiful crushed chest, crushed against the whipping-post by the bull bar of a Kombi called Gertrude.

Hands under my armpits, dragging me. My rubbery legs refusing to work, until –

'That's better.' It's the voice of a street nurse trying to raise a derelict from the dead. 'We've got you upright. Now lean on me. Just a couple more steps and you'll be in the van.'

I feel the small, determined hands under my back as Annie heaves me into Gertrude. Then the door slams shut and another door – it must be the driver's-side door – opens and closes, and the air-cooled flat four starts, followed by the familiar whine of Gertrude in reverse, a screeching stop, the grating of gears, and Annie screaming, 'Hang on!'

We've stopped once, or maybe twice, and I'm no longer in the back of the van, but on the bench-seat next to Annie, trying to remember something.

'Where is she?'

'Dead, crushed against her own whipping-post. Jesus, Rainbow, who the hell was Paris Witherspoon, anyway?'

I shake my head as I try to straighten in my seat. 'Just another one of life's little victims. Where are –?'

'Your hat and your gun? They're on the seat beside you. Meanwhile, I figured you needed to get to the racecourse.'

'How did you –?'

'At first, I thought it was just a woman's jealousy.' She hurries over that one. 'But then I realised that it might be for real, and that there could be a very good reason for my instinctive dislike of Paris Witherspoon. Women get their hooks into men. But I knew her hooks were – different – and that you weren't in danger of being seduced so much as – getting killed.'

'Where are the cops?'

'I threw them.'

'What do you mean *threw them*?'

A smile from Annie, in the harsh afternoon light the warm glow of a soft smile. 'Not in the sense you're thinking. The police pulled Gertrude over and asked what was under the blanket and I told them –'

I see Annie colour. It might be a reflection from the rear-vision, but I don't think so.

'And you told them what?'

'– that you were just another derelict.'

'And they believed you?'

She shrugs. 'They know me, they know what I do. What was there not to believe?'

Chapter 39

DON'T FRIGHTEN THE HORSES

You'd better clean yourself up,' Annie says. She reaches across and pulls open the glovebox. 'Use that cloth there. I'm getting you to a doctor.'

I pick up the cloth and start using it. 'Thanks, Annie. But there's no time for a doctor. We got to save Cameron.' There's dust all over the dashboard but I can see enough of the clock to worry me. 'As it is, we might be too late. You'll have to step on it.'

'We'll go to the doctor afterwards then.'

It hurts to shake my head, but I still shake it. 'No, after that, we got to save Cyril.' I glance around. 'Did you get his horse for him?'

'You forget that's what I do. I pick up things.' She jerks her head towards the rear of the van. 'Lord Haw-Haw's in the back.'

Racecourses are where the money is. They're also where the trouble's going to be. Paris warned me as much just before she clammed up for good. We're in the layby outside the main entrance. I come round to Annie's door after I climb stiffly down out of the van.

'Wait for me?'

'Forever if you like, Rainbow.'

I head for the turnstiles. I've wiped off as much of the blood as I can, but blood tends to spread, and there's something about having blood on you that makes people nervous. I got my collar up and hat pulled low over my eyes but there are still the scratches on the lower part of my face, so I can't blame security for zeroing in on my potential as soon as I show up at the gates. It's becoming a familiar refrain.

'I'm sorry, sir, but I'm afraid I can't let you in looking like that.'

They're trained to be polite. *Don't frighten the horses*, they're taught at their crime-fighting academy. And before that: *Do nothing to put fear into the punters.*

'Not as afraid as you'll be if you don't.'

'And how might that be?'

I don't show him how it might be. Instead, I show him how it is. And I do that by palming him one of Cameron's hundreds. Money talks and the foe-gendarme's listening. He takes the C-note and steps back.

'I'm sorry, sir.'

It's a different kind of sorry to his first one.

I find my way to the marquee. It's big and it's full of men with money. No women, because it's men's day – men in expensive suits, sheikhs in expensive sheets. I make my way towards the big figure wearing the big smile and holding the even bigger glass of champagne.

'You'll find it to be a prime investment,' he's telling an associate.

'I need a word with you, Cameron.'

No more Mr Nice Guy. Cameron notes the change and the champagne spills and the smile's replaced by a frown. 'What are you doing here?'

'You told me to be here, remember? I'm saving your life.' I wave my arm around the marquee. 'Not to mention the lives of your – friends.'

I hesitate on the word because people like Cameron don't have friends, just people that are afraid to say No when he invites them to the races. A knot of muscle – otherwise known as a masseter – gets to work at the edge of his mandible.

'That was just a moment of uncustomary weakness.' He's had too much to drink. In fact, he's had too much of everything. 'This is a racecourse. No-one's lives are under threat here.'

'I know what you been up to, and I also know why you hired me. You got about as much probity as a sparrow. You been fixing races since the year dot. And up until recently, it was enough to slip the odd four-legger a Micky Finn or a bolter, at the same time as you paid off a couple of riders. Yeah, all those things you told me you'd never stoop to.'

The other big punters are glancing in our direction – and Cameron moves me towards the flap-doodle of the doorway.

'But things started to go wrong, didn't they?' I continue. 'Races stopped being predictable. Starting with Cyril Golightly's fall.'

Cameron's gone white under his Bay of Biscay tan. 'This is all conjecture.'

'Somewhere along the way, you got the bright idea of setting up your own private racecourse where you could rehearse races. It was your insurance policy. Why else would you use a ballet choreographer to stage manage races in advance? And it all worked nice and sweet – until your past finally caught up with you.'

'What past?' Cameron grabs my arm and half-drags me from the tent. 'Look, I have a position to maintain, while you – I could have you arrested, do you know that? I knew I made a mistake hiring you. You're supposed to be working for me, not against me. Also I'm on my homeground, which means that with just a flick of my fingers, you'd be gone.'

I shake my head. 'The reason I'm working for you, is that you preferred me' – I glance back at the marquee – 'to be in your tent piddling out rather than on the outside piddling in. You were afraid that left to my own devices, I might discover too much. Which is why you didn't want me to witness you rehearsing your races.'

'Are you threatening me?'

'No, but time is. You choreographed the fifth, remember? This is the big one, the one in which you hope to make a killing for yourself and your – investors. But it just so happens that your nemesis knows that, too, because one of her minions was following me when I paid a visit to your private racecourse. Which means it won't be your killing, but hers. Because the fifth is when she's going to make her play.'

'What nemesis? What play? What the hell are you talking about?'

I glance towards the western end of the devil's playground. A figure wearing a yellow hi-vis work shirt is lugging a black box up the outside of a platform crane, the crane they're building the new grandstand with.

'Racing used to be a matter of horses for courses, but now it's about to become horses for corpses. Because your past has just caught up with you, Mr Justin Cameron, AO.' I do the pause. 'Or should I say, Uncle Ronnie.'

Chapter 40

THE KILLER ON THE CRANE

That's not my name.'

'It might not be now, but it was then.'

'Wh – when?'

'We both know that you destroyed more than one life when you seduced Angela Golightly. But you had history, didn't you? Including when you used to go into a certain bedroom in the house of your trusting sister.'

That's when I grab his mitt – the right mitt, the one he avoided shaking my hand with – and twist it over. He's had plastic surgery, but the scar's gone red against a hand that's as white as Cameron's aristocratic features.

'You got stabbed for it. And today you could get killed for it.'

All the confidence, all the savoir faire – not to mention all the born-to-rule arrogance – is suddenly sucked out like air out of a badly-tied party balloon.

'Is she – was she – has she been –'

'Behind your fall in fortune?' I nod. 'In between her other nefarious work, little Paris Witherspoon also found a way to fix your fixes. She waited for you to put your money on a race, then took steps to reverse your fortunes. It was a nice little version of the Chinese water torture. It didn't matter how many jockeys you paid off, or how often you rehearsed a race, she could always reverse the process.'

He looks nervously about him. 'How did – will she – is she going to –'

'Yeah, if I don't do something about it. And you know, such are my feelings towards you right now that maybe I wouldn't bother doing anything about it if other lives weren't at stake beside yours.'

I glance towards the crane. The figure in the hi-vis work shirt is more than halfway up to its deadly destination. The commentator's started his commentary on race five, telling everyone how they can win just by putting the house – and then some – on the favourite. And that's when I hightail it away from the marquee and towards the crane. The punters scatter. You're not supposed to drop betting slips on the ground, especially before a race, but that's what happens as they get out of the way.

'This is the best field we've seen at Royal Randwick for years, and we've seen some beauties, ladies and gentlemen. Flying Sheikh's the favourite, but that doesn't mean he can't be beaten. This race is wide open, without any shadow of a doubt. Let's take a look at the form.'

I belt through the masses, past the tubs of multi-coloured flowers, whitesides clattering on the tarmac. I get a foot on the first of the two hundred rungs that lead to the platform at the top of the crane.

'So let's look at today's track. Different conditions suit different horses – or as they say, it's horses for courses.'

It's a long climb and there's no longer any sign of the figure in yellow. Which means that by now the killer will be setting up on the platform after which these cranes are named. I reckon I've got a couple of minutes. But I haven't reckoned on the bird.

I'm halfway up and already tiring when the magpie makes its presence known, a black and white bundle of feathers that comes at me out of nowhere. A lot of feathers, but more beak than feathers. Magpies ought to be vegetarians, but tell that to the birds. This one likes me a lot better than is going to be good for my health, because I need both hands to cling to the crane and I'm fifty rungs above ground level, and still climbing.

'It's been hot today but the ground staff have been busy, and we've got some of the best groundstaff in the world at Royal Randwick, so –'

I let go one hand to try and bat the bird away, but that doesn't help. The voice on the Tannoy's still loud but the punters are small as the toy horses are shuffled into the barrier stalls by their even more minuscule jockeys.

The bird's still diving and swooping. Twenty rungs to go. Dizziness assails me with almost as much vigour as the bird, a wave of nausea that makes me want to let go.

Rubbish.

I snap out of the trance long enough to realise that the caller's started calling the race.

But why would he say rubbish?

That's when I remember that *Rubbish* is the name of one of the runners in race five. It's also what Rube used to say whenever it looked like I was thinking of giving up, on anything – whether it was the conjugation of an irregular verb, a ballet move, or a boxing contest.

Fifteen rungs to go.

The magpie's showing no signs of weakening in the straight. If anything, it's got more ferocious. Meanwhile, the horses far below slide easily into their second lap as my hands slide on the rungs. I'm close enough to the top to feel the movement of the crane as the sniper shifts position above me. I realise this isn't just a fix, a dart to the neck of the favourite as it enters the straight. No, this is going to be a massacre.

Five rungs.

Just like with high buildings, there's a natural sway to cranes. The sway's engineered into them. But knowing that doesn't make it any easier to hang on during the swaying, not with the handicap that Mad Maggie's providing as she does her best to dislodge me. I shake my head. It brings my blurry line-of-sight into contact with the ground, together with the gay array of colour spread out far below, and I see it through the eyes of the sniper.

By the size of the box he was carrying, I'd estimate he's got a 7.62mm M134, the kind of weapon they attached to fixed-wing gunships like the AC-47 Dakota – also known as Puff the Magic Dragon, because it's a nightmare, the kind of nightmare they used to gun down unsuspecting civilians in Afghanistan, before they perfected drones.

Chapter 41

ANOTHER FALLEN WOMAN

They're coming into the straight, calls the caller.

I hear a shot as the cabin tips. It's like I'm getting myself into the *Wooden No*. Makes a difference, two hundred pounds heaving itself onto the platform. Enough of a difference for the shooter to straighten after getting off just the one shot and swing the not-so-sweet cherry-bowl of the multifarious-muzzled machine-gun around to the threat that's coming at him from the rear.

Only the gunner isn't a him, it's a her. And it's not some random sniper picked from an orchard, but the dame that purloined my daughter from outside the punters' sweatshop, and after that graced the front desk of Mrs Grundy's, and after that – allegedly, anyway – got herself retrenched for the heretofore unacknowledged crime of being over-enthusiastic in the pursuit of her duties.

There's a look on Phoebe Riesling's face that I never want to see again, but I know I'm going to. A couple of paces. That's all there is between me and certain death – paces I can't possibly take in time – as the sun glistens in a torrid sky above, while, far below, the caller tells whoever's interested after that single shot winged its way into the marquee, that everything's going according to plan. Only it's not the plan that Cameron set in place – courtesy of a choreographer who thought he was all set to become the turf's next George Balanchine – but the plan of Cameron's nemesis, Phoebe Riesling's sister, Paris Witherspoon.

Behind Phoebe's snarl, I glimpse the features of a once-sweet girl before she was hurt – the wide-open eyes, now life-hardened; the once-cherubic mouth, now segued into a slit of fury; and the once-soft, trusting hands of a child that have turned into the talons of an avenging harridan, clawing at the controls of a primed-to-kill machine-gun.

Pity about the magpie. Because suddenly the bird realises there's something else on the platform, and that something has interposed itself between the magpie and a good feed, and the bird's just not going to stand for it.

Instead it's going to fly for it.

It's like Maggie remembers that, from a standing start, it can travel at over 30 miles per hour – that's 60 kilometres in the new money – which means that it covers the distance in one-tenth of a second, or faster than the blink of an eye.

Which is a shame for Phoebe Riesling, because she cops a beak full in the face. She utters a piercing scream and staggers back towards the edge of the platform, arms flailing and hands clawing for a handhold they're never going to find, not in this world, nor in any other.

I hurl myself towards her, reaching out in a vain attempt to save her from falling into the abyss yawning behind her.

But she flings out her arms as she goes out backwards.

For a moment she hangs as if suspended, her yellow hi-vis shirt opening like a bat's wings. It looks as though, by some miracle of engineering, she's going to beat the rap.

But it's only for a moment. Because after that, gravity wreaks its inevitable mischief and Phoebe Riesling becomes nothing more than a saffron-coloured handkerchief fluttering to the ground.

Another fallen woman.

I don't wait for her to land. I don't need to. What I need is to get off this crane as fast as I can without dying in the attempt, and before some joker blames me for the dame's demise, when the real cause was some overgrown mudlark.

I check the marquee before I leave the course. One of the trackside ambulances is in attendance, but it's not an ambulance they need. There's blood on the double-bed sheets that the sheikhs are wearing, and the silk suits of the others – but the blood's not theirs. Phoebe Riesling made her last shot count. Justin Cameron will never again be the winner he once was. In fact Cameron will never be anything he once was, because Justin Cameron AO – also known as Uncle Ronnie – has just received another honour to make up the daily double, together with the one a young girl once inscribed on the palm of his hand: a bullet to the head.

Annie glances over at me from behind the wheel of the van. 'You look terrible. Now can we go to a doctor?'

I shake my head. Lord Haw-Haw is lying on the bench seat between us. 'We got to save Cyril.'

'Where do we go?'

I tell her where Paris said it was, before she decided she wasn't going to tell me.

Night's falling as we near the target, the kind of night with too much darkness in it, when shadows cover the moon and even more shadows lurk in the shadows of the shadows.

'I'd better come with you, Rainbow.'

I hand her the gat, get out of the van, and come round to the driver's side. 'No, stay here. There might be some deaths, and I don't want yours to be one of them.'

'Okay. But don't forget to take his security blanket.' She grabs the pony from the bench seat. 'And be careful, it's heavy.'

A creature skitters across my path as I tuck the horse under my arm and go in. An owl hoots, or maybe it's fate. Black figures multiply about me, silently shrieking. I recognise an old-style telephone booth, the kind that Superman used to change into bright-red underpants in. After that, a fence, followed by a big, yellow toilet block. No challenge. No guards, no dogs. Why should there be? This is the place where the Grundy organisation brings problem gamblers, where Paris Witherspoon – along with her horde of hell's angels – help so many mug punters beat the habit with lots of warm hugs and lollies and dancing. 'Positive reinforcement' Paris called it.

I get myself over the gate and onto a white-gravelled driveway which ends at the toilet block. Two floors of windows. Utter and complete silence. I make my way around to the back of the edifice. The doors are unpanelled and they're locked and kept that way with very big locks, while the windows are of the simple double hung variety, with sashes that slip up and down and ordinary, everyday casement latches on them.

No catch at all. And no dogs, no alarms ... So why don't I –

Because I'm suddenly cautious, that's why. Something's wrong. Third window from the east end is open and inviting. Not much, not enough to be obvious, anyway. A finger's width, that's all. I reach out and then I stop dead, stepping back and ducking as I go, and a shot goes whanging over my head and thuds into the wooden ladder leaning against the wall behind me.

First round to the interloper.

I check the façade and it's then that I see the light.

Chapter 42

THE YELLOW HOUSE

Correction: I see lights in the plural, six of them to be exact, all lined up nice and neat under the eaves on the building's northern side, each in the region of a thousand watts and pointing down at the lawn. Enough to create daylight out of darkness.

I was meant to see them, to see the opportunity and then step back from it. Because in a split second I'd be dazzled by daylight and go down in a flurry of bullets. Which is what will happen if I do what they want me to do. Which is to make a break for it.

So I don't. Instead, in one swift movement – a la Madame Blavatsky's ballet lessons – I do what I've always been told is impossible, the straight-up-in-the-air leap from the prone position, the flying fandango from a lying start rather than the demi-plié position, the ballonne into the air out of nowhere. And not away from the building but towards it, headfirst into the nearest black-faced window, broken shards of three-millimetre glass spraying out around me as the lights come on. The drought-crazed lawn is suddenly turned into a blaze of yellow ochre – just as another bullet heads my way.

I hurl myself through the window, gripping onto the horse, arms up to cover my eyes, my body hammering onto bare floorboards on the other side. There's nothing inside the room but the broken window and a door. I take the door. I'm in a corridor. More doors leading off the corridor, light spills out from under them. And at the end, a set of stairs.

I don't know what I expected, but it wasn't this. I've only had Cyril's truncated words to go by, but if this joint is what I think it is, how come he was able to make the call? All phones would be locked and barred to the inmates. He wouldn't be able to get a message through.

That's when something stirs in my memory. Something beyond the fence. An old-fashioned red telephone box in a deserted country lane. They must have had only a light guard on Cyril because of his legs. They thought he wouldn't be a problem. He must have escaped and got himself on the other side of the gates and thence to the phone booth, from which he telephoned me, using coins left over from gambling.

During which, he was grabbed and probably –

But there's no probably about it, I know what happened for a fact as I race up the corridor, the sound of multifarious footsteps crashing behind me.

If you knew what was going to happen in life, you wouldn't do it. And if I'd known what was going to happen to me in the Yellow House, I might have fled in the opposite direction. But I'm here now, standing outside one of the doors with light spilling from under it. And when I tuck Cyril's horse under my arm and open the door, I'm back in the casino.

The joint might be a lot smaller, but it's still a casino, a shrunken version of the one I rescued Cyril from – with roulette wheels, chocolate wheels, chemin-de-fer tableaus, poker chips in teetering towers on green baize, rows of pokies, and probably far too much oxygen in the air-conditioning. Plus the players. Plus the smell. The cameras are dotted all over the ceiling, their lenses probing the collective agony like machine-guns. I zero-in on a player, a hulking bloke perched in front of a one-armed bandit bearing the graphic of an underdressed lady and the promise: *Win and I'm Yours.*

Up Yours, more like, going by the spasms in the punter's body accompanying the crazy music spinning out of the machine as the win spills into his lap – spasms so prolonged and severe that his eyes start out of his head and his limbs twist as he grips on like grim death while a series of strangled screams issues from his mouth.

Ha-ha-ha, chants the underdressed lady, while a dame with a tray leans down and offers the punter another drink as he collapses, twitching, onto the floor.

I get the hell away and find myself at a table at which another dame is doling out cards to a group that consists of a geezer in a wheelchair, a fresh-faced kid with a crew-cut, a fat man in grubby shorts and grubbier T-shirt, a skeletal joker with something wrong with his head, and a snowy-haired youth in the final stages of early-onset dementia.

The cards go flying as the fat man leaps to his feet, revealing wires leading from his forearms to the connection under the green-baize table as he cries out – his face contorted in a mixture of joy and fear. 'I've won! I've won! I've won!'

The next second he's writhing on the floor, his mouth forming a rictus and his fingers clawing the air, while the heels of his Nikes hammer the parquet.

'I've won! I've won! I've won!' he screams again. Closely followed by, 'No! No! No!'

'Yes, yes, yes,' murmurs the croupier, still smiling as she scoops together the scattered cards.

And, 'Yes! Yes! Yes!' chant the other players.

'You won! Don't you see? You got what you wanted, but it means you have to pay!'

Then, *'Play means pain!'*

'Bet and bleed!'

'Gambles means shambles.'

'You really ought to stop gambling, you know.'

The punters look at each other as though programmed to do just that, as though waiting for their cue. *'In fact, we all should!'*

I'm no Einstein, but it doesn't take an Einstein to get the picture. This is yet another place of torture, where the usual drawn-out agony of a gambler's life is concentrated in a few terrible seconds at the moment of winning, so there can be no doubt in his or anyone else's mind regarding the association.

Gambling equals pain.

Pain equals gambling.

And stopping gambling means release.

As long as the release comes soon enough.

Which it wouldn't if one of the players – correction: one of the Grundy bunch's employees, namely Phoebe Riesling – was over-enthusiastic in the performance of her duties. Positive reinforcement be damned. This is a place of pain, a sado-masochist's paradise, a torturer's hell hole. It's like the players are drugged. When they're not writhing on the floor, they're sitting at the tables and pokies pressing buttons like they're automatons. There's no drugs involved, there's no need for any. Yet another scream rends the air as yet another punter hits the jackpot, at the same time copping several hundred volts of electrically-induced pain to the more sensitive parts of his anatomy. And all the while the cameras whirr.

No-one's come for me yet.

Why not? Because I'm only a threat as long as they don't know where I am and don't know what I'm doing and don't know what I'm seeing. But they do know all that. Because they can see me, the cameras make certain of that, their pigs' snouts following my every move.

Chapter 43

THE WOMEN IN RED

I saw it when I first arrived at the joint, a room perched on top of the Yellow House, much like the watchtower in a jail. It would have been from there that they saw Cyril escape and went after him. And I'm guessing it's from there that they watch the pain of their victims, via the CCTV cameras. I've got to find Cyril and get him out of here. Maybe he's already dead and dumped on the street, put there by somebody's over-enthusiasm. But if he's not, I've got to find him. I've got to do it for Angela Golightly, but I've also got to do it for Cyril.

Too many players, too much action, too much in the way of distraction. Then suddenly there he is. He's won and is lying unconscious, with wires strapped to his arms under a green-baize table, still as still. Apart from the built-up footwear, he's wearing the usual gambler's rig of egg-stained bowl-of-fruit and a stupid expression on his face.

I bend down. 'Come on, Cyril, get up.'

Eyelids flutter. Then, 'Did – you – bring – my – horse?'

I hand him Lord Haw-Haw. I'm happy to be rid of it. It's too heavy. Christ knows how Cyril manages to lug it around.

'Cyril!'

He doesn't move. I try to extract the horse but it's already welded back into place, all freshly stitched together, and somehow bulkier, the hooves awry and the glass eyes staring accusingly at me like I'm some kind of interloper. I shake him but it's no good. He's a lift-and-carry job. I yank the wires off him and hurl them aside and after that I haul Cyril across my shoulders and get us the hell out of there.

Correction.

Try to get us the hell out of there.

There are six of them and they're all wearing tight, scarlet-coloured body-stockings with hoods. None of them is armed, apart from the protective machinery that some god dealt them – bare hands and bare feet, accompanied by the ability and desire to hurt people, employing nothing more than those self-same bare feet and hands. They're moving in unison, with all the delicacy of wildcats.

I've got Cyril to the top of the stairs while the six dames in red are still at the bottom. That means we got the height advantage, but even from where I'm standing, I can see it's not enough.

They start up the stairs after us. The horse with Cyril attached whangs me on the back of the head as I swing away. Then I feint, making as if to dive down towards the women. It's enough to make them hesitate – six right legs poised in the air in perfect unison. The door's behind me and to my left. Somehow, I heft Cyril over my shoulder like I'm about to chuck him, and obtain the immediate satisfaction of seeing the six-pack below me hit Pause.

But the satisfaction's only momentary. Because the Barbarellas start like gazelles up towards me, snarling and flailing as one. I'm not about to wait to see what happens when they arrive. I spin, with Cyril and his horse still over my shoulder, and my whitesides hammer the floorboards as I make for the door at the end of the hall.

I kick it shut behind us. Through the window at the far end, the outside lights have turned night into day. I dump my load and grab the nearest piece of furniture – a steel bed – and jam it under the door knob.

Chapter 44

THE FACE AT THE WINDOW

Cyril reaches for his horse – as if to reassure himself it's still there – and after that, relaxes again.

'Cyril!'

He opens his eyes and for a moment it's as if he can't see, his eyes blinking in the harsh light, sight wavering. 'Where are we?'

'We're in trouble.'

'What kind of trouble?'

'The kind that people don't usually get out of.'

The women in red must have realised the door's impregnable. I can hear them outside now, in the garden. They're not trying to keep quiet.

'You know this joint, Cyril. Is there any way out? Other than the obvious?'

Cyril tucks his horse under one arm and shakes his head. 'I've known more than one victim to exit via the window, because instant death was preferable to what he was experiencing.'

'I thought at first we might make a drop rope out of the cordage, but now that they're down in the garden, it's no longer an option.'

A hard look replaces the calm in Cyril's eyes. 'I been here only a short while but it seems like a lifetime. They love torturing men. They got all these screens in their viewing room. They forced me to watch. And all the time, you know what they were doing?'

I know what they were doing, but I let him tell me anyway.

'They were laughing. It didn't matter that none of us had hurt them. All right, maybe as gamblers we *had* hurt people, but ...' He shakes his head like he wants to clear it of memories he'd rather not have. 'The greater the pain, the more they laughed. Mrs Grundy was here a lot. Part of the treatment was for her to lecture us on how the various women that worked here had been hurt by men. You could see ... But there must have been a better answer than ...'

'They had a lot to laugh about, Cyril. Once upon a time they were victims. At last they were able to get their own back.' I can hear the scrape of something hard on gravel down below. I keep talking to distract Cyril. 'They were enjoying themselves and at the same time they were curing people. They got kicks out of witnessing pain, but all the time they were spitting out punters that were never going to gamble again.'

Cyril nods sadly. 'The trouble was too much enthusiasm, wasn't it? And a few too many corpses.'

It's like death row. We're sitting together – our backs to the wall – me, Cyril and the horse.

'But why didn't some survivors talk when they came out?' Cyril asks.

'Would you? I mean, if you survived? It's like the women that were hurt. They don't want to testify, they just want to forget. Do people that come out of loony bins talk? Or crooks that are released from lock-up? Or soldiers that return from war? All you want to do is forget.' I remember the corpses. 'Apart from which, they didn't want to end up dead.'

It's a conversation stopper, and consequently the conversation stops. There's enough silence in the room to hear the ladder slap against the wall. I keep my eyes on Cyril. I got to keep him talking, keep his mind off what's happening outside, and of the fate worse than death that's awaiting both of us.

'What did they do to you, Cyril?'

He shrugs, taking a firmer hold on Lord Haw-Haw as he does so. 'What didn't they do? They might have cured me of gambling, but they almost killed me in the process.'

The silence that follows is no silence at all. I look past Cyril at the window.

He sees me looking. 'They're coming for us, aren't they?'

I'm too deep in an imaginary dialogue with Rube to notice that Cyril's been edging his way towards the window, his horse under his arm.

'It was them, wasn't it?' he asks.

'Them what?'

He nods towards the window. 'That killed Angel. My fault, but these women lit the fire that killed her.'

498

I don't answer. I don't have to. Cyril knows. And he's not wired like me. But neither is the horse. I know this because in the harsh light from outside, after Cyril wrenches its head off, I see red and black wires sprouting from its neck. And beyond the wires, at the very heart of the toy horse, a red light is flashing.

The horse was fixed all right.

I jump to my feet. The first dame's at the window. But Cyril's waving what's left of his horse at me.

'Back off!'

'What the hell do you think you're doing, Cyril!'

He spins on one of his crippled heels so that he's facing the dame at the window and when he speaks, his voice is muffled because he's turned away from me, the headless horse in his arms.

Chapter 45

THE LOADED HORSE

The woman is balanced on the sill and I can see two more behind her. The horse's head is on the floor but I'm not looking at its head, I'm looking at its neck, where the red light's flashing with increasing intensity like a small, naked heart. Cyril thrusts it towards the window, and the women stay stock-still, as if they know.

'They killed the love of my life. Angela died because I gambled. But in the end they were the ones who killed her.' Pause. 'Only it all started with me, didn't it? I know you're behind me, Rainbow, but it's too late. Lord Haw-Haw's left the barrier. This is one bet I'm going to make a killing on.'

'What would Angel say if she was here?' It's a last, desperate throw of the dice, and when the cubes rattle hollowly on the floorboards, it's little more than the faint echoes of futility.

'You know, in all the time I gambled, I never once asked myself what Angela would say. Oh, sure, at the back of my mind, I had the gambler's fantasy that one day I'd land the big one and Angela would be so proud of me ...'

I take a step forward.

Cyril reaches up with his spare hand and presses something inside Lord Haw-Haw, and the flashing light fuses into a constant crimson glow.

I take a step back. 'Mate, it'll kill you.' I can't think of anything else to say. The women are almost in.

Cyril smiles. It's the first time I've ever seen him smile.

'Not as much as it'll kill them.'

Somehow I imagined he'd throw it.

Instead, clutching Lord Haw-Haw to his pigeon chest, Cyril turns to the window, takes one short step backwards and, with a speed I wouldn't have thought him capable of, hurls himself slap-bang into the arms of his erstwhile tormenters. I do a last-ditch dive behind the steel bed propped against the door.

The blast rocks the Yellow House like a ten-megaton bomb, a massive red, orange and yellow aurora of light eclipsing all else. The building's outside wall collapses in a shower of masonry, the floor turns into a slippy-side, and I find myself clutching the Wheel of Death to stop myself falling.

It's a while before the smoke clears, and when it does, the cloud cover's taken a powder and the sky's full of stars, saying *Star light, star bright* to no-one in particular. The bomb's taken out this side of the building. From down below on the other side – as though from a great distance – I hear a hubbub emanating from the casino room. I grab the length of half-inch, soft matt polyester 16-plait sheath rope enclosing a hawser-laid core of high-tenacity polyester filaments lying beside me, single-hitch it to the whipping-post, and ease myself into the void.

There's not much illumination, and I've got to be grateful for small mercies as I make my way as fast as I can out of this hell hole towards where the rescue vehicle should be, the one with the multi-coloured writing and the flowers on it. The starlight enables me to read the writing on the side. I note with approval the added apostrophe.

'Are you all right?'

I climb in beside Annie, slamming the door on the approaching sirens. 'As right as I'll ever be. One more stop. You know where. And don't spare the horses.'

Chapter 46

THE END OF THE LINE

It's a long drive, but I owe Annie a long explanation.

'In the beginning, it was a story about an evil man called Cameron. But in the end, it was about the victims of people like Cameron, and their victims.'

Annie nods but keeps her eyes on the road. 'And their victims' victims. It's called the vicious cycle. And it started with Cameron's niece, Phoebe Riesling – née Witherspoon.'

'Exactly. Phoebe was the real victim of Uncle Ronnie, which was why she got so enthusiastic when torturing the Grundy clientele – so enthusiastic, in fact, that she ended up killing a few of them. Big sister Paris might have cut Cameron's hand, but Phoebe was the one he was molesting – the girl that had to change her name, which was why the internet history on her was as short as Cyril's legs.'

The night sky does battle with the headlights of the passing traffic. Suddenly, it seems there are no answers at all.

'So the two Witherspoon girls – and others like them that they recruited – went bad, too. There was good reason for how they felt, but they had no right to do what they ended up doing. They decided to get back, not only at the uncle, but at all mankind.

'At first it took a benign form. Paris was the brains – she tried to screw her uncle's pitch by staying one step ahead on the fixing front. I twigged to that early on, but didn't do anything about it because no-one else was getting hurt, except for Cameron. Or so I thought.'

'What do you mean?'

'Cameron was fixing races, only to find that someone was busy *unfixing* them. And that someone was Paris. Which was fine by me – she was simply fixing the fixer. But she went a lot further than that. Her front was the business focused on curing gamblers. For a while that was benign, too. She and her girlfriends had fun torturing people under the guise of curing them.'

'But then something happened ...'

'Yeah. Phoebe started going too far and as a result the clients began dying. And when they did, the protective sister dumped them in a way she thought no-one would notice.'

'Except that you knew there was something about those bodies – something different – which was why you told me to check the pockets, because you had a fair idea what I'd find. But somebody noticed you noticing.'

'That's right. And I also noticed the noticer.' I shift in my seat. 'But I was too long realising the obvious – that I was *meant* to notice her. She wore leopardskin leotards, for God's sake – of course I was meant to notice her.'

Annie picks up the story. 'Because one day Paris knew she'd want to lead you to where she'd be waiting.'

'Yeah, I was onto her, and she realised it. That was when she decided to kill me. She also decided to enjoy herself while she was doing it.'

Annie shudders. 'So instead of sitting beside me, you could have been a corpse in the back of the van, after all ...'

'That was pretty much her intention.'

I try to continue the conversation, but I'm distracted by what lies ahead. Because it doesn't matter how fast Annie drives, we're still not going to make it. I know this in the same way a mug punter knows, even as he places his losing bet, that he's about to do his dough.

The joint's shrouded in darkness. Three wheelie bins stand outside, all of them overflowing. There are fast-food cartons, plastic cups, a broken recorder and an exercise book. I'll go through everything later but there won't be any surprises. Of this I'm sure. I'm also sure of something else: Salina's finally done what she's been threatening to do all along.

This is the big one, not just another simple abscond-and-you'll-learn-to-treat-me-better-as-a-result manoeuvre but the torch-to-the-guts job accompanied by the battery applied to the private parts, a disappearing act to rival any torture that any of life's victims can inflict on any other victim in this world.

It's a variant of the oldest gamble of all – the pea-and-thimble trick. In the trick, the conjuror has three thimbles on his upturned cardboard carton, and the punter has just one chance in three to find which thimble covers the pea. Usually the punter's got a five-spot riding on it. But I've got more than that, a lot more. Because somewhere out there is Salina and she's got the thimble. And under that thimble is Imogene.